THE NERO WOLFE PRIMER
A Mystery Guild Lost Classics Omnibus

THE NERO WOLFE PRIMER:

And Be a Villain
Black Orchids
Champagne for One

by
Rex Stout

Garden City, New York

Contents

A Stout Story

It was sometime in the early to mid 1970s when I was able to convince Rex Stout to "do" the Dick Cavett Show in conjunction with the Viking publication of his latest Nero Wolfe mystery. I remember that it was summer because Rex and I were talking fairly frequently about the Mets' chances to pull off another "Ya gotta believe" year.

Rex kept night watchman's hours and I wasn't allowed to call before 12:30 or 1:00 p.m. After a brief recap of Tug McGraw's relief appearance the evening before, I pitched Cavett. Rex didn't watch much television except for news and ball games, but I had gotten him to check out Cavett's show and he'd agreed to do it. Two of Cavett's producers, Betty Ann Besch and Bridget Potter, loved his books and had assured me that Cavett was a big fan and would treat Rex with dignity and a proper respect for Nero.

The day of the show, Rex drove down from his home in Brewster, New York—even in his later years he wouldn't take the train. He always wanted to be able to get out of town fast on his own schedule. We met at the Oak Room at The Plaza for a pre-show toddy. It was a mild early evening and Rex elected for us to walk across town to the Cavett studio on West 57th Street. As we were crossing to the south side of 57th, a rather Rubenesque young woman in jeans and a tie-dyed "T" shirt rushed up with an autograph book stretched out before her.

"Are you Rex Stout?" she shouted out.

"No, I'm John the Baptist. Watch out for your head," responded Rex as he brushed past her and on up the stage door stairs, his mane of white hair and beard flashing in the sunset reflecting off the Hudson.

—Richard Barber*

* *Rich Barber was director of publicity at The Viking Press in those years.*

AND BE A VILLAIN

Meet it is I set it down,
That one may smile, and smile, and be a villain. . . .

—HAMLET, ACT I

1   FOR THE THIRD TIME I WENT OVER THE FINAL ADDITIONS and subtractions on the first page of Form 1040, to make good and sure. Then I swiveled my chair to face Nero Wolfe, who was seated behind his desk to the right of mine reading a book of poems by a guy named Van Doren, Mark Van Doren. So I thought I might as well use a poetry word.

"It's bleak," I said.

There was no sign that he heard.

"Bleak," I repeated. "If it means what I think it does. Bleak!"

His eyes didn't lift from the page, but he murmured, "What's bleak?"

"Figures." I leaned to slide the Form 1040 across the waxed grain of his desk. "This is March thirteenth. Four thousand three hundred and twelve dollars and sixty-eight cents, in addition to the four quarterly installments already paid. Then we have to send in 1040-ES for 1948, and a check for ten thousand bucks goes with it." I clasped my fingers at the back of my head and asked grimly, "Bleak or not?"

He asked what the bank balance was and I told him. "Of course," I conceded, "that will take care of the two wallops from our rich uncle just mentioned, also a loaf of bread and a sliver of shad roe, but weeks pass and bills arrive, not to be so crude as to speak of paying Fritz and Theodore and me."

Wolfe had put down the poetry and was scowling at the Form 1040, pretending he could add. I raised my voice:

"But you own this house and furniture, except the chair and other items in my room which I bought myself, and you're the boss and you know best. Sure. That electric company bird would have been good for at least a grand over and above expenses on his forgery problem, but you couldn't be bothered. Mrs. What's-her-name would have paid twice that, plenty, for the lowdown on that so-called musician, but you were too busy reading. That lawyer by the name of Clifford was in a bad hole and had to buy help, but he had dandruff. That actress and her gentleman protector—"

"Archie. Shut up."

"Yes, sir. Also what do you do? You come down from your beautiful orchids day before yesterday and breeze in here and tell me merrily to draw another man-size check for that World Government outfit. When I meekly mention that the science of bookkeeping has two main branches, first addition and second subtraction—"

"Leave the room!"

I snarled in his direction, swiveled back to my desk position, got the typewriter in place, inserted paper with carbon, and started to tap out, from my work sheet, Schedule G for line 6 of Schedule C. Time passed and I went on with the job, now and then darting a glance to the right to see if he had had the brass to resume on the book. He hadn't. He was leaning back in his chair, which was big enough for two but not two of him, motionless, with his eyes closed. The tempest was raging. I had a private grin and went on with my work. Somewhat later, when I was finishing Schedule F for line 16 of Schedule C, a growl came from him:

"Archie."

"Yes, sir." I swiveled.

"A man condemning the income tax because of the annoyance it gives him or the expense it puts him to is merely a dog baring its teeth, and he forfeits the privileges of civilized discourse. But it is permissible to criticize it on other and impersonal grounds. A government, like an individual, spends money for any or all of three reasons: because it needs to, because it wants to, or simply because it has it to spend. The last is much the shabbiest. It is arguable, if not manifest, that a substantial proportion of this great spring flood of billions pouring into the Treasury will in effect get spent for that last shabby reason."

"Yeah. So we deduct something? How do I word it?"

Wolfe half opened his eyes. "You are sure of your figures?"

"Only too sure."

"Did you cheat much?"

"Average. Nothing indecent."

"I have to pay the amounts you named?"

"Either that or forfeit some privileges."

"Very well." Wolfe sighed clear down, sat a minute, and straightened in his chair. "Confound it. There was a time when a thousand dinars a year was ample for me. Get Mr. Richards of the Federal Broadcasting Company."

I frowned at him, trying to guess; then, because I knew he was using up a lot of energy sitting up straight, I gave up, found the number in the book, dialed, and, by using Wolfe's name, got through to Richards three minutes under par for a vice-president. Wolfe took his phone, exchanged greetings, and went on:

"In my office two years ago, Mr. Richards, when you handed me a check, you said that you felt you were still in my debt—in spite of the size of the check. So I'm presuming to ask a favor of you. I want some confidential information. What amount of money is involved, weekly let us say, in the radio program of Miss Madeline Fraser?"

"Oh." There was a pause. Richards's voice had been friendly and even warm. Now it backed off a little: "How did you get connected with that?"

"I'm not connected with it, not in any way. But I would appreciate the information—confidentially. Is it too much for me?"

"It's an extremely unfortunate situation, for Miss Fraser, for the network, for the sponsors—everyone concerned. You wouldn't care to tell me why you're interested?"

"I'd rather not." Wolfe was brusque. "I'm sorry I bothered you—"

"You're not bothering me, or if you are you're welcome. The information you want isn't published, but everyone in radio knows it. Everyone in radio knows everything. Exactly what do you want?"

"The total sum involved."

"Well ... let's see ... counting air time, it's on nearly two hundred stations ... production, talent, scripts, everything ... roughly, thirty thousand dollars a week."

"Nonsense," Wolfe said curtly.

"Why nonsense?"

"It's monstrous. That's over a million and a half a year."

"No, around a million and a quarter, on account of the summer vacation."

"Even so. I suppose Miss Fraser gets a material segment of it?"

"Quite material. Everyone knows that too. Her take is around five thousand a week, but the way she splits it with her manager, Miss Koppel, is one thing everyone doesn't know—at least I don't." Richards's voice had warmed up again. "You know, Mr. Wolfe, if you felt like doing me a little favor right back you could tell me confidentially what you want with this."

But all he got from Wolfe was thanks, and he was gentleman enough to take them without insisting on the return favor. After Wolfe had pushed the phone away he remarked to me:

"Good heavens. Twelve hundred thousand dollars!"

I, feeling better because it was obvious what he was up to, grinned at him. "Yes, sir. You would go over big on the air. You could read poetry. By the way, if you want to hear her earn her segment, she's on every Tuesday and Friday morning from eleven to twelve. You'd get pointers. Was that your idea?"

"No." He was gruff. "My idea is to land a job I know how to do. Take your notebook. These instructions will be a little complicated on account of the contingencies to be provided for."

I got my notebook from a drawer.

2   AFTER THREE TRIES THAT SATURDAY AT THE LISTED Manhattan number of Madeline Fraser, with don't answer as the only result, I finally resorted to Lon Cohen of the *Gazette* and he dug it out for me that both Miss Fraser and her manager, Miss Deborah Koppel, were week-ending up in Connecticut.

As a citizen in good standing—anyway pretty good—my tendency was to wish the New York Police Department good luck in its contacts with crime, but I frankly hoped that Inspector Cramer and his homicide scientists wouldn't get Scotch tape on the Orchard case before we had a chance to inspect the contents. Judging from the newspaper accounts I had read, it didn't seem likely that Cramer was getting set to toot a trumpet, but you can never tell how much is being held back, so I was all for driving to Connecticut and horning in on the week end, but Wolfe vetoed it and told me to wait until Monday.

By noon Sunday he had finished the book of poems and was drawing pictures of horses on sheets from his memo pad, testing a theory he had run across somewhere that you can analyze a man's character from the way he draws a horse. I had completed Forms 1040 and 1040-ES and, with checks enclosed, they had been mailed. After lunch I hung around the kitchen a while, listening to Wolfe and Fritz Brenner, the chef and household jewel, arguing whether horse mackerel is as good as Mediterranean tunny fish for *vitello tonnato*—which, as prepared by Fritz, is the finest thing on earth to do with tender young veal. When the argument began to bore me because there was no Mediterranean tunny fish to be had anyhow, I went up to the top floor, to the plant rooms that had been built on the roof, and spent a couple of hours with Theodore Horstmann on the germination records. Then, remembering that on account of a date with a lady I wouldn't have the evening for it, I went down three flights to the office, took the newspapers for five days to my desk, and read everything they had on the Orchard case.

When I had finished I wasn't a bit worried that Monday morning's paper would confront me with a headline that the cops had wrapped it up.

3   THE BEST I WAS ABLE TO GET ON THE PHONE WAS AN
appointment for 3:00 P.M., so at that hour Monday afternoon I entered
the lobby of an apartment house in the upper Seventies between Madison and Park. It was the palace type, with rugs bought by the acre,
but with the effect somewhat spoiled, as it so often is, by a rubber
runner on the main traffic lane merely because the sidewalk was wet
with rain. That's no way to run a palace. If a rug gets a damp dirty
footprint, what the hell, toss it out and roll out another one, that's the
palace spirit.

I told the distinguished-looking hallman that my name was Archie
Goodwin and I was bound for Miss Fraser's apartment. He got a slip
of paper from his pocket, consulted it, nodded, and inquired:

"And? Anything else?"

I stretched my neck to bring my mouth within a foot of his ear,
and whispered to him:

"Oatmeal."

He nodded again, signaled with his hand to the elevator man, who
was standing outside the door of his car fifteen paces away, and said
in a cultivated voice, "Ten B."

"Tell me," I requested, "about this password gag, is it just since
the murder trouble or has it always been so?"

He gave me an icy look and turned his back. I told the back:

"That costs you a nickel. I fully intended to give you a nickel."

With the elevator man I decided not to speak at all. He agreed.
Out at the tenth floor, I found myself in a box no bigger than the
elevator, another palace trick, with a door to the left marked 10A and
one to the right marked 10B. The elevator man stayed there until I

had pushed the button on the latter, and the door had opened and I
had entered.

The woman who had let me in, who might easily have been a
female wrestling champion twenty years back, said, "Excuse me, I'm
in a hurry," and beat it on a trot. I called after her, "My name's Goodwin!" but got no reaction.

I advanced four steps, took off my hat and coat and dropped them
on a chair, and made a survey. I was in a big square sort of a hall,
with doors off to the left and in the wall ahead. To the right, instead
of a wall and doors, it just spread out into an enormous living room
which contained at least twenty different kinds of furniture. My eye
was professionally trained to take in anything from a complicated street
scene to a speck on a man's collar, and really get it, but for the job
of accurately describing that room I would have charged double. Two
of the outstanding items were a chrome-and-red-leather bar with stools
to match and a massive old black walnut table with carved legs and
edges. That should convey the tone of the place.

There was nobody in sight, but I could hear voices. I advanced to
pick out a chair to sit on, saw none that I thought much of, and settled
on a divan ten feet long and four feet wide, covered with green burlap.
A near-by chair had pink embroidered silk. I was trying to decide what
kind of a horse the person who furnished that room would draw, when
company entered the square hall sector from one of the doors in the
far wall—two men, one young and handsome, the other middle-aged
and bald, both loaded down with photographic equipment, including a
tripod.

"She's showing her age," the young man said.

"Age hell," the bald man retorted, "she's had a murder, hasn't
she? Have you ever had a murder?" He caught sight of me and asked
his companion, "Who's that?"

"I don't know, never saw him before." The young man was trying
to open the entrance door without dropping anything. He succeeded,
and they passed through, and the door closed behind them.

In a minute another of the doors in the square hall opened and the
female wrestler appeared. She came in my direction, but, reaching me,
trotted on by, made for a door near a corner off to the left, opened it,
and was gone.

I was beginning to feel neglected.

Ten minutes more and I decided to take the offensive. I was on
my feet and had taken a couple of steps when there was another entrance, again from an inside door at the far side of the square hall, and

I halted. The newcomer headed for me, not at a jerky trot but with a smooth easy flow, saying as she approached:

"Mr. Goodwin?"

I admitted it.

"I'm Deborah Koppel." She offered a hand. "We never really catch up with ourselves around here."

She had already given me two surprises. At first glance I had thought her eyes were small and insignificant, but when she faced me and talked I saw they were quite large, very dark, and certainly shrewd. Also, because she was short and fat, I had expected the hand I took to be pudgy and moist, but it was firm and strong though small. Her complexion was dark and her dress was black. Everything about her was either black or dark, except the gray, almost white by comparison, showing in her night-black hair.

"You told Miss Fraser on the phone," she was saying in her high thin voice, "that you have a suggestion for her from Mr. Nero Wolfe."

"That's right."

"She's very busy. Of course she always is. I'm her manager. Would you care to tell me about it?"

"I'd tell you anything," I declared. "But I work for Mr. Wolfe. His instructions are to tell Miss Fraser, but now, having met you, I'd like to tell her *and* you."

She smiled. The smile was friendly, but it made her eyes look even shrewder. "Very good ad libbing," she said approvingly. "I wouldn't want you to disobey your instructions. Will it take long?"

"That depends. Somewhere between five minutes and five hours."

"By no means five hours. Please be as brief as you can. Come this way."

She turned and started for the square hall and I followed. We went through a door, crossed a room that had a piano, a bed, and an electric refrigerator in it, which left it anybody's guess how to name it, and on through another door into a corner room big enough to have six windows, three on one side and three on another. Every object in it, and it was anything but empty, was either pale yellow or pale blue. The wood, both the trim and the furniture, was painted blue, but other things—rugs, upholstery, curtains, bed coverlet—were divided indiscriminately between the two colors. Among the few exceptions were the bindings of the books on the shelves and the clothes of the blond young man who was seated on a chair. The woman lying on the bed kept to the scheme, with her lemon-colored house gown and her light blue slippers.

The blond young man rose and came to meet us, changing expression on the way. My first glimpse of his face had shown me a gloomy frown, but now his eyes beamed with welcome and his mouth was arranged into a smile that would have done a brush salesman proud. I suppose he did it from force of habit, but it was uncalled for because I was the one who was going to sell something.

"Mr. Goodwin," Deborah Koppel said. "Mr. Meadows."

"Bill Meadows. Just make it Bill, everyone does." His handshake was out of stock but he had the muscle for it. "So you're Archie Goodwin? This is a real pleasure! The next best thing to meeting the great Nero Wolfe himself!"

A rich contralto voice broke in:

"This is my rest period, Mr. Goodwin, and they won't let me get up. I'm not even supposed to talk, but when the time comes that I don't talk—!"

I stepped across to the bed, and as I took the hand Madeline Fraser offered she smiled. It wasn't a shrewd smile like Deborah Koppel's or a synthetic one like Bill Meadows's, but just a smile from her to me. Her gray-green eyes didn't give the impression that she was measuring me, though she probably was, and I sure was measuring her. She was slender but not skinny and she looked quite long, stretched out on the bed. With no makeup on it at all it was quite possible to look at her face without having to resist an impulse to look somewhere else, which was darned good for a woman certainly close to forty and probably a little past it, especially since I personally can see no point in spending eyesight on females over thirty.

"You know," she said, "I have often been tempted—bring chairs up, Bill—to ask Nero Wolfe to be a guest on my program."

She said it like a trained broadcaster, breaking it up so it would sound natural but arranging the inflections so that listeners of any mental age whatever would get it.

"I'm afraid," I told her with a grin, "that he wouldn't accept unless you ran wires to his office and broadcast from there. He never leaves home on business, and rarely for anything at all." I lowered myself onto one of the chairs Bill had brought up, and he and Deborah Koppel took the other two.

Madeline Fraser nodded. "Yes, I know." She had turned on her side to see me without twisting her neck, and the hip curving up under the thin yellow gown made her seem not quite so slender. "Is that just a publicity trick or does he really like it?"

"I guess both. He's very lazy, and he's scared to death of moving objects, especially things on wheels."

"Wonderful! Tell me all about him."

"Some other time, Lina," Deborah Koppel put in. "Mr. Goodwin has a suggestion for you, and you have a broadcast tomorrow and haven't even looked at the script."

"My God, is it Monday already?"

"Monday and half past three," Deborah said patiently.

The radio prima donna's torso popped up to perpendicular as if someone had given her a violent jerk. "What's the suggestion?" she demanded, and flopped back again.

"What made him think of it," I said, "was something that happened to him Saturday. This great nation took him for a ride. Two rides. The Rides of March."

"Income tax? Me too. But what—"

"That's good!" Bill Meadows exclaimed. "Where did you get it? Has it been on the air?"

"Not that I know of. I created it yesterday morning while I was brushing my teeth."

"We'll give you ten bucks for it—no, wait a minute." He turned to Deborah. "What percentage of our audience ever heard of the Ides of March?"

"One-half of one," she said as if she were quoting a published statistic. "Cut."

"You can have it for a dollar," I offered generously. "Mr. Wolfe's suggestion will cost you a lot more. Like everyone in the upper brackets, he's broke." My eyes were meeting the gray-green gaze of Madeline Fraser. "He suggests that you hire him to investigate the murder of Cyril Orchard."

"Oh, Lord," Bill Meadows protested, and brought his hands up to press the heels of his palms against his eyes. Deborah Koppel looked at him, then at Madeline Fraser, and took in air for a deep sigh. Miss Fraser shook her head, and suddenly looked older and more in need of makeup.

"We have decided," she said, "that the only thing we can do about that is forget it as soon as possible. We have ruled it out of conversation."

"That would be fine and sensible," I conceded, "if you could make everyone, including the cops and the papers, obey the rule. But aside from the difficulty of shutting people up about any old kind of a murder, even a dull one, it was simply too good a show. Maybe you don't realize how good. Your program has an eight million audience, twice a week. Your guests were a horse-race tipster and a professor of mathematics from a big university. And smack in the middle of the program one of them makes terrible noises right into the microphone, and keels

over, and pretty soon he's dead, and he got the poison right there on
the broadcast, in the product of one of your sponsors."

I darted glances at the other two and then back to the woman on
the bed. "I knew I might meet any one of a dozen attitudes here, but
I sure didn't expect this one. If you don't know, you ought to, that
one like that doesn't get ruled out of conversation, not only not in a
week, but not in twenty years—not when the question is still open
who provided the poison. Twenty years from now people would still
be arguing about who was it, Madeline Fraser or Deborah Koppel or
Bill Meadows or Nathan Traub or F. O. Savarese or Elinor Vance or
Nancylee Shepherd or Tully Strong—"

The door came open and the female wrestler entered and announced in a hasty breath:

"Mr. Strong is here."

"Send him in, Cora," Miss Fraser told her.

I suppose I would have been struck by the contrast between Tully
Strong and his name if I hadn't known what to expect from his pictures
in the papers. He looked like them in the obvious points—the rimless
spectacles, the thin lips, the long neck, the hair brushed flat—but somehow in the flesh he didn't look as dumb and vacant as the pictures. I
got that much noted while he was being greeted, by the time he turned
to me for the introduction.

"Mr. Strong," Deborah Koppel told me, "is the secretary of our
Sponsors' Council."

"Yes, I know."

"Mr. Goodwin," she told him, "has called with a suggestion from
Nero Wolfe. Mr. Wolfe is a private detective."

"Yes, I know." Tully Strong smiled at me. With lips as thin as his
it is often difficult to tell whether it's a smile or a grimace, but I would
have called it a smile, especially when he added, "We are both famous,
aren't we? Of course you are accustomed to the glare of the spotlight,
but it is quite new to me." He sat down. "What does Mr. Wolfe suggest?"

"He thinks Miss Fraser ought to hire him to look into the murder
of Cyril Orchard."

"Damn Cyril Orchard." Yes, it had been a smile, for now it was
a grimace, and it was quite different. "Damn him to hell!"

"That's pretty tough," Bill Meadows objected, "since he may be
there right now."

Strong ignored him to ask me, "Aren't the police giving us enough
trouble without deliberately hiring someone to give us more?"

"Sure they are," I agreed, "but that's a shortsighted view of it. The person who is really giving you trouble is the one who put the poison in the Hi-Spot. As I was explaining when you came, the trouble will go on for years unless and until he gets tapped on the shoulder. Of course the police may get him, but they've had it for six days now and you know how far they've got. The one that stops the trouble will be the one that puts it where it belongs. Do you know that Mr. Wolfe is smart or shall I go into that?"

"I had hoped," Deborah Koppel put in, "that Mr. Wolfe's suggestion would be something concrete. That he had a . . . an idea."

"Nope." I made it definite. "His only idea is to get paid twenty thousand dollars for ending the trouble."

Bill Meadows let out a whistle. Deborah Koppel smiled at me. Tully Strong protested indignantly:

"Twenty thousand!"

"Not from me," said Madeline Fraser, fully as definite as I had been. "I really must get to work on my broadcast, Mr. Goodwin."

"Now wait a minute." I concentrated on her. "That's only one of my points, getting the trouble over, and not the best one. Look at it this way. You and your program have had a lot of publicity out of this, haven't you?"

She groaned. "Publicity, my God! The man calls it publicity!"

"So it is," I maintained, "but out of the wrong barrel. And it's going to keep coming, still out of the wrong barrel, whether you like it or not. Again tomorrow every paper in town will have your name in a front-page headline. You can't help that, but you can decide what the headline will say. As it stands now you know darned well what it will say. What if, instead of that, it announces that you have engaged Nero Wolfe to investigate the murder of the guest on your program because of your passionate desire to see justice done? The piece would explain the terms of the arrangement: you are to pay the expenses of the investigation—unpadded, we don't pad expenses—and that's all you are to pay unless Mr. Wolfe gets the murderer with evidence to convict. If he comes through you pay him a fee of twenty thousand dollars. Would that get the headline or not? What kind of publicity would it be, still out of the wrong barrel? What percentage of your audience and the general public would it persuade, not only that you and yours are innocent, but that you are a hero to sacrifice a fortune for the sake of justice? Ninety-nine and one-half per cent. Very few of them would stop to consider that both the expenses and the fee will be deductible on your income tax and, in your bracket, the actual cost to you would be around four thousand dollars, no more. In the public mind you would no longer be one of the suspects in a sensational murder case, being hunted—you would be a champion of the people, *hunting* a murderer."

I spread out my hands. "And you would get all that, Miss Fraser, even if Mr. Wolfe had the worst flop of his career and all it cost you was expenses. Nobody could say you hadn't tried. It's a big bargain for you. Mr. Wolfe almost never takes a case on a contingent basis, but when he needs money he breaks rules, especially his own."

Madeline Fraser had closed her eyes. Now she opened them again, and again her smile was just from her to me. "The way you tell it," she said, "it certainly is a bargain.—What do you think, Debby?"

"I think I like it," Miss Koppel said cautiously. "It would have to be discussed with the network and agencies and sponsors."

"Mr. Goodwin."

I turned my head. "Yes, Mr. Strong?"

Tully Strong had removed his spectacles and was blinking at me. "You understand that I am only the secretary of the Council of the sponsors of Miss Fraser's program, and I have no real authority. But I know how they feel about this, two of them in particular, and of course it is my duty to report this conversation to them without delay, and I can tell you off the record that it is extremely probable they would prefer to accept Mr. Wolfe's offer on their own account. For the impression on the public I think they would consider it desirable that Mr. Wolfe should be paid by them—on the terms stated by you. Still off the record, I believe this would apply especially to the makers of Hi-Spot. That's the bottled drink the poison was put into."

"Yeah, I know it is." I looked around at the four faces. "I'm sort of in a hole. I hoped to close a deal with Miss Fraser before I left here, but Miss Koppel says it has to be discussed with others, and now Mr. Strong thinks the sponsors may want to take it over. The trouble is the delay. It's already six days old, and Mr. Wolfe should get to work at once. Tonight if possible, tomorrow at the latest."

"Not to mention," Bill Meadows said, smiling at me, "that he has to get ahead of the cops and keep ahead if he wants to collect. It seems to me— Hello, Elinor!" He left his chair in a hurry. "How about it?"

The girl who had entered without announcement tossed him a nod and a word and came toward the bed with rapid steps. I say girl because, although according to the newspapers Elinor Vance already had under her belt a Smith diploma, a play written and nearly produced, and two years as script writer for the Madeline Fraser program, she looked as if she had at least eight years to go to reach my deadline. As she crossed to us the thought struck me how few there are who still look attractive even when they're obviously way behind on sleep and played out to the point where they're about ready to drop.

"I'm sorry to be so late, Lina," she said all in a breath, "but they kept me down there all day, at the District Attorney's office . . . I couldn't make them understand . . . they're terrible, those men are . . ."

She stopped, and her body started to shake all over.

"Goddam it," Bill Meadows said savagely. "I'll get you a drink."

"I'm already getting it, Bill," Tully Strong called from a side of the room.

"Flop here on the bed," Miss Fraser said, getting her feet out of the way.

"It's nearly five o'clock." It was Miss Koppel's quiet determined voice. "We're going to start to work right now or I'll phone and cancel tomorrow's broadcast."

I stood up, facing Madeline Fraser, looking down at her. "What about it? Can this be settled tonight?"

"I don't see how." She was stroking Elinor Vance's shoulder. "With a broadcast to get up, and people to consult . . ."

"Then tomorrow morning?"

Tully Strong, approaching with the drink for Elinor Vance, handed it to her and then spoke to me:

"I'll phone you tomorrow, before noon if possible."

"Good for you," I told him, and beat it.

4   WITHOUT AT ALL INTENDING TO, I CERTAINLY HAD turned it into a seller's market.

The only development that Monday evening came not from the prospective customers, but from Inspector Cramer of Homicide, in the form of a phone call just before Fritz summoned Wolfe and me to dinner. It was nothing shattering. Cramer merely asked to speak to Wolfe, and asked him:

"Who's paying you on the Orchard case?"

"No one," Wolfe said curtly.

"No? Then Goodwin drives your car up to Seventy-eighth Street just to test the tires?"

"It's my car, Mr. Cramer, and I help to pay for the streets."

It ended in a stalemate, and Wolfe and I moved across the hall to the dining room, to eat fried shrimps and Cape Cod clam cakes. With those items Fritz serves a sour sauce thick with mushrooms which is habit-forming.

Tuesday morning the fun began, with the first phone call arriving before Wolfe got down to the office. Of course that didn't mean sunup, since his morning hours upstairs with Theodore and the orchids are always and forever from nine to eleven. First was Richards of the Federal Broadcasting Company. It is left to my discretion whether to buzz the plant rooms or not, and this seemed to call for it, since Richards had done us a favor the day before. When I got him through to Wolfe it appeared that what he wanted was to introduce another FBC vice-president, a Mr. Beech. What Mr. Beech wanted was to ask why the hell Wolfe hadn't gone straight to the FBC with his suggestion about murder, though he didn't put it that way. He was very affable.

The impression I got, listening in as instructed, was that the network had had its tongue hanging out for years, waiting and hoping for an excuse to hand Wolfe a hunk of dough. Wolfe was polite to him but didn't actually apologize.

Second was Tully Strong, the secretary of the Sponsors' Council, and I conversed with him myself. He strongly hoped that we had made no commitment with Miss Fraser or the network or anyone else because, as he had surmised, some of the sponsors were interested and one of them was excited. That one, he told me off the record, was the Hi-Spot Company, which, since the poison had been served to the victim in a bottle of Hi-Spot, The Drink You Dream Of, would fight for its exclusive right to take Wolfe up. I told him I would refer it to Wolfe without prejudice when he came down at eleven o'clock.

Third was Lon Cohen of the *Gazette*, who said talk was going around and would I kindly remember that on Saturday he had moved heaven and earth for me to find out where Madeline Fraser was, and how did it stand right now? I bandied words with him.

Fourth was a man with a smooth low-pitched voice who gave his name as Nathan Traub, which was one of the names that had been made familiar to the public by the newspaper stories. I knew, naturally, that he was an executive of the advertising agency which handled the accounts of three of the Fraser sponsors, since I had read the papers. He seemed to be a little confused as to just what he wanted, but I gathered that the agency felt that it would be immoral for Wolfe to close any deal with anyone concerned without getting an okay from the agency. Having met a few agency men in my travels, I thought it was nice of them not to extend it to cover any deal with anyone about anything. I told him he might hear from us later.

Fifth was Deborah Koppel. She said that Miss Fraser was going on the air in twenty minutes and had been too busy to talk with the people who must be consulted, but that she was favorably inclined toward Wolfe's suggestion and would give us something definite before the day ended.

So by eleven o'clock, when two things happened simultaneously—Wolfe's entering the office and my turning on the radio and tuning it to the FBC station, WPIT—it was unquestionably a seller's market.

Throughout Madeline Fraser's broadcast Wolfe leaned back in his chair behind his desk with his eyes shut. I sat until I got restless and then moved around, with the only interruptions a couple of phone calls. Bill Meadows was of course on with her, as her stooge and feeder, since that was his job, and the guests for the day were an eminent fashion designer and one of the Ten Best-Dressed Women. The guests were eminently lousy and Bill was nothing to write home about, but there was no getting away from it that Fraser was good. Her voice was good, her timing was good, and even when she was talking about White Birch Soap you would almost as soon leave it on as turn it off. I had listened in on her the preceding Friday for the first time, no doubt along with several million others, and again I had to hand it to her for sitting on a very hot spot without a twitch or a wriggle.

It must have been sizzling hot when she got to that place in the program where bottles of Hi-Spot were opened and poured into glasses—drinks for the two guests and Bill Meadows and herself. I don't know who had made the decision the preceding Friday, her first broadcast after Orchard's death, to leave that in, but if she did she had her nerve. Whoever had made the decision, it had been up to her to carry the ball, and she had sailed right through as if no bottle of Hi-Spot had ever been known even to make anyone belch, let alone utter a shrill cry, claw at the air, have convulsions, and die. Today she delivered again. There was no false note, no quiver, no slack or speedup, nothing; and I must admit that Bill handled it well too. The guests were terrible, but that was the style to which they had accustomed us.

When it was over and I had turned the radio off Wolfe muttered: "That's an extremely dangerous woman."

I would have been more impressed if I hadn't known so well his conviction that all women alive are either extremely dangerous or extremely dumb. So I merely said:

"If you mean she's damn clever I agree. She's awful good."

He shook his head. "I mean the purpose she allows her cleverness to serve. That unspeakable prepared biscuit flour! Fritz and I have tried it. Those things she calls Sweeties! Pfui! And that salad dressing abomination—we have tried that too, in an emergency. What they do to stomachs heaven knows, but that woman is ingeniously and deliberately conspiring in the corruption of millions of palates. She should be stopped!"

"Okay, stop her. Pin a murder on her. Though I must admit, having seen—"

The phone rang. It was Mr. Beech of FBC, wanting to know if we had made any promises to Tully Strong or to anyone else connected with any of the sponsors, and if so whom and what? When he had been attended to I remarked to Wolfe:

"I think it would be a good plan to line up Saul and Orrie and Fred—"

The phone rang. It was a man who gave his name as Owen, saying he was in charge of public relations for the Hi-Spot Company, asking if he could come down to West Thirty-fifth Street on the run for a talk with Nero Wolfe. I stalled him with some difficulty and hung up. Wolfe observed, removing the cap from a bottle of beer which Fritz had brought:

"I must first find out what's going on. If it appears that the police are as stumped as—"

The phone rang. It was Nathan Traub, the agency man, wanting to know everything.

Up till lunch, and during lunch, and after lunch, the phone rang. They were having one hell of a time trying to get it decided how they would split the honor. Wolfe began to get really irritated and so did I. His afternoon hours upstairs with the plants are from four to six, and it was just as he was leaving the office, headed for his elevator in the hall, that word came that a big conference was on in Beech's office in the FBC building on Forty-sixth Street.

At that, when they once got together apparently they dealt the cards and played the hands without any more horsing around, for it was still short of five o'clock when the phone rang once more. I answered it and heard a voice I had heard before that day:

"Mr. Goodwin? This is Deborah Koppel. It's all arranged."

"Good. How?"

"I'm talking on behalf of Miss Fraser. They thought you should be told by her, through me, since you first made the suggestion to her and therefore you would want to know that the arrangement is satisfactory to her. An FBC lawyer is drafting an agreement to be signed by Mr. Wolfe and the other parties."

"Mr. Wolfe hates to sign anything written by a lawyer. Ten to one he won't sign it. He'll insist on dictating it to me, so you might as well give me the details."

She objected. "Then someone else may refuse to sign it."

"Not a chance," I assured her. "The people who have been phoning here all day would sign anything. What's the arrangement?"

"Well, just as you suggested. As you proposed it to Miss Fraser. No one objected to that. What they've been discussing was how to divide it up, and this is what they've agreed on . . ."

As she told it to me I scribbled it in my notebook, and this is how it looked:

	Per cent of expenses	Share of fee
Hi-Spot	50	$10,000
FBC	28	5,500

M. Fraser	15	3,000
White Birch Soap	5	1,000
Sweeties	2	500
	100	$20,000

I called it back to check and then stated, "It suits us if it suits Miss Fraser. Is she satisfied?"

"She agrees to it," Deborah said. "She would have preferred to do it alone, all herself, but under the circumstances that wasn't possible. Yes, she's satisfied."

"Okay. Mr. Wolfe will dictate it, probably in the form of a letter, with copies for all. But that's just a formality and he wants to get started. All we know is what we've read in the papers. According to them there are eight people that the police regard as—uh, possibilities. Their names—"

"I know their names. Including mine."

"Sure you do. Can you have them all here at this office at half past eight this evening?"

"All of them?"

"Yes, ma'am."

"But is that necessary?"

"Mr. Wolfe thinks so. This is him talking through me, to Miss Fraser through you. I ought to warn you, he can be an awful nuisance when a good fee depends on it. Usually when you hire a man to do something he thinks you're the boss. When you hire Wolfe he thinks he's the boss. He's a genius and that's merely one of the ways it shows. You can either take it or fight it. What do you want, just the publicity, or do you want the job done?"

"Don't bully me, Mr. Goodwin. We want the job done. I don't know if I can get Professor Savarese. And that Shepherd girl—she's a bigger nuisance than Mr. Wolfe could ever possibly be."

"Will you get all you can? Half past eight. And keep me informed?"

She said she would. After I had hung up I buzzed Wolfe on the house phone to tell him we had made a sale.

It soon became apparent that we had also bought something. It was only twenty-five to six, less than three-quarters of an hour since I had finished with Deborah Koppel, when the doorbell rang. Sometimes Fritz answers it and sometimes me—usually me, when I'm home and not engaged on something that shouldn't be interrupted. So I marched to the hall and to the front door and pulled it open.

On the stoop was a surprise party. In front was a man-about-town in a topcoat the Duke of Windsor would have worn any day. To his left and rear was a red-faced plump gentleman. Back of them were three more, miscellaneous, carrying an assortment of cases and bags. When I saw what I had to contend with I brought the door with me and held it, leaving only enough of an opening for room for my shoulders.

"We'd like to see Mr. Nero Wolfe," the topcoat said like an old friend.

"He's engaged. I'm Archie Goodwin. Can I help?"

"You certainly can! I'm Fred Owen, in charge of public relations for the Hi-Spot Company." He was pushing a hand at me and I took it. "And this is Mr. Walter B. Anderson, the president of the Hi-Spot Company. May we come in?"

I reached to take the president's hand and still keep my door block intact. "If you don't mind," I said, "it would be a help if you'd give me a rough idea."

"Certainly, glad to! I would have phoned, only this has to be rushed if we're going to make the morning papers. So I just persuaded Mr. Anderson, and collected the photographers, and came. It shouldn't take ten minutes—say a shot of Mr. Anderson looking at Mr. Wolfe as he signs the agreement, or vice versa, and one of them shaking hands, and one of them side by side, bending over in a huddle inspecting some object that can be captioned as a clue—how about that one?"

"Wonderful!" I grinned at him. "But damn it, not today. Mr. Wolfe cut himself shaving, and he's wearing a patch, and vain as he is it would be very risky to aim a camera at him."

That goes to show how a man will degrade himself on account of money. Meaning me. The proper and natural thing to do would have been to kick them off the stoop down the seven steps to the sidewalk, especially the topcoat, and why didn't I do it? Ten grand. Maybe even twenty, for if Hi-Spot had been insulted they might have soured the whole deal.

The effort, including sacrifice of principle, that it took to get them on their way without making them too sore put me in a frame of mind that accounted for my reaction somewhat later, after Wolfe had come down to the office, when I had explained the agreement our clients had come to, and he said:

"No. I will not." He was emphatic. "I will not draft or sign an agreement one of the parties to which is that Sweeties."

I knew perfectly well that was reasonable and even noble. But what pinched me was that I had sacrificed principle without hesitation, and here he was refusing to. I glared at him:

"Very well." I stood up. "I resign as of now. You are simply too conceited, too eccentric, and too fat to work for."

"Archie. Sit down."

"No."

"Yes. I am no fatter than I was five years ago. I am considerably more conceited, but so are you, and why the devil shouldn't we be? Some day there will be a crisis. Either you'll get insufferable and I'll fire you, or I'll get insufferable and you'll quit. But this isn't the day and you know it. You also know I would rather become a policeman and take orders from Mr. Cramer than work for anything or anyone called Sweeties. Your performance yesterday and today has been highly satisfactory."

"Don't try to butter me."

"Bosh. I repeat that I am no fatter than I was five years ago. Sit down and get your notebook. We'll put it in the form of a letter, to all of them jointly, and they can initial our copy. We shall ignore Sweeties"—he made a face—"and add that two per cent and that five hundred dollars to the share of the Federal Broadcasting Company."

That was what we did.

By the time Fritz called us to dinner there had been phone calls from Deborah Koppel and others, and the party for the evening was set.

5

THERE ARE FOUR ROOMS ON THE GROUND FLOOR OF Wolfe's old brownstone house on West Thirty-fifth Street not far from the Hudson River. As you enter from the stoop, on your right are an enormous old oak clothes rack with a mirror, the elevator, the stairs, and the door to the dining room. On your left are the doors to the front room, which doesn't get used much, and to the office. The door to the kitchen is at the rear, the far end of the hall.

The office is twice as big as any of the other rooms. It is actually our living room too, and since Wolfe spends most of his time there you have to allow him his rule regarding furniture and accessories: nothing enters it or stays in it that he doesn't enjoy looking at. He enjoys the contrast between the cherry of his desk and the cardato of his chair, made by Meyer. The bright yellow couch cover has to be cleaned every two months, but he likes bright yellow. The three-foot globe over by the bookshelves is too big for a room that size, but he likes to look at it. He loves a comfortable chair so much that he won't have any other kind in the place, though he never sits on any but his own.

So that evening at least our guests' fannies were at ease, however the rest of them may have felt. There were nine of them present, six invited and three gate-crashers. Of the eight I had wanted Deborah Koppel to get, Nancylee Shepherd hadn't been asked, and Professor F. O. Savarese couldn't make it. The three gate-crashers were Hi-Spot's president and public relations man, Anderson and Owen, who had previously only got as far as the stoop, and Beech, the FBC vice-president.

At nine o'clock they were all there, all sitting, and all looking at

Wolfe. There had been no friction at all except a little brush I had
with Anderson. The best chair in the room, not counting Wolfe's, is
one of red leather which is kept not far from one end of Wolfe's desk.
Soon after entering Anderson had spotted it and squat-claimed it.
When I asked him courteously to move to the other side of the room
he went rude on me. He said he liked it there.

"But," I said, "this chair, and those, are reserved for the candidates."

"Candidates for what?"

"For top billing in a murder trial. Mr. Wolfe would like them sort
of together, so they'll all be under his eye."

"Then arrange them that way."

He wasn't moving. "I can't ask you to show me your stub," I said
pointedly, "because this is merely a private house, and you weren't
invited, and my only argument is the convenience and pleasure of your
host."

He gave me a dirty look but no more words, got up, and went
across to the couch. I moved Madeline Fraser to the red leather chair,
which gave the other five candidates more elbow room in their semicircle fronting Wolfe's desk. Beech, who had been standing talking to
Wolfe, went and took a chair near the end of the couch. Owen had
joined his boss, so I had the three gate-crashers off to themselves,
which was as it should be.

Wolfe's eyes swept the semicircle, starting at Miss Fraser's end.
"You are going to find this tiresome," he said conversationally, "because I'm just starting on this and so shall have to cover details that
you're sick of hearing and talking about. All the information I have
has come from newspapers, and therefore much of it is doubtless in-
accurate and some of it false. How much you'll have to correct me on
I don't know."

"It depends a lot," said Nathan Traub with a smile, "on which
paper you read."

Traub, the agency man, was the only one of the six I hadn't seen
before, having only heard his smooth low-pitched voice on the phone,
when he had practically told me that everything had to be cleared
through him. He was much younger than I had expected, around my
age, but otherwise he was no great surprise. The chief difference between any two advertising executives is that one goes to buy a suit at
Brooks Brothers in the morning and the other one goes in the afternoon. It depends on the conference schedule. The suit this Traub had
bought was a double-breasted gray which went very well with his dark
hair and the healthy color of his cheeks.

"I have read them all." Wolfe's eyes went from left to right again. "I did so when I decided I wanted a job on this case. By the way, I assume you all know who has hired me, and for what?"

There were nods. "We know all about it," Bill Meadows said.

"Good. Then you know why the presence of Mr. Anderson, Mr. Owen, and Mr. Beech is being tolerated. With them here, and of course Miss Fraser, ninety-five per cent of the clients' interest is represented. The only one absent is White Birch Soap."

"They're not absent." Nathan Traub was politely indignant. "I can speak for them."

"I'd rather you'd speak for yourself," Wolfe retorted. "The clients are here to listen, not to speak." He rested his elbows on the arms of his chair and put the tips of his thumbs together. With the gate-crashers put in their places, he went on, "As for you, ladies and gentlemen, this would be much more interesting and stimulating for you if I could begin by saying that my job is to learn which one of you is guilty of murder—and to prove it. Unfortunately we can't have that fillip, since two of the eight—Miss Shepherd and Mr. Savarese—didn't come. I am told that Mr. Savarese had an engagement, and there is a certain reluctance about Miss Shepherd that I would like to know more about."

"She's a nosy little chatterbox." From Tully Strong, who had removed his spectacles and was gazing at Wolfe with an intent frown.

"She's a pain in the neck." From Bill Meadows.

Everybody smiled, some nervously, some apparently meaning it.

"I didn't try to get her," Deborah Koppel said. "She wouldn't have come unless Miss Fraser herself had asked her, and I didn't think that was necessary. She hates all the rest of us."

"Why?"

"Because she thinks we keep her away from Miss Fraser."

"Do you?"

"Yes. We try to."

"Not from me too, I hope." Wolfe sighed down to where a strip of his yellow shirt divided his vest from his trousers, and curled his palms and fingers over the ends of his chair arms. "Now. Let's get at this. Usually when I talk I dislike interruptions, but this is an exception. If you disagree with anything I say, or think me in error, say so at once. With that understood:

"Frequently, twice a week or oftener, you consider the problem of guests for Miss Fraser's program. It is in fact a problem, because you want interesting people, famous ones if possible, but they must be willing to submit to the indignity of lending their presence, and their assent by silence, if nothing more, to the preposterous statements made

by Miss Fraser and Mr. Meadows regarding the products they adver-
tise. Recently—"

"What's undignified about it?"

"There are no preposterous statements!"

"What's this got to do with what we're paying you for?"

"You disagree." Wolfe was unruffled. "I asked for it. Archie, include it in your notes that Mr. Traub and Mr. Strong disagree. You
may ignore Mr. Owen's protest, since my invitation to interrupt did
not extend to him."

He took in the semicircle again. "Recently a suggestion was made
that you corral, as a guest, a man who sells tips on horse races. I
understand that your memories differ as to when that suggestion was
first made."

Madeline Fraser said, "It's been discussed off and on for over a
year."

"I've always been dead against it," Tully Strong asserted.

Deborah Koppel smiled. "Mr. Strong thought it would be im-
proper. He thinks the program should never offend anybody, which is
impossible. Anything and everything offends somebody."

"What changed your mind, Mr. Strong?"

"Two things," said the secretary of the Sponsors' Council. "First,
we got the idea of having the audience vote on it—the air audience—
and out of over fourteen thousand letters ninety-two point six per cent
were in favor. Second, one of the letters was from an assistant professor of mathematics at Columbia University, suggesting that the second
guest on the program should be him, or some other professor, who
could speak as an expert on the law of averages. That gave it a different slant entirely, and I was for it. Nat Traub, for the agency, was
still against it."

"And I still am," Traub declared. "Can you blame me?"

"So," Wolfe asked Strong, "Mr. Traub was a minority of one?"

"That's right. We went ahead. Miss Vance, who does research for
the program in addition to writing scripts, got up a list of prospects. I
was surprised to find, and the others were too, that more than thirty
tip sheets of various kinds are published in New York alone. We boiled
it down to five and they were contacted."

I should have warned them that the use of contact as a verb was
not permitted in that office. Now Wolfe would have it in for him.

Wolfe frowned. "All five were invited?"

"Oh, no. Appointments were made for them to see Miss Fraser—
the publishers of them. She had to find out which one was most likely

to go over on the air and not pull something that would hurt the program. The final choice was left to her."

"How were the five selected?"

"Scientifically. The length of time they had been in business, the quality of paper and printing of the sheets, the opinions of sports writers, things like that."

"Who was the scientist? You?"

"No . . . I don't know . . ."

"I was," a firm quiet voice stated. It was Elinor Vance. I had put her in the chair nearest mine because Wolfe isn't the only one who likes to have things around that he enjoys looking at. Obviously she hadn't caught up on sleep yet, and every so often she had to clamp her teeth to keep her chin from quivering, but she was the only one there who could conceivably have made me remember that I was not primarily a detective, but a man. I was curious how her brown eyes would look if and when they got fun in them again some day. She was going on:

"First I took out those that were plainly impossible, more than half of them, and then I talked it over with Miss Koppel and Mr. Meadows, and I think one or two others—I guess Mr. Strong—yes, I'm sure I did—but it was me more than them. I picked the five names."

"And they all came to see Miss Fraser?"

"Four of them did. One of them was out of town—in Florida."

Wolfe's gaze went to the left. "And you, Miss Fraser, chose Mr. Cyril Orchard from those four?"

She nodded. "Yes."

"How did you do that? Scientifically?"

"No." She smiled. "There's nothing scientific about me. He seemed fairly intelligent, and he had much the best voice of the four and was the best talker, and I liked the name of his sheet, *Track Almanac*—and then I guess I was a little snobbish about it too. His sheet was the most expensive—ten dollars a week."

"Those were the considerations that led you to select him?"

"Yes."

"You had never seen or heard of him before he came to see you as one of the four?"

"I hadn't seen him, but I had heard of him, and I had seen his sheet."

"Oh?" Wolfe's eyes went half shut. "You had?"

"Yes, about a month before that, maybe longer, when the question of having a tipster on the program had come up again, I had subscribed to some of the sheets—three or four of them—to see what they were like. Not in my name, of course. Things like that are done in my manager's name—Miss Koppel. One of them was this *Track Almanac*."

"How did you happen to choose that one?"

"My God, I don't know!" Madeline Fraser's eyes flashed momentarily with irritation. "Do you remember, Debby?"

Deborah shook her head. "I think we phoned somebody."

"The New York State Racing Commission," Bill Meadows offered sarcastically.

"Well." Wolfe leaned forward to push a button on his desk. "I'm going to have some beer. Aren't some of you thirsty?"

That called for an intermission. No one had accepted a previous offer of liquids I had made, but now they made it unanimous in the affirmative, and I got busy at the table at the far wall, already equipped. Two of them joined Wolfe with the beer, brought by Fritz from the kitchen, and the others suited their fancy. I had suggested to Wolfe that it would be fitting to have a case of Hi-Spot in a prominent place on the table, but he had merely snorted. On such occasions he always insisted that a red wine and a chilled white wine must be among those present. Usually they had no takers, but this time there were two, Miss Koppel and Traub, who went for the Montrachet; and, being strongly in favor of the way its taste insists on sneaking all over the inside of your head, I helped out with it. There is only one trouble about serving assorted drinks to a bunch of people in the office on business. I maintain that it is a legitimate item for the expense account for the clients, and Wolfe says no, that what anyone eats or drinks in his house is on him. Another eccentricity. Also he insists that they must all have stands or tables at their elbows for their drinks.

So they did.

6   WOLFE, FOR WHOM THE FIRST BOTTLE OF BEER IS MERELY
a preamble, filled his glass from the second bottle, put the bottle down,
and leaned back.

"What I've been after," he said in his conversational tone again,
"is how that particular individual, Mr. Cyril Orchard, became a guest
on that program. The conclusion from the newspaper accounts is that
none of you, including Miss Shepherd and Mr. Savarese, knew him
from Adam. But he was murdered. Later I'll discuss this with you
severally, but for now I'll just put it to all of you: had you had any
dealings with, or connection with, or knowledge of, Cyril Orchard
prior to his appearance on that program? Other than what I have just
been told?"

Starting with Madeline Fraser, he got either a no or a shake of the
head from each of the six.

He grunted. "I assume," he said, "that the police have unearthed
no contradiction to any of your negatives, since if they had you would
hardly be foolish enough to try to hold to them with me. My whole
approach to this matter is quite different from what it would be if I
didn't know that the police have spent seven days and nights working
on it. They have been after you, and they have their training and
talents; also they have authority and a thousand men—twenty thousand. The question is whether their methods and abilities are up to this
job; all I can do is use my own."

Wolfe came forward to drink beer, used his handkerchief on his
lips, and leaned back again.

"But I need to know what happened—from you, not the newspapers. We now have you in the broadcasting studio Tuesday morning,

a week ago today. The two guests—Mr. Cyril Orchard and Professor Savarese—have arrived. It is a quarter to eleven. The rest of you are there, at or near the table which holds the microphones. Seated at one side of the narrow table are Miss Fraser and Professor Savarese; across from them, facing them, are Mr. Orchard and Mr. Meadows. Voice levels are being taken. About twenty feet from the table is the first row of chairs provided for the studio audience. That audience consists of some two hundred people, nearly all women, many of whom, devoted followers of Miss Fraser, frequently attend the broadcasts. Is that picture correct—not approximately correct, but correct?"

They nodded. "Nothing wrong with it," Bill Meadows said.

"Many of them," Miss Fraser stated, "would come much oftener if they could get tickets. There are always twice as many applications for tickets as we can supply."

"No doubt," Wolfe growled. He had shown great restraint, not telling her how dangerous she was. "But the applicants who didn't get tickets, not being there, do not concern us. An essential element of the picture which I haven't mentioned is not yet visible. Behind the closed door of an electric refrigerator over against the wall are eight bottles of Hi-Spot. How did they get there?"

An answer came from the couch, from Fred Owen. "We always have three or four cases in the studio, in a locked cab——"

"If you please, Mr. Owen." Wolfe wiggled a finger at him. "I want to hear as much as I can of the voices of these six people."

"They were there in the studio," Tully Strong said. "In a cabinet. It's kept locked because if it wasn't they wouldn't be there long."

"Who had taken the eight bottles from the cabinet and put them in the refrigerator?"

"I had." It was Elinor Vance, and I looked up from my notebook for another glance at her. "That's one of my chores every broadcast."

One trouble with her, I thought, is overwork. Script writer, researcher, bartender—what else?

"You can't carry eight bottles," Wolfe remarked, "at one time."

"I know I can't, so I took four and then went back for four more."

"Leaving the cabinet unlocked—no." Wolfe stopped himself. "Those refinements will have to wait." His eyes passed along the line again. "So there they are, in the refrigerator. —By the way, I understand that the presence at the broadcast of all but one of you was routine and customary. The exception was you, Mr. Traub. You very rarely attend. What were you there for?"

"Because I was jittery, Mr. Wolfe." Traub's advertising smile and smooth low-pitched voice showed no resentment at being singled out.

"I still thought having a race tout on the program was a mistake, and I wanted to be on hand."

"You thought there was no telling what Mr. Orchard might say?"

"I knew nothing about Orchard. I thought the whole idea was a stinker."

"If you mean the whole idea of the program, I agree—but that's not what we're trying to decide. We'll go on with the broadcast. First, one more piece of the picture. Where are the glasses they're going to drink from?"

"On a tray at the end of the table," Deborah Koppel said.

"The broadcasting table? Where they're seated at the microphones?"

"Yes."

"Who put them there?"

"That girl, Nancylee Shepherd. The only way to keep her back of the line would be to tie her up. Or of course not let her in, and Miss Fraser will not permit that. She organized the biggest Fraser Girls' Club in the country. So we—"

The phone rang. I reached for it and muttered into it.

"Mr. Bluff," I told Wolfe, using one of my fifteen aliases for the caller. Wolfe got his receiver to his ear, giving me a signal to stay on.

"Yes, Mr. Cramer?"

Cramer's sarcastic voice sounded as if he had a cigar stuck in his mouth, as he probably had. "How are you coming up there?"

"Slowly. Not really started yet."

"That's too bad, since no one's paying you on the Orchard case. So you told me yesterday."

"This is today. Tomorrow's paper will tell you all about it. I'm sorry, Mr. Cramer, but I'm busy."

"You certainly are, from the reports I've got here. Which one is your client?"

"You'll see it in the paper."

"Then there's no reason—"

"Yes. There is. That I'm extremely busy and exactly a week behind you. Good-by, sir."

Wolfe's tone and his manner of hanging up got a reaction from the gate-crashers. Mr. Walter B. Anderson, the Hi-Spot president, demanded to know if the caller had been Police Inspector Cramer, and, told that it was, got critical. His position was that Wolfe should not have been rude to the Inspector. It was bad tactics and bad manners. Wolfe, not bothering to draw his sword, brushed him aside with a couple of words, but Anderson leaped for his throat. He had not yet, he said, signed any agreement, and if that was going to be Wolfe's attitude maybe he wouldn't.

"Indeed." Wolfe's brows went up a sixteenth of an inch. "Then you'd better notify the press immediately. Do you want to use the phone?"

"By God, I wish I could. I have a right to—"

"You have no right whatever, Mr. Anderson, except to pay your share of my fee if I earn it. You are here in my office on sufferance. Confound it, I am undertaking to solve a problem that has Mr. Cramer so nonplused that he desperately wants a hint from me before I've even begun. He doesn't mind my rudeness; he's so accustomed to it that if I were affable he'd haul me in as a material witness. Are you going to use the phone?"

"You know damn well I'm not."

"I wish you were. The better I see this picture the less I like it." Wolfe went back to the line of candidates. "You say, Miss Koppel, that this adolescent busybody, Miss Shepherd, put the tray of glasses on the table?"

"Yes, she—"

"She took them from me," Elinor Vance put in, "when I got them from the cabinet. She was right there with her hand out and I let her take them."

"The locked cabinet that the Hi-Spot is kept in?"

"Yes."

"And the glasses are heavy and dark blue, quite opaque, so that anything in them is invisible?"

"Yes."

"You didn't look into them from the top?"

"No."

"If one of them had something inside you wouldn't have seen it?"

"No." Elinor went on, "If you think my answers are short and quick, that's because I've already answered these questions, and many others, hundreds of times. I could answer them in my sleep."

Wolfe nodded. "Of course. So now we have the bottles in the refrigerator and the glasses on the table, and the program is on the air. For forty minutes it went smoothly. The two guests did well. None of Mr. Traub's fears were realized."

"It was one of the best broadcasts of the year," Miss Fraser said.

"Exceptional," Tully Strong declared. "There were thirty-two studio laughs in the first half hour."

"How did you like the second half?" Traub asked pointedly.

"We're coming to it." Wolfe sighed. "Well, here we are. The moment arrives when Hi-Spot is to be poured, drunk, and eulogized. Who brought it from the refrigerator? You again, Miss Vance?"

"No, me," Bill Meadows said. "It's part of the show for the mikes, me pushing back my chair, walking, opening the refrigerator door and closing it, and coming back with the bottles. Then someone—"

"There were eight bottles in the refrigerator. How many did you get?"

"Four."

"How did you decide which ones?"

"I didn't decide. I always just take the four in front. You realize that all Hi-Spot bottles are exactly alike. There wouldn't be any way to tell them apart, so how would I decide?"

"I couldn't say. Anyway, you didn't?"

"No. As I said, I simply took the four bottles that were nearest to me. That's natural."

"So it is. And carried them to the table and removed the caps?"

"I took them to the table, but about removing the caps, that's something we don't quite agree on. We agree that I didn't do it, because I put them on the table as usual and then got back into my chair, quick, to get on the mike. Someone else always takes the caps from the bottles, not always the same one, and that day Debby—Miss Koppel was right there, and Miss Vance, and Strong, and Traub. I was on the mike and didn't see who removed the caps. The action there is a little tight and needs help, with taking off the caps, pouring into the glasses, and getting the glasses passed around—and the bottles have to be passed around too."

"Who does the passing?"

"Oh, someone—or, rather, more than one. You know, they just get passed—the glasses and bottles both. After pouring into the glasses the bottles are still about half full, so the bottles are passed too."

"Who did the pouring and passing that day?"

Bill Meadows hesitated. "That's what we don't agree about." He was not at ease. "As I said, they were all right there—Miss Koppel and Miss Vance, and Strong and Traub. That's why it was confusing."

"Confusing or not," Wolfe said testily, "it should be possible to remember what happened, so simple a thing as that. This is the detail where, above all others, clarity is essential. We know that Mr. Orchard got the bottle and glass which contained the cyanide, because he drank enough of it to kill him. But we do not know, at least I don't, whether he got it by a whim of circumstance or by the deliberate maneuver of one or more of those present. Obviously that's a vital point. That glass

and bottle were placed in front of Mr. Orchard by somebody—not this
one, or this one, but that one. Who put it there?"

Wolfe's gaze went along the line. They all met it. No one had
anything to say, but neither was anyone impelled to look somewhere
else. Finally Tully Strong, who had his spectacles back on, spoke:

"We simply don't remember, Mr. Wolfe."

"Pfui." Wolfe was disgusted. "Certainly you remember. No wonder Mr. Cramer has got nowhere. You're lying, every one of you."

"No," Miss Fraser objected. "They're not lying really."

"The wrong pronoun," Wolfe snapped at her. "My comment included you, Miss Fraser."

She smiled at him. "You may include me if you like, but I don't.
It's like this. These people are not only associated with one another in
connection with my program, they are friends. Of course they have
arguments—there's always bound to be some friction when two people
are often together, let alone five or six—but they are friends and they
like one another." Her timing and inflections were as good as if she
had been on the air. "This is a terrible thing, a horrible thing, and we
all knew it was the minute the doctor came and looked at him, and
then looked up and said nothing should be touched and no one should
leave. So could you really expect one of them to say—or, since you
include me, could you expect one of us to say—*yes, I gave him the
glass with poison in it?*"

"What was left in the bottle was also poisoned."

"All right, the bottle too. Or could you expect one of us to say,
yes, I saw my friend give him the glass and bottle? And name the
friend?"

"Then you're agreeing with me. That you're all lying."

"Not at all." Miss Fraser was too earnest to smile now. "The pouring and passing the glasses and bottles was commonplace routine, and
there was no reason for us to notice details enough to keep them in
our minds at all. Then came that overwhelming shock, and the con-
fusion, and later came the police, and the strain and tension of it, and
we just didn't remember. That isn't the least bit surprising. What would
surprise me would be if someone did remember, for instance if Mr.
Traub said positively that Mr. Strong put that glass and bottle in front
of Mr. Orchard, it would merely prove that Mr. Traub hates Mr.
Strong, and that would surprise me because I don't believe that any
one of us hates another one."

"Nor," Wolfe murmured dryly, "that any of you hated Mr. Orchard—or wanted to kill him."

"Who on earth could have wanted to kill that man?"

"I don't know. That's what I've been hired to find out—provided the poison reached its intended destination. You say you're not surprised, but I am. I'm surprised the police haven't locked you all up."

"They damn near did," Traub said grimly.

"I certainly thought they would arrest me," Madeline Fraser declared. "That was what was in my mind—it was all that was in my mind—as soon as I heard the doctor say cyanide. Not who had given him that glass and bottle, not even what the effect would be on my program, but the death of my husband. He died of cyanide poisoning six years ago."

Wolfe nodded. "The papers haven't neglected that. It was what leaped first to your mind?"

"Yes, when I heard the doctor say cyanide. I suppose you wouldn't understand—or perhaps you would—anyway it did."

"It did to mine too," Deborah Koppel interposed, in a tone that implied that someone had been accused of something. "Miss Fraser's husband was my brother. I saw him just after he died. Then that day I saw Cyril Orchard, and—" She stopped. Having her in profile, I couldn't see her eyes, but I saw her clasped hands. In a moment she went on, "Yes, it came to my mind."

Wolfe stirred impatiently. "Well. I won't pretend that I'm exasperated that you're such good friends that you haven't been able to remember what happened. If you had, and had told the police, I might not have this job." He glanced at the clock on the wall. "It's after eleven. I had thought it barely possible that I might get a wedge into a crack by getting you here together, but it seems hopeless. You're much too fond of one another. Our time has been completely wasted. I haven't got a thing, not a microscopic morsel, that I hadn't already got from the papers. I may never get anything, but I intend to try. Which of you will spend the night here with me? Not all the night; probably four or five hours. I shall need that long, more or less, with each of you, and I would like to start now. Which of you will stay?"

There were no eager volunteers.

"My Lord!" Elinor Vance protested. "Over and over and over again."

"My clients," Wolfe said, "are your employer, your network, and your sponsors. Mr. Meadows?"

"I've got to take Miss Fraser home," Bill objected. "I could come back."

"I'll take her," Tully Strong offered.

"That's foolish." Deborah Koppel was annoyed. "I live only a block away and we'll take a taxi together."

"I'll go with you," Elinor Vance suggested. "I'll drop you and keep the taxi on uptown."

"I'll ride with you," Tully Strong insisted.

"But you live in the Village!"

"Count me in," Bill Meadows said stubbornly. "I can be back here in twenty minutes. Thank God tomorrow's Wednesday."

"This is all unnecessary," the president of Hi-Spot broke in with authority. He had left the couch and was among the candidates, who were also on their feet. "My car is outside and I can take all of you who are going uptown. You can stay here with Wolfe, Meadows." He turned and stepped to the desk. "Mr. Wolfe, I haven't been greatly impressed this evening. Hardly at all impressed."

"Neither have I," Wolfe agreed. "It's a dreary outlook. I would prefer to abandon it, but you and I are both committed by that press release." Seeing that some of them were heading for the hall, he raised his voice. "If you please? A moment. I would like to make appointments. One of you tomorrow from eleven to one, another from two to four, another in the evening from eight-thirty to twelve, and another from midnight on. Will you decide on that before you go?"

They did so, with me helping them and making notes of the decisions. It took a little discussion, but they were such good friends that there was no argument. The only thing that soured the leave-taking at all was when Owen made an opportunity to pass me a crack about no patch or cut being visible on Wolfe's face. He might at least have had the decency to let it lay.

"I said nothing about his face," I told him coldly. "I said he cut himself shaving. He shaves his legs. I understood you wanted him in kilts for the pictures."

Owen was too offended to speak. Utterly devoid of a sense of humor.

When the others had gone Bill Meadows was honored with the red leather chair. On a low table at his elbow I put a replenished glass, and Fritz put a tray holding three sandwiches made with his own bread, one of minced rabbit meat, one of corned beef, and one of Georgia country ham. I arranged myself at my desk with my notebook, a plate of sandwiches to match Bill's, a pitcher of milk and a glass. Wolfe had only beer. He never eats between dinner and breakfast. If he did he never would be able to say he is no fatter than he was five years ago, which isn't true anyhow.

In a way it's a pleasure to watch Wolfe doing a complete overhaul on a man, or a woman either, and in another way it's enough to make you grit your teeth. When you know exactly what he's after and he's sneaking up on it without the slightest sound to alarm the victim, it's a joy to be there. But when he's after nothing in particular, or if he is you don't know what, and he pokes in this hole a while and then tries another one, and then goes back to the first one, and as far as you can see is getting absolutely nowhere, and the hours go by, and your sandwiches and milk are all gone long ago, sooner or later the time comes when you don't even bother to get a hand in front of your yawns, let alone swallow them.

If, at four o'clock that Wednesday morning, Wolfe had once more started in on Bill Meadows about his connections with people who bet on horse races, or about the favorite topics of conversation among the people we were interested in when they weren't talking shop, or about how he got into broadcasting and did he like it much, I would either have thrown my notebook at him or gone to the kitchen for more milk. But he didn't. He pushed back his chair and manipulated himself to his feet. If anyone wants to know what I had in the notebook he can come to the office any time I'm not busy and I'll read it to him for a dollar a page, but he would be throwing his money away at any price.

I ushered Bill out. When I returned to the office Fritz was there tidying up. He never goes to bed until after Wolfe does. He asked me:

"Was the corned beef juicy, Archie?"

"Good God," I demanded, "do you expect me to remember that far back? That was days ago." I went to spin the knob on the safe and jiggle the handle, remarking to Wolfe:

"It seems we're still in the paddock, not even at the starting post. Who do you want in the morning? Saul and Orrie and Fred and Johnny? For what? Why not have them tail Mr. Anderson?"

"I do not intend," Wolfe said glumly, "to start spending money until I know what I want to buy—not even our clients' money. If this poisoner is going to be exposed by such activities as investigation of sales of potassium cyanide or of sources of it available to these people, it is up to Mr. Cramer and his twenty thousand men. Doubtless they have already done about all they can in those directions, and many others, or he wouldn't have phoned me squealing for help. The only person I want to see in the morning is—who is it? Who's coming at eleven?"

"Debby. Miss Koppel."

"You might have taken the men first, on the off chance that we'd have it before we got to the women." He was at the door to the hall. "Good night."

7

IF, THIRTY-THREE HOURS LATER, AT LUNCH TIME ON Thursday, anyone had wanted to know how things were shaping up, he could have satisfied his curiosity by looking in the dining room and observing Wolfe's behavior at the midday meal, which consisted of corn fritters with autumn honey, sausages, and a bowl of salad. At meals he is always expansive, talkative, and good-humored, but throughout that one he was grim, sullen, and peevish. Fritz was worried stiff.

Wednesday we had entertained Miss Koppel from eleven to one, Miss Fraser from two to four, Miss Vance from eight-thirty in the evening until after eleven, and Nathan Traub from midnight on; and Tully Strong Thursday morning from eleven until lunch time.

We had got hundreds of notebook pages of nothing.

Gaps had of course been filled in, but with what? We even had confessions, but of what? Bill Meadows and Nat Traub both confessed that they frequently bet on horse races. Elinor Vance confessed that her brother was an electroplater, and that she was aware that he constantly used materials which contained cyanide. Madeline Fraser confessed that it was hard to believe that anyone would have put poison into one of the bottles without caring a damn which one of the four broadcasters it got served to. Tully Strong confessed that the police had found his fingerprints on all four of the bottles, and accounted for them by explaining that while the doctor had been kneeling to examine Cyril Orchard, he, Strong, had been horrified by the possibility that there had been something wrong with a bottle of Hi-Spot, the product of the most important sponsor on the Council. In a panic he had seized the four bottles, with the idiotic notion of caching them somewhere, and Miss Fraser and Traub had taken them from him and replaced them on the table. That was a particularly neat confession, since it explained why the cops had got nowhere from prints on the bottles.

Deborah Koppel confessed that she knew a good deal about cyanides, their uses, effects, symptoms, doses, and accessibility, because she had read up on them after the death of her brother six years ago. In all the sessions those were the only two times Wolfe got really disagreeable, when he was asking about the death of Lawrence Koppel—first with Deborah, the sister, and then with Madeline Fraser, the widow. The details had of course been pie for the newspapers during the past week, on account of the coincidence of the cyanide, and one of the tabloids had even gone so far as to run a piece by an expert, discussing whether it had really been suicide, though there hadn't been the slightest question about it at the time or at any time since.

But that wasn't the aspect that Wolfe was disagreeable about. Lawrence Koppel's death had occurred at his home in a little town in Michigan called Fleetville, and what Wolfe wanted to know was whether there had been anyone in or near Fleetville who was named Orchard, or who had relatives named Orchard, or who had later changed his name to Orchard. I don't know how it had entered his head that that was a hot idea, but he certainly wrung it dry and kept going back to it for another squeeze. He spent so much time on it with Madeline Fraser that four o'clock, the hour of his afternoon date with the orchids, came before he had asked her anything at all about horse races.

The interviews with those five were not all that happened that day and night and morning. Wolfe and I had discussions, of the numerous ways in which a determined and intelligent person can get his hands on a supply of cyanide, of the easy access to the bottles in the refrigerator in the broadcasting studio, of the advisability of trying to get Inspector Cramer or Sergeant Purley Stebbins to cough up some data on things like fingerprints. That got us exactly as far as the interviews did. Then there were two more phone calls from Cramer, and some from Lon Cohen and various others; and there was the little detail of arranging for Professor F. O. Savarese to pay us a visit.

Also the matter of arranging for Nancylee Shepherd to come and be processed, but on that we were temporarily stymied. We knew all about her: she was sixteen, she lived with her parents at 829 Wixley Avenue in the Bronx, she had light yellow hair and gray eyes, and her father worked in a storage warehouse. They had no phone, so at four Wednesday, when Miss Fraser had left and Wolfe had gone up to the plants, I got the car from the garage and drove to the Bronx.

829 Wixley Avenue was the kind of apartment house where people live not because they want to, but because they have to. It should have been ashamed of itself and probably was. There was no click when I pushed the button marked Shepherd, so I went to the basement and dug up the janitor. He harmonized well with the building. He said I was way behind time if I expected to get any effective results—that's what he said—pushing the Shepherd button. They had been gone three days now. No, not the whole family, Mrs. Shepherd and the girl. He didn't know where they had gone, and neither did anyone else around there. Some thought they had skipped, and some thought the cops had 'em. He personally thought they might be dead. No, not Mr. Shepherd too. He came home from work every afternoon a little after five, and left every morning at half past six.

A glance at my wrist showing me ten to five, I offered the animal a buck to stick around the front and give me a sign when Shepherd showed up, and the look in his eye told me that I had wasted at least four bits of the clients' money.

It wasn't a long wait. When Shepherd appeared I saw that it wouldn't have been necessary to keep the janitor away from his work, for from the line of the eyebrows it was about as far up to the beginning of his hair as it was down to the point of his chin, and a sketchy description would have been enough. Whoever designs the faces had lost all sense of proportion. As he was about to enter the vestibule I got in front of him and asked without the faintest touch of condescension:

"Mr. Shepherd?"

"Get out," he snarled.

"My name's Goodwin and I'm working for Miss Madeline Fraser. I understand your wife and daughter—"

"Get out!"

"But I only want—"

"Get out!"

He didn't put a hand on me or shoulder me, and I can't understand yet how he got past me to the vestibule without friction, but he did, and got his key in the door. There were of course a dozen possible courses for me, anything from grabbing his coat and holding on to plugging him in the jaw, but while that would have given me emotional release it wouldn't have got what I wanted. It was plain that as long as he was conscious he wasn't going to tell me where Nancylee was, and unconscious he couldn't. I passed.

I drove back down to Thirty-fifth Street, left the car at the curb, went in to the office, and dialed Madeline Fraser's number. Deborah Koppel answered, and I asked her:

"Did you folks know that Nancylee has left home? With her mother?"

Yes, she said, they knew that.

"You didn't mention it when you were here this morning. Neither did Miss Fraser this afternoon."

"There was no reason to mention it, was there? We weren't asked."

"You were asked about Nancylee, both of you."

"But not if she had left home or where she is."

"Then may I ask you now? Where is she?"

"I don't know."

"Does Miss Fraser?"

"No. None of us knows."

"How did you know she was gone?"

"She phoned Miss Fraser and told her she was going."

"When was that?"

"That was . . . that was Sunday."

"She didn't say where she was going?"

"No."

That was the best I could get. When I was through trying and had hung up, I sat and considered. There was a chance that Purley Stebbins of Homicide would be in the mood for tossing me a bone, since Cramer had been spending nickels on us, but if I asked him for it he would want to make it a trade, and I had nothing to offer. So when I reached for the phone again it wasn't that number, but the *Gazette*'s, that I dialed.

Lon Cohen immediately got personal. Where, he wanted to know, had I got the idea that an open press release made an entry in my credit column?

I poohed him. "Some day, chum, you'll get a lulu. Say in about six months, the way we're going. A newspaper is supposed to render public service, and I want some. Did you know that Nancylee Shepherd and her mother have blown?"

"Certainly. The father got sore because she was mixed up in a murder case. He damn near killed two photographers. Father has character."

"Yeah, I've met Father. What did he do with his wife and daughter, bury them?"

"Shipped 'em out of town. With Cramer's permission, as we got it here, and of course Cramer knew where but wasn't giving out. Naturally we thought it an outrage. Is the great public, are the American people, to be deceived and kept in ignorance? No. You must have had a hunch, because we just got it here—it came in less than an hour ago. Nancylee and her mother are at the Ambassador in Atlantic City, sitting room, bedroom, and bath."

"You don't say. Paid for by?"

He didn't know. He agreed that it was intolerable that the American people, of whom I was one, should be uninformed on so vital a point, and before he hung up he said he would certainly do something about it.

When Wolfe came down to the office I reported developments. At that time we still had three more to overhaul, but it was already apparent that we were going to need all we could get, so Wolfe told me to get Saul Panzer on the phone. Saul wasn't in, but an hour later he called back.

Saul Panzer free-lances. He has no office and doesn't need one. He is so good that he demands, and gets, double the market, and any day of the week he gets so many offers that he can pick as he pleases. I have never known him to turn Wolfe down except when he was so tied up he couldn't shake loose.

He took this on. He would take a train to Atlantic City that evening, sleep there, and in the morning persuade Mrs. Shepherd to let Nancylee come to New York for a talk with Wolfe. He would bring her, with Mother if necessary.

As Wolfe was finishing with Saul, Fritz entered with a tray. I looked at him with surprise, since Wolfe seldom takes on beer during the hour preceding dinner, but then, as he put the tray on the desk, I saw it wasn't beer. It was a bottle of Hi-Spot, with three glasses. Instead of turning to leave, Fritz stood by.

"It may be too cold," Fritz suggested.

With a glance of supercilious distaste at the bottle, Wolfe got the opener from his top drawer, removed the cap, and started pouring.

"It seems to me," I remarked, "like a useless sacrifice. Why suffer? If Orchard had never drunk Hi-Spot before he wouldn't know whether it tasted right or not, and even if he didn't like it they were on the air and just for politeness he would have gulped some down." I took the glass that Fritz handed me, a third full. "Anyway he drank enough to kill him, so what does it matter what we think?"

"He may have drunk it before." Wolfe held the glass to his nose, sniffed, and made a face. "At any rate, the murderer had to assume that he might have. Would the difference in taste be too great a hazard?"

"I see." I sipped. "Not so bad." I sipped again. "The only way we can really tell is to drink this and then drink some cyanide. Have you got some?"

"Don't bubble, Archie." Wolfe put his glass down after two little tastes. "Good heavens. What the devil is in it, Fritz?"

Fritz shook his head. "Ipecac?" he guessed. "Horehound? Would you like some sherry?"

"No. Water. I'll get it." Wolfe got up, marched to the hall, and turned toward the kitchen. He believes in some good healthy exercise before dinner.

That evening, Wednesday, our victims were first Elinor Vance and then Nathan Traub. It was more than three hours after midnight when Wolfe finally let Traub go, which made two nights in a row.

Thursday morning at eleven we started on Tully Strong. In the middle of it, right at noon, there was a phone call from Saul Panzer. Wolfe took it, giving me the sign to stay on. I knew from the tone of Saul's voice, just pronouncing my name, that he had no bacon.

"I'm at the Atlantic City railroad station," Saul said, "and I can either catch a train to New York in twenty minutes or go jump in the ocean, whichever you advise. I couldn't get to Mrs. Shepherd just by asking, so I tried a trick but it didn't work. Finally she and the daughter came down to the hotel lobby, but I thought it would be better to wait until they came outside, if they came, and they did. My approach was one that has worked a thousand times, but it didn't with her. She called a cop and wanted him to arrest me for annoying her. I made another try later, on the phone again, but four words was as far as I got. Now it's no use. This is the third time I've flopped on you in ten years, and that's too often. I don't want you to pay me, not even expenses."

"Nonsense." Wolfe never gets riled with Saul. "You can give me the details later, if there are any I should have. Will you reach New York in time to come to the office at six o'clock?"

"Yes."

"Good. Do that."

Wolfe resumed with Traub. As I have already mentioned, the climax of that two hours' hard work was when Traub confessed that he frequently bet on horse races. As soon as he had gone Wolfe and I went to the dining room for the lunch previously described, corn fritters with autumn honey, sausages, and a bowl of salad. Of course what added to his misery was the fact that Savarese was expected at two o'clock, because he likes to have the duration of a meal determined solely by the inclination of him and the meal, not by some extraneous phenomenon like the sound of a doorbell.

But the bell rang right on the dot.

8

YOU HAVE HEARD OF THE EXCEPTION THAT PROVES THE rule. Professor F. O. Savarese was it.

The accepted rule is that an Italian is dark and, if not actually a runt, at least not tall; that a professor is dry and pedantic, with eye trouble; and that a mathematician really lives in the stratosphere and is here just visiting relatives. Well, Savarese was an Italian-American professor of mathematics, but he was big and blond and buoyant, two inches taller than me, and he came breezing in like a March morning wind.

He spent the first twenty minutes telling Wolfe and me how fascinating and practical it would be to work out a set of mathematical formulas that could be used in the detective business. His favorite branch of mathematics, he said, was the one that dealt with the objective numerical measurement of probability. Very well. What was any detective work, any kind at all, but the objective measurement of probability? All he proposed to do was to add the word *numerical*, not as a substitute or replacement, but as an ally and reinforcement.

"I'll show you what I mean," he offered. "May I have paper and pencil?"

He had bounded over to me before I could even uncross my legs, took the pad and pencil I handed him, and bounded back to the red leather chair. When the pencil had jitterbugged on the pad for half a minute he tore off the top sheet and slid it across the desk to Wolfe, then went to work on the next sheet and in a moment tore that off and leaped to me with it.

"You should each have one," he said, "so you can follow me."

I wouldn't try to pretend I could put it down from memory, but I still have both of those sheets, in the folder marked ORCHARD, and this is what is on them:

$$u = \frac{1}{V_{2\pi} \cdot D} \left\{ 1 - \tfrac{1}{2}\, k \left(\frac{X}{D} - \tfrac{1}{3}\, \frac{X^3}{D^3} \right) \right\} e^{-\tfrac{1}{2}\, X^3/D^2}$$

"That," Savarese said, his whole face smiling with eager interest and friendliness and desire to help, "is the second approximation of the normal law of error, sometimes called the generalized law of error. Let's apply it to the simplest kind of detective problem, say the question which one of three servants in a house stole a diamond ring from a locked drawer. I should explain that X is the deviation from the mean, D is the standard deviation, k is—"

"Please!" Wolfe had to make it next door to a bellow, and did. "What are you trying to do, change the subject?"

"No." Savarese looked surprised and a little hurt. "Am I? What was the subject?"

"The death of Mr. Cyril Orchard and your connection with it."

"Oh. Of course." He smiled apologetically and spread his hands, palms up. "Perhaps later? It is one of my favorite ideas, the application of the mathematical laws of probability and error to detective problems, and a chance to discuss it with you is a golden opportunity."

"Another time. Meanwhile"—Wolfe tapped the generalized law of error with a finger tip—"I'll keep this. Which one of the people at that broadcast placed that glass and bottle in front of Mr. Orchard?"

"I don't know. I'm going to find it very interesting to compare your handling of me with the way the police did it. What you're trying to do, of course, is to proceed from probability toward certainty, as close as you can get. Say you start, as you see it, with one chance in five that I poisoned Orchard. Assuming that you have no subjective bias, your purpose is to move as rapidly as possible from that position, and you don't care which direction. Anything I say or do will move you one way or the other. If one way, the one-in-five will become one-in-four, one-in-three, and so on until it becomes one-in-one and a minute fraction, which will be close enough to affirmative certainty so that you will say you know that I killed Orchard. If it goes the other way, your one-in-five will become one-in-ten, one-in-one-hundred, one-in-one-thousand; and when it gets to one-in-ten-billion you will be close enough to negative certainty so that you will say you know that I did not kill Orchard. There is a formula—"

"No doubt." Wolfe was controlling himself very well. "If you want to compare me with the police you'll have to let me get a word in now and then. Had you ever seen Mr. Orchard before the day of the broadcast?"

"Oh, yes, six times. The first time was thirteen months earlier, in February 1947. You're going to find me remarkably exact, since the police have had me over all this, back and forth. I might as well give you everything I can that will move you toward affirmative certainty, since subjectively you would prefer that direction. Shall I do that?"

"By all means."

"I thought that would appeal to you. As a mathematician I have always been interested in the application of the calculation of probabilities to the various forms of gambling. The genesis of normal distributions—"

"Not now," Wolfe said sharply.

"Oh—of course not. There are reasons why it is exceptionally difficult to calculate probabilities in the case of horse races, and yet people bet hundreds of millions of dollars on them. A little over a year ago, studying the possibilities of some formulas, I decided to look at some tip sheets, and subscribed to three. One of them was the *Track Almanac,* published by Cyril Orchard. Asked by the police why I chose that one, I could only say that I didn't know. I forget. That is suspicious, for them and you; for me, it is simply a fact that I don't remember. One day in February last year a daily double featured by Orchard came through, and I went to see him. He had some intelligence, and if he had been interested in the mathematical problems involved I could have made good use of him, but he wasn't. In spite of that I saw him occasionally, and he once spent a week end with me at the home of a friend in New Jersey. Altogether, previous to that broadcast, I had seen him, been with him, six times. That's suspicious, isn't it?"

"Moderately," Wolfe conceded.

Savarese nodded. "I'm glad to see you keep as objective as possible. But what about this? When I learned that a popular radio program on a national network had asked for opinions on the advisability of having a horse race tipster as a guest, I wrote a letter strongly urging it, asked for the privilege of being myself the second guest on the program, and suggested that Cyril Orchard should be the tipster invited." Savarese smiled all over, beaming. "What about your one-in-five now?"

Wolfe grunted. "I didn't take that position. You assumed it for me. I suppose the police have that letter you wrote?"

"No, they haven't. No one has it. It seems that Miss Fraser's staff doesn't keep correspondence more than two or three weeks, and my letter has presumably been destroyed. If I had known that in time I might have been less candid in describing the letter's contents to the police, but on the other hand I might not have been. Obviously my treatment of that problem had an effect on my calculations of the probability of my being arrested for murder. But for a free decision I would have had to know, first, that the letter had been destroyed, and, second, that the memories of Miss Fraser's staff were vague about its contents. I learned both of those facts too late."

Wolfe stirred in his chair. "What else on the road to affirmative certainty?"

"Let's see." Savarese considered. "I think that's all, unless we go into observation of distributions, and that should be left for a secondary formula. For instance, my character, a study of which, *a posteriori,* would show it to be probable that I would commit murder for the sake of a sound but revolutionary formula. One detail of that would be my personal finances. My salary as an assistant professor is barely enough to live on endurably, but I paid ten dollars a week for that *Track Almanac.*"

"Do you gamble? Do you bet on horse races?"

"No. I never have. I know too much—or rather, I know too little. More than ninety-nine per cent of the bets placed on horse races are outbursts of emotion, not exercises of reason. I restrict my emotions to the activities for which they are qualified." Savarese waved a hand. "That starts us in the other direction, toward a negative certainty, with its conclusion that I did not kill Orchard, and we might as well go on with it. Items:

"I could not have managed that Orchard got the poison. I was seated diagonally across from him, and I did not help pass the bottles. It cannot be shown that I have ever purchased, stolen, borrowed, or possessed any cyanide. It cannot be established that I would, did, or shall profit in any way from Orchard's death. When I arrived at the broadcasting studio, at twenty minutes to eleven, everyone else was already there and I would certainly have been observed if I had gone to the refrigerator and opened its door. There is no evidence that my association with Orchard was other than as I have described it, with no element of animus or of any subjective attitude."

Savarese beamed. "How far have we gone? One-in-one-thousand?"

"I'm not with you," Wolfe said with no element of animus. "I'm not on that road at all, nor on any road. I'm wandering around poking at things. Have you ever been in Michigan?"

For the hour that was left before orchid time Wolfe fired questions

at him, and Savarese answered him briefly and to the point. Evidently
the professor really did want to compare Wolfe's technique with that
of the police, for, as he gave close attention to each question as it was
asked, he had more the air of a judge or referee sizing something up
than of a murder suspect, guilty or innocent, going through an ordeal.
The objective attitude.

He maintained it right up to four o'clock, when the session ended,
and I escorted the objective attitude to the front door, and Wolfe went
to his elevator.

A little after five Saul Panzer arrived. Coming only up to the middle of my ear, and of slight build, Saul doesn't even begin to fill the
red leather chair, but he likes to sit in it, and did so. He is pretty
objective too, and I have rarely seen him either elated or upset about
anything that had happened to him, or that he had caused to happen
to someone else, but that day he was really riled.

"It was bad judgment," he told me, frowning and glum. "Rotten
judgment. I'm ashamed to face Mr. Wolfe. I had a good story ready,
one that I fully expected to work, and all I needed was ten minutes
with the mother to put it over. But I misjudged her. I had discussed
her with a couple of the bellhops, and had talked with her on the phone,
and had a good chance to size her up in the hotel lobby and when she
came outside, and I utterly misjudged her. I can't tell you anything
about her brains or character, I didn't get that far, but she certainly
knows how to keep the dogs off. I came mighty close to spending the
day in the pound."

He told me all about it, and I had to admit it was a gloomy tale.
No operative likes to come away empty from as simple a job as that,
and Saul Panzer sure doesn't. To get his mind off of it, I mixed him
a highball and got out a deck of cards for a little congenial gin. When
six o'clock came and brought Wolfe down from the plant rooms, ending the game, I had won something better than three bucks.

Saul made his report. Wolfe sat behind his desk and listened, without interruption or comment. At the end he told Saul he had nothing
to apologize for, asked him to phone after dinner for instructions, and
let him go. Left alone with me, Wolfe leaned back and shut his eyes
and was not visibly even breathing. I got at my typewriter and tapped
out a summary of Saul's report, and was on my way to the cabinet to
file it when Wolfe's voice came:

"Archie."

"Yes, sir."

"I am stripped. This is no better than a treadmill."

"Yes, sir."

"I have to talk with that girl. Get Miss Fraser."

I did so, but we might as well have saved the nickel. Listening in on my phone, I swallowed it along with Wolfe. Miss Fraser was sorry that we had made little or no progress. She would do anything she could to help, but she was afraid, in fact she was certain, that it would be useless for her to call Mrs. Shepherd at Atlantic City and ask her to bring her daughter to New York to see Wolfe. There was no doubt that Mrs. Shepherd would flatly refuse. Miss Fraser admitted that she had influence with the child, Nancylee, but asserted that she had none at all with the mother. As for phoning Nancylee and persuading her to scoot and come on her own, she wouldn't consider it. She couldn't very well, since she had supplied the money for the mother and daughter to go away.

"You did?" Wolfe allowed himself to sound surprised. "Miss Koppel told Mr. Goodwin that none of you knew where they had gone."

"We didn't, until we saw it in the paper today. Nancylee's father was provoked, and that's putting it mildly, by all the photographers and reporters and everything else, and he blamed it on me, and I offered to pay the expense of a trip for them, but I didn't know where they decided to go."

We hung up, and discussed the outlook. I ventured to suggest two or three other possible lines of action, but Wolfe had his heart set on Nancylee, and I must admit I couldn't blame him for not wanting to start another round of conferences with the individuals he had been working on. Finally he said, in a tone that announced he was no longer discussing but telling me:

"I have to talk with that girl. Go and bring her."

I had known it was coming. "Conscious?" I asked casually.

"I said with her, not to her. She must be able to talk. You could revive her after you get her here. I should have sent you in the first place, knowing how you are with young women."

"Thank you very much. She's not a young woman, she's a minor. She wears socks."

"Archie."

"Yes, sir."

"Get her."

9 I HAD A BAD BREAK. AN IDEA THAT CAME TO ME AT THE dinner table, while I was pretending to listen to Wolfe telling how men with mustaches a foot long used to teach mathematics in schools in Montenegro, required, if it was to bear fruit, some information from the janitor at 829 Wixley Avenue. But when, immediately after dinner, I drove up there, he had gone to the movies and I had to wait over an hour for him. I got what I hoped would be all I needed, generously ladled out another buck of Hi-Spot money, drove back downtown and put the car in the garage, and went home and up to my room. Wolfe, of course, was in the office, and the door was standing open, but I didn't even stop to nod as I went by.

In my room I gave my teeth an extra good brush, being uncertain how long they would have to wait for the next one, and then did my packing for the trip by putting a comb and hairbrush in my topcoat pocket. I didn't want to have a bag to take care of. Also I made a phone call. I made it there instead of in the office because Wolfe had put it off on me without a trace of a hint regarding ways and means, and if he wanted it like that okay. In that case there was no reason why he should listen to me giving careful and explicit instructions to Saul Panzer. Downstairs again, I did pause at the office door to tell him good night, but that was all I had for him.

Tuesday night I had had a little over three hours' sleep, and Wednesday night about the same. That night, Thursday, I had less than three, and only in snatches. At six-thirty Friday morning, when I emerged to the cab platform at the Atlantic City railroad station, it was still half dark, murky, chilly, and generally unattractive. I had me a good yawn, shivered from head to foot, told a taxi driver I was his customer but he would please wait for me a minute, and then stepped to the taxi just behind him and spoke to the driver of it:

"This time of day one taxi isn't enough for me, I always need two. I'll take the one in front and you follow, and when we stop we'll have a conference."

"Where you going?"

"Not far." I pushed a dollar bill at him. "You won't get lost."

He nodded without enthusiasm and kicked his starter. I climbed into the front cab and told the driver to pull up somewhere in the vicinity of the Ambassador Hotel. It wasn't much of a haul, and a few minutes later he rolled to the curb, which at that time of day had space to spare. When the other driver stopped right behind us I signaled to him, and he came and joined us.

"I have enemies," I told them.

They exchanged a glance and one of them said, "Work it out yourself, bud, we're just hackies. My meter says sixty cents."

"I don't mean that kind of enemies. It's wife and daughter. They're ruining my life. How many ways are there for people to leave the Ambassador Hotel? I don't mean dodges like fire escapes and coal chutes, just normal ways."

"Two," one said.

"Three," the other said.

"Make up your minds."

They agreed on three, and gave me the layout.

"Then there's enough of us," I decided. "Here." I shelled out two finifs, with an extra single for the one who had carried me to even them up. "The final payment will depend on how long it takes, but you won't have to sue me. Now listen."

They did so.

Ten minutes later, a little before seven, I was standing by some kind of a bush with no leaves on it, keeping an eye on the ocean-front entrance of the Ambassador. Gobs of dirty gray mist being batted around by icy gusts made it seem more like a last resort than a resort. Also I was realizing that I had made a serious mistake when I had postponed breakfast until there would be time to do it right. My stomach had decided that since it wasn't going to be needed any more it might as well try shriveling into a ball and see how I liked that. I tried to kid it along by swallowing, but because I hadn't brushed my teeth it didn't taste like me at all, so I tried spitting instead, but that only made my stomach shrivel faster. After less than half an hour of it, when my watch said a quarter past seven, I was wishing to God I had done my planning better when one of my taxis came dashing around a corner to a stop, and the driver called to me and opened the door.

"They're off, bud."

"The station?"

"I guess so. That way." He made a U turn and stepped on the gas. "They came out the cab entrance and took one there. Tony's on their tail."

I didn't have to spur him on because he was already taking it hop, skip, and jump. My wrist watch told me nineteen past—eleven minutes before the seven-thirty for New York would leave. Only four of them had been used up when we did a fancy swerve and jerked to a stop in front of the railroad station. I hopped out. Just ahead of us a woman was paying her driver while a girl stood at her elbow.

"Duck, you damn fool," my driver growled at me. "They ain't blind, are they?"

"That's all right," I assured him. "They know I'm after them. It's a war of nerves."

Tony appeared from somewhere, and I separated myself from another pair of fives and then entered the station. There was only one ticket window working, and mother and child were at it, buying. I moseyed on to the train shed, still with three minutes to go, and was about to glance over my shoulder to see what was keeping them when they passed me on the run, holding hands, daughter in front and pulling Mom along. From the rear I saw them climb on board the train, but I stayed on the platform until the signal had been given and the wheels had started to turn, and then got on.

The diner wasn't crowded. I had a double orange juice, griddle cakes with broiled ham, coffee, French toast with sausage cakes, grape jelly, and more coffee. My stomach and I made up, and we agreed to forget it ever happened.

I decided to go have a look at the family, and here is something I'm not proud of. I had been so damn hungry that no thought of other stomachs had entered my head. But when, three cars back, I saw them and the look on their faces, the thought did come. Of course they were under other strains too, one in particular, but part of that pale, tight, anguished expression unquestionably came from hunger. They had had no time to grab anything on the way, and their manner of life was such that the idea of buying a meal on a train might not even occur to them.

I went back to the end of the car, stood facing the occupants, and called out:

"Get your breakfast in the dining car, three cars ahead! Moderate prices!"

Then I passed down the aisle, repeating it at suitable intervals, once right at their seat. It worked. They exchanged some words and then got up and staggered forward. Not only that, I had made other sales too: a woman, a man, and a couple.

By the time the family returned we were less than an hour from New York. I looked them over as they came down the aisle. Mother was small and round-shouldered and her hair was going gray. Her nose still looked thin and sharp-pointed, but not as much so as it had when she was starving. Nancylee was better-looking, and much more intelligent-looking, than I would have expected from her pictures in the papers or from Saul's description. She had lots of medium-brown hair coming below her shoulders, and blue eyes, so dark that you had to be fairly close to see the blue, that were always on the go. She showed no trace either of Mom's pointed nose or of Pop's acreage of brow. If I had been in high school I would gladly have bought her a Coke or even a sundae.

Danger would begin, I well knew, the minute they stepped off the train at Pennsylvania Station and mounted the stairs. I had decided what to do if they headed for a taxi or bus or the subway, or if Mom started to enter a phone booth. So I was right on their heels when the moment for action came, but the only action called for was a pleasant walk. They took the escalator to the street level, left the station by the north exit, and turned left. I trailed. At Ninth Avenue they turned uptown, and at Thirty-fifth Street left again. That cinched it that they were aiming straight for Wolfe's house, non-stop, and naturally I was anything but crestfallen, but what really did my heart good was the timing. It was exactly eleven o'clock, and Wolfe would get down from the plant rooms and settled in his chair just in time to welcome them.

So it was. West of Tenth Avenue they began looking at the numbers, and I began to close up. At our stoop they halted, took another look, and mounted the steps. By the time they were pushing the button I was at the bottom of the stoop, but they had taken no notice of me. It would have been more triumphant if I could have done it another way, but the trouble was that Fritz wouldn't let them in until he had checked with Wolfe. So I took the steps two at a time, used my key and flung the door open, and invited them:

"Mrs. Shepherd? Go right in."

She crossed the threshold. But Nancylee snapped at me:

"You were on the train. There's something funny about this."

"Mr. Wolfe's expecting you," I said, "if you want to call that funny. Anyway, come inside to laugh, so I can shut the door."

She entered, not taking her eyes off of me. I asked them if they wanted to leave their things in the hall, and they didn't, so I escorted them to the office. Wolfe, in his chair behind his desk, looked undecided for an instant and then got to his feet. I really appreciated that. He never rises when men enter, and his customary routine when a woman enters is to explain, if he feels like taking the trouble, that he keeps his chair because getting out of it and back in again is a more serious undertaking for him than for most men. I knew why he was breaking his rule. It was a salute to me, not just for producing them, but for getting them there exactly at the first minute of the day that he would be ready for them.

"Mrs. Shepherd," I said, "this is Mr. Nero Wolfe. Miss Nancylee Shepherd."

Wolfe bowed. "How do you do, ladies."

"My husband," Mom said in a scared but determined voice. "Where's my husband?"

"He'll be here soon," Wolfe assured her. "He was detained. Sit down, madam."

I grinned at him and shook my head. "Much obliged for trying to help, but that's not the line." I shifted the grin to the family. "I'll have to explain not only to you but to Mr. Wolfe too. Have you got the telegram with you? Let me have it a minute?"

Mom would have opened her handbag, but Nancylee stopped her. "Don't give it to him!" She snapped at me, "You let us out of here right now!"

"No," I said, "not right now, but I will in about five minutes if you still want to go. What are you afraid of? Didn't I see to it that you got some breakfast? First I would like to explain to Mr. Wolfe, and then I'll explain to you." I turned to Wolfe. "The telegram Mrs. Shepherd has in her bag reads as follows: *Take first train to New York and go to office of Nero Wolfe at 918 West Thirty-fifth Street. He is paying for this telegram. Bring Nan with you. Meet me there. Leave your things in your hotel room. Shake a leg. Al.* Saul sent it from a telegraph office in the Bronx at six-thirty this morning. You will understand why I had to go up there again to see the janitor. The *shake a leg* made it absolutely authentic, along with other things."

"Then Father didn't send it!" Nancylee was glaring at me. "I thought there was something funny about it!" She took her mother's arm. "Come on, we're going!"

"Where, Nan?"

"We're leaving here!"

"But where are we going?" Near-panic was in Mom's eyes and voice. "Home?"

"That's the point," I said emphatically. "That's just it. Where? You have three choices. First, you can go home, and when the head of the family comes from work you can tell him how you were taken in by a fake telegram. Your faces show how much that appeals to you. Second, you can take the next train back to Atlantic City, but in that case I phone immediately, before you leave, to Mr. Shepherd at the warehouse where he works, and tell him that you're here with a wild tale about a telegram, and of course he'll want to speak to you. So again you would have to tell him about being fooled by a fake telegram."

Mom looked as if she needed some support, so I moved a chair up behind her and she sat.

"You're utterly awful," Nancylee said. "Just utterly!"

I ignored her and continued to her mother. "Or, third, you can stay here and Mr. Wolfe will discuss some matters with Nancylee, and ask her some questions. It may take two hours, or three, or four, so the sooner he gets started the better. You'll get an extra good lunch. As soon as Mr. Wolfe is through I'll take you to the station and put you on a train for Atlantic City. We'll pay your fare both ways and all expenses, such as taxi fare, and your breakfast, and dinner on the train going back. Mr. Shepherd, whom I have met, will never know anything about it." I screwed my lips. "Those are the only choices I can think of, those three."

Nancylee sat down and—another indication of her intelligence— in the red leather chair.

"This is terrible," Mom said hopelessly. "This is the worst thing . . . you don't look like a man that would do a thing like this. Are you absolutely sure my husband didn't send that telegram? Honestly?"

"Positively not," I assured her. "He doesn't know a thing about it and never will. There's nothing terrible about it. Long before bedtime you'll be back in that wonderful hotel room."

She shook her head as if all was lost.

"It's not so wonderful," Nancylee asserted. "The shower squirts sideways and they won't fix it." Suddenly she clapped a hand to her mouth, went pop-eyed, and sprang from the chair.

"Jumping cats!" she squealed. "Where's your radio? It's Friday! She's broadcasting!"

"No radio," I said firmly. "It's out of order. Here, let me take your coat and hat."

10

DURING THE ENTIRE PERFORMANCE, EXCEPT WHEN WE knocked off for lunch, Mrs. Shepherd sat with sagging shoulders on one of the yellow chairs. Wolfe didn't like her there and at various points gave her suggestions, such as going up to the south room for a nap or up to the top to look at the orchids, but she wasn't moving. She was of course protecting her young, but I swear I think her main concern was that if she let us out of her sight we might pull another telegram on her signed Al.

I intend to be fair and just to Nancylee. It is quite true that this is on record, on a page of my notebook:

W: You have a high regard for Miss Fraser, haven't you, Miss Shepherd?

N: Oh, yes! She's simply utterly!

On another page:

W: Why did you leave high school without graduating, if you were doing so well?

N: I was offered a modeling job. Just small time, two dollars an hour not very often and mostly legs, but the cash was simply sweet!

W: You're looking forward to a life of that—modeling?

N: Oh, no! I'm really very serious-minded. *Am* I! I'm going into radio. I'm going to have a program like Miss Fraser—you know, human and get the laughs, but worthwhile and *good*. How often have you been on the air, Mr. Wolfe?

On still another page:

W: How have you been passing your time at Atlantic City?

N: Rotting away. That place is as dead as last week's date. Simply stagnating. Utterly!

Those are verbatim, and there are plenty more where they came from, but there are other pages to balance them. She could talk to the point when she felt like it, as for instance when she explained that she would have been suspicious of the telegram, and would have insisted that her mother call her father at the warehouse by long distance, if she hadn't learned from the papers that Miss Fraser had engaged Nero Wolfe to work on the case. And when he got her going on the subject of Miss Fraser's staff, she not only showed that she had done a neat little job of sizing them up, but also conveyed it to us without including anything that she might be called upon either to prove or to eat.

It was easy to see how desperate Wolfe was from the way he confined himself, up to lunch time, to skating around the edges, getting her used to his voice and manner and to hearing him ask any and every kind of question. By the time Fritz summoned us to the dining room I couldn't see that he had got the faintest flicker of light from any direction.

When we were back in the office and settled again, with Mom in her same chair and Nancylee dragging on a cigarette as if she had been at it for years, Wolfe resumed as before, but soon I noticed that he was circling in toward the scene of the crime. After getting himself up to date on the East Bronx Fraser Girls' Club and how Nancylee had organized it and put it at the top, he went right on into the studio and began on the Fraser broadcasts. He learned that Nancylee was always there on Tuesday, and sometimes on Friday too. Miss Fraser had promised her that she could get on a live mike some day, at least for a line or two. On the network! Most of the time she sat with the audience, front row, but she was always ready to help with anything, and frequently she was allowed to, but only on account of Miss Fraser. The others thought she was a nuisance.

"Are you?" Wolfe asked.

"You bet I am! But Miss Fraser doesn't think so because she knows I think she's the very hottest thing on the air, simply super, and then there's my club, so you see how that is. The old ego mego."

You can see why I'd like to be fair and just to her.

Wolfe nodded as man to man. "What sort of things do you help with?"

"Oh." She waved a hand. "Somebody drops a page of script, I pick it up. One of the chairs squeaks, I hear it first and bring another one. The day it happened, I got the tray of glasses from the cabinet and took them to the table."

"You did? The day Mr. Orchard was a guest?"

"Sure, I often did that."

"Do you have a key to the cabinet?"

"No, Miss Vance has. She opened it and got the tray of glasses out." Nancylee smiled. "I broke one once, and did Miss Fraser throw a fit? No definitely. She just told me to bring a paper cup, that's how super she is."

"Marvelous. When did that happen?"

"Oh, a long while ago, when they were using the plain glasses, before they changed to the dark blue ones."

"How long ago was it?"

"Nearly a year, it must be." Nancylee nodded. "Yes, because it was when they first started to drink Hi-Spot on the program, and the first few times they used plain clear glasses and then they had to change—"

She stopped short.

"Why did they have to change?"

"I don't know."

I expected Wolfe to pounce, or at least to push. There was no doubt about it. Nancylee had stopped herself because she was saying, or starting to say, something that she didn't intend to let out, and when she said she didn't know she was lying. But Wolfe whirled and skated off:

"I suspect to get them so heavy they wouldn't break." He chuckled as if that were utterly amusing. "Have you ever drunk Hi-Spot, Miss Shepherd?"

"Me? Are you kidding? When my club got to the top they sent me ten cases. Truckloads!"

"I don't like it much. Do you?"

"Oh . . . I guess so. I guess I adore it, but not too much at a time. When I get my program and have Shepherd Clubs I'm going to work it a different way." She frowned. "Do you think Nancylee Shepherd is a good radio name, or is Nan Shepherd better, or should I make one up? Miss Fraser's name was Oxhall, and she married a man named Koppel but he died, and when she got into radio she didn't want to use either of them and made one up."

"Either of yours," Wolfe said judiciously, "would be excellent. You must tell me some time how you're going to handle your clubs. Do you think Hi-Spot has pepper in it?"

"I don't know, I never thought. It's a lot of junk mixed together. Not at all frizoo."

"No," Wolfe agreed, "not frizoo. What other things do you do to help out at the broadcasts?"

"Oh, just like I said."

"Do you ever help pass the glasses and bottles around—to Miss Fraser and Mr. Meadows and the guests?"

"No, I tried to once, but they wouldn't let me."

"Where were you—the day we're talking about—while that was being done?"

"Sitting on the piano bench. They want me to stay in the audience while they're on the air, but sometimes I don't."

"Did you see who did the passing—to Mr. Orchard, for instance?"

Nancylee smiled in good-fellowship. "Now you'd like to know that, wouldn't you? But I didn't. The police asked me that about twenty million times."

"No doubt. I ask you once. Do you ever take the bottles from the cabinet and put them in the refrigerator?"

"Sure, I often do that—or I should say I help. That's Miss Vance's job, and she can't carry them all at once, so she has to make two trips, so quite often she takes four bottles and I take three."

"I see. I shouldn't think she would consider you a nuisance. Did you help with the bottles that Tuesday?"

"No, because I was looking at the new hat Miss Fraser had on, and I didn't see Miss Vance starting to get the bottles."

"Then Miss Vance had to make two trips, first four bottles and then three?"

"Yes, because Miss Fraser's hat was really something for the preview. Utterly first run! It had—"

"I believe you." Wolfe's voice sharpened a little, though perhaps only to my experienced ear. "That's right, isn't it, first four bottles and then three?"

"Yes, that's right."

"Making a total of seven?"

"Oh, you can add!" Nancylee exclaimed delightedly. She raised her right hand with four fingers extended, then her left hand with three, and looked from one to the other. "Correct. Seven!"

"Seven," Wolfe agreed. "I can add, and you can, but Miss Vance and Mr. Meadows can't. I understand that only four bottles are required for the program, but that they like to have extra ones in the refrigerator to provide for possible contingencies. But Miss Vance and Mr. Meadows say that the total is eight bottles. You say seven. Miss Vance says that they are taken from the cabinet to the refrigerator in two lots, four and four. You say four and three."

Wolfe leaned forward. "Miss Shepherd." His voice cut. "You will explain to me immediately, and satisfactorily, why they say eight and you say seven. Why?"

She didn't look delighted at all. She said nothing.

"Why?" It was the crack of a whip.

"I don't know!" she blurted.

I had both eyes on her, and even from a corner of one, with the other one shut, it would have been as plain as daylight that she did know, and furthermore that she had clammed and intended to stay clammed.

"Pfui." Wolfe wiggled a finger at her. "Apparently, Miss Shepherd, you have the crackbrained notion that whenever the fancy strikes you you can say you don't know, and I'll let it pass. You tried it about the glasses, and now this. I'll give you one minute to start telling me why the others said the customary number of bottles taken to the refrigerator is eight, and you say seven. —Archie, time it."

I looked at my wrist, and then back at Nancylee. But she merely stayed a clam. Her face showed no sign that she was trying to make one up, or even figuring what would happen if she didn't. She was simply utterly not saying anything. I let her have an extra ten seconds, and then announced:

"It's up."

Wolfe sighed. "I'm afraid, Miss Shepherd, that you and your mother will not return to Atlantic City. Not today. It is—"

A sound of pain came from Mom—not a word, just a sound. Nancy cried:

"But you promised—"

"No. I did not. Mr. Goodwin did. You can have that out with him, but not until after I have given him some instructions." Wolfe turned to me. "Archie, you will escort Miss Shepherd to the office of Inspector Cramer. Her mother may accompany you or go home, as she prefers. But first take this down, type it, and take it with you. Two carbons. A letter to Inspector Cramer."

Wolfe leaned back, closed his eyes, pursed his lips, and in a moment began:

"Regarding the murder of Cyril Orchard, I send you this information by Mr. Goodwin, who is taking Miss Nancylee Shepherd to you. He will explain how Miss Shepherd was brought to New York from Atlantic City. Paragraph.

"I suggest that Miss Madeline Fraser should be arrested without delay, charged with the murder of Cyril Orchard. It is obvious that the members of her staff are joined in a conspiracy. At first I assumed that their purpose was to protect her, but I am now convinced that I was wrong. At my office Tuesday evening it was ludicrously transparent that they were all deeply concerned about Miss Fraser's getting home safely, or so I then thought. I now believe that their concern was of a very different kind. Paragraph.

"That evening, here, Mr. Meadows was unnecessarily explicit and explanatory when I asked him how he decided which bottles to take from the refrigerator. There were various other matters which aroused my suspicion, plainly pointing to Miss Fraser, among them their pretense that they cannot remember who placed the glass and bottle in front of Mr. Orchard, which is of course ridiculous. Certainly they remember; and it is not conceivable that they would conspire unanimously to defend one of their number from exposure, unless that one were Miss Fraser. They are moved, doubtless, by varying considerations—loyalty, affection, or merely the desire to keep their jobs, which they will no longer have after Miss Fraser is arrested and disgraced—and, I hope, punished as the law provides. Paragraph.

"All this was already in my mind, but not with enough conviction to put it to you thus strongly, so I waited until I could have a talk with Miss Shepherd. I have now done that. It is plain that she too is in the conspiracy, and that leaves no doubt that it is Miss Fraser who is being shielded from exposure, since Miss Shepherd would do anything for her but nothing for any of the others. Miss Shepherd has lied to me twice that I am sure of, once when she said that she didn't know why the glasses that they drank from were changed, and once when she would give no explanation of her contradiction of the others regarding the number of bottles put in the refrigerator. Mr. Goodwin will give you the details of that. Paragraph.

"When you have got Miss Fraser safely locked in a cell, I would suggest that in questioning her you concentrate on the changing of the glasses. That happened nearly a year ago, and therefore it seems likely that the murder of Mr. Orchard was planned far in advance. This should make it easier for you, not harder, especially if you are able to persuade Miss Shepherd, by methods available to you, to tell all she knows about it. I do not—*Archie!*"

If Nancylee had had a split personality and it had been the gungirl half of her that suddenly sprang into action, I certainly would have been caught with my fountain pen down. But she didn't pull a gat. All she did was come out of her chair like a hurricane, get to me before I could even point the pen at her, snatch the notebook and hurl it across the room, and turn to blaze away at Wolfe:

"That's a lie! It's all a lie!"

"Now, Nan," came from Mrs. Shepherd, in a kind of shaky hopeless moan.

I was on my feet at the hurricane's elbow, feeling silly. Wolfe snapped at me:

"Get the notebook and we'll finish. She's hysterical. If she does it again put her in the bathroom."

Nancylee was gripping my coat sleeve. "No!" she cried. "You're a stinker, you know you are! Changing the glasses had nothing to do with it! And I don't know why they changed them, either—you're just a stinker—"

"Stop it!" Wolfe commanded her. "Stop screaming. If you have anything to say, sit down and say it. Why did they change the glasses?"

"I don't know!"

In crossing the room for it I had to detour around Mom, and, doing so, I gave her a pat on the shoulder, but I doubt if she was aware of it. From her standpoint there was nothing left. When I got turned around again Nancylee was still standing there, and from the stiffness of her back she looked put for the day. But as I reached my desk suddenly she spoke, no screaming:

"I honestly don't know why they changed the glasses, because I was just guessing, but if I tell you what I was guessing I'll have to tell you something I promised Miss Fraser I would never tell anybody."

Wolfe nodded. "As I said. Shielding Miss Fraser."

"I'm not shielding her! She doesn't have to be shielded!"

"Don't get hysterical again. What was it you guessed?"

"I want to phone her."

"Of course you do. To warn her. So she can get away."

Nancylee slapped a palm on his desk.

"Don't do that!" he thundered.

"You're such a stinker!"

"Very well. Archie, lock her in the bathroom and phone Mr. Cramer to send for her."

I stood up, but she paid no attention to me. "All right," she said, "then I'll tell her how you made me tell, and my mother can tell her too. When they got the new glasses I didn't know why, but I noticed right away, the broadcast that day, about the bottles too. That day Miss Vance didn't take eight bottles, she only took seven. If it hadn't been for that I might not have noticed, but I did, and when they were broadcasting I saw that the bottle they gave Miss Fraser had a piece of tape on it. And every time after that it has always been seven bottles, and they always give Miss Fraser the one with tape on it. So I thought there was some connection, the new glasses and the tape on the bottle, but I was just guessing."

"I wish you'd sit down, Miss Shepherd. I don't like tipping my head back."

"I wouldn't care if you broke your old neck!"

"Now, Nan," her mother moaned.

Nancylee went to the red leather chair and lowered herself onto the edge of it.

"You said," Wolfe murmured, "that you promised Miss Fraser not to tell about this. When did you promise, recently?"

"No, a long time ago. Months ago. I was curious about the tape on the bottle, and one day I asked Miss Vance about it, and afterward Miss Fraser told me it was something very personal to her and she made me promise never to tell. Twice since then she has asked me if I was keeping the promise and I told her I was and I always would. And now here I am! But you saying she should be arrested for murder . . . just because I said I didn't know . . ."

"I gave other reasons."

"But she won't be arrested now, will she? The way I've explained?"

"We'll see. Probably not." Wolfe sounded comforting. "No one has ever told you what the tape is on the bottle for?"

"No."

"Haven't you guessed?"

"No, I haven't, and I'm not going to guess now. I don't know what it's for or who puts it on or when they put it on, or anything about it except what I've said, that the bottle they give Miss Fraser has a piece of tape on it. And that's been going on a long time, nearly a year, so it couldn't have anything to do with that man getting murdered just last week. So I hope you're satisfied."

"Fairly well," Wolfe conceded.

"Then may I phone her now?"

"I'd rather you didn't. You see, she has hired me to investigate this murder, and I'd prefer to tell her about this myself—and apologize for suspecting her. By the way, the day Mr. Orchard was poisoned— did Miss Fraser's bottle have tape on it that day as usual?"

"I didn't notice it that day, but I suppose so, it always did."

"You're sure you didn't notice it?"

"What do you think? Am I lying again?"

Wolfe shook his head. "I doubt it. You don't sound like it. But one thing you can tell me, about the tape. What was it like and where was it on the bottle?"

"Just a piece of Scotch tape, that's all, around the neck of the bottle, down nearly to where the bottle starts to get bigger."

"Always in the same place?"

"Yes."

"How wide is it?"

"You know, Scotch tape, about that wide." She held a thumb and fingertip about half an inch apart.

"What color?"

"Brown—or maybe it looks brown because the bottle is."

"Always the same color?"

"Yes."

"Then it couldn't have been very conspicuous."

"I didn't say it was conspicuous. It wasn't."

"You have good eyesight, of course, at your age." Wolfe glanced at the clock and turned to me. "When is the next train for Atlantic City?"

"Four-thirty," I told him.

"Then you have plenty of time. Give Mrs. Shepherd enough to cover all expenses. You will take her and her daughter to the station. Since they do not wish it to be known that they have made this trip, it would be unwise for them to do any telephoning, and of course you will make sure that they board the right train, and that the train actually starts. As you know, I do not trust trains either to start or, once started, to stop."

"We're going back," Mom said, unbelieving but daring to hope.

11 THERE WAS ONE LITTLE INCIDENT I SHOULDN'T SKIP, on the train when I had found their seats for them and was turning to go. I had made no effort to be sociable, since their manner, especially Nancylee's, had made it plain that if I had stepped into a manhole they wouldn't even have halted to glance down in. But as I turned to go Mom suddenly reached up to pat me on the shoulder. Apparently the pat I had given her at one of her darkest moments had been noticed after all, or maybe it was because I had got them Pullman seats. I grinned at her, but didn't risk offering to shake hands in farewell. I ride my luck only so far.

Naturally another party was indicated, but I didn't realize how urgent it was until I got back to the office and found a note, on a sheet from Wolfe's memo pad, waiting for me under a paperweight on my desk—he being, as per schedule, up in the plant rooms. The note said:

> AG—
> Have all seven of them here at six o'clock.
> NW

Just like snapping your fingers. I scowled at the note. Why couldn't it be after dinner, allowing more time both to get them and to work on them? Not to mention that I already had a fairly good production record for the day, with the 11:00 A.M. delivery I had made. My watch said ten to five. I swallowed an impulse to mount to the plant rooms and give him an argument, and reached for the phone.

I ran into various difficulties, including resistance to a summons on such short notice, with which I was in complete sympathy. Bill

Meadows balked good, saying that he had already told Wolfe everything he knew, including the time he had thrown a baseball through a
windowpane, and I had to put pressure on him with menacing hints.
Madeline Fraser and Deborah Koppel were reluctant but had to admit
that Wolfe should either be fired or given all possible help. They
agreed to bring Elinor Vance. Nathan Traub, whom I got first, at his
office, was the only one who offered no objection, though he commented that he would have to call off an important appointment. The
only two I fell down on were Savarese and Strong. The professor had
left town for the week end, I supposed to hunt formulas, and Tully
Strong just couldn't be found, though I tried everywhere, including all
the sponsors.

Shortly before six I phoned up to Wolfe to report. The best he had
for me was a grunt. I remarked that five out of seven, at that hour on
a Friday, was nothing to be sneezed at. He replied that seven would
have been better.

"Yeah," I agreed. "I've sent Savarese and Strong telegrams signed
Al, but what if they don't get them on time?"

So there were five. Wolfe doesn't like to be seen, by anyone but
Fritz or me, sitting around waiting for people, I imagine on the theory
that it's bad for his prestige, and therefore he didn't come down to the
office until I passed him the word that all five were there. Then he
favored us by appearing. He entered, bowed to them, crossed to his
chair, and got himself comfortable. It was cozier and more intimate
than it had been three days earlier, with the gatecrashers absent.

There was a little conversation. Traub offered some pointed remarks about Wolfe's refusal to admit reporters for an interview. Ordinarily, with an opening like that, Wolfe counters with a nasty
crusher, but now he couldn't be bothered. He merely waved it away.

"I got you people down here," he said, perfectly friendly, "for a
single purpose, and if you're not to be late for your dinners we'd better
get at it. Tuesday evening I told you that you were all lying to me,
but I didn't know then how barefaced you were about it. Why the
devil didn't you tell me about the piece of tape on Miss Fraser's
bottle?"

They all muffed it badly, even Miss Fraser, with the sole exception
of Traub. He alone looked just bewildered.

"Tape?" he asked. "What tape?"

It took the other four an average of three seconds even to begin
deciding what to do about their faces.

"Who is going to tell me about it?" Wolfe inquired. "Not all of
you at once. Which one?"

"But," Bill Meadows stammered, "we don't know what you're talking about."

"Nonsense." Wolfe was less friendly. "Don't waste time on that. Miss Shepherd spent most of the day here and I know all about it." His eyes stopped on Miss Fraser. "She couldn't help it, madam. She did quite well for a child, and she surrendered only under the threat of imminent peril to you."

"What's this all about?" Traub demanded.

"It's nothing, Nat," Miss Fraser assured him. "Nothing of any importance. Just a little . . . a sort of joke . . . among us . . . that you don't know about . . ."

"Nothing to it!" Bill Meadows said, a little too loud. "There's a perfectly simple—"

"Wait, Bill." Deborah Koppel's voice held quiet authority. Her gaze was at Wolfe. "Will you tell us exactly what Nancylee said?"

"Certainly," Wolfe assented. "The bottle served to Miss Fraser on the broadcast is always identified with a strip of Scotch tape. That has been going on for months, nearly a year. The tape is either brown, the color of the bottle, or transparent, is half an inch wide, and encircles the neck of the bottle near the shoulder."

"Is that all she told you?"

"That's the main thing. Let's get that explained. What's the tape for?"

"Didn't Nancylee tell you?"

"She said she didn't know."

Deborah was frowning. "Why, she must know! It's quite simple. As we told you, when we get to the studio the day of a broadcast Miss Vance takes the bottles from the cabinet and puts them in the refrigerator. But that gives them only half an hour or a little longer to get cold, and Miss Fraser likes hers as cold as possible, so a bottle for her is put in earlier and the tape put on to tell it from the others."

"Who puts it there and when?"

"Well—that depends. Sometimes one of us puts it there the day before . . . sometimes it's one left over from the preceding broadcast . . ."

"Good heavens," Wolfe murmured. "I didn't know you were an imbecile, Miss Koppel."

"I am not an imbecile, Mr. Wolfe."

"I'll have to have more than your word for it. I presume the explanation you have given me was concocted to satisfy the casual curiosity of anyone who might notice the tape on the bottle—and, incidentally, I wouldn't be surprised if it was offered to Miss Shepherd and after further observation she rejected it. That's one thing she didn't tell me. For that purpose the explanation would be adequate—except with Miss Shepherd—but to try it on me! I'll withdraw the 'imbecile,' since I blurted it at you without warning, but I do think you might have managed something a little less flimsy."

"It may be flimsy," Bill Meadows put in aggressively, "but it happens to be true."

"My dear sir." Wolfe was disgusted. "You too? Then why didn't it satisfy Miss Shepherd, if it was tried on her, and why was she sworn to secrecy? Why weren't all the bottles put in the refrigerator in advance, to get them all cold, instead of just the one for Miss Fraser? There are—"

"Because someone—" Bill stopped short.

"Precisely," Wolfe agreed with what he had cut off. "Because hundreds of people use that studio between Miss Fraser's broadcasts, and someone would have taken them from the refrigerator, which isn't locked. That's what you were about to say, but didn't, because you realized there would be the same hazard for one bottle as for eight." Wolfe shook his head. "No, it's no good. I'm tired of your lies; I want the truth; and I'll get it because nothing else can meet the tests I am now equipped to apply. Why is the tape put on the bottle?"

They looked at one another.

"No," Deborah Koppel said to anybody and everybody.

"What *is* all this?" Traub demanded peevishly.

No one paid any attention to him.

"Why not," Wolfe inquired, "try me with the same answer you have given the police?"

No reply.

Elinor Vance spoke, not to Wolfe. "It's up to you, Miss Fraser. I think we have to tell him."

"No," Miss Koppel insisted.

"I don't see any other way out of it, Debby," Madeline Fraser declared. "You shouldn't have told him that silly lie. It wasn't good enough for him and you know it." Her gray-green eyes went to Wolfe. "It would be fatal for me, for all of us, if this became known. I don't suppose you would give me your word to keep it secret?"

"How could I, madam?" Wolfe turned a palm up. "Under the circumstances? But I'll share it as reluctantly, and as narrowly, as the circumstances will permit."

"All right. Damn that Cyril Orchard, for making this necessary.

The tape on the bottle shows that it is for me. My bottle doesn't contain Hi-Spot. I can't drink Hi-Spot."

"Why not?"

"It gives me indigestion."

"Good God!" Nathan Traub cried, his smooth low-pitched voice transformed into a squeak.

"I can't help it, Nat," Miss Fraser told him firmly, "but it does."

"And that," Wolfe demanded, "is your desperate and fatal secret?"

She nodded. "My Lord, could anything be worse? If that got around? If Leonard Lyons got it, for instance? I stuck to it the first few times, but it was no use. I wanted to cut that from the program, serving it, but by that time the Hi-Spot people were crazy about it, especially Anderson and Owen, and of course I couldn't tell them the truth. I tried faking it, not drinking much, but even a few sips made me sick. It must be an allergy."

"I congratulate you," Wolfe said emphatically.

"Good God," Traub muttered. He pointed a finger at Wolfe. "It is absolutely essential that this get to no one. No one whatever!"

"It's out now," Miss Koppel said quietly but tensely. "It's gone now."

"So," Wolfe asked, "you used a substitute?"

"Yes." Miss Fraser went on: "It was the only way out. We used black coffee. I drink gallons of it anyhow, and I like it either hot or cold. With sugar in it. It looks enough like Hi-Spot, which is dark brown, and of course in the bottle it can't be seen anyway, and we changed to dark blue glasses so it couldn't be seen that it didn't fizz."

"Who makes the coffee?"

"My cook, in my apartment."

"Who bottles it?"

"She does—my cook—she puts it in a Hi-Spot bottle, and puts the cap on."

"When, the day of the broadcast?"

"No, because it would still be hot, or at least warm, so she does it the day before and puts it in the refrigerator."

"Not at the broadcasting studio?"

"Oh, no, in my kitchen."

"Does she put the tape on it?"

"No, Miss Vance does that. In the morning she gets it—she always comes to my apartment to go downtown with me—and she puts the tape on it, and takes it to the studio in her bag, and puts it in the refrigerator there. She has to be careful not to let anyone see her do that."

"I feel better," Bill Meadows announced abruptly. He had his handkerchief out and was wiping his forehead.

"Why?" Wolfe asked him.

"Because I knew this had to come sooner or later, and I'm glad it was you that got it instead of the cops. It's been a cockeyed farce, all this digging to find out who had it in for this guy Orchard. Nobody wanted to poison Orchard. The poison was in the coffee and Orchard got it by mistake."

That finished Traub. A groan came from him, his chin went down, and he sat shaking his head in despair.

Wolfe was frowning. "Are you trying to tell me that the police don't know that the poisoned bottle held coffee?"

"Oh, sure, they know that." Bill wanted to help now. "But they've kept it under their hats. You notice it hasn't been in the papers. And none of us has spilled it, you can see why we wouldn't. They know it was coffee all right, but they think it was meant for Orchard, and it wasn't, it was meant for Miss Fraser."

Bill leaned forward and was very earnest. "Damn it, don't you see what we're up against? If we tell it and it gets known, God help the program! We'd get hooted off the air. But as long as we don't tell it, everybody thinks the poison was meant for Orchard, and that's why I said it was a farce. Well, we didn't tell, and as far as I'm concerned we never would."

"How have you explained the coffee to the police?"

"We haven't explained it. We didn't know how the poison got in the bottle, did we? Well, we didn't know how the coffee got there either. What else could we say?"

"Nothing, I suppose, since you blackballed the truth. How have you explained the tape?"

"We haven't explained it."

"Why not?"

"We haven't been asked to."

"Nonsense. Certainly you have."

"I haven't."

"Thanks, Bill." It was Madeline Fraser, smiling at him. "But there's no use trying to save any pieces." She turned to Wolfe. "He's trying to protect me from—don't they call it tampering with evidence? You remember that after the doctor came Mr. Strong took the four bottles from the table and started off with them, just a foolish impulse he had, and Mr. Traub and I took them from him and put them back on the table."

Wolfe nodded.

"Well, that was when I removed the tape from the bottle."

"I see. Good heavens! It's a wonder all of you didn't collectively gather them up, and the glasses, and march to the nearest sink to wash up." Wolfe went back to Bill. "You said Mr. Orchard got the poisoned coffee by mistake. How did that happen?"

"Traub gave it to him. Traub didn't—"

Protests came at him from both directions, all of them joining in. Traub even left his chair to make it emphatic.

Bill got a little flushed, but he was stubborn and heedless. "Since we're telling it," he insisted, "we'd better tell it all."

"You're not sure it was Nat," Miss Koppel said firmly.

"Certainly I'm sure! You know damn well it was! You know damn well we all saw—all except Lina—that Orchard had her bottle, and of course it was Traub that gave it to him, because Traub was the only one that didn't know about the tape. Anyhow I saw him! —That's the way it was, Mr. Wolfe. But when the cops started on us apparently we all had the same idea—I forget who started it—that it would be best not to remember who put the bottle in front of Orchard. So we didn't. Now that you know about the tape, I do remember, and if the others don't they ought to."

"Quit trying to protect me, Bill," Miss Fraser scolded him. "It was my idea, about not remembering. I started it."

Again several of them spoke at once. Wolfe showed them a palm:

"Please! —Mr. Traub. Manifestly it doesn't matter whether you give me a yes or a no, since you alone were not aware that one of the bottles had a distinction; but I ask you pro forma, did you place that bottle before Mr. Orchard?"

"I don't know," Traub said belligerently, "and I don't care. Meadows doesn't know either."

"But you did help pass the glasses and bottles around?"

"I've told you I did. I thought it was fun." He threw up both hands. "Fun!"

"There's one thing," Madeline Fraser put in, for Wolfe. "Mr. Meadows said that they all saw that Mr. Orchard had my bottle, except me. That's only partly true. I didn't notice it at first, but when I lifted the glass to drink and smelled the Hi-Spot I knew someone else had my glass. I went ahead and faked the drinking, and as I went on with the script I saw that the bottle with the tape on it was a little nearer to him than to me—as you know, he sat across from me. I had to decide quick what to do—not me with the Hi-Spot, but him with the coffee. I was afraid he would blurt out that it tasted like coffee, especially since he had taken two big gulps. I was feeling relieved that apparently he wasn't going to, when he sprang up with that terrible cry . . . so what Mr. Meadows said was only partly true. I suppose he was protecting me some more, but I'm tired of being protected by everybody."

"He isn't listening, Lina," Miss Koppel remarked.

It was a permissible conclusion, but not necessarily sound. Wolfe had leaned back in his chair and closed his eyes, and even to me it might have seemed that he was settling for a snooze but for two details: first, dinner time was getting close, and second, the tip of his right forefinger was doing a little circle on the arm of his chair, around and around. The silence held for seconds, made a minute, and started on another one.

Someone said something.

Wolfe's eyes came half open and he straightened up.

"I could," he said, either to himself or to them, "ask you to stay to dinner. Or to return after dinner. But if Miss Fraser is tired of being protected, I am tired of being humbugged. There are things I need to know, but I don't intend to try to pry them out of you without a lever. If you are ready to let me have them, I'm ready to take them. You know what they are as well as I do. It now seems obvious that this was an attempt to kill Miss Fraser. What further evidence is there to support that assumption, and what evidence is there, if any, to contradict it? Who wants Miss Fraser to die, and why? Particularly, who of those who had access to the bottle of coffee, at any time from the moment it was bottled at her apartment to the moment when it was served at the broadcast? And so on. I won't put all the questions; you know what I want. Will any of you give it to me—any of it?"

His gaze passed along the line. No one said a word.

"One or more of you," he said, "might prefer not to speak in the presence of the others. If so, do you want to come back later? This evening?"

"If I had anything to tell you," Bill Meadows asserted, "I'd tell you now."

"You sure would," Traub agreed.

"I thought not," Wolfe said grimly. "To get anything out of you another Miss Shepherd would be necessary. One other chance: if you prefer not even to make an appointment in the presence of the others, we are always here to answer the phone. But I would advise you not to delay." He pushed his chair back and got erect. "That's all I have for you now, and you have nothing for me."

They didn't like that much. They wanted to know what he was

going to do. Especially and unanimously, they wanted to know what about their secret. Was the world going to hear of what a sip of Hi-Spot did to Madeline Fraser? On that Wolfe refused to commit himself. The stubbornest of the bunch was Traub. When the others finally left he stayed behind, refusing to give up the fight, even trying to follow Wolfe into the kitchen. I had to get rude to get rid of him.

When Wolfe emerged from the kitchen, instead of bearing left toward the dining room he returned to the office, although dinner was ready.

I followed. "What's the idea? Not hungry?"

"Get Mr. Cramer."

I went to my desk and obeyed.

Wolfe got on.

"How do you do, sir." He was polite but far from servile. "Yes. No. No, indeed. If you will come to my office after dinner, say at nine o'clock, I'll tell you why you haven't got anywhere on that Orchard case. No, not only that, I think you'll find it helpful. No, nine o'clock would be better."

He hung up, scowled at me, and headed for the dining room. By the time he had seated himself, tucked his napkin in the V of his vest, and removed the lid from the onion soup, letting the beautiful strong steam sail out, his face had completely cleared and he was ready to purr.

12

Inspector Cramer, adjusted to ease in the red leather chair, with beer on the little table at his elbow, manipulated his jaw so that the unlighted cigar made a cocky upward angle from the left side of his mouth.

"Yes," he admitted. "You can have it all for a nickel. That's where I am. Either I'm getting older or murderers are getting smarter."

He was in fact getting fairly gray and his middle, though it would never get into Wolfe's class, was beginning to make pretensions, but his eyes were as sharp as ever and his heavy broad shoulders showed no inclination to sink under the load.

"But," he went on, sounding more truculent than he actually was because keeping the cigar where he wanted it made him talk through his teeth, "I'm not expecting any nickel from you. You don't look as if you needed anything. You look as pleased as if someone had just given you a geranium."

"I don't like geraniums."

"Then what's all the happiness about? Have you got to the point where you're ready to tell Archie to mail out the bills?"

He not only wasn't truculent; he was positively mushy. Usually he called me Goodwin. He called me Archie only when he wanted to peddle the impression that he regarded himself as one of the family, which he wasn't.

Wolfe shook his head. "No, I'm far short of that. But I am indeed pleased. I like the position I'm in. It seems likely that you and your trained men—up to a thousand of them, I assume, on a case as blazoned as this one—are about to work like the devil to help me earn a fee. Isn't that enough to give me a smirk?"

"The hell you say." Cramer wasn't so sugary. "According to the papers your fee is contingent."

"So it is."

"On what you do. Not on what we do."

"Of course," Wolfe agreed. He leaned back and sighed comfortably. "You're much too clearsighted not to appraise the situation, which is a little peculiar, as I do. Would you like me to describe it?"

"I'd love it. You're a good describer."

"Yes, I think I am. You have made no progress, and after ten days you are sunk in a morass, because there is a cardinal fact which you have not discovered. I have. I have discovered it by talking with the very persons who have been questioned by you and your men many times, and it was not given to me willingly. Only by intense and sustained effort did I dig it out. Then why should I pass it on to you? Why don't I use it myself, and go on to triumph?"

Cramer put his beer glass down. "You're telling me."

"That was rhetoric. The trouble is that, while without this fact you can't even get started, with it there is still a job to be done; that job will require further extended dealing with these same people, their histories and relationships; and I have gone as far as I can with them unless I hire an army. You already have an army. The job will probably need an enormous amount of the sort of work for which your men are passably equipped, some of them even adequately, so why shouldn't they do it? Isn't it the responsibility of the police to catch a murderer?"

Cramer was now wary and watchful. "From you," he said, "that's one hell of a question. More rhetoric?"

"Oh, no. That one deserves an answer. Yours, I feel sure, is yes, and the newspapers agree. So I submit a proposal: I'll give you the fact, and you'll proceed to catch the murderer. When that has been done, you and I will discuss whether the fact was essential to your success; whether you could possibly have got the truth and the evidence without it. If we agree that you couldn't, you will so inform my clients, and I shall collect my fee. No document will be required; an oral statement will do; and of course only to my clients. I don't care what you say to journalists or to your superior officers."

Cramer grunted. He removed the cigar from his mouth, gazed at the mangled end suspiciously as if he expected to see a bug crawling, and put it back where it belonged. Then he squinted at Wolfe:

"Would you repeat that?"

Wolfe did so, as if he were reading it off, without changing a word.

Cramer grunted again. "You say if we agree. You mean if you agree with me, or if I agree with you?"

"Bah. It couldn't be plainer."

"Yeah. When you're plainest you need looking at closest. What if I've already got this wonderful fact?"

"You didn't have it two hours ago. If you have it now, I have nothing to give and shall get nothing. If when I divulge it you claim to have had it, you'll tell me when and from whom you got it." Wolfe stirred impatiently. "It is, of course, connected with facts in your possession—for instance, that the bottle contained sugared coffee instead of Hi-Spot."

"Sure, they've told you that."

"Or that your laboratory has found traces of a certain substance, in a band half an inch wide, encircling the neck of the bottle."

"They haven't told you *that*." Cramer's eyes got narrower. "There are only six or seven people who could have told you that, and they all get paid by the City of New York, and by God you can name him before we go any farther."

"Pfui." Wolfe was disgusted. "I have better use for my clients' money than buying information from policemen. Why don't you like my proposal? What's wrong with it? Frankly, I hope to heaven you accept it, and immediately. If you don't I'll have to hire two dozen men and begin all over again on those people, and I'd rather eat baker's bread—almost."

"All right." Cramer did not relax. "Hell, I'd do anything to save you from that. I'm on. Your proposal, as you have twice stated it, provided I get the fact, and all of it, here and now."

"You do. Here it is, and Mr. Goodwin will have a typed copy for you. But first—a little detail—I owe it to one of my clients to request that one item of it be kept confidential, if it can possibly be managed."

"I can't keep murder evidence confidential."

"I know you can't. I said if it can possibly be managed."

"I'll see, but I'm not promising, and if I did promise I probably wouldn't keep it. What's the item? Give it to me first."

"Certainly. Miss Fraser can't drink Hi-Spot because it gives her indigestion."

"What the hell." Cramer goggled at him. "Orchard didn't drink Hi-Spot, he drank coffee, and it didn't give him indigestion, it killed him."

Wolfe nodded. "I know. But that's the item, and on behalf of my clients I ask that it be kept undisclosed if possible. This is going to take some time, perhaps an hour, and your glass and bottle are empty. Archie?"

I got up and bartended without any boyish enthusiasm because I wasn't very crazy about the shape things were taking. I was keeping my fingers crossed. If Wolfe was starting some tricky maneuver and only fed him a couple of crumbs, with the idea of getting a full-sized loaf, not baker's bread, in exchange, that would be one thing, and I was ready to applaud if he got away with it. If he really opened the bag and dumped it out, letting Cramer help himself, that would be something quite different. In that case he was playing it straight, and that could only mean that he had got fed up with them, and really intended to sit and read poetry or draw horses and let the cops earn his fee for him. That did not appeal to me. Money may be everything, but it makes a difference how you get it.

He opened the bag and dumped it. He gave Cramer all we had. He even quoted, from memory, the telegram that had been sent to Mom Shepherd, and as he did so I had to clamp my jaw to keep from making one of four or five remarks that would have fitted the occasion. I had composed that telegram, not him. But I kept my trap shut. I do sometimes ride him in the presence of outsiders, but rarely for Cramer to hear, and not when my feelings are as strong as they were then.

Also Cramer had a lot of questions to ask, and Wolfe answered them like a lamb. And I had to leave my chair so Cramer could rest his broad bottom on it while he phoned his office.

"Rowcliff? Take this down, but don't broadcast it." He was very crisp and executive, every inch an inspector. "I'm at Wolfe's office, and he did have something, and for once I think he's dealing off the top of the deck. We've got to start all over. It's one of those goddam babies where the wrong person got killed. It was intended for the Fraser woman. I'll tell you when I get there, in half an hour, maybe a little more. Call in everybody that's on the case. Find out where the Commissioner is, and the D.A. Get that Elinor Vance and that Nathan Traub, and get the cook at the Fraser apartment. Have those three there by the time I come. We'll take the others in the morning. Who was it went to Michigan—oh, I remember, Darst. Be sure you don't miss him, I want to see him . . ."

And so forth. After another dozen or so executive orders Cramer hung up and returned to the red leather chair.

"What else?" he demanded.

"That's all," Wolfe declared. "I wish you luck."

Having dropped his chewed-up cigar in my wastebasket when he usurped my chair, Cramer got out another one and stuck it in his mouth without looking at it. "I'll tell you," he said. "You gave me a fact, no doubt about that, but this is the first time I ever saw you turn out all your pockets, so I sit down again. Before I leave I'd like to sit here a couple of minutes and ask myself, what for?"

Wolfe chuckled. "Didn't I just hear you telling your men to start to work for me?"

"Yeah, I guess so." The cigar slanted up. "It seems plausible, but I've known you to seem plausible before. And I swear to God if there's a gag in this it's buried too deep for me. You don't even make any suggestions."

"I have none."

And he didn't. I saw that. And there wasn't any gag. I didn't wonder that Cramer suspected him, considering what his experiences with him had been in the past years, but to me it was only too evident that Wolfe had really done a strip act, to avoid overworking his brain. I have sat in that office with him too many hours, and watched him put on his acts for too many audiences, not to know when he is getting up a charade. I certainly don't always know what he is up to, but I do know when he is up to nothing at all. He was simply utterly going to let the city employees do it.

"Would you suggest, for instance," Cramer inquired, "to haul Miss Fraser in on a charge of tampering with evidence? Or the others for obstructing justice?"

Wolfe shook his head. "My dear sir, you are after a murderer, not tamperers or obstructers. Anyway you can't get convictions on charges like that, except in very special cases, and you know it. You are hinting that it isn't like me to expose a client to such a charge, but will you arrest her? No. What you will do, I hope, is find out who it is that wants to kill her. How could I have suggestions for you? You know vastly more about it than I do. There are a thousand lines of investigation, in a case like this, on which I haven't moved a finger; and doubtless you have explored all of them. I won't insult you by offering a list of them. I'll be here, though, I'm always here, should you want a word with me."

Cramer got up and went.

13   I CAN'T DENY THAT FROM A PURELY PRACTICAL POINT
of view the deal that Wolfe made with Cramer that Friday evening
was slick, even fancy, and well designed to save wear and tear on
Wolfe's energy and the contents of his skull. No matter how it added
up at the end it didn't need one of Professor Savarese's formulas to
show how probable it was that the fact Wolfe had furnished Cramer
would turn out to be an essential item. That was a good bet at almost
any odds.

But.

There was one fatal flaw in the deal. The city scientists, in order
to earn Wolfe's fee for him while he played around with his toys, had
to crack the case. That was the joker. I have never seen a more completely uncracked case than that one was, a full week after Wolfe had
made his cute little arrangement to have his detective work done by
proxy. I kept up to date on it both by reading the newspapers and by
making jaunts down to Homicide headquarters on Twentieth Street,
for chats with Sergeant Purley Stebbins or other acquaintances, and
twice with Cramer himself. That was humiliating, but I did want to
keep myself informed somehow about the case Wolfe and I were working on. For the first time in history I was perfectly welcome at Homicide, especially after three or four days had passed. It got to be
pathetic, the way they would greet me like a treasured pal, no doubt
thinking it was just possible I had come to contribute another fact. God
knows they needed one. For of course they were reading the papers
too, and the press was living up to one of its oldest traditions by
bawling hell out of the cops for bungling a case which, by prompt and
competent—you know how it goes.

So far the public had not been informed that Hi-Spot gave Miss Fraser indigestion. If the papers had known that!

Wolfe wasn't lifting a finger. It was not, properly speaking, a relapse. Relapse is my word for it when he gets so offended or disgusted by something about a case, or so appalled by the kind or amount of work it is going to take to solve it, that he decides to pretend he has never heard of it, and rejects it as a topic of conversation. This wasn't like that. He just didn't intend to work unless he had to. He was perfectly willing to read the pieces in the papers, or to put down his book and listen when I returned from one of my visits to Homicide. But if I tried to badger him into some mild exertion like hiring Saul and Fred and Orrie to look under some stones, or even thinking up a little errand for me, he merely picked up his book again.

If any of the developments, such as they were, meant anything to him, he gave no sign of it. Elinor Vance was arrested, held as a material witness, and after two days released on bail. The word I brought from Homicide was that there was nothing to it except that she had by far the best opportunity to put something in the coffee, with the exception of the cook. Not that there weren't plenty of others; the list had been considerably lengthened by the discovery that the coffee had been made, bottled, and kept overnight in Miss Fraser's apartment, with all the coming and going there.

Then there was the motive-collecting operation. In a murder case you can always get some motives together, but the trouble is you can never be sure which ones are sunfast for the people concerned. It all depends. There was the guy in Brooklyn a few years ago who stabbed a dentist in and around the heart eleven times because he had pulled the wrong tooth. In this case the motive assortment was about average, nothing outstanding but fairly good specimens. Six months ago Miss Fraser and Bill Meadows had had a first-class row, and she had fired him and he had been off the program for three weeks. They both claimed that they now dearly loved each other.

Not long ago Nat Traub had tried to persuade a soup manufacturer, one of the Fraser sponsors, to leave her and sign up for an evening comedy show, and Miss Fraser had retaliated by talking the sponsor into switching to another agency. Not only that, there were vague hints that Miss Fraser had started a campaign for a similar switch by other sponsors, including Hi-Spot, but they couldn't be nailed down. Again, she and Traub insisted that they were awful good friends.

The Radio Writers Guild should have been delighted to poison Miss Fraser on account of her tough attitude toward demands of the Guild for changes in contracts, and Elinor Vance was a member of the

Guild in good standing. As for Tully Strong, Miss Fraser had opposed the formation of a Sponsors' Council, and still didn't like it, and of course if there were no Council there would be no secretary.

And so on. As motives go, worth tacking up but not spectacular. The one that would probably have got the popular vote was Deborah Koppel's. Somebody in the D.A.'s office had induced Miss Fraser to reveal the contents of her will. It left ten grand each to a niece and nephew, children of her sister who lived in Michigan, and all the rest to Deborah. It would be a very decent chunk, somewhere in six figures, with the first figure either a 2 or a 3, certainly worth a little investment in poison for anyone whose mind ran in that direction. There was, however, not the slightest indication that Deborah's mind did. She and Miss Fraser, then Miss Oxhall, had been girlhood friends in Michigan, had taught at the same school, and had become sisters-in-law when Madeline had married Deborah's brother Lawrence.

Speaking of Lawrence, his death had of course been looked into again, chiefly on account of the coincidence of the cyanide. He had been a photographer and therefore, when needing cyanide, all he had to do was reach to a shelf for it. What if he hadn't killed himself after all? Or what if, even if he had, someone thought he hadn't, believed it was his wife who had needed the cyanide in order to collect five thousand dollars in insurance money, and had now arranged, after six years, to even up by giving Miss Fraser a dose of it herself?

Naturally the best candidate for that was Deborah Koppel. But they couldn't find one measly scrap to start a foundation with. There wasn't the slightest evidence, ancient or recent, that Deborah and Madeline had ever been anything but devoted friends, bound together by mutual interest, respect, and affection. Not only that, the Michigan people refused to bat an eye at the suggestion that Lawrence Koppel's death had not been suicide. He had been a neurotic hypochondriac, and the letter he had sent to his best friend, a local lawyer, had cinched it. Michigan had been perfectly willing to answer New York's questions, but for themselves they weren't interested.

Another of the thousand lines that petered out into nothing was the effort to link up one of the staff, especially Elinor Vance, with Michigan. They had tried it before with Cyril Orchard, and now they tried it with the others. No soap. None of them had ever been there.

Wolfe, as I say, read some of this in the papers, and courteously listened to the rest of it, and much more, from me. He was not, however, permitted to limit himself strictly to the role of spectator. Cramer came to our office twice during that week, and Anderson, the Hi-Spot president, once; and there were others.

There was Tully Strong, who arrived Saturday afternoon, after a six-hour session with Cramer and an assortment of his trained men. He had probably been pecked at a good deal, as all of them had, since they had told the cops a string of barefaced lies, and he was not in good humor. He was so sore that when he put his hands on Wolfe's desk and leaned over at him to make some remarks about treachery, and his spectacles slipped forward nearly to the tip of his nose, he didn't bother to push them back in place.

His theory was that the agreement with Wolfe was null and void because Wolfe had violated it. Whatever happened, Wolfe not only would not collect his fee, he would not even be reimbursed for expenses. Moreover, he would be sued for damages. His disclosure of a fact which, if made public, would inflict great injury on Miss Fraser and her program, the network, and Hi-Spot, was irresponsible and inexcusable, and certainly actionable.

Wolfe told him bosh, he had not violated the agreement.

"No?" Strong straightened up. His necktie was to one side and his hair needed a comb and brush. His hand went up to his spectacles, which were barely hanging on, but instead of pushing them back he removed them. "You think not? You'll see. And, besides, you have put Miss Fraser's life in danger! I was trying to protect her! We all were!"

"All?" Wolfe objected. "Not all. All but one."

"Yes, all!" Strong had come there to be mad and would have no interference. "No one knew, no one but us, that it was meant for her! Now everybody knows it! Who can protect her now? I'll try, we all will, but what chance have we got?"

It seemed to me he was getting illogical. The only threat to Miss Fraser, as far as we knew, came from the guy who had performed on the coffee, and surely we hadn't told him anything he didn't already know.

I had to usher Tully Strong to the door and out. If he had been capable of calming down enough to be seated for a talk I would have been all for it, but he was really upset. When Wolfe told me to put him out I couldn't conscientiously object. At that he had spunk. Anybody could have told from one glance at us that if I was forced to deal with him physically I would have had to decide what to do with my other hand, in case I wanted to be fully occupied, but when I took hold of his arm he jerked loose and then turned on me as if stretching me out would be pie. He had his specs in one hand, too. I succeeded in herding him out without either of us getting hurt.

As was to be expected, Tully Strong wasn't the only one who had the notion that Wolfe had committed treason by giving their fatal secret to the cops. They all let us know it, too, either by phone or in person. Nat Traub's attitude was specially bitter, probably because of the item that had been volunteered by Bill Meadows, that Traub had served the bottle and glass to Orchard. Cramer's crew must have really liked that one, and I could imagine the different keys they used playing it for Traub to hear. One thing I preferred not to imagine was what we would have got from Mr. Walter B. Anderson, the Hi-Spot president, and Fred Owen, the director of public relations, if anyone had told them the full extent of Wolfe's treachery. Apparently they were still ignorant about the true and horrible reason why one of the bottles had contained coffee instead of The Drink You Dream Of.

Another caller, this one Monday afternoon, was the formula hound, Professor Savarese. He too came to the office straight from a long conference with the cops, and he too was good and mad, but for a different reason. The cops had no longer been interested in his association with Cyril Orchard, or in anything about Orchard at all, and he wanted to know why. They had refused to tell him. They had reviewed his whole life, from birth to date, all over again, but with an entirely different approach. It was plain that what they were after now was a link between him and Miss Fraser. Why? What new factor had entered? The intrusion of a hitherto unknown and unsuspected factor would raise hell with his calculation of probabilities, but if there was one he had to have it, and quick. This was the first good chance he had ever had to test his formulas on the most dramatic of all problems, a murder case, from the inside, and he wasn't going to tolerate any blank spaces without a fight.

What was the new factor? Why was it now a vital question whether he had had any previous association, direct or indirect, with Miss Fraser?

Up to a point Wolfe listened to him without coming to a boil, but he finally got annoyed enough to call on me again to do some more ushering. I obeyed in a halfhearted way. For one thing, Wolfe was passing up another chance to do a dime's worth of work himself, with Savarese right there and more than ready to talk, and for another, I was resisting a temptation. The question had popped into my head, how would this figure wizard go about getting Miss Fraser's indigestion into a mathematical equation? It might not be instructive to get him to answer it, but at least it would pass the time, and it would help as much in solving the case as anything Wolfe was doing. But, not wanting to get us any more deeply involved in treachery than we already were, I skipped it.

I ushered him out.

Anyhow, that was only Monday. By the time four more days had passed and another Friday arrived, finishing a full week since we had supplied Cramer with a fact, I was a promising prospect for a strait jacket. That evening, as I returned to the office with Wolfe after an unusually good dinner which I had not enjoyed, the outlook for the next three or four hours revolted me. As he got himself adjusted comfortably in his chair and reached for his book, I announced:

"I'm going to my club."

He nodded, and got his book open.

"You do not even," I said cuttingly, "ask me which club, though you know damn well I don't belong to any. I am thoroughly fed up with sitting here day after day and night after night, waiting for the moment when the idea will somehow seep into you that a detective is supposed to detect. You are simply too goddam lazy to live. You think you're a genius. Say you are. If in order to be a genius myself I had to be as self-satisfied, as overweight, and as inert as you are, I like me better this way."

Apparently he was reading.

"This," I said, "is the climax I've been leading up to for a week— or rather, that you've been leading me up to. Sure, I know your alibi, and I'm good and sick of it—that there is nothing we can do that the cops aren't already doing. Of all the sausage." I kept my voice dry, factual, and cultured. "If this case is too much for you why don't you try another one? The papers are full of them. How about the gang that stole a truckload of cheese yesterday right here on Eleventh Avenue? How about the fifth-grade boy that hit his teacher in the eye with a jelly bean? Page fifty-eight in the *Times*. Or, if everything but murder is beneath you, what's wrong with the political and economic fortune-teller, a lady named Beula Poole, who got shot in the back of her head last evening? Page one of any paper. You could probably sew that one up before bedtime."

He turned over a page.

"Tomorrow," I said, "is Saturday. I shall draw my pay as usual. I'm going to a fight at the Garden. Talk about contrasts—you in that chair and a couple of good middleweights in a ring."

I blew.

But I didn't go to the Garden. My first stop was the corner drugstore, where I went to a phone booth and called Lon Cohen of the *Gazette*. He was in, and about through, and saw no reason why I shouldn't buy him eight or ten drinks, provided he could have a two-inch steak for a chaser.

So an hour later Lon and I were at a corner table at Pietro's. He had done well with the drinks and had made a good start on the steak. I was having highballs, to be sociable, and was on my third, along with my second pound of peanuts. I hadn't realized how much I had short-changed myself on dinner, sitting opposite Wolfe, until I got into the spirit of it with the peanuts.

We had discussed the state of things from politics to prizefights, by no means excluding murder. Lon had had his glass filled often enough, and had enough of the steak in him, to have reached a state of mind where he might reasonably be expected to be open to suggestion. So I made an approach by telling him, deadpan, that in my opinion the papers were riding the cops too hard on the Orchard case.

He leered at me. "For God's sake, has Cramer threatened to take your license or something?"

"No, honest," I insisted, reaching for peanuts, "this one is really tough and you know it. They're doing as well as they can with what they've got. Besides that, it's so damn commonplace. Every paper always does it—after a week start crabbing and after two weeks start screaming. It's got so everybody always expects it and nobody ever reads it. You know what I'd do if I ran a newspaper? I'd start running stuff that people would read."

"Jesus!" Lon gawked at me. "What an idea! Give me a column on it. Who would teach 'em to read?"

"A column," I said, "would only get me started. I need at least a page. But in this particular case, where it's at now, it's a question of an editorial. This is Friday night. For Sunday you ought to have an editorial on the Orchard case. It's still hot and the public still loves it. But—"

"I'm no editor, I'm a news man."

"I know, I'm just talking. Five will get you ten that your sheet will have an editorial on the Orchard case Sunday, and what will it say? It will be called OUR PUBLIC GUARDIANS, and it will be the same old crap, and not one in a thousand will read beyond the first line. Phooey. If it was me I would call it TOO OLD OR TOO FAT, and I wouldn't mention the cops once. Nor would I mention Nero Wolfe, not by name. I would refer to the blaze of publicity with which a certain celebrated private investigator entered the Orchard case, and to the expectations it aroused. That his record seemed to justify it. That we see now how goofy it was, because in ten days he hasn't taken a trick. That the reason may be that he is getting too old, or too fat, or merely that he hasn't got what it takes when a case is really tough, but no matter what the reason is, this shows us that for our protection from vicious criminals we must rely on our efficient and well-trained police force, and not on any so-called brilliant geniuses. I said I wouldn't mention the cops, but I think I'd better, right at the last. I could add a sentence that while they may have got stuck in the mud on the Orchard case, they are the brave men who keep the structure of our society from you know."

Lon, having swallowed a hunk of steak, would have spoken, but I stopped him:

"They would read that, don't think they wouldn't. I know you're not an editor, but you're the best man they've got and you're allowed to talk to editors, aren't you? I would love to see an editorial like that tried, just as an experiment. So much so that if a paper ran it I would want to show my appreciation the first opportunity I get, by stretching a point a hell of a ways to give it first crack at some interesting little item."

Lon had his eyebrows up. "If you don't want to bore me, turn it the other side up so the interesting little item will be on top."

"Nuts. Do you want to talk about it or not?"

"Sure, I'll talk about anything."

I signaled the waiter for refills.

14   I WOULD GIVE ANYTHING IN THE WORLD, ANYWAY UP
to four bits, to know whether Wolfe saw or read that editorial before
I showed it to him late Sunday afternoon. I think he did. He always
glances over the editorials in three papers, of which the *Gazette* is one,
and if his eye caught it at all he must have read it. It was entitled THE
FALSE ALARM, and it carried out the idea I had given Lon to a T.

I knew of course that Wolfe wouldn't do any spluttering, and I
should have realized that he probably wouldn't make any sign or offer
any comment. But I didn't, and therefore by late afternoon I was in a
hole. If he hadn't read it I had to see that he did, and that was risky.
It had to be done right or he would smell an elephant. So I thought it
over: what would be the natural thing? How would I naturally do it if
I suddenly ran across it?

What I did do was turn in my chair to grin at him and ask casually:
"Did you see this editorial in the *Gazette* called THE FALSE
ALARM?"

He grunted. "What's it about?"

"You'd better read it." I got up, crossed over, and put it on his
desk. "A funny thing, it gave me the feeling I had written it myself.
It's the only editorial I've seen in weeks that I completely agree with."

He picked it up. I sat down facing him, but he held the paper so
that it cut off my view. He isn't a fast reader, and he held the pose
long enough to read it through twice, but that's exactly what he would
have done if he already knew it by heart and wanted me to think
otherwise.

"Bah!" The paper was lowered. "Some little scrivener who doubtless has ulcers and is on a diet."

"Yeah, I guess so. The rat. The contemptible louse. If only he knew how you've been sweating and stewing, going without sleep—"

"Archie. Shut up."

"Yes, sir."

I hoped to God I was being natural.

That was all for then, but I was not licked. I had never supposed that he would tear his hair or pace up and down. A little later an old friend of his, Marko Vukčić, dropped in for a Sunday evening snack— five kinds of cheese, guava jelly, freshly roasted chestnuts, and almond tarts. I was anxious to see if he would show the editorial to Marko, which would have been a bad sign. He didn't. After Marko had left, to return to Rusterman's Restaurant, which was the best in New York because he managed it, Wolfe settled down with his book again, but hadn't turned more than ten pages before he dogeared and closed it and tossed it to a far corner of his desk. He then got up, crossed the room to the big globe, and stood and studied geography. That didn't seem to satisfy him any better than the book, so he went and turned on the radio. After dialing to eight different stations, he muttered to himself, stalked back to his chair behind his desk, and sat and scowled. I took all this in only from a corner of one eye, since I was buried so deep in a magazine that I didn't even know he was in the room.

He spoke. "Archie."

"Yes, sir?"

"It has been nine days."

"Yes, sir."

"Since that tour de force of yours. Getting that Miss Shepherd here."

"Yes, sir."

He was being tactful. What he meant was that it had been nine days since he had passed a miracle by uncovering the tape on the bottle and Miss Fraser's indigestion, but he figured that if he tossed me a bone I would be less likely either to snarl or to gloat. He went on:

"It was not then flighty to assume that a good routine job was all that was needed. But the events of those nine days have not supported that assumption."

"No, sir."

"Get Mr. Cramer."

"As soon as I finish this paragraph."

I allowed a reasonable number of seconds to go by, but I admit I wasn't seeing a word. Then, getting on the phone, I was prepared to settle for less than the inspector himself, since it was Sunday evening, and hoped that Wolfe was too, but it wasn't necessary. Cramer was there, and Wolfe got on and invited him to pay us a call.

"I'm busy." Cramer sounded harassed. "Why, have you got something?"

"Yes."

"What?"

"I don't know. I won't know until I've talked with you. After we've talked your busyness may be more productive than it has been."

"The hell you say. I'll be there in half an hour."

That didn't elate me at all. I hadn't cooked up a neat little scheme, and devoted a whole evening to it, and bought Lon Cohen twenty bucks' worth of liquids and solids, just to prod Wolfe into getting Cramer in to talk things over. As for his saying he had something, that was a plain lie. All he had was a muleheaded determination not to let his ease and comfort be interfered with.

So when Cramer arrived I didn't bubble over. Neither did he, for that matter. He marched into the office, nodded a greeting, dropped into the red leather chair, and growled:

"I wish to God you'd forget you're eccentric and start moving around more. Busy as I am, here I am. What is it?"

"My remark on the phone," Wolfe said placidly, "may have been blunt, but it was justified."

"What remark?"

"That your busyness could be more productive. Have you made any progress?"

"No."

"You're no further along than you were a week ago?"

"Further along to the day I retire, yes. Otherwise no."

"Then I'd like to ask some questions about that woman, Beula Poole, who was found dead in her office Friday morning. The papers say that you say it was murder. Was it?"

I gawked at him. This was clear away from me. When he jumped completely off the track like that I never knew whether he was stalling, being subtle, or trying to show me how much of a clod I was. Then I saw a gleam in Cramer's eye which indicated that even he had left me far behind, and all I could do was gawk some more.

Cramer nodded. "Yeah, it was murder. Why, looking for another client so I can earn another fee for you?"

"Do you know who did it?"

"No."

"No glimmer? No good start?"

"No start at all, good or bad."

"Tell me about it."

Cramer grunted. "Most of it has been in the papers, all but a detail or two we've saved up." He moved further back in the chair, as if he might stay longer than he had thought. "First you might tell me what got you interested, don't you think?"

"Certainly. Mr. Cyril Orchard, who got killed, was the publisher of a horse race tip sheet for which subscribers paid ten dollars a week, an unheard-of price. Miss Beula Poole, who also got killed, was the publisher of a sheet which purported to give inside advance information on political and economic affairs, for which subscribers paid the same unheard-of price of ten dollars a week."

"Is that all?"

"I think it's enough to warrant a question or two. It is true that Mr. Orchard was poisoned and Miss Poole was shot, a big variation in method. Also that it is now assumed that Mr. Orchard was killed by misadventure, the poison having been intended for another, whereas the bullet that killed Miss Poole must have been intended for her. But even so, it's a remarkable coincidence—sufficiently so to justify some curiosity, at least. For example, it might be worth the trouble to compare the lists of subscribers of the two publications."

"Yeah, I thought so too."

"You did?" Wolfe was a little annoyed, as he always was at any implication that someone else could be as smart as him. "Then you've compared them. And?"

Cramer shook his head. "I didn't say I'd compared them, I said I'd thought of it. What made me think of it was the fact that it couldn't be done, because there weren't any lists to compare."

"Nonsense. There must have been. Did you look for them?"

"Sure we did, but too late. In Orchard's case there was a little bad management. His office, a little one-room hole in a building on Forty-second Street, was locked, and there was some fiddling around looking for an employee or a relative to let us in. When we finally entered by having the superintendent admit us, the next day, the place had been cleaned out—not a piece of paper or an address plate or anything else. It was different with the woman, Poole, because it was in her office that she was shot—another one-room hole, on the third floor of an old building on Nineteenth Street, only four blocks from my place. But her body wasn't found until nearly noon the next day, and by the time we got there that had been cleaned out too. The same way. Nothing."

Wolfe was no longer annoyed. Cramer had had two coincidences and he had had only one. "Well." He was purring. "That settles it. In spite of variations, it is now more than curiosity. Of course you have inquired?"

"Plenty. The sheets were printed at different shops, and neither of them had a list of subscribers or anything else that helps. Neither Orchard nor the woman employed any help. Orchard left a widow and two children, but they don't seem to know a damn thing about his business, let alone who his subscribers were. Beula Poole's nearest relatives live out West, in Colorado, and they don't know anything, apparently not even how she was earning a living. And so on. As for the routine, all covered and all useless. No one seen entering or leaving—it's only two flights up—no weapon, no fingerprints that help any, nobody heard the shot—"

Wolfe nodded impatiently. "You said you hadn't made any start, and naturally routine has been followed. Any discoverable association of Miss Poole with Mr. Orchard?"

"If there was we can't discover it."

"Where were Miss Fraser and the others at the time Miss Poole was shot?"

Cramer squinted at him. "You think it might even develop that way?"

"I would like to put the question. Wouldn't you?"

"Yeah. I have. You see, the two offices being cleaned out is a detail we've saved up." Cramer looked at me. "And you'll kindly not peddle it to your pal Cohen of the *Gazette*." He went on to Wolfe: "It's not so easy because there's a leeway of four or five hours on when she was shot. We've asked all that bunch about it, and no one can be checked off."

"Mr. Savarese? Miss Shepherd? Mr. Shepherd?"

"What?" Cramer's eyes widened. "Where the hell does Shepherd come in?"

"I don't know. Archie doesn't like him, and I have learned that it is always quite possible that anyone he doesn't like may be a murderer."

"Oh, comic relief. The Shepherd girl was in Atlantic City with her mother, and still is. On Savarese I'd have to look at the reports, but I know he's not checked off because nobody is. By the way, we've dug up two subscribers to Orchard's tip sheet, besides Savarese and the Fraser woman. With no result. They bet on the races and they subscribed, that's all, according to them."

"I'd like to talk with them," Wolfe declared.

"You can. At my office any time."

"Pfui. As you know, I never leave this house on business. If you'll give Archie their names and addresses he'll attend to it."

Cramer said he'd have Stebbins phone and give them to me. I never saw him more cooperative, which meant that he had never been more frustrated.

They kept at it a while longer, but Cramer had nothing more of any importance to give Wolfe, and Wolfe hadn't had anything to give Cramer to begin with. I listened with part of my brain, and with the other part tried to do a little offhand sorting and arranging. I had to admit that it would take quite a formula to have room for the two coincidences as such, and therefore they would probably have to be joined together somehow, but it was no part-brain job for me. Whenever dough passes without visible value received the first thing you think of is blackmail, so I thought of it, but that didn't get me anywhere because there were too many other things in the way. It was obvious that the various aspects were not yet in a condition that called for the application of my particular kind of talent.

After Cramer had gone Wolfe sat and gazed at a distant corner of the ceiling with his eyes open about a thirty-second of an inch. I sat and waited, not wanting to disturb him, for when I saw his lips pushing out, and in again, and out and in, I knew he was exerting himself to the limit, and I was perfectly satisfied. There had been a good chance that he would figure that he had helped all he could for a while, and go back to his reading until Cramer made a progress report or somebody else got killed. But the editorial had stung him good. Finally he transferred the gaze to me and pronounced my name.

"Yes, sir," I said brightly.

"Your notebook. Take this."

I got ready.

"Former subscribers to the publication of Cyril Orchard, or to that of Beula Poole, should communicate with me immediately. Put it in three papers, the *Gazette*, the *News*, and the *Herald-Tribune*. A modest display, say two inches. Reply to a box number. A good page if possible."

"And I'll call for the replies? It saves time."

"Then do so."

I put paper in the typewriter. The phone rang. It was Sergeant Purley Stebbins, to give me the names and addresses of the two Orchard subscribers they had dug up.

15   So beginning Monday morning we were again a
going concern, instead of a sitting-and-waiting one, but I was not in
my element. I like a case you can make a diagram of. I don't object
to complications, that's all right, but if you're out for bear it seems
silly to concentrate on hunting for moose tracks. Our fee depended on
our finding out how and why Orchard got cyanided by drinking Madeline Fraser's sugared coffee, and here we were spending our time and
energy on the shooting of a female named Beula Poole. Even granting
it was one and the same guy who pinched the lead pencils and spilled
ink on the rug, if you've been hired to nail him for pencil stealing
that's what you should work at.

I admit that isn't exactly fair, because most of our Monday activities had to do with Orchard. Wolfe seemed to think it was important
for him to have a talk with those two subscribers, so instead of using
the phone I went out after them. I had one of them in the office waiting
for him at 11:00 A.M.—an assistant office manager for a big tile company. Wolfe spent less than a quarter of an hour on him, knowing, of
course, that the cops had spent more and had checked him. He had
bet on the races for years. In February a year ago he had learned that
a Hialeah daily double featured in a sheet called *Track Almanac* had
come through for a killing, and he had subscribed, though the ten bucks
a week was a sixth of his salary. He had stayed with it for nine weeks
and then quit. So much for him.

The other one was a little different. Her name was Marie Leconne,
and she owned a snooty beauty parlor on Madison Avenue. She
wouldn't have accepted my invitation if she hadn't been under the
illusion that Wolfe was connected with the police, though I didn't

precisely tell her so. That Monday evening she was with us a good two hours, but left nothing of any value behind. She had subscribed to *Track Almanac* in August, seven months ago, and had remained a subscriber up to the time of Orchard's death. Prior to subscribing she had done little or no betting on the races; she was hazy about whether it was little, or no. Since subscribing she had bet frequently, but she firmly refused to tell where, through whom, or in what amounts. Wolfe, knowing that I occasionally risk a finif, passed me a hint to have some conversation with her about pertinent matters like horses and jockeys, but she declined to cooperate. All in all she kept herself nicely under control, and flew off the handle only once, when Wolfe pressed her hard for a plausible reason why she had subscribed to a tip sheet at such a price. That aggravated her terribly, and since the one thing that scares Wolfe out of his senses is a woman in a tantrum, he backed away fast.

He did keep on trying, from other angles, but when she finally left all we knew for sure was that she had not subscribed to *Track Almanac* in order to get guesses on the ponies. She was slippery, and nobody's fool, and Wolfe had got no further than the cops in opening her up.

I suggested to Wolfe: "We might start Saul asking around in her circle."

He snorted. "Mr. Cramer is presumably attending to that, and, anyway, it would have to be dragged out of her inch by inch. The advertisement should be quicker."

It was quicker, all right, in getting results, but not the results we were after. There had not been time to make the Monday papers, so the ad's first appearance was Tuesday morning. Appraising it, I thought it caught the eye effectively for so small a space. After breakfast, which I always eat in the kitchen with Fritz while Wolfe has his in his room on a tray, and after dealing with the morning mail and other chores in the office, I went out to stretch my legs and thought I might as well head in the direction of the Herald-Tribune Building. Expecting nothing so soon but thinking it wouldn't hurt to drop in, I did so. There was a telegram. I tore it open and read:

> CALL MIDLAND FIVE THREE SEVEN
> EIGHT FOUR LEAVE MESSAGE FOR
> DUNCAN GIVING APPOINTMENT

I went to a phone booth and put a nickel in the slot, with the idea of calling Cramer's office to ask who Midland 5-3784 belonged to, but changed my mind. If it happened that this led to a hot trail we

didn't want to be hampered by city interference, at least I didn't. However, I thought I might as well get something for my nickel and dialed
another number. Fritz answered, and I asked him to switch it to the
plant rooms.

"Yes, Archie?" Wolfe's voice came, peevish. He was at the bench,
repotting, as I knew from his schedule, and he hates to be interrupted
at that job. I told him about the telegram.

"Very well, call the number. Make an appointment for eleven
o'clock or later."

I walked back home, went to my desk, dialed the Midland number,
and asked for Mr. Duncan. Of course it could have been Mrs. or Miss,
but I preferred to deal with a man after our experience with Marie
Leconne. A gruff voice with an accent said that Mr. Duncan wasn't
there and was there a message.

"Will he be back soon?"

"I don't know. All I know is that I can take a message."

I thereupon delivered one, that Mr. Duncan would be expected at
Nero Wolfe's office at eleven o'clock, or as soon thereafter as possible.

He didn't come. Wolfe descended in his elevator sharp at eleven
as usual, got himself enthroned, rang for beer, and began sorting plant
cards he had brought down with him. I had him sign a couple of checks
and then started to help with the cards. At half past eleven I asked if
I should ring the Midland number to see if Duncan had got the message, and he said no, we would wait until noon.

The phone rang. I went to my desk and told it:

"Nero Wolfe's office, Goodwin speaking."

"I got your message for Duncan. Let me speak to Mr. Wolfe,
please."

I covered the transmitter and told Wolfe: "He says Duncan, but
it's a voice I've heard. It's not a familiar voice, but by God I've heard
it. See if you have."

Wolfe lifted his instrument.

"Yes, Mr. Duncan? This is Nero Wolfe."

"How are you?" the voice asked.

"I'm well, thank you. Do I know you, sir?"

"I really don't know. I mean I don't know if you would recognize
me, seeing me, because I don't know how foolishly inquisitive you
may have been. But we have talked before, on the phone."

"We have?"

"Yes. Twice. On June ninth, nineteen forty-three, I called to give
you some advice regarding a job you were doing for General Carpen-

ter. On January sixteenth, nineteen forty-six, I called to speak about the advisability of limiting your efforts in behalf of a Mrs. Tremont."

"Yes. I remember."

I remembered too. I chalked it against me that I hadn't recognized the voice with the first six words, though it had been over two years since I had heard it—hard, slow, precise, and cold as last week's corpse. It was continuing:

"I was pleased to see that you did limit your efforts as I suggested. That showed—"

"I limited them because no extension of them was required to finish the job I was hired for. I did not limit them because you suggested it, Mr. Zeck." Wolfe was being fairly icy himself.

"So you know my name." The voice never changed.

"Certainly. I went to some trouble and expense to ascertain it. I don't pay much attention to threats, I get too many of them, but at least I like to know who the threatener is. Yes, I know your name, sir. Is that temerarious? Many people know Mr. Arnold Zeck."

"You have had no occasion to. This, Mr. Wolfe, does *not* please me."

"I didn't expect it to."

"No. But I am much easier to get along with when I am pleased. That's why I sent you that telegram and am talking with you now. I have strong admiration for you, as I've said before. I wouldn't want to lose it. It would please me better to keep it. Your advertisement in the papers has given me some concern. I realize that you didn't know that, you couldn't have known it, so I'm telling you. The advertisement disturbs me. It can't be recalled; it has appeared. But it is extremely important that you should not permit it to lead you into difficulties that will be too much for you. The wisest course for you will be to drop the matter. You understand me, don't you, Mr. Wolfe?"

"Oh yes, I understand you. You put things quite clearly, Mr. Zeck, and so do I. I have engaged to do something, and I intend to do it. I haven't the slightest desire either to please you or to displease you, and unless one or the other is inherent in my job you have no reason to be concerned. You understand me, don't you?"

"Yes. I do. But now you know."

The line went dead.

Wolfe cradled the phone and leaned back in his chair, with his eyes closed to a slit. I pushed my phone away, swiveled, and gazed at him through a minute's silence.

"So," I said. "That sonofabitch. Shall I find out about the Midland number?"

Wolfe shook his head. "Useless. It would be some little store that merely took a message. Anyway, he has a number of his own."

"Yeah. He didn't know you knew his name. Neither did I. How did that happen?"

"Two years ago I engaged some of Mr. Bascom's men without telling you. He had sounded as if he were a man of resource and resolution, and I didn't want to get you involved."

"It's the Zeck with the place in Westchester, of course?"

"Yes. I should have signaled you off as soon as I recognized his voice. I tell you nothing because it is better for you to know nothing. You are to forget that you know his name."

"Like that." I snapped my fingers, and grinned at him. "What the hell? Does he eat human flesh, preferably handsome young men?"

"No. He does worse." Wolfe's eyes came half open. "I'll tell you this. If ever, in the course of my business, I find that I am committed against him and must destroy him, I shall leave this house, find a place where I can work—and sleep and eat if there is time for it—and stay there until I have finished. I don't want to do that, and therefore I hope I'll never have to."

"I see. I'd like to meet this bozo. I think I'll make his acquaintance."

"You will not. You'll stay away from him." He made a face. "If this job leads me to that extremity—well, it will or it won't." He glanced at the clock. "It's nearly noon. You'd better go and see if any more answers have arrived. Can't you telephone?"

16 THERE WERE NO MORE ANSWERS. THAT GOES NOT only for Tuesday noon, but for the rest of the day and evening, and Wednesday morning, and Wednesday after lunch. Nothing doing.

It didn't surprise me. The nature of the phone call from the man whose name I had been ordered to forget made it seem likely that there was something peculiar about the subscribers to *Track Almanac* and *What to Expect*, which was the name of the political and economic dope sheet published by the late Beula Poole. But even granting that there wasn't, that as far as they were concerned it was all clean and straight, the two publishers had just been murdered, and who would be goop enough to answer such an ad just to get asked a lot of impertinent questions? In the office after lunch Wednesday I made a remark to that effect to Wolfe, and got only a growl for reply.

"We might at least," I insisted, "have hinted that they would get their money back or something."

No reply.

"We could insert it again and add that. Or we could offer a reward for anyone who would give us the name of an Orchard or Poole subscriber."

No reply.

"Or I could go up to the Fraser apartment and get into conversation with the bunch, and who knows?"

"Yes. Do so."

I looked at him suspiciously. He meant it.

"Now?"

"Yes."

"You sure are hard up when you start taking suggestions from me."

I pulled the phone to me and dialed the number. It was Bill Meadows who answered, and he sounded anything but gay, even when he learned it was me. After a brief talk, however, I was willing to forgive him. I hung up and informed Wolfe:

"I guess I'll have to postpone it. Miss Fraser and Miss Koppel are both out. Bill was a little vague, but I gather that the latter has been tagged by the city authorities for some reason or other, and the former is engaged in trying to remove the tag. Maybe she needs help. Why don't I find out?"

"I don't know. You might try."

I turned and dialed Watkins 9-8241. Inspector Cramer wasn't available, but I got someone just as good, or sometimes I think even better, Sergeant Stebbins.

"I need some information," I told him, "in connection with this fee you folks are earning for Mr. Wolfe."

"So do we," he said frankly. "Got any?"

"Not right now. Mr. Wolfe and I are in conference. How did Miss Koppel hurt your feelings, and where is she, and if you see Miss Fraser give her my love."

He let out a roar of delight. Purley doesn't laugh often, at least when he's on duty, and I resented it. I waited until I thought he might hear me and then demanded:

"What the hell is so funny?"

"I never expected the day to come," he declared. "You calling me to ask where your client is. What's the matter, is Wolfe off his feed?"

"I know another one even better. Call me back when you're through laughing."

"I'm through. Haven't you heard what the Koppel dame did?"

"No. I only know what you tell me."

"Well, this isn't loose yet. We may want to keep it a while if we can, I don't know."

"I'll help you keep it. So will Mr. Wolfe."

"That's understood?"

"Yes."

"Okay. Of course they've all been told not to leave the jurisdiction. This morning Miss Koppel took a cab to La-Guardia. She was nabbed as she was boarding the nine o'clock plane for Detroit. She says she wanted to visit her sick mother in Fleetville, which is eighty miles from Detroit. But she didn't ask permission to go, and the word we get is that her mother is no sicker than she has been for a year. So we

charged her as a material witness. Does that strike you as highhanded?
Do you think it calls for a shakeup?"

"Get set for another laugh. Where's Miss Fraser?"

"With her lawyer at the D.A.'s office discussing bail."

"What kind of reasons have you got for Miss Koppel taking a trip
that are any better than hers?"

"I wouldn't know. Now you're out of my class. If you want to go
into details like that, Wolfe had better ask the Inspector."

I tried another approach or two, but either Purley had given me
all there was or the rest was in another drawer which he didn't feel
like opening. I hung up and relayed the news to Wolfe.

He nodded as if it were no concern of his. I glared at him:

"It wouldn't interest you to have one or both of them stop in for
a chat on their way home? To ask why Miss Koppel simply had to go
to Michigan would be vulgar curiosity?"

"Bah. The police are asking, aren't they?" Wolfe was bitter. "I've
spent countless hours with those people, and got something for it only
when I had a whip to snap. Why compound futility? I need another
whip. Call those newspapers again."

"Am I still to go up there? After the ladies get home?"

"You might as well."

"Yeah." I was savage. "At least I can compound some futility."

I phoned all three papers. Nothing. Being in no mood to sit and
concentrate on germination records, I announced that I was going out
for a walk, and Wolfe nodded absently. When I got back it was after
four o'clock and he had gone up to the plant rooms. I fiddled around,
finally decided that I might as well concentrate on something and the
germination records were all I had, and got Theodore's reports from
the drawer, but then I thought why not throw away three more nickels?
So I started dialing again.

Herald-Tribune, nothing. *News*, nothing. But the *Gazette* girl said
yes, they had one. The way I went for my hat and headed for Tenth
Avenue to grab a taxi, you might have thought I was on my way to a
murder.

The driver was a philosopher. "You don't see many eager happy
faces like yours nowadays," he told me.

"I'm on my way to my wedding."

He opened his mouth to speak again, then clamped it shut. He
shook his head resolutely. "No. Why should I spoil it?"

I paid him off outside the *Gazette* building and went in and got
my prize. It was a square pale-blue envelope, and the printed return
on the flap said:

Mrs. W. T. Michaels
890 East End Avenue
New York City 28

Inside was a single sheet matching the envelope, with small neat handwriting on it:

Box P304:
  Regarding your advertisement, I am not a former subscriber to either of the publications, but I may be able to tell you something. You may write me, or call Lincoln 3-4808, but do not phone before ten in the morning or after five-thirty in the afternoon. That is important.

                                        Hilda Michaels

It was still forty minutes this side of her deadline, so I went straight to a booth and dialed the number. A female voice answered. I asked to speak to Mrs. Michaels.

"This is Mrs. Michaels."

"This is the *Gazette* advertiser you wrote to, Box P304. I've just read—"

"What's your name?" She had a tendency to snap.

"My name is Goodwin, Archie Goodwin. I can be up there in fifteen minutes or less—"

"No, you can't. Anyway, you'd better not. Are you connected with the Police Department?"

"No. I work for Nero Wolfe. You may have heard of Nero Wolfe, the detective?"

"Of course. This isn't a convent. Was that his advertisement?"

"Yes. He—"

"Then why didn't he phone me?"

"Because I just got your note. I'm phoning from a booth in the *Gazette* building. You said not—"

"Well, Mr. Goodman, I doubt if I can tell Mr. Wolfe anything he would be interested in. I really doubt it."

"Maybe not," I conceded. "But he would be the best judge of that. If you don't want me to come up there, how would it be if you called on Mr. Wolfe at his office? West Thirty-fifth Street—it's in the phone book. Or I could run up now in a taxi and—"

"Oh, not now. Not today. I might be able to make it tomorrow—or Friday—"

I was annoyed. For one thing, I would just as soon be permitted to finish a sentence once in a while, and for another, apparently she had read the piece about Wolfe being hired to work on the Orchard case, and my name had been in it, and it had been spelled correctly. So I took on weight:

"You don't seem to realize what you've done, Mrs. Michaels. You—"

"Why, what have I done?"

"You have landed smack in the middle of a murder case. Mr. Wolfe and the police are more or less collaborating on it. He would like to see you about the matter mentioned in his advertisement, not tomorrow or next week, but quick. I think you ought to see him. If you try to put it off because you've begun to regret sending this note he'll be compelled to consult the police, and then what? Then you'll—"

"I didn't say I regret sending the note."

"No, but the way you—"

"I'll be at Mr. Wolfe's office by six o'clock."

"Good! Shall I come—"

I might have known better than to give her another chance to chop me off. She said that she was quite capable of getting herself transported, and I could well believe it.

17   THERE WAS NOTHING SNAPPY ABOUT HER APPEAR-
ance. The mink coat, and the dark red woolen dress made visible when
the coat had been spread over the back of the red leather chair, unquestionably meant well, but she was not built to cooperate with
clothes. There was too much of her and the distribution was all wrong.
Her face was so well padded that there was no telling whether there
were any bones underneath, and the creases were considerably more
than skin deep. I didn't like her. From Wolfe's expression it was plain,
to me, that he didn't like her. As for her, it was a safe bet that she
didn't like anybody.

Wolfe rustled the sheet of pale-blue paper, glanced at it again, and
looked at her. "You say here, madam, that you may be able to tell me
something. Your caution is understandable and even commendable.
You wanted to find out who had placed the advertisement before committing yourself. Now you know. There is no need—"

"That man threatened me," she snapped. "That's not the way to
get me to tell something—if I have something to tell."

"I agree. Mr. Goodwin is headstrong. —Archie, withdraw the
threat."

I did my best to grin at her as man to woman. "I take it back,
Mrs. Michaels. I was so anxious—"

"If I tell you anything," she said to Wolfe, ignoring me, "it will
be because I want to, and it will be completely confidential. Whatever
you do about it, of course I have nothing to say about that, but you
will give me your solemn word of honor that my name will not be
mentioned to anyone. No one is to know I wrote you or came to see
you or had anything to do with it."

Wolfe shook his head. "Impossible. Manifestly impossible. You are not a fool, madam, and I won't try to treat you as if you were. It is even conceivable that you might have to take the witness stand in a murder trial. I know nothing about it, because I don't know what you have to tell. Then how could I—"

"All right," she said, surrendering. "I see I made a mistake. I must be home by seven o'clock. Here's what I have to tell you: somebody I know was a subscriber to that *What to Expect* that was published by that woman, Beula Poole. I distinctly remember, one day two or three months ago, I saw a little stack of them somewhere—in some house or apartment or office. I've been trying to remember where it was, and I simply can't. I wrote you because I thought you might tell me something that would make me remember, and I'm quite willing to try, but I doubt if it will do any good."

"Indeed." Wolfe's expression was fully as sour as hers. "I said you're not a fool. I suppose you're prepared to stick to that under any circum—"

"Yes, I am."

"Even if Mr. Goodwin gets headstrong again and renews his threat?"

"That!" She was contemptuous.

"It's very thin, Mrs. Michaels. Even ridiculous. That you would go to the bother of answering that advertisement, and coming down here—"

"I don't mind being ridiculous."

"Then I have no alternative." Wolfe's lips tightened. He released them. "I accept your conditions. I agree, for myself and for Mr. Goodwin, who is my agent, that we will not disclose the source of our information, and that we will do our utmost to keep anyone from learning it. Should anyone ascertain it, it will be against our will and in spite of our precautions in good faith. We cannot guarantee; we can only promise; and we do so."

Her eyes had narrowed. "On your solemn word of honor."

"Good heavens. That ragged old patch? Very well. My solemn word of honor. Archie?"

"My solemn word of honor," I said gravely.

Her head made an odd ducking movement, reminding me of a fat-cheeked owl I had seen at the zoo getting ready to swoop on a mouse.

"My husband," she said, "has been a subscriber to that publication, *What to Expect*, for eight months."

But the owl had swooped because it was hungry, whereas she was swooping just to hurt. It was in her voice, which was still hers but quite different when she said the word husband.

"And that's ridiculous," she went on, "if you want something ridiculous. He hasn't the slightest interest in politics or industry or the stock market or anything like that. He is a successful doctor and all he ever thinks about is his work and his patients, especially his women patients. What would he want with a thing like that *What to Expect?* Why should he pay that Beula Poole money every week, month after month? I have my own money, and for the first few years after we married we lived on my income, but then he began to be successful, and now he doesn't need my money any more. And he doesn't—"

Abruptly she stood up. Apparently the habit had got so strong that sometimes she even interrupted herself. She was turning to pick up her coat.

"If you please," Wolfe said brusquely. "You have my word of honor and I want some details. What has your husband—"

"That's all," she snapped. "I don't intend to answer any silly questions. If I did you'd be sure to give me away, you wouldn't be smart enough not to, and the details don't matter. I've told you the one thing you need to know, and I only hope—"

She was proceeding with the coat, and I had gone to her to help.

"Yes, madam, what do you hope?"

She looked straight at him. "I hope you've got some brains. You don't look it."

She turned and made for the hall, and I followed. Over the years I have opened that front door to let many people out of that house, among them thieves, swindlers, murderers, and assorted crooks, but it has never been a greater pleasure than on that occasion. Added to everything else, I had noticed when helping her with her coat that her neck needed washing.

It had not been news to us that her husband was a successful doctor. Between my return to the office and her arrival there had been time for a look at the phone book, which had him as an M.D. with an office address in the Sixties just off Park Avenue, and for a call to Doc Vollmer. Vollmer had never met him, but knew his standing and reputation, which were up around the top. He had a good high-bracket practice, with the emphasis on gynecology.

Back in the office I remarked to Wolfe, "There goes my pendulum again. Lately I've been swinging toward the notion of getting myself a little woman, but good Godalmighty. Brother!"

He nodded, and shivered a little. "Yes. However, we can't reject it merely because it's soiled. Unquestionably her fact is a fact; other-

wise she would have contrived an elaborate support for it." He glanced
at the clock. "She said she had to be home by seven, so he may still
be in his office. Try it."

I found the number and dialed it. The woman who answered firmly
intended to protect her employer from harassment by a stranger, but I
finally sold her.

Wolfe took it. "Dr. Michaels? This is Nero Wolfe, a detective.
Yes, sir, so far as I know there is only one of that name. I'm in a little
difficulty and would appreciate some help from you."

"I'm just leaving for the day, Mr. Wolfe. I'm afraid I couldn't
undertake to give you medical advice on the phone." His voice was
low, pleasant, and tired.

"It isn't medical advice I need, doctor. I want to have a talk with
you about a publication called *What to Expect*, to which you subscribed. The difficulty is that I find it impractical to leave my house.
I could send my assistant or a policeman to see you, or both, but I
would prefer to discuss it with you myself, confidentially. I wonder if
you could call on me this evening after dinner?"

Evidently the interrupting mania in the Michaels family was confined to the wife. Not only did he not interrupt, he didn't even take a
cue. Wolfe tried again:

"Would that be convenient, sir?"

"If I could have another moment, Mr. Wolfe. I've had a hard day
and am trying to think."

"By all means."

He took ten seconds. His voice came, even tireder:

"I suppose it would be useless to tell you to go to hell. I would
prefer not to discuss it on the phone. I'll be at your office around nine
o'clock."

"Good. Have you a dinner engagement, doctor?"

"An engagement? No. I'm dining at home. Why?"

"It just occurred to me—could I prevail on you to dine with me?
You said you were just leaving for the day. I have a good cook. We
are having fresh pork tenderloin, with all fiber removed, done in a
casserole, with a sharp brown sauce moderately spiced. There will not
be time to chambrer a claret properly, but we can have the chill off.
We shall of course not approach our little matter until afterward, with
the coffee—or even after that. Do you happen to know the brandy
labeled Remisier? It is not common. I hope this won't shock you, but
the way to do it is to sip it with bites of Fritz's apple pie. Fritz is my
cook."

"I'll be damned. I'll be there—what's the address?"

Wolfe gave it to him, and hung up.

"I'll be damned too," I declared. "A perfect stranger? He may put horse-radish on oysters."

Wolfe grunted. "If he had gone home to eat with that creature things might have been said. Even to the point of repudiation by her and defiance by him. I thought it prudent to avoid that risk."

"Nuts. There's no such risk and you know it. What you're trying to avoid is to give anyone an excuse to think you're human. You were being kind to your fellow man and you'd rather be caught dead. The idea of the poor devil going home to dine with that female hyena was simply too much for your great big warm heart, and you were so damn impetuous you even committed yourself to letting him have some of that brandy of which there are only nineteen bottles in the United States and they're all in your cellar."

"Bosh." He arose. "You would sentimentalize the multiplication table." He started for the kitchen, to tell Fritz about the guest, and to smell around.

18

AFTER DINNER FRITZ BROUGHT US A SECOND POT OF coffee in the office, and also the brandy bottle and big-bellied glasses. Most of the two hours had been spent, not on West Thirty-fifth Street in New York, but in Egypt. Wolfe and the guest had both spent some time there in days gone by, and they had settled on that for discussion and a few arguments.

Dr. Michaels, informally comfortable in the red leather chair, put down his coffee cup, ditched a cigarette, and gently patted his midriff. He looked exactly like a successful Park Avenue doctor, middle-aged, well-built and well-dressed, worried but self-assured. After the first hour at the table the tired and worried look had gone, but now, as he cocked an eye at Wolfe after disposing of the cigarette, his forehead was wrinkled again.

"This has been a delightful recess," he declared. "It has done me a world of good. I have dozens of patients for whom I would like to prescribe a dinner with you, but I'm afraid I'd have to advise you not to fill the prescription." He belched, and was well-mannered enough not to try to cheat on it. "Well. Now I'll stop masquerading as a guest and take my proper role. The human sacrifice."

Wolfe disallowed it. "I have no desire or intention to gut you, sir."

Michaels smiled. "A surgeon might say that too, as he slits the skin. No, let's get it done. Did my wife phone you, or write you, or come to see you?"

"Your wife?" Wolfe's eyes opened innocently. "Has there been any mention of your wife?"

"Only by me, this moment. Let it pass. I suppose your solemn word of honor has been invoked—a fine old phrase, really, solemn word of honor—" He shrugged. "I wasn't actually surprised when you asked me about that blackmail business on the phone, merely momentarily confused. I had been expecting something of the sort, because it didn't seem likely that such an opportunity to cause me embarrassment—or perhaps worse—would be missed. Only I would have guessed it would be the police. This is much better, much."

Wolfe's head dipped forward, visibly, to acknowledge the compliment. "It may eventually reach the police, doctor. There may be no help for it."

"Of course, I realize that. I can only hope not. Did she give you the anonymous letters, or just show them to you?"

"Neither. But that 'she' is your pronoun, not mine. With that understood—I have no documentary evidence, and have seen none. If there is some, no doubt I could get it." Wolfe sighed, leaned back, and half closed his eyes. "Wouldn't it be simpler if you assume that I know nothing at all, and tell me about it?"

"I suppose so, damn it." Michaels sipped some brandy, used his tongue to give all the membranes a chance at it, swallowed, and put the glass down. "From the beginning?"

"If you please."

"Well . . . it was last summer, nine months ago, that I first learned about the anonymous letters. One of my colleagues showed me one that he had received by mail. It strongly hinted that I was chronically guilty of—uh, unethical conduct—with women patients. Not long after that I became aware of a decided change in the attitude of one of my oldest and most valued patients. I appealed to her to tell me frankly what had caused it. She had received two similar letters. It was the next day—naturally my memory is quite vivid on this—that my wife showed me two letters, again similar, that had come to her."

The wrinkles on his forehead had taken command again. "I don't have to explain what that sort of thing could do to a doctor if it kept up. Of course I thought of the police, but the risk of possible publicity, or even spreading of rumor, through a police inquiry, was too great. There was the same objection, or at least I thought there was, to hiring a private investigator. Then, the day after my wife showed me the letters—no, two days after—I had a phone call at my home in the evening. I presume my wife listened to it on the extension in her room—but you're not interested in that. I wish to God you were—" Michaels abruptly jerked his head up as if he had heard a noise somewhere. "Now what did I mean by that?"

"I have no idea," Wolfe murmured. "The phone call?"

"It was a woman's voice. She didn't waste any words. She said she understood that people had been getting letters about me, and if it annoyed me and I wanted to stop it I could easily do so. If I would subscribe for one year to a publication called *What to Expect*—she gave me the address—there would be no more letters. The cost would be ten dollars a week, and I could pay as I pleased, weekly, monthly, or the year in advance. She assured me emphatically that there would be no request for renewal, that nothing beyond the one year's subscription would be required, that the letters would stop as soon as I subscribed, and that there would be no more."

Michaels turned a hand to show a palm. "That's all. I subscribed. I sent ten dollars a week for a while—eight weeks—and then I sent a check for four hundred and forty dollars. So far as I know there have been no more letters—and I think I would know."

"Interesting," Wolfe murmured. "Extremely."

"Yes," Michaels agreed. "I can understand your saying that. It's what a doctor says when he runs across something rare like a lung grown to a rib. But if he's tactful he doesn't say it in the hearing of the patient."

"You're quite right, sir. I apologize. But this is indeed a rarity— truly remarkable! If the execution graded as high as the conception . . . what were the letters like, typed?"

"Yes. Plain envelopes and plain cheap paper, but the typing was perfect."

"You said you sent a check. That was acceptable?"

Michaels nodded. "She made that clear. Either check or money order. Cash would be accepted, but was thought inadvisable on account of the risk in the mails."

"You see? Admirable. What about her voice?"

"It was medium in pitch, clear and precise, educated—I mean good diction and grammar—and matter-of-fact. One day I called the number of the publication—as you probably know, it's listed—and asked for Miss Poole. It was Miss Poole talking, she said. I discussed a paragraph in the latest issue, and she was intelligent and informed about it. But her voice was soprano, jerky and nervous, nothing like the voice that had told me how to get the letters stopped."

"It wouldn't be. That was what you phoned for?"

"Yes. I thought I'd have that much satisfaction at least, since there was no risk in it."

"You might have saved your nickel." Wolfe grimaced. "Dr. Michaels, I'm going to ask you a question."

"Go ahead."

"I don't want to, but though the question is intrusive it is also important. And it will do no good to ask it unless I can be assured of a completely candid reply or a refusal to answer at all. You would be capable of a fairly good job of evasion if you were moved to try, and I don't want that. Will you give me either candor or silence?"

Michaels smiled. "Silence is so awkward. I'll give you a straight answer or I'll say 'no comment.' "

"Good. How much substance was there in the hints in those letters about your conduct?"

The doctor looked at him, considered, and finally nodded his head. "It's intrusive, all right, but I'll take your word for it that it's important. You want a full answer?"

"As full as possible."

"Then it must be confidential."

"It will be."

"I accept that. I don't ask for your solemn word of honor. There was not even a shadow of substance. I have never, with any patient, even approached the boundaries of professional decorum. But I'm not like you; I have a deep and intense need for the companionship of a woman. I suppose that's why I married so early—and so disastrously. Possibly her money attracted me too, though I would vigorously deny it; there are bad streaks in me. Anyway, I do have the companionship of a woman, but not the one I married. She has never been my patient. When she needs medical advice she goes to some other doctor. No doctor should assume responsibility for the health of one he loves or one he hates."

"This companionship you enjoy—it could not have been the stimulus for the hints in the letters?"

"I don't see how. All the letters spoke of women patients—in the plural, and patients."

"Giving their names?"

"No, no names."

Wolfe nodded with satisfaction. "That would have taken too much research for a wholesale operation, and it wasn't necessary." He came forward in his chair to reach for the push button. "I am greatly obliged to you, Dr. Michaels. This has been highly distasteful for you, and you have been most indulgent. I don't need to prolong it, and I won't. I foresee no necessity to give the police your name, and I'll even engage not to do so, though heaven only knows what my informant will do. Now we'll have some beer. We didn't get it settled about the pointed arches in the Tulun mosque."

"If you don't mind," the guest said, "I've been wondering if it would be seemly to tip this brandy bottle again."

So he stayed with the brandy while Wolfe had beer. I excused myself and went out for a breath of air, for while they were perfectly welcome to do some more settling about the pointed arches in the Tulun mosque, as far as I was concerned it had been attended to long ago.

It was past eleven when I returned, and soon afterward Michaels arose to go. He was far from being pickled, but he was much more relaxed and rosy than he had been when I let him in. Wolfe was so mellow that he even stood up to say good-by, and I didn't see his usual flicker of hesitation when Michaels extended a hand. He doesn't care about shaking hands indiscriminately.

Michaels said impulsively, "I want to ask you something."

"Then do so."

"I want to consult you professionally—your profession. I need help. I want to pay for it."

"You will, sir, if it's worth anything."

"It will be, I'm sure. I want to know, if you are being shadowed, if a man is following you, how many ways are there of eluding him, and what are they, and how are they executed?"

"Good heavens." Wolfe shuddered. "How long has this been going on?"

"For months."

"Well. —Archie?"

"Sure," I said. "Glad to."

"I don't want to impose on you," Michaels lied. He did. "It's late."

"That's okay. Sit down."

I really didn't mind, having met his wife.

19

THAT, I THOUGHT TO MYSELF AS I WAS BRUSHING MY hair Thursday morning, covered some ground. That was a real step forward.

Then, as I dropped the brush into the drawer, I asked aloud, "Yeah? Toward what?"

In a murder case you expect to spend at least half your time barking up wrong trees. Sometimes that gets you irritated, but what the hell, if you belong in the detective business at all you just skip it and take another look. That wasn't the trouble with this one. We hadn't gone dashing around investigating a funny sound only to learn it was just a cat on a fence. Far from it. We had left all that to the cops. Every move we had made had been strictly pertinent. Our two chief discoveries—the tape on the bottle of coffee and the way the circulation department of *What to Expect* operated—were unquestionably essential parts of the picture of the death of Cyril Orchard, which was what we were working on.

So it was a step forward. Fine. When you have taken a step forward, the next thing on the program is another step in the same direction. And that was the pebble in the griddle cake I broke a tooth on that morning. Bathing and dressing and eating breakfast, I went over the situation from every angle and viewpoint, and I had to admit this: if Wolfe had called me up to his room and asked for a suggestion on how I should spend the day, I would have been tongue-tied.

What I'm doing, if you're following me, is to justify what I did do. When he did call me up to his room, and wished me a good morning, and asked how I had slept, and told me to phone Inspector

Cramer and invite him to pay us a visit at eleven o'clock, all I said was:

"Yes, sir."

There was another phone call which I had decided to make on my own. Since it involved a violation of a law Wolfe had passed I didn't want to make it from the office, so when I went out for a stroll to the bank to deposit a check from a former client who was paying in installments, I patronized a booth. When I got Lon Cohen I told him I wanted to ask him something that had no connection with the detective business, but was strictly private. I said I had been offered a job at a figure ten times what he was worth, and fully half what I was, and, while I had no intention of leaving Wolfe, I was curious. Had he ever heard of a guy named Arnold Zeck, and what about him?

"Nothing for you," Lon said.

"What do you mean, nothing for me?"

"I mean you don't want a Sunday feature, you want the lowdown, and I haven't got it. Zeck is a question mark. I've heard that he owns twenty Assemblymen and six district leaders, and I've also heard that he is merely a dried fish. There's a rumor that if you print something about him that he resents your body is washed ashore at Montauk Point, mangled by sharks, but you know how the boys talk. One little detail—this is between us?"

"Forever."

"There's not a word on him in our morgue. I had occasion to look once, several years ago—when he gave his yacht to the Navy. Not a thing, which is peculiar for a guy that gives away yachts and owns the highest hill in Westchester. What's the job?"

"Skip it. I wouldn't consider it. I thought he still had his yacht."

I decided to let it lay. If the time should come when Wolfe had to sneak outdoors and look for a place to hide, I didn't want it blamed on me.

Cramer arrived shortly after eleven. He wasn't jovial, and neither was I. When he came, as I had known him to, to tear Wolfe to pieces, or at least to threaten to haul him downtown or send a squad with a paper signed by a judge, he had fire in his eye and springs in his calves. This time he was so forlorn he even let me hang up his hat and coat for him. But as he entered the office I saw him squaring his shoulders. He was so used to going into that room to be belligerent that it was automatic. He growled a greeting, sat, and demanded:

"What have you got this time?"

Wolfe, lips compressed, regarded him a moment and then pointed a finger at him. "You know, Mr. Cramer, I begin to suspect I'm a jackass. Three weeks ago yesterday, when I read in the paper of Mr. Orchard's death, I should have guessed immediately why people paid him ten dollars a week. I don't mean merely the general idea of black-mail; that was an obvious possibility; I mean the whole operation, the way it was done."

"Why, have you guessed it now?"

"No. I've had it described to me."

"By whom?"

"It doesn't matter. An innocent victim. Would you like to have me describe it to you?"

"Sure. Or the other way around."

Wolfe frowned. "What? You know about it?"

"Yeah, I know about it. I do now." Cramer wasn't doing any bragging. He stayed glum. "Understand I'm saying nothing against the New York Police Department. It's the best on earth. But it's a large organization, and you can't expect everyone to know what everybody else did or is doing. My part of it is Homicide. Well. In September nineteen forty-six, nineteen months ago, a citizen lodged a complaint with a precinct detective sergeant. People had received anonymous letters about him, and he had got a phone call from a man that if he subscribed to a thing called *Track Almanac* for one year there would be no more letters. He said the stuff in the letters was lies, and he wasn't going to be swindled, and he wanted justice. Because it looked as if it might be a real job the sergeant consulted his captain. They went together to the *Track Almanac* office, found Orchard there, and jumped him. He denied it, said it must have been someone trying to queer him. The citizen listened to Orchard's voice, both direct and on the phone, and said it hadn't been his voice on the phone, it must have been a confederate. But no lead to a confederate could be found. Nothing could be found. Orchard stood pat. He refused to let them see his subscription list, on the ground that he didn't want his customers pestered, which was within his rights in the absence of a charge. The citizen's lawyer wouldn't let him swear a warrant. There were no more anonymous letters."

"Beautiful," Wolfe murmured.

"What the hell is so beautiful?"

"Excuse me. And?"

"And nothing. The captain is now retired, living on a farm in Rhode Island. The sergeant is still a sergeant, as he should be, since apparently he doesn't read the papers. He's up in a Bronx precinct, specializing on kids that throw stones at trains. Just day before yes-terday the name Orchard reminded him of something! So I've got that.

I've put men onto the other Orchard subscribers that we know about, except the one that was just a sucker—plenty of men to cover anybody at all close to them, to ask about anonymous letters. There have been no results on Savarese or Madeline Fraser, but we've uncovered it on the Leconne woman, the one that runs a beauty parlor. It was the same routine—the letters and the phone call, and she fell for it. She says the letters were lies, and it looks like they were, but she paid up to get them stopped, and she pushed us off, and you too, because she didn't want a stink."

Cramer made a gesture. "Does that describe it?"

"Perfectly," Wolfe granted.

"Okay. You called me, and I came because I swear to God I don't see what it gets me. It was you who got brilliant and made it that the poison was for the Fraser woman, not Orchard. Now that looks crazy, but what don't? If it was for Orchard after all, who and why in that bunch? And what about Beula Poole? Were she and Orchard teaming it? Or was she horning in on his list? By God, I never saw anything like it! Have you been giving me a runaround? I want to know!"

Cramer pulled a cigar from his pocket and got his teeth closed on it.

Wolfe shook his head. "Not I," he declared. "I'm a little dizzy myself. Your description was sketchy, and it might help to fill it in. Are you in a hurry?"

"Hell no."

"Then look at this. It is important, if we are to see clearly the connection of the two events, to know exactly what the roles of Mr. Orchard and Miss Poole were. Let us say that I am an ingenious and ruthless man, and I decide to make some money by blackmailing wholesale, with little or no risk to myself."

"Orchard got poisoned," Cramer growled, "and she got shot."

"Yes," Wolfe agreed, "but I didn't. I either know people I can use or I know how to find them. I am a patient and resourceful man. I supply Orchard with funds to begin publication of *Track Almanac*. I have lists prepared, with the greatest care, of persons with ample incomes from a business or profession or job that would make them sensitive to my attack. Then I start operating. The phone calls are made neither by Orchard nor by me. Of course Orchard, who is in an exposed position, has never met me, doesn't know who I am, and probably isn't even aware that I exist. Indeed, of those engaged in the operation, very few know that I exist, possibly only one."

Wolfe rubbed his palms together. "All this is passably clever. I am taking from my victims only a small fraction of their income, and

I am not threatening them with exposure of a fearful secret. Even if I knew their secrets, which I don't, I would prefer not to use them in the anonymous letters; that would not merely harass them, it would fill them with terror, and I don't want terror, I only want money. Therefore, while my lists are carefully compiled, no great amount of research is required, just enough to get only the kind of people who would be least likely to put up a fight, either by going to the police or by any other method. Even should one resort to the police, what will happen? You have already answered that, Mr. Cramer, by telling what did happen."

"That sergeant was dumb as hell," Cramer grumbled.

"Oh, no. There was the captain too. Take an hour sometime to consider what you would have done and see where you come out. What if one or two more citizens had made the same complaint? Mr. Orchard would have insisted that he was being persecuted by an enemy. In the extreme case of an avalanche of complaints, most improbable, or of an exposure by an exceptionally capable policeman, what then? Mr. Orchard would be done for, but I wouldn't. Even if he wanted to squeal, he couldn't, not on me, for he doesn't know me."

"He has been getting money to you," Cramer objected.

"Not to me. He never gets within ten miles of me. The handling of the money is an important detail and you may be sure it has been well organized. Only one man ever gets close enough to me to bring me money. It shouldn't take me long to build up a fine list of subscribers to *Track Almanac*—certainly a hundred, possibly five hundred. Let us be moderate and say two hundred. That's two thousand dollars a week. If Mr. Orchard keeps half, he can pay all expenses and have well over thirty thousand a year for his net. If he has any sense, and he has been carefully chosen and is under surveillance, that will satisfy him. For me, it's a question of my total volume. How many units do I have? New York is big enough for four or five, Chicago for two or three, Detroit, Philadelphia, and Los Angeles for two each, at least a dozen cities for one. If I wanted to stretch it I could easily get twenty units working. But we'll be moderate again and stop at twelve. That would bring me in six hundred thousand dollars a year for my share. My operating costs shouldn't be more than half that; and when you consider that my net is really net, with no income tax to pay, I am doing very well indeed."

Cramer started to say something, but Wolfe put up a hand:

"Please. As I said, all that is fairly clever, especially the avoidance of real threats about real secrets, but what makes it a masterpiece is the limitation of the tribute. All blackmailers will promise that this time is the last, but I not only make the promise, I keep it. I have an inviolable rule never to ask for a subscription renewal."

"You can't prove it."

"No, I can't. But I confidently assume it, because it is the essence, the great beauty, of the plan. A man can put up with a pain—and this was not really a pain, merely a discomfort, for people with good incomes—if he thinks he knows when it will stop, and if it stops when the time comes. But if I make them pay year after year, with no end in sight, I invite sure disaster. I'm too good a businessman for that. It is much cheaper and safer to get four new subscribers a week for each unit; that's all that is needed to keep it at a constant two hundred subscribers."

Wolfe nodded emphatically. "By all means, then, if I am to stay in business indefinitely, and I intend to, I must make that rule and rigidly adhere to it; and I do so. There will of course be many little difficulties, as there are in any enterprise, and I must also be prepared for an unforeseen contingency. For example, Mr. Orchard may get killed. If so I must know of it at once, and I must have a man in readiness to remove all papers from his office, even though there is nothing there that could possibly lead to me. I would prefer to have no inkling of the nature and extent of my operations reach unfriendly parties. But I am not panicky; why should I be? Within two weeks one of my associates—the one who makes the phone calls for my units that are managed by females—begins phoning the *Track Almanac* subscribers to tell them that their remaining payments should be made to another publication called *What to Expect*. It would have been better to discard my *Track Almanac* list and take my loss, but I don't know that. I only find it out when Miss Poole also gets killed. Luckily my surveillance is excellent. Again an office must be cleaned out, and this time under hazardous conditions and with dispatch. Quite likely my man has seen the murderer, and can even name him; but I'm not interested in catching a murderer; what I want is to save my business from these confounded interruptions. I discard both those cursed lists, destroy them, burn them, and start plans for two entirely new units. How about a weekly sheet giving the latest shopping information? Or a course in languages, any language? There are numberless possibilities."

Wolfe leaned back. "There's your connection, Mr. Cramer."

"The hell it is," Cramer mumbled. He was rubbing the side of his nose with his forefinger. He was sorting things out. After a moment he went on, "I thought maybe you were going to end up by killing both of them yourself. That would be a connection too, wouldn't it?"

"Not a very plausible one. Why would I choose that time and place and method for killing Mr. Orchard? Or even Miss Poole—why there in her office? It wouldn't be like me. If they had to be disposed of surely I would have made better arrangements than that."

"Then you're saying it was a subscriber."

"I make the suggestion. Not necessarily a subscriber, but one who looked at things from the subscriber's viewpoint."

"Then the poison was intended for Orchard after all."

"I suppose so, confound it. I admit that's hard to swallow. It's sticking in my throat."

"Mine too." Cramer was skeptical. "One thing you overlooked. You were so interested in pretending it was you, you didn't mention who it really is. This patient ruthless bird that's pulling down over half a million a year. Could I have his name and address?"

"Not from me," Wolfe said positively. "I strongly doubt if you could finish him, and if you tried he would know who had named him. Then I would have to undertake it, and I don't want to tackle him. I work for money, to make a living, not just to keep myself alive. I don't want to be reduced to that primitive extremity."

"Nuts. You've been telling me a dream you had. You can't stand it for anyone to think you don't know everything, so you even have the brass to tell me to my face that you know his name. You don't even know he exists, any more than Orchard did."

"Oh yes I do. I'm much more intelligent than Mr. Orchard."

"Have it your way," Cramer conceded generously. "You trade orchids with him. So what? He's not in my department. If he wasn't behind these murders I don't want him. My job is homicide. Say you didn't dream it, say it's just as you said, what comes next? How have I gained an inch or you either? Is that what you got me here for, to tell me about your goddam units in twelve different cities?"

"Partly. I didn't know your precinct sergeant had been reminded of something. But that wasn't all. Do you feel like telling me why Miss Koppel tried to get on an airplane?"

"Sure I feel like it, but I can't because I don't know. She says to see her sick mother. We've tried to find another reason that we like better, but no luck. She's under bond not to leave the state."

Wolfe nodded. "Nothing seems to fructify, does it? What I really wanted was to offer a suggestion. Would you like one?"

"Let me hear it."

"I hope it will appeal to you. You said that you have had men working in the circles of the Orchard subscribers you know about, and that there have been no results on Professor Savarese or Miss Fraser.

You might have expected that, and probably did, since those two have given credible reasons for having subscribed. Why not shift your aim to another target? How many men are available for that sort of work?"

"As many as I want."

"Then put a dozen or more onto Miss Vance—or, rather, onto her associates. Make it thorough. Tell the men that the object is not to learn whether anonymous letters regarding Miss Vance have been received. Tell them that that much has been confidently assumed, and that their job is to find out what the letters said, and who got them and when. It will require pertinacity to the farthest limit of permissible police conduct. The man good enough actually to secure one of the letters will be immediately promoted."

Cramer sat scowling. Probably he was doing the same as me, straining for a quick but comprehensive flashback of all the things that Elinor Vance had seen or done, either in our presence or to our knowledge. Finally he inquired:

"Why her?"

Wolfe shook his head. "If I explained you would say I was telling you another dream. I assure you that in my opinion the reason is good."

"How many letters to how many people?"

Wolfe's brows went up. "My dear sir! If I knew that would I let you get a finger in it? I would have her here ready for delivery, with evidence. What the deuce is wrong with it? I am merely suggesting a specific line of inquiry on a specific person whom you have already been tormenting for over three weeks."

"You're letting my finger in now. If it's any good why don't you hire men with your clients' money and sail on through?"

Wolfe snorted. He was disgusted. "Very well," he said. "I'll do that. Don't bother about it. Doubtless your own contrivances are far superior. Another sergeant may be reminded of something that happened at the turn of the century."

Cramer stood up. I thought he was going to leave without a word, but he spoke. "That's pretty damn cheap, Wolfe. You would never have heard of that sergeant if I hadn't told you about him. Freely."

He turned and marched out. I made allowances for both of them because their nerves were on edge. After three weeks for Cramer, and more than two for Wolfe, they were no closer to the killer of Cyril Orchard than when they started.

20   I HAVE TO ADMIT THAT FOR ME THE TOSS TO ELINOR Vance was a passed ball. It went by me away out of reach. I halfway expected that now at last we would get some hired help, but when I asked Wolfe if I should line up Saul and Fred and Orrie he merely grunted. I wasn't much surprised, since it was in accordance with our new policy of letting the cops do it. It was a cinch that Cramer's first move on returning to his headquarters would be to start a pack sniffing for anonymous letters about Elinor Vance.

After lunch I disposed of a minor personal problem by getting Wolfe's permission to pay a debt, though that wasn't the way I put it. I told him that I would like to call Lon Cohen and give him the dope on how subscriptions to *Track Almanac* and *What to Expect* had been procured, of course without any hint of a patient ruthless master mind who didn't exist, and naming no names. My arguments were (a) that Wolfe had fished it up himself and therefore Cramer had no copyright, (b) that it was desirable to have a newspaper under an obligation, (c) that it would serve them right for the vicious editorial they had run, and (d) that it might possibly start a fire somewhere that would give us a smoke signal. Wolfe nodded, but I waited until he had gone up to the plant rooms to phone Lon to pay up. If I had done it in his hearing he's so damn suspicious that some word, or a shade of a tone, might have started him asking questions.

Another proposal I made later on didn't do so well. He turned it down flat. Since it was to be assumed that I had forgotten the name Arnold Zeck, I used Duncan instead. I reminded Wolfe that he had told Cramer that it was likely that an employee of Duncan's had seen the killer of Beula Poole, and could even name him. What I proposed was to call the Midland number and leave a message for Duncan to phone Wolfe. If and when he did so Wolfe would make an offer: if Duncan would come through on the killer, not for quotation of course, Wolfe would agree to forget that he had ever heard tell of anyone whose name began with Z—pardon me, D.

All I got was my head snapped off. First, Wolfe would make no such bargain with a criminal, especially a dysgenic one; and second, there would be no further communication between him and that nameless buzzard unless the buzzard started it. That seemed shortsighted to me. If he didn't intend to square off with the bird unless he had to, why not take what he could get? After dinner that evening I tried to bring it up again, but he wouldn't discuss it.

The following morning, Friday, we had a pair of visitors that we hadn't seen for quite a while: Walter B. Anderson, the Hi-Spot president, and Fred Owen, the director of public relations. When the door-bell rang a little before noon and I went to the front and saw them on the stoop, my attitude was quite different from what it had been the first time. They had no photographers along, and they were clients in good standing entitled to one hell of a beef if they only knew it, and there was a faint chance that they had a concealed weapon, maybe a hatpin, to stick into Wolfe. So without going to the office to check I welcomed them across the threshold.

Wolfe greeted them without any visible signs of rapture, but at least he didn't grump. He even asked them how they did. While they were getting seated he shifted in his chair so he could give his eyes to either one without excessive exertion for his neck muscles. He actually apologized:

"It isn't astonishing if you gentlemen are getting a little impatient. But if you are exasperated, so am I. I had no idea it would drag on like this. No murderer likes to be caught, naturally; but this one seems to have an extraordinary aversion to it. Would you like me to describe what has been accomplished?"

"We know pretty well," Owen stated. He was wearing a dark brown double-breasted pin-stripe that must have taken at least five fittings to get it the way it looked.

"We know too well," the president corrected him. Usually I am tolerant of the red-faced plump type, but every time that geezer opened his mouth I wanted to shut it and not by talking.

Wolfe frowned. "I've admitted your right to exasperation. You needn't insist on it."

"We're not exasperated with you, Mr. Wolfe," Owen declared.

"I am," the president corrected him again. "With the whole damn thing and everything and everyone connected with it. For a while I've been willing to string along with the idea that there can't be any argument against a Hooper in the high twenties, but I've thought I might be wrong and now I know I was. My God, blackmail! Were you responsible for that piece in the *Gazette* this morning?"

"Well . . ." Wolfe was being judicious. "I would say that the responsibility rests with the man who conceived the scheme. I discovered and disclosed it—"

"It doesn't matter." Anderson waved it aside. "What does matter is that my company and my product cannot and will not be connected in the public mind with blackmail. That's dirty. That makes people gag."

"I absolutely agree," Owen asserted.

"Murder is moderately dirty too," Wolfe objected.

"No," Anderson said flatly. "Murder is sensational and exciting, but it's not like blackmail and anonymous letters. I'm through. I've had enough of it."

He got a hand in his breast pocket and pulled out an envelope, from which he extracted an oblong strip of blue paper. "Here's a check for your fee, the total amount. I can collect from the others—or not. I'll see. Send me a bill for expenses to date. You understand, I'm calling it off."

Owen had got up to take the check and hand it to Wolfe. Wolfe took a squint at it and let it drop to the desk.

"Indeed." Wolfe picked up the check, gave it another look, and dropped it again. "Have you consulted the other parties to our arrangement?"

"No, and I don't intend to. What do you care? That's the full amount, isn't it?"

"Yes, the amount's all right. But why this headlong retreat? What has suddenly scared you so?"

"Nothing has scared me." Anderson came forward in his chair. "Look, Wolfe. I came down here myself to make sure there's no slip-up on this. The deal is off, beginning right now. If you listened to the Fraser program this morning you didn't hear my product mentioned. I'm paying that off too, and clearing out. If you think I'm scared you don't know me. I don't scare. But I know how to take action when the circumstances require it, and that's what I'm doing."

He left his chair, leaned over Wolfe's desk, stretched a short fat arm, and tapped the check with a short stubby forefinger. "I'm no welcher! I'll pay your expenses just like I'm paying this! I'm not blaming you, to hell with that, but from this minute—you—are—not—working—for—me!"

With the last six words the finger jabbed the desk, at the rate of about three jabs to a word.

"Come on Fred," the president commanded, and the pair tramped out to the hall.

I moseyed over as far as the office door to see that they didn't make off with my new twenty-dollar gray spring hat, and, when they were definitely gone, returned to my desk, sat, and commented to Wolfe:

"He seems to be upset."

"Take a letter to him."

I got my notebook and pen. Wolfe cleared his throat.

"Not dear Mr. Anderson, dear sir. Regarding our conversation at my office this morning, I am engaged with others as well as you, and, since my fee is contingent upon a performance, I am obliged to continue until the performance is completed. The check you gave me will be held in my safe until that time."

I looked up. "Sincerely?"

"I suppose so. There's nothing insincere about it. When you go out to mail it go first to the bank and have the check certified."

"That shifts the contingency," I remarked, opening the drawer where I kept letterheads, "to whether the bank stays solvent or not."

It was at that moment, the moment when I was putting the paper in the typewriter, that Wolfe really settled down to work on the Orchard case. He leaned back, shut his eyes, and began exercising his lips. He was like that when I left on my errand, and still like that when I got back. At such times I don't have to tiptoe or keep from rustling papers; I can bang the typewriter or make phone calls or use the vacuum cleaner and he doesn't hear it.

All the rest of that day and evening, up till bedtime, except for intermissions for meals and the afternoon conclave in the plant rooms, he kept at it, with no word or sign to give me a hint what kind of trail he had found, if any. In a way it was perfectly jake with me, for at least it showed that he had decided we would do our own cooking, but in another way it wasn't so hot. When it goes on hour after hour, as it did that Friday, the chances are that he's finding himself just about cornered, and there's no telling how desperate he'll be when he picks a hole to bust out through. A couple of years ago, after spending most of a day figuring one out, he ended up with a charade that damn near got nine human beings asphyxiated with ciphogene, including him and me, not to mention Inspector Cramer.

When both the clock and my wrist watch said it was close to midnight, and there he still was, I inquired politely:

"Shall we have some coffee to keep awake?"

His mutter barely reached me: "Go to bed."

I did so.

21 I NEEDN'T HAVE WORRIED. HE DID GIVE BIRTH, BUT not to one of his fantastic freaks. The next morning, Saturday, when Fritz returned to the kitchen after taking up the breakfast tray he told me I was wanted.

Since Wolfe likes plenty of air at night but a good warm room at breakfast time it had been necessary, long ago, to install a contraption that would automatically close his window at 6:00 A.M. As a result the eight o'clock temperature permits him to have his tray on a table near the window without bothering to put on a dressing gown. Seated there, his hair not yet combed, his feet bare, and all the yardage of his yellow pajamas dazzling in the morning sun, he is something to blink at, and it's too bad that Fritz and I are the only ones who ever have the privilege.

I told him it was a nice morning, and he grunted. He will not admit that a morning is bearable, let alone nice, until, having had his second cup of coffee, he has got himself fully dressed.

"Instructions," he growled.

I sat down, opened my notebook, and uncapped my pen. He instructed:

"Get some ordinary plain white paper of a cheap grade; I doubt if any of ours will do. Say five by eight. Type this on it, single-spaced, no date or salutation."

He shut his eyes. "Since you are a friend of Elinor Vance, this is something you should know. During her last year at college the death of a certain person was ascribed to natural causes and was never properly investigated. Another incident that was never investigated was the disappearance of a jar of cyanide from the electroplating shop of Miss

Vance's brother. It would be interesting to know if there was any connection between those two incidents. Possibly an inquiry into both of them would suggest such a connection."

"That all?"

"Yes. No signature. No envelope. Fold the paper and soil it a little; give it the appearance of having been handled. This is Saturday, but an item in the morning paper tells of the withdrawal of Hi-Spot from sponsorship of Miss Fraser's program, so I doubt if those people will have gone off for week ends. You may even find that they are together, conferring; that would suit our purpose best. But either together or singly, see them; show them the anonymous letter; ask if they have ever seen it or one similar to it; be insistent and as pestiferous as possible."

"Including Miss Vance herself?"

"Let circumstances decide. If they are together and she is with them, yes. Presumably she has already been alerted by Mr. Cramer's men."

"The professor? Savarese?"

"No, don't bother with him." Wolfe drank coffee. "That's all."

I stood up. "I might get more or better results if I knew what we're after. Are we expecting Elinor Vance to break down and confess? Or am I nagging one of them into pulling a gun on me, or what?"

I should have known better, with him still in his pajamas and his hair tousled.

"You're following instructions," he said peevishly. "If I knew what you're going to get I wouldn't have had to resort to this shabby stratagem."

"Shabby is right," I agreed, and left him.

I would of course obey orders, for the same reason that a good soldier does, namely he'd better, but I was not filled with enough zeal to make me hurry my breakfast. My attitude as I set about the preliminaries of the operation was that if this was the best he could do he might as well have stayed dormant. I did not believe that he had anything on Elinor Vance. He does sometimes hire Saul or Orrie or Fred without letting me know what they're up to or, more rarely, even that they're working for him, but I can always tell by seeing if money has been taken from the safe. The money was all present or accounted for. You can judge my frame of mind when I state that I halfway suspected that he had picked on Elinor merely because I had gone to a little trouble to have her seated nearest to me the night of the party.

He was, however, right about the week ends. I didn't start on the phone calls until nine-thirty, not wanting to get them out of bed for something which I regarded as about as useful as throwing rocks at the moon. The first one I tried, Bill Meadows, said he hadn't had breakfast yet and he didn't know when he would have some free time, because he was due at Miss Fraser's apartment at eleven for a conference and there was no telling how long it would last. That indicated that I would have a chance to throw at two or more moons with one stone, and another couple of phone calls verified it. There was a meeting on. I did the morning chores, buzzed the plant rooms to inform Wolfe, and left a little before eleven and headed uptown.

To show you what a murder case will do to people's lives, the password routine had been abandoned. But it by no means followed that it was easier than it had been to get up to apartment 10B. Quite the contrary. Evidently journalists and others had been trying all kinds of dodges to get a ride in the elevator, for the distinguished-looking hallman wasn't a particle interested in what I said my name was, and he steeled himself to betray no sign of recognition. He simply used the phone, and in a few minutes Bill Meadows emerged from the elevator and walked over to us. We said hello.

"Strong said you'd probably show up," he said. Neither his tone nor his expression indicated that they had been pacing up and down waiting for me. "Miss Fraser wants to know if it's something urgent."

"Mr. Wolfe thinks it is."

"All right, come on."

He was so preoccupied that he went into the elevator first.

I decided that if he tried leaving me alone in the enormous living room with the assorted furniture, to wait until I was summoned, I would just stick to his heels, but that proved to be unnecessary. He couldn't have left me alone there because that was where they were.

Madeline Fraser was on the green burlap divan, propped against a dozen cushions. Deborah Koppel was seated on the piano bench. Elinor Vance perched on a corner of the massive old black walnut table. Tully Strong had the edge of his sitter on the edge of the pink silk chair, and Nat Traub was standing. That was all as billed, but there was an added attraction. Also standing, at the far end of the long divan, was Nancylee Shepherd.

"It was Goodwin," Bill Meadows told them, but they would probably have deduced it anyhow, since I had dropped my hat and coat in the hall and was practically at his elbow. He spoke to Miss Fraser:

"He says it's something urgent."

Miss Fraser asked me briskly, "Will it take long, Mr. Goodwin?" She looked clean and competent, as if she had had a good night's sleep, a shower, a healthy vigorous rub, and a thorough breakfast.

I told her I was afraid it might.

"Then I'll have to ask you to wait." She was asking a favor. She certainly had the knack of being personal without making you want to back off. "Mr. Traub has to leave soon for an appointment, and we have to make an important decision. You know, of course, that we have lost a sponsor. I suppose I ought to feel low about it, but I really don't. Do you know how many firms we have had offers from, to take the Hi-Spot place? Sixteen!"

"Wonderful!" I admired. "Sure, I'll wait." I crossed to occupy a chair outside the conference zone.

They forgot, immediately and completely, that I was there. All but one: Nancylee. She changed position so she could keep her eyes on me, and her expression showed plainly that she considered me tricky, ratty, and unworthy of trust.

"We've got to start eliminating," Tully Strong declared. He had his spectacles off, holding them in his hand. "As I understand it there are just five serious contenders."

"Four," Elinor Vance said, glancing at a paper she held. "I've crossed off Fluff, the biscuit dough. You said to, didn't you, Lina?"

"It's a good company," Traub said regretfully. "One of the best. Their radio budget is over three million."

"You're just making it harder, Nat," Deborah Koppel told him. "We can't take all of them. I thought your favorite was Meltettes."

"It is," Traub agreed, "but these are all very fine accounts. What do you think of Meltettes, Miss Fraser?" He was the only one of the bunch who didn't call her Lina.

"I haven't tried them." She glanced around. "Where are they?"

Nancylee, apparently not so concentrated on me as to miss any word or gesture of her idol, spoke up: "There on the piano, Miss Fraser. Do you want them?"

"We have got to eliminate," Strong insisted, stabbing the air with his spectacles for emphasis. "I must repeat, as representative of the other sponsors, that they are firmly and unanimously opposed to Sparkle, if it is to be served on the program as Hi-Spot was. They never liked the idea and they don't want it resumed."

"It's already crossed off," Elinor Vance stated. "With Fluff and Sparkle out, that leaves four."

"Not on account of the sponsors," Miss Fraser put in. "We just happen to agree with them. They aren't going to decide this. We are."

"You mean you are, Lina." Bill Meadows sounded a little irritated. "What the hell, we all know that. You don't want Fluff because Cora made some biscuits and you didn't like 'em. You don't want Sparkle because they want it served on the program, and God knows I don't blame you."

Elinor Vance repeated, "That leaves four."

"All right, eliminate!" Strong persisted.

"We're right where we were before," Deborah Koppel told them. "The trouble is, there's no real objection to any of the four, and I think Bill's right, I think we have to put it up to Lina."

"I am prepared," Nat Traub announced, in the tone of a man burning bridges, "to say that I will vote for Meltettes."

For my part, I was prepared to say that I would vote for nobody. Sitting there taking them in, as far as I could tell the only strain they were under was the pressure of picking the right sponsor. If, combined with that, one of them was contending with the nervous wear and tear of a couple of murders, he was too good for me. As the argument got warmer it began to appear that, though they were agreed that the final word was up to Miss Fraser, each of them had a favorite among the four entries left. That was what complicated the elimination.

Naturally, on account of the slip of paper I had in my pocket, I was especially interested in Elinor Vance, but the sponsor problem seemed to be monopolizing her attention as completely as that of the others. I would of course have to follow instructions and proceed with my errand as soon as they gave me a chance, but I was beginning to feel silly. While Wolfe had left it pretty vague, one thing was plain, that I was supposed to give them a severe jolt, and I doubted if I had what it would take. When they got worked up to the point of naming the winner—settling on the lucky product that would be cast for the role sixteen had applied for—bringing up the subject of an anonymous letter, even one implying that one of them was a chronic murderer, would be an anticlimax. With a serious problem like that just triumphantly solved, what would they care about a little thing like murder?

But I was dead wrong. I found that out incidentally, as a by-product of their argument. It appeared that two of the contenders were deadly rivals, both clawing for children's dimes: a candy bar called Happy Andy and a little box of tasty delights called Meltettes. It was the latter that Traub had decided to back unequivocally, and he, when the question came to a head which of those two to eliminate, again asked Miss Fraser if she had tried Meltettes. She told him no. He asked if she had tried Happy Andy. She said yes. Then, he insisted, it was only fair for her to try Meltettes.

"All right," she agreed. "There on the piano, Debby, that little red box. Toss it over."

"No!" a shrill voice cried. It was Nancylee. Everyone looked at her. Deborah Koppel, who had picked up the little red cardboard box, asked her:

"What's the matter?"

"It's dangerous!" Nancylee was there, a hand outstretched. "Give it to me. I'll eat one first!"

It was only a romantic kid being dramatic, and all she rated from that bunch, if I had read their pulses right, was a laugh and a brush-off, but that was what showed me I had been dead wrong. There wasn't even a snicker. No one said a word. They all froze, staring at Nancylee, with only one exception. That was Deborah Koppel. She held the box away from Nancylee's reaching hand and told her contemptuously:

"Don't be silly."

"I mean it!" the girl cried. "Let me—"

"Nonsense." Deborah pushed her back, opened the flap of the box, took out an object, popped it into her mouth, chewed once or twice, swallowed, and then spat explosively, ejecting a spray of little particles.

I was the first, by maybe a tenth of a second, to realize that there was something doing. It wasn't so much the spitting, for that could conceivably have been merely her way of voting against Meltettes, as it was the swift terrible contortion of her features. As I bounded across to her she left the piano bench with a spasmodic jerk, got erect with her hands flung high, and screamed:

"Lina! Don't! Don't let—"

I was at her, with a hand on her arm, and Bill Meadows was there too, but her muscles all in convulsion took us along as she fought toward the divan, and Madeline Fraser was there to meet her and get supporting arms around her. But somehow the three of us together failed to hold her up or get her onto the divan. She went down until her knees were on the floor, with one arm stretched rigid across the burlap of the divan, and would have gone the rest of the way but for Miss Fraser, also on her knees.

I straightened, wheeled, and told Nat Traub: "Get a doctor quick." I saw Nancylee reaching to pick up the little red cardboard box and snapped at her: "Let that alone and behave yourself." Then to the rest of them: "Let everything alone, hear me?"

22 AROUND FOUR O'CLOCK I COULD HAVE GOT PERMISsion to go home if I had insisted, but it seemed better to stay as long as there was a chance of picking up another item for my report. I had already phoned Wolfe to explain why I wasn't following his instructions.

All of those who had been present at the conference were still there, very much so, except Deborah Koppel, who had been removed in a basket when several gangs of city scientists had finished their part of it. She had been dead when the doctor arrived. The others were still alive but not in a mood to brag about it.

At four o'clock Lieutenant Rowcliff and an assistant D.A. were sitting on the green burlap divan, arguing whether the taste of cyanide should warn people in time to refrain from swallowing. That seemed pointless, since whether it should or not it usually doesn't, and anyway the only ones who could qualify as experts are those who have tried it, and none of them is available. I moved on. At the big oak table another lieutenant was conversing with Bill Meadows, meanwhile referring to notes on loose sheets of paper. I went on by. In the dining room a sergeant and a private were pecking away at Elinor Vance. I passed through. In the kitchen a dick with a pug nose was holding a sheet of paper, one of a series, flat on the table while Cora, the female wrestler, put her initials on it.

Turning and going back the way I had come, I continued on to the square hall, opened a door at its far end, and went through. This, the room without a name, was more densely populated than the others. Tully Strong and Nat Traub were on chairs against opposite walls. Nancylee was standing by a window. A dick was seated in the center of the room, another was leaning against a wall, and Sergeant Purley Stebbins was sort of strolling around.

That called the roll, for I knew that Madeline Fraser was in the room beyond, her bedroom, where I had first met the bunch of them, having a talk with Inspector Cramer. The way I knew that, I had just been ordered out by Deputy Commissioner O'Hara, who was in there with them.

The first series of quickies, taking them one at a time on a gallop, had been staged in the dining room by Cramer himself. Cramer and an assistant D.A. had sat at one side of the table, with the subject across from them, and me seated a little to the rear of the subject's elbow. The theory of that arrangement was that if the subject's memory showed a tendency to conflict with mine, I could tip Cramer off by sticking out my tongue or some other signal without being seen by the subject. The dick-stenographer had been at one end of the table, and other units of the personnel had hung around.

Since they were by no means strangers to Cramer and he was already intimately acquainted with their biographies, he could keep it brief and concentrate chiefly on two points: their positions and movements during the conference, and the box of Meltettes. On the former there were some contradictions on minor details, but only what you might expect under the circumstances; and I, who had been there, saw no indication that anyone was trying to fancy it up.

On the latter, the box of Meltettes, there was no contradiction at all. By noon Friday, the preceding day, the news had begun to spread that Hi-Spot was bowing out, though it had not yet been published. For some time Meltettes had been on the Fraser waiting list, to grab a vacancy if one occurred. Friday morning Nat Traub, whose agency had the Meltettes account, had phoned his client the news, and the client had rushed him a carton of its product by messenger. A carton held forty-eight of the little red cardboard boxes. Traub, wishing to lose no time on a matter of such urgency and importance, and not wanting to lug the whole carton, had taken one little box from it and dropped it in his pocket, and hotfooted it to the FBC building, arriving at the studio just before the conclusion of the Fraser broadcast. He had spoken to Miss Fraser and Miss Koppel on behalf of Meltettes and handed the box to Miss Koppel.

Miss Koppel had passed the box on to Elinor Vance, who had put it in her bag—the same bag that had been used to transport sugared coffee in a Hi-Spot bottle. The three women had lunched in a near-by restaurant and then gone to Miss Fraser's apartment, where they had been joined later by Bill Meadows and Tully Strong for an exploratory discussion of the sponsor problem. Soon after their arrival at the apartment Elinor had taken the box of Meltettes from her bag and given it to Miss Fraser, who had put it on the big oak table in the living room.

That had been between two-thirty and three o'clock Friday afternoon, and that was as far as it went. No one knew how or when the box had been moved from the oak table to the piano. There was a blank space, completely blank, of about eighteen hours, ending around nine o'clock Saturday morning, when Cora, on a dusting mission, had seen it on the piano. She had picked it up for a swipe of the dustcloth on the piano top and put it down again. Its next appearance was two hours later, when Nancylee, soon after her arrival at the apartment, had spotted it and been tempted to help herself, even going so far as to get her clutches on it, but had been scared off when she saw that Miss Koppel's eye was on her. That, Nancylee explained, was how she had known where the box was when Miss Fraser had asked.

As you can see, it left plenty of room for inch-by-inch digging and sifting, which was lucky for everybody from privates to inspectors who are supposed to earn their pay, for there was no other place to dig at all. Relationships and motives and suspicions had already had all the juice squeezed out of them. So by four o'clock Saturday afternoon a hundred grown men, if not more, were scattered around the city, doing their damnedest to uncover another little splinter of a fact, any old fact, about that box of Meltettes. Some of them, of course, were getting results. For instance, word had come from the laboratory that the box, as it came to them, had held eleven Meltettes; that one of them, which had obviously been operated on rather skillfully, had about twelve grains of cyanide mixed into its insides; and that the other ten were quite harmless, with no sign of having been tampered with. Meltettes, they said, fitted snugly into the box in pairs, and the cyanided one had been on top, at the end of the box which opened.

And other reports, including of course fingerprints. Most of them had been relayed to Cramer in my presence. Whatever he may have thought they added up to, it looked to me very much like a repeat performance by the artist who had painted the sugared coffee picture: so many crossing lines and overlapping colors that no resemblance to any known animal or other object was discernible.

Returning to the densely populated room with no name after my tour of inspection, I made some witty remark to Purley Stebbins and lowered myself into a chair. As I said, I could probably have bulled my way out and gone home, but I didn't want to. What prospect did it offer? I would have fiddled around until Wolfe came down to the office, made my report, and then what? He would either have grunted in disgust, found something to criticize, and lowered his iron curtain again, or he would have gone into another trance and popped out around midnight with some bright idea like typing an anonymous letter about Bill Meadows flunking in algebra his last year in high school. I preferred to stick around in the faint hope that something would turn up.

And something did. I had abandoned the idea of making some sense out of the crossing lines and overlapping colors, given up trying to get a rise out of Purley, and was exchanging hostile glares with Nancylee, when the door from the square hall opened and a lady entered. She darted a glance around and told Purley Inspector Cramer had sent for her. He crossed to the far door which led to Miss Fraser's bedroom, opened it, and closed it after she had passed through.

I knew her by sight but not her name, and even had an opinion of her, namely that she was the most presentable of all the female dicks I had seen. With nothing else to do, I figured out what Cramer wanted with her, and had just come to the correct conclusion when the door opened again and I got it verified. Cramer appeared first, then Deputy Commissioner O'Hara. Cramer spoke to Purley:

"Get 'em all in here."

Purley flew to obey. Nat Traub asked wistfully, "Have you made any progress, Inspector?"

Cramer didn't even have the decency to growl at him, let alone reply. That seemed unnecessarily rude, so I told Traub:

"Yeah, they've reached an important decision. You're all going to be frisked."

It was ill-advised, especially with O'Hara there, since he has never forgiven me for being clever once, but I was frustrated and edgy. O'Hara gave me an evil look and Cramer told me to close my trap.

The others came straggling in with their escorts. I surveyed the lot and would have felt genuinely sorry for them if I had known which one to leave out. There was no question now about the kind of strain they were under, and it had nothing to do with picking a sponsor.

Cramer addressed them:

"I want to say to you people that as long as you cooperate with us we have no desire to make it any harder for you than we have to. You can't blame us for feeling we have to bear down on you, in view of the fact that all of you lied, and kept on lying, about the bottle that the stuff came out of that killed Orchard. I called you in here to tell you that we're going to search your persons. The position is this, we would be justified in taking you all down and booking you as material witnesses, and that's what we'll do if any of you object to the search.

Miss Fraser made no objection. A policewoman is in there with her now. The women will be taken in there one at a time. The men will be taken by Lieutenant Rowcliff and Sergeant Stebbins, also one at a time, to another room. Does anyone object?"

It was pitiful. They were in no condition to object, even if he had announced his intention of having clusters of Meltettes tattooed on their chests. Nobody made a sound except Nancylee, who merely shrilled:

"Oh, I never!"

I crossed my legs and prepared to sit it out. And so I did, up to a point. Purley and Rowcliff took Tully Strong first. Soon the female dick appeared and got Elinor Vance. Evidently they were being thorough, for it was a good eight minutes before Purley came back with Strong and took Bill Meadows, and the lady took just as long with Elinor Vance. The last two on the list were Nancylee in one direction and Nat Traub in the other.

That is, they were the last two as I had it. But when Rowcliff and Purley returned with Traub and handed Cramer some slips of paper, O'Hara barked at them:

"What about Goodwin?"

"Oh, him?" Rowcliff asked.

"Certainly him! He was here, wasn't he?"

Rowcliff looked at Cramer. Cramer looked at me.

I grinned at O'Hara. "What if I object, Commissioner?"

"Try it! That won't help you any!"

"The hell it won't. It will either preserve my dignity or start a string of firecrackers. What do you want to bet my big brother can't lick your big brother?"

He took a step toward me. "You resist, do you?"

"You're damn right I do." My hand did a half circle. "Before twenty witnesses."

He wheeled. "Send him down, Inspector. To my office. Charge him. Then have him searched."

"Yes, sir." Cramer was frowning. "First, would you mind stepping into another room with me? Perhaps I haven't fully explained the situation—"

"I understand it perfectly! Wolfe has cooperated, so you say—to what purpose? What has happened? Another murder! Wolfe has got you all buffaloed, and I'm sick and tired of it! Take him to my office!"

"No one has got me buffaloed," Cramer rasped. "Take him, Purley. I'll phone about a charge."

23 THERE WERE TWO THINGS I LIKED ABOUT DEPUTY
Commissioner O'Hara's office. First, it was there that I had been clever
on a previous occasion, and therefore it aroused agreeable memories,
and second, I like nice surroundings and it was the most attractive
room at Centre Street, being on a corner with six large windows, and
furnished with chairs and rugs and other items which had been paid
for by O'Hara's rich wife.

I sat at ease in one of the comfortable chairs. The contents of my
pockets were stacked in a neat pile on a corner of O'Hara's big shiny
mahogany desk, except for one item which Purley Stebbins had in his
paw. Purley was so mad his face was a red sunset, and he was stut-
tering.

"Don't be a g-goddam fool," he exhorted me. "If you clam it with
O'Hara when he gets here he'll jug you sure as hell, and it's after six
o'clock so where'll you spend the night?" He shook his paw at me,
the one holding the item taken from my pocket. "Tell me about this!"

I shook my head firmly. "You know, Purley," I said without ran-
cor, "this is pretty damn ironic. You frisked that bunch of suspects and
got nothing at all—I could tell that from the way you and Rowcliff
looked. But on me, absolutely innocent of wrongdoing, you find what
you think is an incriminating document. So here I am, sunk, facing
God knows what kind of doom. I try to catch a glimpse of the future,
and what do I see?"

"Oh, shut up!"

"No, I've got to talk to someone." I glanced at my wrist. "As you
say, it's after six o'clock. Mr. Wolfe has come down from the plant
rooms, expecting to find me awaiting him in the office, ready for my

report of the day's events. He'll be disappointed. You know how he'll feel. Better still, you know what he'll do. He'll be so frantic he'll start looking up numbers and dialing them himself. I am offering ten to one that he has already called the Fraser apartment and spoken to Cramer. How much of it do you want? A dime? A buck?"

"Can it, you goddam ape." Purley was resigning. "Save it for O'Hara, he'll be here pretty soon. I hope they give you a cell with bedbugs."

"I would prefer," I said courteously, "to chat."

"Then chat about this."

"No. For the hundredth time, no. I detest anonymous letters and I don't like to talk about them."

He went to a chair and sat facing me. I got up, crossed to bookshelves, selected CRIME AND CRIMINALS, by Mercier, and returned to my seat with it.

Purley had been wrong. O'Hara was not there pretty soon. When I glanced at my wrist every ten minutes or so I did it on the sly because I didn't want Purley to think I was getting impatient. It was a little past seven when I looked up from my book at the sound of a buzzer. Purley went to a phone on the desk and had a talk with it. He hung up, returned to his chair, sat, and after a moment spoke:

"That was the Deputy Commissioner. He is going to have his dinner. I'm to keep you here till he comes."

"Good," I said approvingly. "This is a fascinating book."

"He thinks you're boiling. You bastard."

I shrugged.

I kept my temper perfectly for another hour or more, and then, still there with my book, I became aware that I was starting to lose control. The trouble was that I had begun to feel hungry, and that was making me sore. Then there was another factor: what the hell was Wolfe doing? That, I admit, was unreasonable. Any phoning he did would be to Cramer or O'Hara, or possibly someone at the D.A.'s office, and with me cooped up as I was I wouldn't hear even an echo. If he had learned where I was and tried to get me, they wouldn't have put him through, since Purley had orders from O'Hara that I was to make no calls. But what with feeling hungry and getting no word from the outside world, I became aware that I was beginning to be offended, and that would not do. I forced my mind away from food and other aggravating aspects, including the number of revolutions the minute hand of my watch had made, and turned another page.

It was ten minutes to nine when the door opened and O'Hara and Cramer walked in. Purley stood up. I was in the middle of a paragraph and so merely flicked one eye enough to see who it was. O'Hara hung his hat and coat on a rack, and Cramer dropped his on a chair. O'Hara strode to his desk, crossing my bow so close that I could easily have tripped him by stretching a leg.

Cramer looked tired. Without spending a glance on me he nodded at Purley.

"Has he opened up?"

"No, sir. Here it is." Purley handed him the item.

They had both had it read to them on the phone, but they wanted to see it. Cramer read it through twice and then handed it to O'Hara. While that was going on I went to the shelves and replaced the book, had a good stretch and yawn, and returned to my chair.

Cramer glared down at me. "What have you got to say?"

"More of the same," I told him. "I've explained to the sergeant, who has had nothing to eat by the way, that that thing has no connection whatever with any murder or any other crime, and therefore questions about it are out of order."

"You've been charged as a material witness."

"Yeah, I know, Purley showed it to me. Why don't you ask Mr. Wolfe? He might be feeling generous."

"The hell he might. We have. Look, Goodwin—"

"I'll handle him, Inspector." O'Hara speaking. He was an energetic cuss. He had gone clear around his desk to sit down, but now he arose and came clear around it again to confront me. I looked up at him inquiringly, not a bit angry.

He was trying to control himself. "You can't possibly get away with it," he stated. "It's incredible that you have the gall to try it, both you and Wolfe. Anonymous letters are a central factor in this case, a vital factor. You went up to that apartment today to see those people, and you had in your pocket an anonymous letter about one of them, practically accusing her of murder. Do you mean to tell me that you take the position that that letter has no connection with the crimes under investigation?"

"I sure do. Evidently Mr. Wolfe does too." I made a gesture. "Corroboration."

"You take and maintain that position while aware of the penalty that may be imposed upon conviction for an obstruction of justice?"

"I do."

O'Hara turned and blurted at Cramer, "Get Wolfe down here! Damn it, we should have hauled him in hours ago!"

This, I thought to myself, is something like. Now we ought to see some fur fly.

But we didn't, at least not as O'Hara had it programed. What interfered was a phone call. The buzzer sounded, and Purley, seeing that his superiors were too worked up to hear it, went to the desk and answered. After a word he told Cramer, "For you, Inspector," and Cramer crossed and got it. O'Hara stood glaring down at me, but, having his attention called by a certain tone taken by Cramer's voice, turned to look that way. Finally Cramer hung up. The expression on his face was that of a man trying to decide what it was he just swallowed.

"Well?" O'Hara demanded.

"The desk just had a call," Cramer said, "from the WPIT newsroom. WPIT is doing the script for the ten o'clock newscast, and they're including an announcement received a few minutes ago from Nero Wolfe. Wolfe announces that he has solved the murder cases, all three of them, with no assistance from the police, and that very soon, probably sometime tomorrow, he will be ready to tell the District Attorney the name of the murderer and to furnish all necessary information. WPIT wants to know if we have any comment."

Of course it was vulgar, but I couldn't help it. I threw back my head and let out a roar. It wasn't so much the news itself as it was the look on O'Hara's face as the full beauty of it seeped through to him.

"The fat bum!" Purley whimpered.

I told O'Hara distinctly: "The next time Cramer asks you to step into another room with him I'd advise you to step."

He didn't hear me.

"It wasn't a question," Cramer said, "of Wolfe having me buffaloed. With him the only question is what has he got and how and when will he use it. If that goes on the air I would just as soon quit."

"What—" O'Hara stopped to wet his lips. "What would you suggest?"

Cramer didn't answer. He pulled a cigar from his pocket, slow motion, got it between his teeth, took it out again and hurled it for the wastebasket, missing by two feet, walked to a chair, sat down, and breathed.

"There are only two things," he said. "Just let it land is one. The other is to ask Goodwin to call him and request him to recall the announcement—and tell him he'll be home right away to report." Cramer breathed again. "I won't ask Goodwin that. Do you want to?"

"No! It's blackmail!" O'Hara yelled in pain.

"Yeah," Cramer agreed. "Only when Wolfe does it there's nothing anonymous about it. The newscast will be on in thirty-five minutes."

O'Hara would rather have eaten soap. "It may be a bluff," he pleaded. "Pure bluff!"

"Certainly it may. And it may not. It's easy enough to call it— just sit down and wait. If you're not going to call on Goodwin I guess I'll have to see if I can get hold of the Commissioner." Cramer stood up.

O'Hara turned to me. I have to hand it to him, he looked me in the eye as he asked:

"Will you do it?"

I grinned at him. "That warrant Purley showed me is around somewhere. It will be vacated?"

"Yes."

"Okay, I've got witnesses." I crossed to the desk and began returning my belongings to the proper pockets. The anonymous letter was there where O'Hara had left it when he had advanced to overwhelm me, and I picked it up and displayed it. "I'm taking this," I said, "but I'll let you look at it again if you want to. May I use the phone?"

I circled the desk, dropped into O'Hara's personal chair, pulled the instrument to me, and asked the male switchboard voice to get Mr. Nero Wolfe. The voice asked who I was and I told it. Then we had some comedy. After I had waited a good two minutes there was a knock on the door and O'Hara called come in. The door swung wide open and two individuals entered with guns in their hands, stern and alert. When they saw the arrangements they stopped dead and looked foolish.

"What do you want?" O'Hara barked.

"The phone," one said. "Goodwin. We didn't know . . ."

"For Christ's sake!" Purley exploded. "Ain't I here?" It was a breach of discipline, with his superiors present.

They bumped at the threshold, getting out, pulling the door after them. I couldn't possibly have been blamed for helping myself to another hearty laugh, but there's a limit to what even a Deputy Commissioner will take, so I choked it off and sat tight until there was a voice in my ear that I knew better than any other voice on earth.

"Archie," I said.

"Where are you?" The voice was icy with rage, but not at me.

"I'm in O'Hara's office, at his desk, using his phone. I am half starved. O'Hara, Cramer, and Sergeant Stebbins are present. To be perfectly fair, Cramer and Purley are innocent. This boneheaded play was a solo by O'Hara. He fully realizes his mistake and sincerely apologizes. The warrant for my arrest is a thing of the past. The letter

about Miss Vance is in my pocket. I have conceded nothing. I'm free
to go where I please, including home. O'Hara requests, as a personal
favor, that you kill the announcement you gave WPIT. Can that be
done?"

"It can if I choose. It was arranged through Mr. Richards."

"So I suspected. You should have seen O'Hara's face when the
tidings reached him. If you choose, and all of us here hope you do,
go ahead and kill it and I'll be there in twenty minutes or less. Tell
Fritz I'm hungry."

"Mr. O'Hara is a nincompoop. Tell him I said so. I'll have the
announcement suspended temporarily, but there will be conditions.
Stay there. I'll phone you shortly."

I cradled the phone, leaned back, and grinned at the three inquiring
faces. "He'll call back. He thinks he can head it off temporarily, but
he's got some idea about conditions." I focused on O'Hara. "He said
to tell you that he says you're a nincompoop, but I think it would be
more tactful not to mention it, so I won't."

"Someday," O'Hara said through his teeth, "he'll land on his
nose."

They all sat down and began exchanging comments. I didn't listen
because my mind was occupied. I was willing to chalk up for Wolfe
a neat and well-timed swagger, and to admit that it got the desired
results, but now what? Did he really have anything at all, and if so
how much? It had better be fairly good. Cramer and Stebbins were
not exactly ready to clasp our hands across the corpses, and as for
O'Hara, I only hoped to God that when Wolfe called back he wouldn't
tell me to slap the Deputy Commissioner on the back and tell him it
had been just a prank and wasn't it fun? All in all, it was such a
gloomy outlook that when the buzzer sounded and I reached for the
phone I would just as soon have been somewhere else.

Wolfe's voice asked if they were still there and I said yes. He said
to tell them that the announcement had been postponed and would not
be broadcast at ten o'clock, and I did so. Then he asked for my report
of the day's events.

"Now?" I demanded. "On the phone?"

"Yes," he said. "Concisely, but including all essentials. If there is
a contradiction to demolish I must know it."

Even with the suspicion gnawing at me that I had got roped in for
a supporting role in an enormous bluff, I did enjoy it. It was a situation
anyone would appreciate. There I was, in O'Hara's chair at his desk
in his office, giving a detailed report to Wolfe of a murder I had
witnessed and a police operation I had helped with, and for over half

an hour those three bozos simply utterly had to sit and listen. Whatever position they might be in all too soon, all they could do now was take it and like it. I did enjoy it. Now and then Wolfe interrupted with a question, and when I had finished he took me back to fill in a few gaps. Then he proceeded to give me instructions, and as I listened it became apparent that if it was a bluff at least he wasn't going to leave me behind the enemy lines to fight my way out. I asked him to repeat it to make sure I had it straight. He did so.

"Okay," I said. "Tell Fritz I'm hungry." I hung up and faced the three on chairs:

"I'm sorry it took so long, but he pays my salary and what could I do? As I told you, the announcement has been postponed. He is willing to kill it, but that sort of depends. He thinks it would be appropriate for Inspector Cramer and Sergeant Stebbins to help with the windup. He would appreciate it if you will start by delivering eight people at his office as soon as possible. He wants the five who were at the Fraser apartment today, not including the girl, Nancylee, or Cora the cook. Also Savarese. Also Anderson, president of the Hi-Spot Company, and Owen, the public relations man. All he wants you to do is to get them there, and to be present yourselves, but with the understanding that he will run the show. With that provision, he states that when you leave you will be prepared to make an arrest and take the murderer with you, and the announcement he gave WPIT will not be made. You can do the announcing." I arose and moved, crossing to a chair over by the wall near the door to reclaim my hat and coat. Then I turned:

"It's after ten o'clock, and if this thing is on I'm not going to start it on an empty stomach. In my opinion, even if all he has in mind is a game of blind man's buff, which I doubt, it's well worth it. Orchard died twenty-five days ago. Beula Poole nine days. Miss Koppel ten hours. You could put your inventory on a postage stamp." I had my hand on the doorknob. "How about it? Feel like helping?"

Cramer growled at me, "Why Anderson and Owen? What does he want them for?"

"Search me. Of course he likes a good audience."

"Maybe we can't get them."

"You can try. You're an inspector and murder is a very bad crime."

"It may take hours."

"Yeah, it looks like an all-night party. If I can stand it you can, not to mention Mr. Wolfe. All right, then we'll be seeing you." I opened the door and took a step, but turned:

"Oh, I forgot, he told me to tell you, this anonymous letter about Elinor Vance is just some homemade bait that didn't get used. I typed it myself this morning. If you get a chance tonight you can do a sample on my machine and compare."

O'Hara barked ferociously, "Why the hell didn't you say so?"

"I didn't like the way I was asked, Commissioner. The only man I know of more sensitive than me is Nero Wolfe."

24   It was not surprising that Cramer delivered the whole order. Certainly none of those people could have been compelled to go out into the night, and let themselves be conveyed to Nero Wolfe's office, or any place else, without slapping a charge on them, but it doesn't take much compelling when you're in that kind of a fix. They were all there well before midnight.

Wolfe stayed up in his room until they all arrived. I had supposed that while I ate my warmed-over cutlets he would have some questions or instructions for me, and probably both, but no. If he had anything he already had it and needed no contributions from me. He saw to it that my food was hot and my salad crisp and then beat it upstairs.

The atmosphere, as they gathered, was naturally not very genial, but it wasn't so much tense as it was glum. They were simply sunk. As soon as Elinor Vance got onto a chair she rested her elbows on her knees and buried her face in her hands, and stayed that way. Tully Strong folded his arms, let his head sag until his chin met his chest, and shut his eyes. Madeline Fraser sat in the red leather chair, which I got her into before President Anderson arrived, looking first at one of her fellow beings and then at another, but she gave the impression that she merely felt she ought to be conscious of something and they would do as well as anything else.

Bill Meadows, seated near Elinor Vance, was leaning back with his hands clasped behind his head, glaring at the ceiling. Nat Traub was a sight, with his necktie off center, his hair mussed, and his eyes bloodshot. His facial growth was the kind that needs shaving twice a day, and it hadn't had it. He was so restless he couldn't stay in his chair, but when he left it there was no place he wanted to go, so all

he could do was sit down again. I did not, on that account, tag him
for it, since he had a right to be haggard. A Meltette taken from a box
delivered by him had poisoned and killed someone, and it wasn't hard
to imagine how his client had reacted to that.

Two conversations were going on. Professor Savarese was telling
Purley Stebbins something at length, presumably the latest in formulas,
and Purley was making himself an accessory by nodding now and then.
Anderson and Owen, the Hi-Spot delegates, were standing by the
couch talking with Cramer, and, judging from the snatches I caught,
they might finally decide to sit down and they might not. They had
been the last to arrive. I, having passed the word to Wolfe that the
delivery had been completed, was wondering what was keeping him
when I heard the sound of his elevator.

They were so busy with their internal affairs that Traub and I were
the only ones who were aware that our host had joined us until he
reached the corner of his desk and turned to make a survey. The conversations stopped. Savarese bounded across to shake hands. Elinor
Vance lifted her head, showing such a woebegone face that I had to
restrain an impulse to take the anonymous letter from my pocket and
tear it up then and there. Traub sat down for the twentieth time. Bill
Meadows unclasped his hands and pressed his finger tips against his
eyes. President Anderson sputtered:

"Since when have you been running the Police Department?"

That's what a big executive is supposed to do, go straight to the
point.

Wolfe, getting loose from Savarese, moved to his chair and got
himself arranged in it. I guess it's partly his size, unquestionably impressive, which holds people's attention when he is in motion, but his
manner and style have a lot to do with it. You get both suspense and
surprise. You know he's going to be clumsy and wait to see it, but by
gum you never do. First thing you know there he is, in his chair or
wherever he was bound for, and there was nothing clumsy about it at
all. It was smooth and balanced and efficient.

He looked up at the clock, which said twenty to twelve, and remarked to the audience, "It's late, isn't it?" He regarded the Hi-Spot
president:

"Let's not start bickering, Mr. Anderson. You weren't dragged
here by force, were you? You were impelled either by concern or
curiosity. In either case you won't leave until you hear what I have to
say, so why not sit down and listen? If you want to be contentious
wait until you learn what you have to contend with. It works better
that way."

He took in the others. "Perhaps, though, I should answer Mr. Anderson's question, though it was obviously rhetorical. I am not running the Police Department, far from it. I don't know what you were told when you were asked to come here, but I assume you know that nothing I say is backed by any official authority, for I have none. Mr. Cramer and Mr. Stebbins are present as observers. That is correct, Mr. Cramer?"

The Inspector, seated on the corner of the couch, nodded. "They understand that."

"Good. Then Mr. Anderson's question was not only rhetorical, it was gibberish. I shall—"

"I have a question!" a voice said, harsh and strained.

"Yes, Mr. Meadows, what is it?"

"If this isn't official, what happens to the notes Goodwin is making?"

"That depends on what we accomplish. They may never leave this house, and end up by being added to the stack in the cellar. Or a transcription of them may be accepted as evidence in a courtroom. —I wish you'd sit down, Mr. Savarese. It's more tranquil if everyone is seated."

Wolfe shifted his center of gravity. During his first ten minutes in a chair minor adjustments were always required.

"I should begin," he said with just a trace of peevishness, "by admitting that I am in a highly vulnerable position. I have told Mr. Cramer that when he leaves here he will take a murderer with him; but though I know who the murderer is, I haven't a morsel of evidence against him, and neither has anyone else. Still—"

"Wait a minute," Cramer growled.

Wolfe shook his head. "It's important, Mr. Cramer, to keep this unofficial—until I reach a certain point, if I ever do—so it would be best for you to say nothing whatever." His eyes moved. "I think the best approach is to explain how I learned the identity of the murderer—and by the way, here's an interesting point: though I was already close to certitude, it was clinched for me only two hours ago, when Mr. Goodwin told me that there were sixteen eager candidates for the sponsorship just abandoned by Hi-Spot. That removed my shred of doubt."

"For God's sake," Nat Traub blurted, "let the fine points go! Let's have it!"

"You'll have to be patient, sir," Wolfe reproved him. "I'm not merely reporting, I'm doing a job. Whether a murderer gets arrested, and tried, and convicted, depends entirely on how I handle this. There is no evidence, and if I don't squeeze it out of you people now, tonight, there may never be any. The trouble all along, both for the police and for me, has been that no finger pointed without wavering. In going for a murderer as well concealed as this one it is always necessary to trample down improbabilities to get a path started, but it is foolhardy to do so until a direction is plainly indicated. This time there was no such plain indication, and, frankly, I had begun to doubt if there would be one—until yesterday morning, when Mr. Anderson and Mr. Owen visited this office. They gave it to me."

"You're a liar!" Anderson stated.

"You see?" Wolfe upturned a palm. "Some day, sir, you're going to get on the wrong train by trying to board yours before it arrives. How do you know whether I'm a liar or not until you know what I'm saying? You did come here. You gave me a check for the full amount of my fee, told me that I was no longer in your hire, and said that you had withdrawn as a sponsor of Miss Fraser's program. You gave as your reason for withdrawal that the practice of blackmail had been injected into the case, and you didn't want your product connected in the public mind with blackmail because it is dirty and makes people gag. Isn't that so?"

"Yes. But—"

"I'll do the butting. After you left I sat in this chair twelve straight hours, with intermissions only for meals, using my brain on you. If I had known then that before the day was out sixteen other products were scrambling to take your Hi-Spot's place, I would have reached my conclusion in much less than twelve hours, but I didn't. What I was exploring was the question, what had happened to you? You had been so greedy for publicity that you had even made a trip down here to get into a photograph with me. Now, suddenly, you were fleeing like a comely maiden from a smallpox scare. Why?"

"I told you—"

"I know. But that wasn't good enough. Examined with care, it was actually flimsy. I don't propose to recite all my twistings and windings for those twelve hours, but first of all I rejected the reason you gave. What, then? I considered every possible circumstance and all conceivable combinations. That you were yourself the murderer and feared I might sniff you out; that you were not the murderer, but the blackmailer; that, yourself innocent, you knew the identity of one of the culprits, or both, and did not wish to be associated with the disclosure; and a thousand others. Upon each and all of my conjectures I brought to bear what I knew of you—your position, your record, your temperament, and your character. At the end only one supposition wholly

satisfied me. I concluded that you had somehow become convinced
that someone closely connected with that program, which you were
sponsoring, had committed the murders, and that there was a possibility that that fact would be discovered. More: I concluded that it was
not Miss Koppel or Miss Vance or Mr. Meadows or Mr. Strong, and
certainly not Mr. Savarese. It is the public mind that you are anxious
about, and in the public mind those people are quite insignificant. Miss
Fraser is that program, and that program is Miss Fraser. It could only
be her. You knew, or thought you knew, that Miss Fraser herself had
killed Mr. Orchard, and possibly Miss Poole too, and you were getting
as far away from her as you could as quickly as you could. Your face
tells me you don't like that."

"No," Anderson said coldly, "and you won't either before you hear
the last of it. You through?"

"Good heavens, no. I've barely started. As I say, I reached that
conclusion, but it was nothing to crow about. What was I to do with
it? I had a screw I could put on you, but it seemed unwise to be hasty
about it, and I considered a trial of other expedients. I confess that the
one I chose to begin with was feeble and even sleazy, but it was at
breakfast this morning, before I had finished my coffee and got
dressed, and Mr. Goodwin was fidgety and I wanted to give him something to do. Also, I had already made a suggestion to Mr. Cramer
which was designed to give everyone the impression that there was
evidence that Miss Vance had been blackmailed, that she was under
acute suspicion, and that she might be charged with murder at any
moment. There was a chance, I thought, that an imminent threat to
Miss Vance, who is a personable young woman, might impel somebody to talk."

"So you started that," Elinor Vance said dully.

Wolfe nodded. "I'm not boasting about it. I've confessed it was
worse than second-rate, but I thought Mr. Cramer might as well try it;
and this morning, before I was dressed, I could devise nothing better
than for Mr. Goodwin to type an anonymous letter about you and take
it up there—a letter which implied that you had committed murder at
least twice."

"Goddam pretty," Bill Meadows said.

"He didn't do it," Elinor said.

"Yes, he did," Wolfe disillusioned her. "He had it with him, but
didn't get to use it. The death of Miss Koppel was responsible not
only for that, but for other things as well—for instance, for this gathering. If I had acted swiftly and energetically on the conclusion I
reached twenty-four hours ago, Miss Koppel might be alive now. I

owe her an apology but I can't get it to her. What I can do is what I'm doing."

Wolfe's eyes darted to Anderson and fastened there. "I'm going to put that screw on you, sir. I won't waste time appealing to you, in the name of justice or anything else, to tell me why you abruptly turned tail and scuttled. That would be futile. Instead, I'll tell you a homely little fact: Miss Fraser drank Hi-Spot only the first few times it was served on her program, and then had to quit and substitute coffee. She had to quit because your product upset her stomach. It gave her a violent indigestion."

"That's a lie," Anderson said. "Another lie."

"If it is it won't last long. —Miss Vance. Some things aren't as important as they once were. You heard what I said. Is it true?"

"Yes."

"Mr. Strong?"

"I don't think this—"

"Confound it, you're in the same room and the same chair! Is it true or not?"

"Yes."

"Mr. Meadows?"

"Yes."

"That should be enough. —So, Mr. Anderson—"

"A put-up job," the president sneered. "I left their damn program."

Wolfe shook his head. "They're not missing you. They had their choice of sixteen offers. No, Mr. Anderson, you're in a pickle. Blackmail revolts you, and you're being blackmailed. It is true that newspapers are reluctant to offend advertisers, but some of them couldn't possibly resist so picturesque an item as this, that the product Miss Fraser puffed so effectively to ten million people made her so ill that she didn't dare swallow a spoonful of it. Indeed yes, the papers will print it; and they'll get it in time for Monday morning."

"You sonofabitch." Anderson was holding. "They won't touch it. Will they, Fred?"

But the director of public relations was frozen, speechless with horror.

"I think they will," Wolfe persisted. "One will, I know. And open publication might be better than the sort of talk that would get around when once it's started. You know how rumors get distorted; fools would even say that it wasn't necessary to add anything to Hi-Spot to poison Mr. Orchard. Really, the blackmail potential of this is very high. And what do you have to do to stop it? Something hideous and insupportable? Not at all. Merely tell me why you suddenly decided to scoot."

Anderson looked at Owen, but Owen was gazing fixedly at Wolfe as at the embodiment of evil.

"It will be useless," Wolfe said, "to try any dodge. I'm ready for you. I spent all day yesterday on this, and I doubt very much if I'll accept anything except what I have already specified: that someone or something had persuaded you that Miss Fraser herself was in danger of being exposed as a murderer or a blackmailer. However, you can try."

"I don't have to try." He was a stubborn devil. "I told you yesterday. That was my reason then, and it's my reason now."

"Oh, for God's sake!" Fred Owen wailed. "Oh, my God!"

"Goddam it," Anderson blurted at him, "I gave my word! I'm sewed up! I promised!"

"To whom?" Wolfe snapped.

"All right," Owen said bitterly, "keep your word and lose your shirt. This is ruin! This is dynamite!"

"To whom?" Wolfe persisted.

"I can't tell you, and I won't. That was part of the promise."

"Indeed. Then that makes it simple." Wolfe's eyes darted left. "Mr. Meadows, a hypothetical question. If it was you to whom Mr. Anderson gave the pledge that keeps him from speaking, do you now release him from it?"

"It wasn't me," Bill said.

"I didn't ask you that. You know what a hypothetical question is. Please answer to the if. If it was you, do you release him?"

"Yes. I do."

"Mr. Traub, the same question. With that if, do you release him?"

"Yes."

"Miss Vance? Do you?"

"Yes."

"Mr. Strong. Do you?"

Of course Tully Strong had had time, a full minute, to make up his mind what to say. He said it:

"No!"

25   Eleven pairs of eyes fastened on Tully Strong.

"Aha," Wolfe muttered. He leaned back, sighed deep, and looked pleased.

"Remarkable!" a voice boomed. It was Professor Savarese. "So simple!"

If he expected to pull some of the eyes his way, he got cheated. They stayed on Strong.

"That was a piece of luck," Wolfe said, "and I'm grateful for it. If I had started with you, Mr. Strong, and got your no, the others might have made it not so simple."

"I answered a hypothetical question," Tully asserted, "and that's all. It doesn't mean anything."

"Correct," Wolfe agreed. "In logic, it doesn't. But I saw your face when you realized what was coming, the dilemma you would be confronted with in a matter of seconds, and that was enough. Do you now hope to retreat into logic?"

Tully just wasn't up to it. Not only had his face been enough when he saw it coming; it was still enough. The muscles around his thin tight lips quivered as he issued the command to let words through.

"I merely answered a hypothetical question," was the best he could do. It was pathetic.

Wolfe sighed again. "Well. I suppose I'll have to light it for you. I don't blame you, sir, for being obstinate about it, since it may be assumed that you have behaved badly. I don't mean your withholding information from the police; most people do that, and often for reasons much shoddier than yours. I mean your behavior to your employers. Since you are paid by the eight sponsors jointly your loyalty to them is indivisible; but you did not warn all of them that Miss Fraser was, or might be, headed for disgrace and disaster, and that therefore they had better clear out; apparently you confined it to Mr. Anderson. For value received or to be received, I presume—a good job?"

Wolfe shrugged. "But now it's all up." His eyes moved. "By the way, Archie, since Mr. Strong will soon be telling us how he knew it was Miss Fraser, you'd better take a look. She's capable of anything, and she's as deft as a bear's tongue. Look in her bag."

Cramer was on his feet. "I'm not going—"

"I didn't ask you," Wolfe snapped. "Confound it, don't you see how ticklish this is? I'm quite aware I've got no evidence yet, but I'm not going to have that woman displaying her extraordinary dexterity in my office. Archie?"

I had left my chair and stepped to the other end of Wolfe's desk, but I was in a rather embarrassing position. I am not incapable of using force on a woman, since after all men have never found anything else to use on them with any great success when it comes right down to it, but Wolfe had by no means worked up to a point where the audience was with me. And when I extended a hand toward the handsome leather bag in Madeline Fraser's lap, she gave me the full force of her gray-green eyes and told me distinctly:

"Don't touch me."

I brought the hand back. Her eyes went to Wolfe:

"Don't you think it's about time I said something? Wouldn't it look better?"

"No." Wolfe met her gaze. "I'd advise you to wait, madam. All you can give us now is a denial, and of course we'll stipulate that. What else can you say?"

"I wouldn't bother with a denial," she said scornfully. "But it seems stupid for me to sit here and let this go on indefinitely."

"Not at all." Wolfe leaned toward her. "Let me assure you of one thing, Miss Fraser, most earnestly. It is highly unlikely, whatever you say or do from now on, that I shall ever think you stupid. I am too well convinced of the contrary. Not even if Mr. Goodwin opens your bag and finds in it the gun with which Miss Poole was shot."

"He isn't going to open it."

She seemed to know what she was talking about. I glanced at Inspector Cramer, but the big stiff wasn't ready yet to move a finger. I picked up the little table that was always there by the arm of the red leather chair, moved it over to the wall, went and brought one of the small yellow chairs, and sat, so close to Madeline Fraser that if we had spread elbows they would have touched. That meant no more notes, but Wolfe couldn't have everything. As I sat down by her, putting in motion the air that had been there undisturbed, I got a faint whiff of a spicy perfume, and my imagination must have been pretty active because I was reminded of the odor that had reached me that day in her apartment, from the breath of Deborah Koppel as I tried to get her onto the divan before she collapsed. It wasn't the same at all except in my fancy. I asked Wolfe:

"This will do, won't it?"

He nodded and went back to Tully Strong. "So you have not one reason for reluctance, but several. Even so, you can't possibly stick it. It has been clearly demonstrated to Mr. Cramer that you are withholding important information directly pertinent to the crimes he is investigating, and you and others have already pushed his patience pretty far. He'll get his teeth in you now and he won't let go. Then there's Mr. Anderson. The promise he gave you is half gone, now that we know it was you he gave it to, and with the threat I'm holding over him he can't reasonably be expected to keep the other half."

Wolfe gestured. "And all I really need is a detail. I am satisfied that I know pretty well what you told Mr. Anderson. What happened yesterday, just before he took alarm and leaped to action? The morning papers had the story of the anonymous letters—the blackmailing device by which people were constrained to make payments to Mr. Orchard and Miss Poole. Then that story had supplied a missing link for someone. Who and how? Say it was Mr. Anderson. Say that he received, some weeks ago, an anonymous letter or letters blackguarding Miss Fraser. He showed them to her. He received no more letters. That's all he knew about it. A little later Mr. Orchard was a guest on the Fraser program and got poisoned, but there was no reason for Mr. Anderson to connect that event with the anonymous letters he had received. That was what the story in yesterday's papers did for him; they made that connection. It was now perfectly plain: anonymous letters about Miss Fraser; Miss Fraser's subscription to *Track Almanac*; the method by which those subscriptions were obtained; and Mr. Orchard's death by drinking poisoned coffee ostensibly intended for Miss Fraser. That did not convict Miss Fraser of murder, but at a minimum it made it extremely inadvisable to continue in the role of her sponsor. So Mr. Anderson skedaddled."

"I got no anonymous letters," Anderson declared.

"I believe you." Wolfe didn't look away from Tully Strong. "I rejected, tentatively, the assumption that Mr. Anderson had himself received the anonymous letters, on various grounds, but chiefly because it would be out of character for him to show an anonymous letter to the subject of it. He would be much more likely to have the letter's allegations investigated, and there was good reason to assume that that had not been done. So I postulated that it was not Mr. Anderson, but some other person, who had once received an anonymous letter or letters about Miss Fraser and who was yesterday provided with a missing link. It was a permissible guess that that person was one of those now present, and so I tried the experiment of having the police insinuate an imminent threat to Miss Vance, in the hope that it would loosen a tongue. I was too cautious. It failed lamentably; and Miss Koppel died."

Wolfe was talking only to Strong. "Of course, having no evidence, I have no certainty that the information you gave Mr. Anderson concerned anonymous letters. It is possible that your conviction, or suspicion, about Miss Fraser, had some other basis. But I like my assumption because it is neat and comprehensive; and I shall abandon it only under compulsion. It explains everything, and nothing contradicts it. It will even explain, I confidently expect, why Mr. Orchard and Miss Poole were killed. Two of the finer points of their operation were these, that they demanded only a small fraction of the victim's income, limited to one year, and that the letters did not expose, or threaten to expose, an actual secret in the victim's past. Even if they had known such secrets they would not have used them. But sooner or later—this is a point on which Mr. Savarese could speak with the authority of an expert, but not now, some other time—sooner or later, by the law of averages, they would use such a secret by inadvertence. Sooner or later the bugaboo they invented would be, for the victim, not a mischievous libel, but a real and most dreadful terror."

Wolfe nodded. "Yes. So it happened. The victim was shown the letter or letters by some friend—by you, Mr. Strong—and found herself confronted not merely by the necessity of paying an inconsequential tribute, but by the awful danger of some disclosure that was not to be borne; for she could not know, of course, that the content of the letter had been fabricated and that its agreement with reality was sheer accident. So she acted. Indeed, she acted! She killed Mr. Orchard. Then she learned, from a strange female voice on the phone, that Mr. Orchard had not been the sole possessor of the knowledge she thought he had, and again she acted. She killed Miss Poole."

"My God," Anderson cut in, "you're certainly playing it strong, with no cards."

"I am, sir," Wolfe agreed. "It's time I got dealt to, don't you think? Surely I've earned at least one card. You can give it to me, or Mr.

Strong can. What more do you want, for heaven's sake? Rabbits from a hat?"

Anderson got up, moved, and was confronting the secretary of the Sponsors' Council. "Don't be a damn fool, Tully," he said with harsh authority. "He knows it all, you heard him. Go ahead and get rid of it!"

"This is swell for me," Tully said bitterly.

"It would have been swell for Miss Koppel," Wolfe said curtly, "if you had spoken twenty hours ago. How many letters did you get?"

"Two."

"When?"

"February. Around the middle of February."

"Did you show them to anyone besides Miss Fraser?"

"No, just her, but Miss Koppel was there so she saw them too."

"Where are they now?"

"I don't know. I gave them to Miss Fraser."

"What did they say?"

Tully's lips parted, stayed open a moment, and closed again.

"Don't be an ass," Wolfe snapped. "Mr. Anderson is here. What did they say?"

"They said that it was lucky for Miss Fraser that when her husband died no one had been suspicious enough to have the farewell letters he wrote examined by a handwriting expert."

"What else?"

"That was all. The second one said the same thing, only in a different way."

Wolfe's eyes darted to Anderson. "Is that what he told you, sir?"

The president, who had returned to the couch, nodded. "Yes, that's it. Isn't it enough?"

"Plenty, in the context." Wolfe's head jerked around to face the lady at my elbow. "Miss Fraser. I've heard of only one farewell letter your husband wrote, to a friend, a local attorney. Was there another? To you, perhaps?"

"I don't think," she said, "that it would be very sensible for me to try to help you." I couldn't detect the slightest difference in her voice. Wolfe had understated it when he said she was an extremely dangerous woman. "Especially," she went on, "since you are apparently accepting those lies. If Mr. Strong ever got any anonymous letters he never showed them to me—nor to Miss Koppel, I'm sure of that."

"I'll be damned!" Tully Strong cried, and his specs fell off as he gawked at her.

It was marvelous, and it certainly showed how Madeline Fraser got people. Tully had been capable of assuming that she had killed a couple of guys, but when he heard her come out with what he knew to be a downright lie he was flabbergasted.

Wolfe nodded at her. "I suppose," he admitted, "it would be hopeless to expect you to be anything but sensible. You are aware that there is still no evidence, except Mr. Strong's word against yours. Obviously the best chance is the letter your husband wrote to his friend, since the threat that aroused your ferocity concerned it." His face left us, to the right. "Do you happen to know, Mr. Cramer, whether that letter still exists?"

Cramer was right up with him. He had gone to the phone on my desk and was dialing. In a moment he spoke:

"Dixon there? Put him on. Dixon? I'm at Wolfe's office. Yeah, he's got it, but by the end of the tail. Two things quick. Get Darst and have him phone Fleetville, Michigan. He was out there and knows 'em. Before Lawrence Koppel died he wrote a letter to a friend. We want to know if that letter still exists and where it is, and they're to get it if they can and keep it, but for God's sake don't scare the friend into burning it or eating it. Tell Darst it's so important it's the whole case. Then get set with a warrant for an all-day job on the Fraser woman's apartment. What we're looking for is cyanide, and it can be anywhere—the heel of a shoe, for instance. You know the men to get—only the best. Wolfe got it by the tail with one of his crazy dives into a two-foot tank, and now we've got to hang onto it. What? Yes, damn it, of course it's her! Step on it!"

He hung up, crossed to me, thumbed me away, moved the chair aside, and stood by Miss Fraser's chair, gazing down at her. Keeping his gaze where it was, he rumbled:

"You might talk a little more, Wolfe."

"I could talk all night," Wolfe declared. "Miss Fraser is worth it. She had good luck, but most of the bad luck goes to the fumblers, and she is no fumbler. Her husband's death must have been managed with great skill, not so much because she gulled the authorities, which may have been no great feat, but because she completely deceived her husband's sister, Miss Koppel. The whole operation with Mr. Orchard was well conceived and executed, with the finest subtlety in even the lesser details—for instance, having the subscription in Miss Koppel's name. It was simple to phone Mr. Orchard that that money came from her, Miss Fraser. But best of all was the climax—getting the poisoned coffee served to the intended victim. That was one of her pieces of luck, since apparently Mr. Traub, who didn't know about the taped bottle, innocently put it in front of Mr. Orchard, but she would have managed without it. At that narrow table, with Mr. Orchard just across from her, and with the broadcast going on, she could have manipulated it with no difficulty, and probably without anyone becoming aware of any manipulation. Certainly without arousing any suspicion of intent, before or after."

"Okay," Cramer conceded. "That doesn't worry me. And the Poole thing doesn't either, since there's nothing against it. But the Koppel woman?"

Wolfe nodded. "That was the masterpiece. Miss Fraser had in her favor, certainly, years of intimacy during which she had gained Miss Koppel's unquestioning loyalty, affection, and trust. They held stead-fast even when Miss Koppel saw the anonymous letters Mr. Strong had received. It is quite possible that she received similar letters her-self. We don't know, and never will, I suppose, what finally gave birth to the worm of suspicion in Miss Koppel. It wasn't the newspaper story of the anonymous letters and blackmailing, since that appeared yesterday, Friday, and it was on Wednesday that Miss Koppel tried to take an airplane to Michigan. We may now assume, since we know that she had seen the anonymous letters, that something had made her suspicious enough to want to inspect the farewell letter her brother had sent to his friend, and we may certainly assume that Miss Fraser, when she learned what her dearest and closest friend had tried to do, knew why."

"That's plain enough," Cramer said impatiently. "What I mean—"

"I know. You mean what I meant when I said it was a masterpiece. It took resourcefulness, first-rate improvisation, and ingenuity to make use of the opportunity offered by Mr. Traub's delivery of the box of Meltettes; and only a maniacal stoicism could have left those deadly tidbits there on the piano where anybody might casually have eaten one. Probably inquiry would show that it was not as haphazard as it seems; that it was generally known that the box was there to be sam-pled by Miss Fraser and therefore no one would loot it. But the actual performance, as Mr. Goodwin described it to me, was faultless. There was then no danger to a bystander, for if anyone but Miss Koppel had started to eat one of the things Miss Fraser could easily have prevented it. If the box had been handed to Miss Fraser, she could either have postponed the sampling or have taken one from the second layer in-stead of the top. What chance was there that Miss Koppel would eat one of the things? One in five, one in a thousand? Anyway, she played for that chance, and again she had luck; but it was not all luck, and she performed superbly."

"This is incredible," Madeline Fraser said. "I knew I was strong,

but I didn't know I could do this. Only a few hours ago my dearest
friend Debby died in my arms. I should be with her, sitting with her
through the night, but here I am, sitting here, listening to this . . . this
nightmare . . ."

"Cut," Bill Meadows said harshly. "Night and nightmare. Cut
one."

The gray-green eyes darted at him. "So you're ratting, are you,
Bill?"

"Yes, I'm ratting. I saw Debby die. And I think he's got it. I think
you killed her."

"Bill!" It was Elinor Vance, breaking. "Bill, I can't stand it!" She
was on her feet, shaking all over. "I can't!"

Bill put his arms around her, tight. "All right, kid. I hope to God
she gets it. You were there too. What if you had decided to eat one?"

The phone rang and I got it. It was for Cramer. Purley went and
replaced him beside Miss Fraser, and he came to the phone. When he
hung up he told Wolfe:

"Koppel's friend still has that letter, and it's safe."

"Good," Wolfe said approvingly. "Will you please get her out of
here? I've been wanting beer for an hour, and I'm not foolhardy
enough to eat or drink anything with her in the house." He looked
around. "The rest of you are invited to stay if you care to. You must
be thirsty."

But they didn't like it there. They went.

26

THE EXPERTS WERE ENTHUSIASTIC ABOUT THE LETTER Lawrence Koppel had written to his friend. They called it one of the cleverest forgeries they had ever seen. But what pleased Wolfe most was the finding of the cyanide. It was in the hollowed-out heel of a house slipper, and was evidently the leavings of the supply Mrs. Lawrence Koppel had snitched six years ago from her husband's shelf.

It was May eighteenth that she was sentenced on her conviction for the first-degree murder of Deborah Koppel. They had decided that was the best one to try her for. The next day, a Wednesday, a little before noon, Wolfe and I were in the office checking over catalogues when the phone rang. I went to my desk for it.

"Nero Wolfe's office, Archie Goodwin speaking."

"May I speak to Mr. Wolfe, please?"

"Who is it?"

"Tell him a personal matter."

I covered the transmitter. "Personal matter," I told Wolfe. "A man whose name I have forgotten."

"What the devil! Ask him."

"A man," I said distinctly, "whose name I have forgotten."

"Oh." He frowned. He finished checking an item and then picked up the phone on his desk, while I stayed with mine. "This is Nero Wolfe."

"I would know the voice anywhere. How are you?"

"Well, thank you. Do I know you?"

"Yes. I am calling to express my appreciation of your handling of the Fraser case, now that it's over. I am pleased and thought you should know it. I have been, and still am, a little annoyed, but I am satisfied that you are not responsible. I have good sources of information. I congratulate you on keeping your investigation within the limits I prescribed. That has increased my admiration of you."

"I like to be admired," Wolfe said curtly. "But when I undertake an investigation I permit prescription of limits only by the requirements of the job. If that job had taken me across your path you would have found me there."

"Then that is either my good fortune—or yours."

The connection went.

I grinned at Wolfe. "He's an abrupt bastard."

Wolfe grunted. I returned to my post at the end of his desk and picked up my pencil.

"One little idea," I suggested. "Why not give Dr. Michaels a ring and ask if anyone has phoned to switch his subscription? No, that won't do, he's paid up. Marie Leconne?"

"No. I invite trouble only when I'm paid for it. And to grapple with him the pay would have to be high."

"Okay." I checked an item. "You'd be a problem in a foxhole, but the day may come."

"It may. I hope not. Have you any Zygopetalum crinitum on that page?"

"Good God no. It begins with a Z!"

BLACK ORCHIDS

PART I

I don't know how many guesses there have been in the past year, around bars and dinner tables, as to how Nero Wolfe got hold of the black orchids. I have seen three different ones in print—one in a Sunday newspaper magazine section last summer, one in a syndicated New York gossip column a couple of months ago, and one in a press association dispatch, at the time that a bunch of the orchids unexpectedly appeared at a certain funeral service at the Belford Memorial Chapel.

So here in this book are two separate Nero Wolfe cases, two different sets of people. The first is the lowdown on how Wolfe got the orchids. The second tells how he solved another murder, but it leaves a mystery, and that's what's biting me. If anyone who knows Wolfe better than I do—but wait till you read it.

Archie Goodwin

1   MONDAY AT THE FLOWER SHOW, TUESDAY AT THE Flower Show, Wednesday at the Flower Show. Me, Archie Goodwin. How's that?

I do not deny that flowers are pretty, but a million flowers are not a million times prettier than one flower. Oysters are good to eat, but who wants to eat a carload?

I didn't particularly resent it when Nero Wolfe sent me up there Monday afternoon and, anyway, I had been expecting it. After all the ballyhoo in the special Flower Show sections of the Sunday papers, it was a cinch that some member of our household would have to go take a look at those orchids, and as Fritz Brenner couldn't be spared from the kitchen that long, and Theodore Horstmann was too busy in the plant rooms on the roof, and Wolfe himself could have got a job in a physics laboratory as an Immovable Object if the detective business ever played out, it looked as if I would be elected. I was.

When Wolfe came down from the plant rooms at six P.M. Monday and entered the office, I reported:

"I saw them. It was impossible to snitch a sample."

He grunted, lowering himself into his chair. "I didn't ask you to."

"Who said you did, but you expected me to. There are three of them in a glass case and the guard has his feet glued."

"What color are they?"

"They're not black."

"Black flowers are never black. What color are they?"

"Well." I considered. "Say you take a piece of coal. Not anthracite. Cannel coal."

"That's black."

"Wait a minute. Spread on it a thin coating of open kettle molasses. That's it."

"Pfui. You haven't the faintest notion what it would look like. Neither have I."

"I'll go buy a piece of coal and we'll try it."

"No. Is the labellum uniform?"

I nodded. "Molasses on coal. The labellum is large, not as large as aurea, about like truffautiana. Cepals lanceolate. Throat tinged with orange—"

"Any sign of wilting?"

"No."

"Go back tomorrow and look for wilting on the edges of the petals. You know it, the typical wilting after pollination. I want to know if they've been pollinated."

So I went up there again Tuesday after lunch. That evening at six I added a few details to my description and reported no sign of wilting.

I sat at my desk, in front of his against the wall, and aimed a chilly stare at him.

"Will you kindly tell me," I requested, "why the females you see at a flower show are the kind of females who go to a flower show? Ninety per cent of them? Especially their legs? Does it have to be like that? Is it because, never having any flowers sent to them, they have to go there in order to see any? Or is it because—"

"Shut up. I don't know. Go back tomorrow and look for wilting."

I might have known, with his mood getting blacker every hour, all on account of three measly orchid plants, that he was working up to a climax. But I went again Wednesday, and didn't get home until nearly seven o'clock. When I entered the office he was there at his desk with two empty beer bottles on the tray and pouring a third one into the glass.

"Did you get lost?" he inquired politely.

I didn't resent that because I knew he half meant it. He has got to the point where he can't quite understand how a man can drive from 35th Street and Tenth Avenue to 44th and Lexington and back again with nobody to lead the way. I reported no wilting, and sat at my desk and ran through the stuff he had put there, and then swiveled to face him and said:

"I'm thinking of getting married."

His half-open lids didn't move, but his eyes did, and I saw them.

"We might as well be frank," I said. "I've been living in this house with you for over ten years, writing your letters, protecting you from bodily harm, keeping you awake, and wearing out your tires and my shoes. Sooner or later one of my threats to get married will turn out not to be a gag. How are you going to know? How do you know this isn't it?"

He made a noise of derision and picked up his glass.

"Okay," I said. "But you're enough of a psychologist to know what it means when a man is irresistibly impelled to talk about a girl to someone. Preferably, of course, to someone who is sympathetic. You can imagine what it means when I want to talk about her to *you*. What is uppermost in my mind is that this afternoon I saw her washing her feet."

He put the glass down. "So you went to a movie. In the afternoon. Did it occur—"

"No, sir, not a movie. Flesh and bone and skin. Have you ever been to a flower show?"

Wolfe closed his eyes and sighed.

"Anyway," I went on, "you've seen pictures of the exhibits, so you know that the millionaires and big firms do things up brown. Like Japanese gardens and rock gardens and roses in Picardy. This year Rucker and Dill, the seed and nursery company, have stolen the show. They've got a woodland glade. Bushes and dead leaves and green stuff and a lot of little flowers and junk, and some trees with white flowers, and a little brook with a pool and rocks; and it's inhabited. There's a man and a girl having a picnic. They're there all day from eleven to six thirty and from eight to ten in the evening. They pick flowers. They eat a picnic lunch. They sit on the grass and read. They play mumblety-peg. At four o'clock the man lies down and covers his face with a newspaper and takes a nap, and the girl takes off her shoes and stockings and dabbles her feet in the pool. That's when they crowd the ropes. Her face and figure are plenty good enough, but her legs are absolutely artistic. Naturally she has to be careful not to get her skirt wet, and the stream comes tumbling from the rocks into the pool. Speaking as a painter—"

Wolfe snorted. "Pah! You couldn't paint a—"

"I didn't say painting as a painter, I said speaking as a painter. I know what I like. The arrangement of lines into harmonious composition. It gets me. I like to study—"

"She is too long from the knees down."

I looked at him in amazement.

He wiggled a finger at a newspaper on the desk.

"There's a picture of her in the *Post*. Her name is Anne Tracy. She's a stenographer in Rucker and Dill's office. Her favorite dish is blueberry pie with ice cream."

"She is not a stenographer!" I was on my feet. "She's a secretary! W. G. Dill's!" I found the page in the *Post*. "A damn important job. I admit they look a little long here, but it's a bad picture. Wrong angle. There was a better one in the *Times* yesterday, and an article—"

"I saw it. I read it."

"Then you ought to have an inkling of how I feel." I sat down again. "Men are funny," I said philosophically. "That girl with that face and figure and legs has been going along living with her pop and mom and taking dictation from W. G. Dill, who looks like a frog in spite of being the president of the Atlantic Horticultural Society—he was around there today—and who knew about her or paid any attention to her? But put her in a public spot and have her take off her shoes and stockings and wiggle her toes in a man-made pool on the third floor of Grand Central Palace, and what happens? Billy Rose goes to look at her. Movie scouts have to be chased off the grass of the woodland glade. Photographers engage in combat. Lewis Hewitt takes her out to dinner—"

"Hewitt?" Wolfe opened his eyes and scowled at me. "Lewis Hewitt?"

I knew that the sound of that name would churn his beer for him. Lewis Hewitt was the millionaire in whose greenhouse, on his Long Island estate, the black orchids had been produced—thereby creating in Wolfe an agony of envy that surpassed any of his previous childish performances.

"Yep," I said cheerfully. "Lew himself, in his two hundred dollar topcoat and Homburg and gloves made of the belly-skin of a baby gazelle fed on milk and honey, and a walking stick that makes your best Malacca look like a piece of an old fishing pole. I saw her go out with him less than an hour ago, just before I left. And pinned to her left shoulder was a black orchid! He must have cut it for her himself. She becomes the first female in captivity to wear a black orchid. And only last week she was typing with her lovely fingers, 'Yours of the ninth received and contents noted.' "

I grinned at him. "But Lew will have to get out the spray for the insects. Men are flocking in there who don't know a stamen from a stigma. The guy having the picnic with her inside the ropes smirks fatuously. His name is Harry Gould and he is one of Dill's gardeners. A gray-haired geezer that needs a shave gazes at her as if he was about to say his prayers—I've seen him twice. A wholesome young fellow with a serious chin wanders by and pretends he's not looking at her. His name is Fred Updegraff. Updegraff Nurseries, Erie, Pennsylvania. They've got an exhibit not far off. And there's a lot more, but chiefly there's me. Your friend Lew is going to have me to contend with. She smiled at me today without meaning to, and I blushed from head to foot. My intentions are honorable but they are not vague. Look at that picture of her and then take a slant at this." I lifted a heel to the corner of the desk and pulled my trouser leg up to the knee. "In your mind's eye strip off the shoe and sock and garter and apply your knowledge of cross-pollination. What would be the result—"

"Pfui," Wolfe said. "Don't scar the desk. You will return there tomorrow and look for edge-wilt, and you will be here at six o'clock."

But it didn't work out that way. At lunch the next day his envy and curiosity finally foamed up to the climax. He put down his coffee cup, assumed the expression of a man prepared to brave all hardship or hazard for the sake of a Cause, and told me:

"Please bring the sedan around. I'm going up there and look at those confounded freaks myself."

2   So Thursday was my fourth day at the Flower Show in a row. It was the biggest mob of the week, and getting Nero Wolfe through and up to the fourth floor where the orchids were was like a destroyer making a way through a mine field for a battleship. We were halted a couple of times by acquaintances who wanted to exchange greetings, and as we passed the Rucker and Dill woodland glade on the third floor Wolfe stopped to look it over. There was a line of spectators three deep all the way around the ropes. Harry and Anne were playing mumblety-peg. When a flash bulb made a flare she didn't flicker an eyelash.

"Look at her teeth when she smiles," I said. "Look at her hair like fine-spun open kettle molasses. She was more self-conscious the first day or two. A year of this would spoil her. Look at the leaves on the peony bushes, turning yellow, pining away because she'll be with them only one more day—"

"They are not peonies. They are azaleas and laurel, and they have a disease."

"Call it a disease if you want to. They're pining—"

He had started off, and I nearly knocked three women down getting around in front of him for interference.

At the orchid benches up on the fourth floor he disregarded everything else—though there was, for one thing, the finest display of B. thorntoni I had ever seen—and planted himself in front of the glass case. A card in the corner said, "Unnamed hybrid by Mr. Lewis Hewitt. The only three plants in existence." They certainly were something different, and I had been through all the big establishments several times, not to mention the twenty thousand plants Wolfe had, with hundreds of varieties. I stood to one side and watched Wolfe's face. He mumbled something to himself, and then just stood and looked, with his expanse of face five inches from the glass of the case. His emotions didn't show, but from the twitching of a muscle on his neck I knew he was boiling inside. For a quarter of an hour he didn't budge, not even when women bumped against him trying to get a peek at the orchids, though ordinarily he hates to have anyone touching him. Then he backed away and I thought he was through.

"It's hot in here," he said, and was taking off his overcoat. I took it to hold for him.

"Ah, Mr. Wolfe," a voice said. "This is indeed a compliment! What do you think of them?"

It was Lewis Hewitt. Wolfe shook hands with him. He had on another hat and topcoat and gloves, but the same walking stick as the day before—a golden-yellow Malacca with reddish-brown mottles. Any good appraiser would have said $830 as is, on the hoof. He was tall enough to look down at Wolfe with a democratic smile below his aristocratic nose.

"They're interesting," Wolfe said.

Interesting. Ha ha.

"Aren't they marvelous?" Hewitt beamed. "If I had time I'd take one from the case so you could have a good look, but I'm on my way upstairs to judge some roses and I'm already late. Will you be here a little later? Please do.—Hello, Wade. I'm running."

He went. The "Wade" was for a little guy who had come up while he was talking. As this newcomer exchanged greetings with Wolfe I regarded him with interest, for it was no other than W. G. Dill himself, the employer of my future wife. In many ways he was the exact opposite of Lewis Hewitt, for he looked up at Wolfe instead of down, he wore an old brown suit that needed pressing, and his sharp gray eyes gave the impression that they wouldn't know how to beam.

"You probably don't remember me," he was telling Wolfe. "I was at your house one day with Raymond Plehn—"

"I remember. Certainly, Mr. Dill."

"I just saw Plehn downstairs and he told me you were here. I was going to phone you this afternoon. I wonder if you'd do something for me?"

"That depends—"

"I'll explain. Let's step aside away from this jostling." They moved, and I followed suit. "Do you know anything about the Kurume yellows?"

"I've heard of them." Wolfe was frowning but trying to be courteous. "I've read of them in horticultural journals. A disease fatal to broad-leaved evergreens, thought to be fungus. First found two years ago on some Kurume azaleas imported from Japan by Lewis Hewitt. You had some later, I believe, and so did Watson in Massachusetts. Then Updegraff lost his entire plantation, several acres, of what he called rhodaleas."

"You do know about them."

"I remember what I read."

"Did you see my exhibit downstairs?"

"I glanced at it as I passed." Wolfe grimaced. "The crowd. I came to see these hybrids. That's a fine group of Cypripedium pubescens you have. Very fine. The Fissipes—"

"Did you see the laurel and azaleas?"

"Yes. They look sick."

"They are sick. They're dying. The Kurume yellows. The under side of the leaves shows the typical brown spots. Some scoundrel deliberately infected those plants, and I'd give a good deal to know who it was. I intend to know who it was!"

Wolfe looked sympathetic, and he really was sympathetic. Between plant growers a fatal fungus makes a bond. "It's too bad your exhibit was spoiled," he said. "But why a personal devil? Why a deliberate miscreant?"

"It was."

"Have you evidence?"

"No. Evidence is what I want."

"My dear sir. You are a child beating the stick it tripped on. You had that disease once on your place. A nest of spores in a bit of soil—"

Dill shook his head. "The disease was at my Long Island place. These plants came from my place in New Jersey. The soil could not possibly have become contaminated."

"With fungi almost anything is possible. A tool taken from one place to the other, a pair of gloves—"

"I don't believe it." Dill's voice indicated that nothing was going to make him believe it. "With the care we take. I am convinced it was done deliberately and maliciously, to ruin my exhibit. And I'm going to know who it was. I'll pay you a thousand dollars to find out for me."

Wolfe abandoned the ship. Not physically, but mentally. His face went bland and blank. "I don't believe I could undertake it, Mr. Dill."

"Why not? You're a detective, aren't you? Isn't that your business?"

"It is."

"This is a job for a detective. Isn't it?"

"No."

"Why not?"

"Because you wouldn't walk across the continent to take a swim in the Pacific Ocean. The effort and expense are out of proportion to the object sought. You say you have no evidence. Do you suspect anyone in particular?"

"No. But I absolutely intend—"

I butted in. I said to Wolfe, "I've got to go and judge some Brussels sprouts," and I beat it.

I did have a destination in mind, but mostly I wanted to be somewhere else. What with a couple of lucrative cases we had handled since the first of the year, the budget was balanced for months to come, but even so it always gave me the nettles to hear Wolfe turn down a job, and I didn't want to start riding him right there in front of Hewitt's hybrids. To avoid the mob, I opened a door marked "Private" and descended a flight of stairs. This part was not open to the public. On the floor below I made my way through a jungle of packing cases and trees and bushes and spraying equipment and so on, and went along a corridor and turned right with it. This stretch of the corridor extended almost the length of the building, but I knew there was an exit halfway. Along the left wall were cluttered more trees and shrubs and paraphernalia, surplus from the exhibits, and along the right wall, which was the partition between the corridor and the main room, were doors with cards on them, all closed, leading into the exhibits themselves from the back. As I passed the one with a card tacked on it saying "Rucker and Dill," I threw a kiss at it.

Through the door further on I entered the main room. There was even more of a crowd than when Wolfe and I had passed by half an hour earlier. I dodged through the field as far as the rustic scene which had labels on the rope-posts reading "Updegraff Nurseries, Erie, Penna." The exhibits on this side were a series of peninsulas jutting into the main room, with aisles between them extending back to the partition, on which they were based. I skirted the band of spectators taking in the Updegraff arrangement and halted beside a runty specimen who was standing there by the rope scowling at the foliage.

"Hello, Pete," I said.

He nodded and said hello.

I had met Pete day before yesterday. I didn't really like him. In fact I disliked him. His eyes didn't match and that, together with a scar on his nose, made him look unreliable. But he had been hospitable and made me at home around the place.

"Your peonies look nice," I said socially.

Someone tittered on my left and made a remark which probably wasn't intended for my ear but I have good ears. I turned and saw a pair of vintage Helen Hokinsons from Bronxville. I stared and compelled an eye.

"Yes, madam, peonies," I said. "What's a Cymbidium miranda? You don't know. I've known that since I was knee-high to a grasshopper. What's a Phalaenopsis? Do you know?"

"No, I don't, but I know those are rhododendrons. Peonies! Come, Alice."

I watched them waddle off and turned back to Pete. "Excuse me for chasing your audience, but it's none of her business if I prefer to call them peonies. What were you scowling at? Looking for the Kurume yellows?"

His head jerked around at me. "What about the Kurume yellows?" he demanded.

"Nothing. Just conversation. I heard Dill saying his woodland glade has got it and I wondered if it was spreading. You don't need to look at me like that. I haven't got it."

His left eye blinked but the off-color one didn't. "When did you hear Dill say that?"

"Just a while ago."

"So. What I suspected." He stretched himself as high as he could up on his toes, looking in all directions at the throng. "Did you see my boss?"

"No. I just came—"

Pete darted off. Apparently I had started something. But he went off to the left, towards the front, so I didn't follow him. I turned right, past a rose garden and a couple of other exhibits to Rucker and Dill's.

The crowd was about the same as before; it was only a quarter past three and they wouldn't begin surging against the ropes until four o'clock, when Harry would lie down for a nap and Anne would take off her shoes and stockings, positively never seen before at a flower show in the history of the world. I got behind some dames not tall enough to obstruct the view. Mumblety-peg was over, and Harry was making a slingshot and Anne was knitting. What she was working on didn't look as if it might be something I would be able to use, but anyway what I was interested in was her and not her output, which is a normal and healthy attitude during courtship. She sat there on the grass knitting as if there were no one within miles. Harry was nothing like as good an actor as she was. He didn't look at the spectators' faces, and of course he said nothing, since it was all pantomime and neither of them ever spoke, but by movements and glances he gave it away that he was conscious of the audience every minute.

Naturally I was jealous of him, but aside from that he impressed me as a good deal of a wart. He was about my age and he put something on his hair to make it slick. His hair and eyes were dark and he smirked. Also he was cocky. One reason I had picked Anne was that while they were eating lunch Tuesday Harry had put his hand on her arm and she had pulled away, and it wasn't an invitation to try it again. There had been further indications that she was resolved to keep herself innocent and unsullied for me, though of course she had no way of knowing that it was for me until I got a chance to speak to her. I admit her letting Hewitt decorate her with orchids and take her to dinner had been a bitter pill to swallow, but after all I had no right to expect her to be too spiritual to eat, with her legs.

All of a sudden Harry jumped to his feet and yelled, "Hey!"

It was the first word I had ever heard him utter.

Everyone, including me, looked in the direction of his stare.

"You, Updegraff!" Harry yelled. "Get out of that!"

It was the wholesome young man with the serious chin who had been identified for me as Pete's boss, Fred Updegraff, by Pete himself. At the right corner where the exhibit ended at the partition, he had straddled the rope, stretched an arm and snipped off a peony twig or maybe laurel with a pruning shears, picked up the twig, and was making off with it.

"I'll report that!" Harry yelled.

The crowd muttered and ejaculated with indignation, and for a second I thought we might see a lynching as an added attraction for the most dramatic flower show on record, but all that happened was that two women and a man trotted after Updegraff and started remonstrating with him as he kept going. Believe it or not, Anne never looked up and didn't miss a stroke with her needles. A born actress.

My watch said 3:25. It would be over half an hour before the big scene started, and I didn't dare leave Wolfe alone that long in a strange place, so I regretfully dragged myself away. Retracing my steps, I kept an eye out for Pete, thinking to tell him that his boss had resorted to crime, but he wasn't visible. Taking the corridor again as a short cut, I saw it was inhabited by a sample who didn't strike me as the flower show type, either for back stage or out front. She was standing there not far from the door with the Rucker and Dill card on it, a fancy little trick in a gray coat with Fourteenth Street squirrel on the collar, with a little blue hat and a blue leather handbag under her arm, and as I approached she looked at me with an uneasy eye and a doubtful smile.

I asked her, "You lost, sister?"

"No," she said, and the smile got confident. "I'm waiting for some-one."

"Me?"

"Nothing like you."

"That's good. It could have been me a week ago, but now I'm booked."

I went on.

Upstairs I found that Wolfe had stayed put, and W. G. Dill was still with him. Apparently the question of tracking down the gazook who had spoiled Dill's exhibit had been settled one way or the other, for they were arguing about inoculated peat and sterile flasks for germination. I sat down on a vacant spot on a bench. After a while Dill departed and Wolfe went back to the glass case and started peering again, and a few minutes later here came Lewis Hewitt, with his topcoat over his arm. He glanced around as if he was looking for something and asked Wolfe:

"Did I leave my stick here?"

"I haven't seen it. Archie?"

"No, sir."

"Damn it," Hewitt said. "I do leave sticks around, but I wouldn't like to lose that one. Well. Do you want to inspect one of those beauties?"

"Very much. Even without an inspection, I'd like to buy one."

"I imagine you would." Hewitt chuckled. "Plehn offered ten thousand for one the other day." He took a key from his pocket and leaned over the case. "I'm afraid I'm going to be regarded as a miser, but I can't bear to let one go."

"I'm not a commercial grower," Wolfe said ingratiatingly. "I'm an amateur like you."

"I know," Hewitt conceded, lifting out one of the pots as if it was made of star bubbles and angels' breath, "but, my dear fellow, I simply couldn't part with one."

From there on the scene was painful. Wolfe was so damn sweet to him I had to turn my head away to conceal my feelings. He flattered him and yessed him and smiled at him until I expected any minute to hear him offer to dust off his shoes, and the worst of it was, it was obvious he wasn't getting anywhere and wasn't going to. When Hewitt went on and on with a discourse about ovules and pollen tubes, Wolfe beamed at him as if he was fascinated and, finally, when Hewitt offered to present him with a couple of C. hassellis, Wolfe thanked him as if they were just what he asked Santa Claus for, though he had twenty specimens as good or better under his own glass. At a quarter past four I began to fidget. Not only would I have liked to give Wolfe a kick in the fundament for being such a sap, but also I wanted to conduct him past the woodland glade and prove to him that he was wrong when he said my affianced was too long from the knees down, and the big scene would end at four thirty, when Anne would flip water out of the pool onto her co-picnicker to wake him from his nap. That always got a big laugh.

So I was relieved when they started off. Ordinarily Wolfe would have had me carry the two pots of C. hassellis, but he toted them himself, one in each hand, to show Hewitt how precious he thought they were. The big toad-eater. But the worst was yet to come. We went by the back stairs, and, at my suggestion, along the corridor on the floor below, and there on the floor at the base of the door to Rucker and Dill's exhibit, I saw an object I recognized. I halted and told Hewitt:

"There's your cane."

Hewitt stood and looked at it and demanded, "How in the name of heaven did it get there?"

And by gum, Wolfe told me to pick it up for him!

I should have resigned on the spot, but I didn't want to make a scene in front of Hewitt, so I stooped and grabbed it. There was a piece of green string looped on the crook and I brushed it off and extended the crook end toward Hewitt, controlling an impulse to jab him in the ribs. He thanked me democratically and we went on.

"Curious," Hewitt said. "I certainly didn't leave it there. Very odd."

A door ahead of us opened and a man emerged. The door had a card on it, UPDEGRAFF NURSERIES, and the man was the twig-snitcher, Fred Updegraff. At sight of us he stopped, and stood there as we went by. A little farther on, after passing two more doors with exhibitors' cards on them, I swerved to one that wasn't labeled and turned the knob and opened it.

"Where are you going?" Wolfe demanded.

"The water nymph. The pool episode. I thought you might—"

"Bosh. That bedlam—"

"It's really worth seeing," Hewitt declared. "Charming. Perfectly charming. Really delightful. I'll come too."

He headed for the door I was holding open, and Wolfe followed him like an orderly after a colonel, his hands full of potted plants. It would have been comical if it hadn't been disgusting. I kept in front so as not to have to look at him.

At the glade the audience was five and six deep around the ropes to the point on either side where the bushes were in the way, but all three of us were tall enough to get a good view. Anne was putting on a swell performance, dabbling with her toes and swishing around. Her knees were beautiful. I was proud of her. Harry was stretched out in the usual spot for his nap, his head on a grassy mound alongside the rocks and bushes, with a newspaper over his face. The audience was chattering. Anne kicked water onto a cluster of flowers that hung over the pool, and glistening drops fell from the petals.

"Charming," Hewitt said.

"Delightful," Wolfe said. "Archie, will you kindly take these plants? Be very careful—"

Pretending not to hear him, I moved off to the right. Partly I thought he needed some ignoring, but also I wanted to get a better look at Harry's right leg and foot. They were twisted into a strange and unnatural position for a man pretending to take a nap. I stretched tiptoe to get a good look over heads and hats and decided that either his shoe hurt him or he was doing a yogi leg exercise, and went back to Anne just as she took another glance at her wrist watch. She swished once more, swung her feet out of the pool, cast a mischievous eye on her companion, reached into the pool with her cupped hand, and sloshed water over Harry's shirt. The audience screeched with glee.

But Harry didn't take his cue. He was supposed to jerk himself up and blink and look mad, but he didn't move. Anne stared at him in astonishment. Someone called:

"Douse him again!"

I had a quick hunch it wasn't funny, with his leg twisted like that. Pushing through to the front, I got over the rope. As I started across the grass a guard yelled at me, and so did some of the spectators, but I kept going and was bent over Harry when the guard grabbed my arm.

"Hey, you—"

"Shut up." I shook him off and lifted the newspaper enough to see Harry's face, and after one glimpse dropped the paper back over it. As I did that I sniffed. I thought I smelled something, a faint something that I recognized.

"What is it? What's the matter?" a voice above me asked.

It was the first time I had ever heard Anne's voice, but I didn't reply or look up at her because I was seeing something about the moss which clung to the face of the rocks just back of Harry's head. On account of the shrubs and rocks I couldn't get around to see the top of his head, so I reached a hand to feel of it, and the end of my finger went right into a hole in his skull, away in, and it was like sticking your finger into a warm apple pie. I pulled away and started wiping my finger off on the grass, and realized with a shock that the two white things there were Anne's bare feet. I nearly got blood on them.

3   I STOOD UP AND TOLD ANNE, "PUT ON YOUR SHOES AND stockings."

"What—"

"Do as I tell you." I had the guard by the sleeve and stabbed into his sputterings, "Get a cop." By the way his mouth fell open I saw he was too dumb even for something as simple as that without a fireside chat, so I turned to call to Hewitt and there was Fred Updegraff inside the ropes headed for us. His eyes were on Anne, but when I intercepted him and told him to get a cop he about-faced without a word and went. Wolfe's voice barked above the din:

"What the devil are you doing in there?"

I ignored him again and raised my voice to address the multitude: "Ladies and gentlemen. That's all for today. Mr. Gould has had an attack. If you're sensible you'll go and look at flowers. If you're morbid or have got the itch you'll stay where you are—outside the ropes—"

A flash bulb flared at the left. Sympathetic murmurs arose, but they seemed to be a hundred percent morbid. At the right a guy with a camera came diving under the rope, but that was something for which arrangements had already been made inside the guard's head and he responded promptly and adequately. I was gratified to see that Anne appeared to have a modicum of wits. She must have seen the color of what I had wiped from my finger, but she was sitting on the grass getting her feet shod, hastily but efficiently.

"Archie!" Wolfe's voice came in his most menacing tone. I knew what was eating him. He wanted me to get out of there and drive him home, and he thought I was showing off, and he knew I was sore. As he called my name again I turned my back on him to welcome the law. A big flatfoot with no neck shoved through the crowd to the rope and got over it and strode across the grass. I blocked his way at Harry's feet.

"What's wrong with him?" he asked gruffly.

I moved aside and let him pass. He stooped and got a corner of the newspaper and jerked it off.

"Archie!" Wolfe bellowed.

Some of the spectators could see Harry's face and they were reacting. The ropes were bellied in, taut, with the pressure from behind. The guard was charging across the grass at them and Anne was on her feet again and Fred Updegraff was there.

"Hell, he's dead," the cop said.

"You guessed it," I conceded. "Shall I get some help?"

"Go ahead."

I won't say that I already knew things I didn't know, but I already had stirrings above the ears and, besides, I didn't want Wolfe to bust a lung, so I went that way and found him standing with Hewitt a few paces to the rear of the throng.

"Hold everything," I muttered to him.

"Confound you—"

"I said hold everything." I cantered off to the phone booths at the front of the room, parted with a nickel and dialed a number and got connected with Extension 19, gave my name and asked for Inspector Cramer. His voice came:

"What do you want?"

"Me? Nothing. I'm helping with the chores. Wolfe and I are up at the Flower Show—"

"I'm busy!"

"Okay. Now you're busier. Rucker and Dill's exhibit, third floor, Flower Show. Man murdered. Shot through the top of the head. Lying there on the grass guarded by one bull-necked bull who will never be an inspector. That's all."

"Wait a min—"

"Can't. I'm busy."

I slid out of the booth and dodged through the traffic back across the room. In that short time the mob surrounding the glade had doubled in size. A glance showed me that the cop and the guard had got reinforcements and Anne and Fred Updegraff were not in sight, and Wolfe and Hewitt had retreated to the other side of the rose garden next door. W. G. Dill was with them. Wolfe glared at me as I approached. He was still hanging onto those measly plants and was speechless with rage.

". . . feel a sort of responsibility," Hewitt was saying. "I am Honorary Chairman of the Committee. I don't like to shirk responsibility, but what can I do—just look at them—"

"That policeman," Dill said. "Imbecile. Wouldn't let me in my own exhibit. Broke my shoulder blade. It feels like it." He worked his shoulder up and down, grimacing. "There's the doctor—no—"

"A doctor won't help any. He's dead."

They looked at me. Dill stopped working his shoulder. "Dead? Dead!" He darted off and burrowed into the crowd.

"You said he had an attack," Hewitt regarded me accusingly. "How can he be dead? What did he die of?"

"He ceased breathing."

"Archie," Wolfe said in his most crushing tone. "Stop that. I asked you an hour ago to take these plants. Take them, and take me home."

"Yes, sir." I took the plants. "But I can't leave yet. I'm looking—"

"Good heavens," Hewitt said. "What a calamity . . . poor Dill . . . I must see . . . excuse me. . . ." He marched off towards the main stair.

At that instant I caught sight of an object I had been halfway expecting to see. I only got a glimpse of the gray coat with its collar of Fourteenth Street squirrel, for she came from the other side and disappeared into the crowd. I put the pots on the floor at the edge of the rose garden and dashed off before Wolfe could say a word. I didn't care how sore it made him because he had it coming to him after his degrading performance with Hewitt, but I admit I glanced back over my shoulder as I went to see if he was throwing something. His face was purple. I'll bet he lost ten pounds that afternoon.

I skirted the throng and went into it on the other side. In a minute I saw her, squirming through to the front. I took it easy working through to her because I didn't want to make myself conspicuous, and, getting right behind her, saw that the blue leather bag was under her right arm. I shifted Wolfe's coat to my own right arm and under its cover got my fingers on the end of the bag and pulled gently. It started coming, and she was so interested in what she was trying to see around the people still in front of her that she didn't notice it even when the bag was out from under her arm and safely under Wolfe's coat. I kept an eye on her as I backed out, apologizing to the flower lovers as I went, and as soon as I was in the clear turned and made for the stairs.

In the men's room on the second floor I spent a nickel to achieve privacy and sat down and opened the bag, which was monogrammed "RL." It inventoried about as usual, handkerchief and compact and purse and so on, but it also had what I was after, her name and address. They were on an envelope addressed to Miss Rose Lasher, 326 Morrow Street, New York City, which checked with the RL on the bag. I copied it in my notebook. The letter inside was from Ellie and explained why she hadn't paid back the two dollars. And another item was more than I had bargained for. It was a clipping from the *Gazette* of a picture of Harry and Anne playing mumblety-peg. It had cut edges, not torn, and was neatly folded.

I put everything back in, went back to the third floor, worked my way into the crowd, not taking it so easy this time, found her in the front row against the rope, and put my hand on her shoulder. Her head twisted around.

"Will you please—" she began indignantly.

"Okay, sister. It's me. Here's your bag."

"My bag!"

"You dropped it and I risked life and limb to get it. It's yours, isn't it?"

"Sure it's mine!" She grabbed it.

"Say thank you."

She mumbled something and was through with me. I glanced at the scene. The cast had been augmented. The contents of two radio police cars, four of them in uniform, were there in the glade, one of them standing at Harry's feet watching a doctor, who was on his knees applying a stethoscope. W. G. Dill stood at the cop's side, his hands in his pockets, scowling. There was no sign that anyone had got interested in the moss on the rocks. I backed out again without bruising anyone seriously and circled around to the rose garden to rejoin Wolfe.

He wasn't there.

He was gone. The two pots were there on the floor, but he wasn't anywhere.

The damn hippopotamus, I thought. He'll get lost. He'll be kidnapped. He'll fall in a hole. He'll catch cold.

I went back down to the men's room on the second floor and yelled his name in front of the private apartments, but no soap. I went up to the fourth, to the orchid benches. No. I went down to the ground floor and out the main exit and to where I had parked the car on 46th Street, but he wasn't in it. It was trying to snow in March gusts. I spat at a snowflake as it sailed by. Our little Nero, I thought, out on such a night and no coat. The big fat flumpus. I'll put salt on his grapefruit. It was a quarter past five.

I stood and applied logic to it. Had he taken a taxi home? Not the way he hated taxis. What, as I had left him standing there, what had been his most burning desires? That was easy. To shoot me, to sit down, and to drink beer. He couldn't shoot me because I wasn't there. Where might he have found a chair?

I went back and paid four bits to get in again, mounted one flight, and made my way across the grain of the traffic to the corner of the room where a door said OFFICE. People were standing around, and one of them plucked at my sleeve as I put my hand on the knob, and I recognized him. It was the gray-haired geezer I had seen on previous days looking at Anne from a distance as if he was saying his prayers. He looked worried under an old felt hat, and his fingers on my sleeve were trembling.

"Please," he said, "if you're going in there will you please give this to Miss Anne Tracy?"

"Is she in there?"

"Yes, she went in—I saw her go in—"

I took the folded piece of paper and said I'd see that Miss Tracy got it, opened the door and entered, and was in an anteroom containing a tired-looking woman at a desk. I smiled at her irresistibly to keep her quiet, unfolded the piece of paper, and read what it said.

Dear daughter,

    I hope there is no serious trouble. I am outside here. If there is anything I can do let me know.

                              Your father.

It was written with a pencil on cheap white paper. I folded it up again, thinking that one of the first jobs to tackle would be to buy my father-in-law a new hat.

"Do you want something?" the woman at the desk asked in a sad and skeptical tone. I told her I had an important message for Miss Anne Tracy, and she opened her mouth and then decided not to use it any more and motioned to one of three doors. I opened it and passed through, and the first thing I saw was Nero Wolfe sitting in a chair almost big enough for him, with a tray on a table beside him holding four beer bottles, and a glass in his hand.

You can't beat logic.

On another chair right in front of him, facing him, was Anne. Propped against a desk at the left was Lewis Hewitt. A man I didn't know was at another desk writing something, and another one was standing by a window with Fred Updegraff.

Wolfe saw me enter. I saw him see me. But he went on talking to Anne without dropping a stitch:

". . . a matter of nerves, yes, but primarily it depends on oxygenation of the blood. The most remarkable case of self-control I ever saw was in Albania in 1915, displayed by a donkey, I mean a four-legged donkey, which toppled over a cliff—"

I was standing by him. "Excuse me," I said icily. "For you, Miss Tracy." I extended the paper.

She looked up at me, looked at the paper, took it, unfolded it, and read it.

"Oh," she said. She glanced around and looked up at me again. "Where is he?"

"Outside."

"But I . . ." Her brow wrinkled. "Would you tell him . . . no . . . I'll go. . . ."

She got up and started for the door. I went to open it for her, saw that Hewitt had the same intention, quickened my step, beat him to the knob, and swung it open. Anne was walking through, and then she wasn't. A man barging through from the other side ran smack into her and nearly knocked her over, and I grabbed her arm to help her get her balance. I beat Hewitt to that too.

"Pardon me," the intruder said. His eyes swept the room and everything in it and went back to Anne. "Are you Anne Tracy?"

"She is Miss Anne Tracy," Hewitt said, "and that is scarcely the way—"

Anne was sidling by to get to the door. The man put an arm out to stop her.

"Where are you going?"

"I'm going to see my father."

"Where is he?"

Another arm got in on it. Fred Updegraff arrived and his hand came out and contacted the intruder's ribs and gave a healthy shove.

"Learn some manners," he said gruffly. "What business is—"

"Permit me," I interposed. "This is Inspector Cramer of the Homicide Squad." I indicated another man on the door sill. "And Sergeant Purley Stebbins."

"Even so," Lewis Hewitt said in a tone of displeasure. "It is scarcely necessary to restrain Miss Tracy by force. She merely wishes to speak with her father. I am Lewis Hewitt, Inspector. May I ask—"

"Where is your father?"

"Just outside the door," I said.

"Go with her, Purley. All right, Miss Tracy. Come back in here, please."

Purley went out at her heels. That cleared the doorway for another man to enter, W. G. Dill. His lips were in a thinner line than ever, and without looking at anybody or saying anything he crossed to a chair by the rear wall and sat down.

"Hello, Wolfe," Cramer said.

"How do you do, Inspector." With only two grunts, one under par, Wolfe got to his feet and moved forward. "Come, Archie. We'll only be in the way."

"No," Cramer said meaningly.

"No?" Wolfe halted. "No what?"

"Goodwin won't be in the way. On the contrary. At least until I get through with him:"

"He's going to drive me home."

"Not now he isn't."

"May I ask what this is all about?" Hewitt was still displeased. "This surveillance of Miss Tracy? This attitude—"

"Certainly, Mr. Hewitt. Sit down." Cramer waved at chairs, of which there were plenty. "Everybody sit down. This is going to be— ah, Miss Tracy, did you find your father? Good. Pull that chair around for Miss Tracy, Purley. Sit down, Goodwin."

I attended to the chair for Anne myself, then turned to face the Inspector.

"No, thanks. I'm nervous."

"You are," Cramer growled. "The day you're nervous I'll shave with a butter knife. How did you know that man had been shot in the top of the head when you called me on the phone?"

Some of them made noises, but Anne didn't. Her head jerked up and her nostrils tightened, but that was all. I admired her more all the time. Hewitt exclaimed, "Shot!" and Fred Updegraff demanded, "What man?"

"Harry Gould," I told him. I grinned at Cramer. "As you see, I didn't blab around. I saved it for you—"

"How did you know?"

"Good heavens," Hewitt said blankly. He rose half out of his chair and then dropped back again.

"It was nothing to write home about," I said. "I looked at his face and he looked dead. I smelled cordite. I saw a jagged hole in the moss at the back of his head, and the moss was puffed out. I couldn't see the top of his head from where I was, but I felt of it, and my finger went in a hole. By the way, don't build a theory from some blood on the grass about where his knees were. I wiped my finger there."

I saw Anne gulp.

"Confound you," Wolfe said angrily, "I might have known."

"Why did you go to him in the first place?" Cramer demanded. "You climbed the ropes and ran to him. Why did you do that?"

"Because he didn't move when Miss Tracy threw water on him, and because I had already noticed that his leg and foot were twisted in an unnatural position."

"Why did you notice that?"

"Ah," I said, "now you've got me. I give up. I'm trapped. Why does anybody notice anything?"

"Especially a nervous man like you," he said sarcastically. "What were you doing there? Why did you come here?"

"I brought Mr. Wolfe."

"Did he come here on a case?"

"You know damn well he didn't. He never goes anywhere on a case. He came to look at flowers."

"Why were you there at that particular exhibit?"

"For the same reason that other people were. To watch Miss Tracy dabble her feet in the pool."

"Did you know Miss Tracy? Or Gould?"

"No."

"Did you, Wolfe?"

"No," Wolfe said.

Cramer resumed with me. "And smelling the cordite and seeing the hole in the moss and feeling the one in his head, how did you figure someone had shot him? By lying hidden in the bushes and aiming through a crack in the rocks?"

"Now have a heart, Inspector." I grinned at him. "If you're not careful you'll trap me again. At the moment I didn't do much figuring, but that was over an hour ago and you know what my brain is when it gets started. Gould took his nap at the same hour each day, and he put his head in exactly the same spot—"

"How do you know that?"

"Mr. Wolfe has been sending me here to look at orchids. That's a matter I'd rather not dwell on. The pile of rocks was only eight or nine inches from his head. Place a gun among the rocks at the right height, wedge it in, aimed the right way, and replace the moss. The rocks and the moss would muffle the report so that no one would notice it in that big noisy room—or what if they did notice it? Fasten a string to the trigger—make it green string so it won't be seen among the foliage. At the proper time, which will be anywhere between four and four thirty, pull the string."

"Pull the string how? From where?"

"Oh, suit yourself." I waved a hand. "Hide in the bushes and after you've pulled it sneak out the door at the back of the exhibit that leads to the corridor. Or if the string's long enough, run it through the crack at the bottom of the door and then you can pull it from the corridor, which would be safer. Or if you want to be fancy, tie the string to the doorknob and it will be pulled by whoever opens the door from the corridor side. Or if you want to be still fancier, run the string around the trunk of a bush and have its end a loop dangling into the pool, and take off your shoes and stockings and swish your feet around in the pool, and catch the loop with your toes and give it a jerk, and who would ever suspect—"

"That's a lie!"

That blurted insult came from Fred Updegraff. He confronted me, and his chin was not only serious, it was bigoted, and anyone might have thought I was a caterpillar eating his best peony.

"Nonsense!" came another blurt, from W. G. Dill, who didn't leave his chair.

"It seems to me—" Lewis Hewitt began sarcastically.

"Pooh," I said. "You cavaliers. I wouldn't harm a hair of her head. Don't you suppose the Inspector had thought of that? I know how his mind works—"

"Can it," Cramer growled. "The way your mind works." His eyes were narrowed at me. "We'll discuss that a little later, when I'm through with Miss Tracy. The gun was wedged among the rocks and covered with the moss, and the string was tied to the trigger, and the string was green, so you're quite a guesser—"

"How long was the string?"

"Long enough to reach. What else do you know?"

I shook my head. "If you can't tell guessing from logic—"

"What else do you know?"

"Nothing at present."

"We'll see." Cramer looked around. "If there's a room where I can go with Miss Tracy—"

The man who had been writing at a desk stood up. "Certainly, Inspector. That door there—"

"Who are you?"

"I'm Jim Hawley of the house staff. I don't think there's anyone in there—I'll see—"

But there was an interruption. The door to the anteroom opened, and in came a delegation of four. In front was a dick whom I recognized as a member of the squad, next came a lady, next my friend Pete with unmatched eyes, and bringing up the rear a cop in uniform. The lady wore a gray coat with a squirrel collar and had a blue leather bag under her arm, but I didn't presume on old acquaintance by speaking to her.

4   CRAMER TOOK IN THE INFLUX WITH A GLANCE AND asked, "What have you got, Murphy?"

"Yes, sir." The dick stood with his shoulders straight. He was the military type. "At or about half past four o'clock this young woman was seen in the corridor opening the door leading to the Rucker and Dill exhibit."

"Who saw her?"

"I did," Pete spoke up.

"Who are you?"

"I am Pete Arango. I work for Updegraff Nurseries. That's my boss there, Mr. Updegraff. I went through the door at the back of our exhibit, into the corridor, to get some cookies, and I—"

"To get what?"

"Cookies. I eat cookies. In my locker in the corridor."

"Okay. You eat cookies. And saw what?"

"I saw her opening that door. Rucker and Dill. After all what happened. I remembered it and I told a cop—"

"Did she go inside?"

Pete shook his head. "She saw me and she shut the door."

"Did she say anything?"

"No, she didn't have anything to say."

"Did you?"

"No, I went to my locker and got the cookies, and she must have gone away because when I came back she wasn't there. Then when I got back on the floor and saw—"

Cramer turned to the young woman. "What's your name?"

"None of your business!" she snapped.

"Yes, sir," the dick said. "She won't co-operate."

"What do you mean, I won't co-operate?" She was indignant, but I wouldn't have said she looked scared. "I admit I opened the door and looked in, don't I? I got into the corridor by mistake and I was looking for a way out. And why should I have to tell you my name and get my name in the papers—"

"Why didn't you get out the way you got in?"

"Because I got in away around at the other side, and I just thought . . . hey! Hello there!"

Everyone looked the way she was looking, which resulted in all of us looking at Fred Updegraff. Fred himself turned red and was turning redder, as he met her gaze.

"Well," he said, and seemed to think he had said something.

"It was you," she said, "there with the door open, stooping down there peeking in when you heard me."

"Sure," Fred acknowledged, "sure it was me."

"The Rucker and Dill door?" Cramer demanded.

"Yes."

"Were you looking for a way out too?"

"No."

"What were you looking for?"

"I was—" Fred swallowed it. He looked red and flustered, and then all of a sudden he looked relieved. There was no telling what sort of idea had popped into his head that relieved him and pleased him so much, but he certainly showed it. He spoke louder as if he didn't want anyone to miss it: "I was looking at Miss Tracy. I've been doing that all week. My name is Fred Updegraff and I'm an exhibitor here. I was looking at Miss Tracy!" It sounded as if he almost thought he was singing it.

Cramer was unimpressed. "I'll have a talk with you later, Mr. Updegraff." He turned to the sergeant. "Purley, you stay here with Mr. Updegraff and Goodwin and this young woman and this man Pete. Murphy, come with me and Miss Tracy. The rest of you can go if you want—"

"Just a minute." Hewitt, who hadn't sat down again, moved a step. "I am Lewis Hewitt."

"So I understand," Cramer grunted.

"And I have responsibilities here as the Honorary Chairman of the Committee. Without any wish to interfere with the performance of your duties, I feel that Miss Tracy, who is only a young girl, should properly be protected from any undue annoyance or unpleasantness—"

"Allow me, Hewitt," W. G. Dill had got up and walked over. He

faced Cramer. "I'm Miss Tracy's employer and I suppose I ought to
look after her. If you don't mind I'll go along with her."

I was keeping tabs on Anne, knowing that the best time to get the
lowdown on a woman is when she's under stress. I thought she was
doing fine. After four straight days in a glaring spotlight as the star
attraction of a flower show, with such by-products as having her picture taken with Billy Rose and dining out with Lewis Hewitt, here she
was kerplunk in the mire with murder-mud ready to splatter all over
her, and so far she had done nothing to forfeit my respect, even when
I had explained how you could pull a trigger with your toes. But at
this juncture she wasn't so hot. She might have spoken up with something suitable about being armored in her virtue and not needing to be
looked after by any sourpuss employer or millionaire orchid fancier,
but all she did was deadpan W. G. Dill without opening her trap. I
began to suspect she either had depths I hadn't plumbed or was a bit
limited in the mental area—but don't get me wrong, I was still faithful.
Even as a deadpan, the sight of her face—for the mental side of life
you can go to the library.

She went off with Cramer. Cramer informed both Hewitt and Dill
that it wasn't necessary for them to protect her against annoyance, and
took her and Murphy through the door that had been indicated to an
inner room. But not without another brief delay.

"Mr. Cramer! If you please?"

It was Nero Wolfe speaking. I concealed a grin. Of course he was
going to request, or demand, depending on which he thought would
work best, that I be allowed to drive him home. I hoped Cramer would
say yes. Then, after we got in the sedan and he started raving, I would
let him rave, and when he was through I would stick my little dagger
in his ribs and give it a twist. It wasn't often I had a chance like that.

Cramer had turned. "What do you want?"

"I want," Wolfe said, "to finish a discussion I was having with
Mr. Hewitt about orchids."

"Go ahead—"

"And not in a menagerie. In decent privacy. We can find a room
somewhere."

"Go ahead. I said the rest of you could go—"

"And Mr. Goodwin must be present to take notes. He will be
available when you want him. You can't legally detain him, anyhow,
unless you are prepared—"

Cramer snorted in exasperation. "Oh, for God's sake. Discuss orchids. All I want is Goodwin when I want him."

He crossed the sill with the other two, and the door was closed behind them. I glared at Wolfe without any attempt to cover it, and Purley Stebbins gazed at him suspiciously. Neither of us was making any impression on Wolfe, who had got up from his chair and was speaking to Lewis Hewitt in an undertone. Hewitt, frowning, nodded without enthusiasm, and moved toward the door to the anteroom with Wolfe at his heels.

"Come, Archie," Wolfe said.

Purley blocked me. "Where you going?"

"The other end of the anteroom," Hewitt said. "A room there."

Purley hated it. He did hate it. Me detained and going through doors like that. He didn't even smile when I playfully stuck a thumb in his ribs as I went by.

The room at the other end of the anteroom wasn't much more than a cubbyhole, with one window, a couple of small wooden tables, and four wooden chairs. The sad woman in the anteroom came in and turned on the light and went out again and closed the door. Wolfe scowled at the skimpy chairs and darted a glance at me, but I ignored it because I was in no mood to lug in the comfortable seat he had left in the other room. He compressed his lips and sat down, taking care to center himself on what seat there was.

"Sit down, Mr. Hewitt," he invited.

Hewitt stood. "This is an odd performance." He looked at me and back at Wolfe. "What you can possibly have to say to me so confidential as to require—"

"I have," Wolfe said brusquely. "I assure you."

"About orchids? That seems hardly—"

"Not orchids. Murder. I know who shot that man."

Hewitt's eyes opened wide. "You know who shot him?"

"I do."

"But my dear Mr. Wolfe." Hewitt was displeased but courteous. "That is scarcely a matter to discuss confidentially with me. The proper authorities—"

"I prefer to discuss it with you first. I suggest that we keep our voices as low as possible. It's quite possible that a policeman has his ear at the door—"

"Bosh! This melodramatic—"

"Please, Mr. Hewitt. Don't sneer at melodrama; that's only a point of view. I wish to give you a fresh point of view on the death of Harry Gould. The shot was fired by my assistant, Mr. Goodwin.—Please let me finish. First to establish the fact. Archie?"

I had sat down. The fat bum had taken my dagger away from me. I looked at him and said bitterly, "What if I let you down?"

"You won't. Anyway, you can't. I saw the piece of string you brushed off of it. And I wish to say that your performance this afternoon has been satisfactory. Completely satisfactory throughout. Was there a tug when you picked it up? That's the only detail I lack."

"What the devil is all this?" Hewitt demanded without courtesy. "If you actually—"

"Please, Mr. Hewitt. And keep your voice down. I'll state the situation as briefly as possible. Should I report it to Mr. Cramer—"

"There was a tug," I said. "A little jerk. I didn't especially notice it at the time because I was sore as hell."

Wolfe nodded. "I know you were. My report to Mr. Cramer would be this: that Lewis Hewitt said he had lost his cane. A little later, in the corridor on the third floor, we saw the cane lying on the floor with its crook against the crack under the door leading to the Rucker and Dill exhibit. That was at twenty minutes past four. Mr. Goodwin picked up the cane, and as he did so felt a tug. He calls it a little jerk, but he is exceptionally strong and was in a savage emotional state. Looped on the crook of the cane was a piece of green string which he brushed off before he handed it to its owner."

"I saw no string," Hewitt snapped.

"Maybe not," Wolfe admitted. "People who inherit wealth don't have to bother to see things. But certainly Mr. Goodwin saw it, and so did I, and he felt the tug. The tug was unquestionably the pulling of the trigger and the breaking of the string. That would be my report to Mr. Cramer, since those are the facts."

"I tell you I saw no string!"

"But we did. Keep your voice down, Mr. Hewitt. And Mr. Goodwin touched it. Surely you don't suppose we cooked this up?"

"I don't—" Hewitt looked at the door, and then at me, and then back at Wolfe. "No. I don't suppose you did. But it's inconceivable—" He stopped and stared. "What's that?"

"The piece of string," Wolfe said.

The son of a gun had pulled it out of his vest pocket. I got up for a look, and it was it. I said, "Good here," and sat down. Hewitt sat down too. He looked as if he had to do something and that was all he could think of.

"You and Mr. Dill and Mr. Goodwin left me there," Wolfe said. "Standing there alone. He left those plants there on the floor—and by the way, I have better hassellis than those, much better, my own growing. At a certain point my head began to work, which was remarkable under the circumstances. I don't say that I foresaw this moment precisely, but I saw enough to impel me to go to the corridor and find this piece of string on the floor and pick it up. It is indubitably the piece that was looped on the crook of your cane. By comparing it with the piece left attached to the trigger, Mr. Cramer can establish our surmise as a certainty. That is, he can if I let him have it. Do you think I should do that?"

"Good heavens," Hewitt muttered. "My stick. Good heavens, do you realize—*my* stick!"

"Exactly," Wolfe agreed. "Don't talk so loud. I do realize. Whoever rigged up that affair made a loop at the end of the string that could be passed under the door. It may have been an afterthought, ad libbing, suggested by the sight of your cane where you had left it, to pass the loop over the cane and leave it lying there for the first passerby to pick up. If that hadn't happened before half past four I imagine he would have attended to it himself. I do realize what a story that will be for the newspapers. I doubt if it would lead to any official suspicion that you rigged it up yourself, but the public mind—at least some of it—is even less subtle than Mr. Cramer's."

"Good heavens," Hewitt moaned. "This . . ." He clenched his fingers, and released them, and clenched them again. "This is horrible."

"Oh, I wouldn't say horrible. Disagreeable."

"Horrible. For me. For a Hewitt. Horrible!"

"Perhaps for a Hewitt," Wolfe conceded. "Then all the more reason why this may interest you. I want those orchid plants. All three of them."

That changed things entirely. The change, showing itself on Hewitt's face, took perhaps two seconds all told. Up to then nothing had been threatened but his peace of mind or maybe his reputation, at most his life and liberty. But this was something else again; this threatened his property. It put stone in his heart and steel in his jaw. He eyed Wolfe with a shrewd and stubborn stare.

"I see," he hissed. "So that's it. To put it plainly, blackmail. Blackmail! No! I won't do it!"

Wolfe sighed. "You won't?"

"No!"

"Very well. Then I won't get the orchids, but I'll be saved a lot of trouble. Archie, get Mr. Cramer in here. Tell him it's urgent. I'll not perch on this confounded milking stool any longer than I have to."

I arose and started for the door, not hastily. I knew it was in the bag because Hewitt hadn't raised his voice. It was only a war of nerves.

"Blackmail," Hewitt said through his teeth.

"Go on, Archie," Wolfe said. I put my hand on the knob.

"Wait a minute," Hewitt said. I turned my head but kept my hand on the knob.

"One of them," Hewitt said. "Select any one."

I went back and sat down.

Wolfe sighed and shook his head. "All three. I won't haggle. I'm going to have to work for them. You may call it blackmail to relieve your feelings, but what about me? It's possible that this evidence I'm withholding from Mr. Cramer is vital evidence, and I don't intend to shield a murderer. If I withhold it I'll have to find the murderer myself, and enough evidence to convict him without this. And if I fail I'll have to tell Mr. Cramer all about it, which would be deplorable, and shall have to return the plants to you, which would be unthinkable. So I shan't fail."

"Two of them," Hewitt said. "Two plants. To be delivered to you when you have satisfactorily performed your part of the bargain." He may have inherited it, but he certainly knew how to hang onto it.

"No," Wolfe said. "All three, and I take them home with me now. You can trust me. I can't trust you, because if it turns out that you killed the man yourself and I get you for it, I'd never get them."

"Do you—" Hewitt was goggle-eyed. "You have the effrontery— you dare to suggest—"

"Not at all. I suggest nothing. I consider contingencies, and I'd be a fool if I didn't." Wolfe put a hand on the edge of the table for leverage and lifted himself from the milking stool. "I'm going home where there is a chair to sit on, and go to work. If you'll please take Mr. Goodwin upstairs and give him the plants so I can take them with me . . ."

5 OF COURSE I HAD A CARD UP MY SLEEVE. WOLFE HAD taken my dagger away and done the twisting himself, in Hewitt's ribs instead of his own, but I still had a card.

I had a chance to make arrangements for playing it while Wolfe went around, after we returned to the other room, inviting people to lunch. That was actually what he did. Anyhow he invited W. G. Dill and Fred Updegraff; I heard that much. Apparently he intended to spend the evening thinking it out, and have them all to lunch the next day to announce the result. Hewitt declined my help on the orchid portage from upstairs. It seemed as if he didn't like me. When Wolfe had finished the inviting he calmly opened, without knocking, the door into the room where Cramer had gone with Anne, and disappeared within.

I approached Purley Stebbins, stationed on a chair near the door to the anteroom, and grinned at him reassuringly. He was always upset in the presence of either Wolfe or me, and the two of us together absolutely gave him the fidgets. He gave me a glancing eye and let out a growl.

"Look, Purley," I said cordially, "here's one for the notebook. That lady over there." She was sitting by the far wall with her coat still on and the blue leather bag under her arm. "She's a phony. She's really a Chinese spy. So am I. We were sent to do this job by Hoo Flung Dung. If you don't believe it watch us talk code."

"Go to hell," Purley suggested.

"Yeah? You watch."

I ambled across the room and stood right in front of her so Purley couldn't see her face.

"Hello, dear old friend," I said not too loud.

"You've got a nerve," she said. "Beat it."

"Nerve? Me?"

"Beat it. 'Dear old friend!' I never saw you before."

"Aha!" I smiled down at her. "Not a chance in the world. If I tell them I saw you in that corridor at half past three waiting for someone, they'll believe me, don't think they won't, and you'll have to start all over again about opening that door at half past four because you got there by mistake and were looking for a way out. Think fast and don't tell me to beat it again or we part forever. And control your face and keep your voice down."

Her fingers were twisting under a fold of the coat. "What do you want?"

"I want to get to know you better. I'll be leaving here in a minute to drive my boss home, but I'll be back before long for a little talk with the Inspector. Then I'll go to the news movie in Grand Central and you'll be there in the back row. Won't you?"

"Yes."

"You're sure."

"Yes."

"You'd better be. If you are, it's all right that you never saw me before. If you put over your song and dance there may be a tail on you when you leave. Don't try to shake him. We'll take care of that when we leave the movie. Understand?"

"Yes."

"Righto. Stick to me and you'll wear black orchids."

I started to go back to Purley to kid him out of any suspicions that might be pecking at the shell, but a door opened and Wolfe emerged, and Cramer stood on the sill and spoke:

"Purley! Goodwin's taking Wolfe home and will be back in half an hour."

"Yeah," Purley said disrespectfully.

"Come, Archie," Wolfe said.

We waited in the anteroom, and in a few minutes here came Lewis Hewitt, followed by a guard balancing the glass case on his upper limbs. The transfer was made to me without ceremony, after Wolfe peered through the glass for a good gloating look, and off we went. When we got to where I had parked the car Wolfe got in the back, always a major operation, and I deposited the case on the floor at his feet. Ten minutes later we arrived at the old house on West 35th Street near the river, and the sigh he heaved as he deposited his weight and volume in a chair that had been made for them was a record for both depth and duration.

"You'd better get back up there," he said. "I regret it and I resent it, but I gave Mr. Cramer my word. Theodore will attend to the plants. Get back for dinner if you can. We're having saucisse minuit."

He was being sweet. "I didn't give Cramer my word," I suggested.

"No." He wiggled a finger at me. "Archie! No shenanigan."

"I'll see. But I need refreshment."

I went to the kitchen and put two bowls of crackers and milk where they belonged, meanwhile chinning with Fritz and getting sniffs of the sausage he was preparing. Eating crackers and milk and smelling saucisse minuit simultaneously is like sitting with your arm around a country lass while watching Hedy Lamarr raise the temperature. I told Fritz to save some for me if I was late getting back, and departed.

It was 7:15 when I entered the big inside room of the offices on the second floor of Grand Central Palace. There were a dozen or more people in there, most of whom were new to me, but including W. G. Dill and Lewis Hewitt. Updegraff wasn't in sight, and neither was Anne Tracy, and neither was the girl friend I had a date with. Her absence made it desirable to get troublesome without delay, but it wasn't necessary because in a couple of minutes the door to the inner room opened and Pete Arango came out, and I got a sign from Purley and went in. Cramer was there with a dick I had never seen and Murphy with a notebook. His unlighted cigar was chewed halfway to the end and he looked unjubilant.

"Now," I said brightly, taking a seat, "what can I do to help?"

"Join a circus," Cramer said. "By God, you'll clown at your own funeral. What have you been hanging around here all week for?"

That was all it amounted to, a bunch of whats and whys and whens and four pages of the notebook filled, and my wit wasted on the homicide squad as usual. As a matter of fact, the wit was below par because I wanted to get out of there for my date, since it appeared that she had had her session and been turned loose. So I kept it fairly succinct and tried to co-operate on details, and we were about running out of material when the door opened and in came an undersized dick with a flat nose. Cramer looked at him and demanded:

"What the hell are you doing back here?"

The dick's mouth opened and shut again. It didn't want to say what it had to say. On the second try it got it out:

"I lost her."

Cramer groaned and looked speechless.

"It wasn't my fault," the dick said, "I swear it wasn't, Inspector.

That damn subway. A local rolled in and stopped and she hung back like waiting for an express and then the last second she dived through—"

"Can it," Cramer said. "Choke on it. My God. The wonder to me is that—what does it matter what the wonder to me is? What's that name and address?"

Murphy flipped back through the pages of his notebook and stopped at one. "Ruby Lawson. One fourteen Sullivan Street."

The dick got out his memo book and wrote it down. "I don't think it was deliberate," he said. "I think she just changed her mind. I think she just—"

"You think? You say you think?"

"Yes, Inspector, I—"

"Get out. Take another man, take Dorsey, and go to that address and look into her. Don't pick her up. Keep on her. And for God's sake don't think. It's repulsive, the idea of you thinking."

The thinker made himself scarce. Naturally I was now itching to be on my way, so I leaned back comfortably and crossed my legs and began, "You know, when I am tailing someone and they go into a subway station, it is my invariable custom—"

"You can go," Cramer snapped. "On out. If I want you, which God forbid, I know where to get you."

"But I think—"

"I said go!"

I got up leisurely and went out leisurely, and on my way through the outer room paused for a friendly word with Purley, but when I got to the stairs outside I stepped on it. It was at least a hundred to one that I had been stood up, but nevertheless I hotfooted it to the Lexington Avenue entrance of Grand Central Station and on to the newsreel theater, parted with money, and entered. She wasn't in the back row, and I didn't waste time inspecting any other rows. Since she had given a phony name and address to Cramer, and had been smart enough to make it one that matched the RL on her bag, I figured she probably wouldn't be letting grass come up between her toes. Out in the lighted corridor I took a hasty glance at a page in my memo book, considered patronizing the subway and decided no, and headed for 46th Street where I had parked the car.

My high-hatting the subway nearly lost me a trick, for it was slow work at that hour getting around on to Park Avenue, but once headed downtown I made good time.

Number 326 Morrow Street, down at the southern fringe of Greenwich Village, was one of those painted brick fronts that were painted too long ago. There were supposed to be two lights on black iron brackets at the entrance to the vestibule, but only one was working. I parked across the street and moseyed over. Inside the vestibule was the usual row of mailboxes and bell pushes, and the card below one of them had LASHER printed on it. That was okay, but what made it interesting was that on the same card, above LASHER, another name was printed: GOULD. I was leaning over looking at it when the inside door opened and there she was.

It was easy to see that high-hatting the subway had nearly cost me a trick, because she had a traveling bag in her hand and was stooping to pick up a suitcase with the hand she had used to open the door with.

"Allow me," I said, extending a hand. "That looks heavy."

She gave me one startled glance and dropped the suitcase and sat down on it and started to cry. She didn't cover her face with her hands or anything like that, she just burst.

I waited a minute for a lull. "Look," I said, "you're blocking the way in case anyone wants to come in or go out. Let's take these things—"

"You dirty—" The crying interferred with it. "You lousy—"

"No," I said firmly. "No, sister. You stood me up. You humiliated me." I picked up the traveling bag which she had also dropped. "Let's go."

"He's dead," she said. She wasn't bothering about small things like tears. "He's dead, ain't he? Hasn't anybody got any heart at all? The way I had to sit up there—sit there and pretend—" She stopped and chewed her lip, and all of a sudden she stood up and blazed at me. "Who are you, anyway? How did you know who I was? How did you get here so quick? You're a detective, that's what you are, you're a lousy detective—"

"No." I gripped her arm. "If you mean a city employee, no. My name is Archie Goodwin and I work for Nero Wolfe. My car's outside and I'm taking you up to Wolfe's place for a little conference. He's got one of the biggest hearts in the world, encased in a ton of blubber."

Of course she balked. She even defied me to call a cop, but then she started to cry again, and during that deluge I picked up the bag and suitcase and herded her out and across the street to the car. All the way up to 35th Street she cried and I had to lend her a handkerchief.

With my hands full of luggage, I had her precede me up the stoop and ring the bell for Fritz to let us in. He did so, and helped her off with her coat like a head waiter helping the Duchess of Windsor, one of the nicest things about Fritz being that to him anything in a skirt is a lady.

"Mr. Wolfe is at dinner," he announced.

"I'll bet he is. Take Miss Lasher to the office."

I took the luggage with me to the dining room, set it down against the wall, and approached the table. There he was, floating in clouds of bliss. He looked from the luggage to me.

"What's that? Those aren't your bags."

"No, sir," I agreed. "They are the property of an object I brought with me named Rose Lasher, who may help you hang onto those orchids. She is bereaved and hungry and I'm hungry. Shall I stay with her in the office—"

"Hungry? Bring her in here. There's plenty."

I went to the office and returned with her. She had stopped crying but sure was forlorn.

"Miss Lasher," I said, "this is Nero Wolfe. He never discusses business at the table, so we'll eat first and go into things later." I held a chair for her.

"I don't want to eat," she said in a thin voice. "I can't eat."

She ate seven sausages, which was nothing against her grief. Fritz's saucisse minuit would make Gandhi a gourmet.

6   "AND NOW," WOLFE DEMANDED, "WHAT IS MISS LASHER here for?"

Dinner was over and we were settled in the office. Wolfe was seated behind his desk, leaning back with his fingers laced over his sausage mausoleum, his eyes half closed. I was at my desk, and Rose was in a red leather chair facing Wolfe. The set of her lips didn't indicate that the meal had made her one of us.

I recited particulars, briefly but completely.

"Indeed." Wolfe inclined his head a sixteenth of an inch. "Satisfactory, Archie." The head turned. "You must have a lot to tell, Miss Lasher. Tell it, please."

She looked sullen. "Tell what?"

"Start at the end. Where did you hide in that corridor from half past three to half past four and whom and what did you see?"

"I didn't hide. I went out and went back and the second time I saw that man opening that door. Then I went—"

"No. That won't do. You were waiting to intercept Mr. Gould when he came out, and you hid. The police won't like it that you lied to them and gave them a false name and address and were running away. So I may not tell the police if you tell me the truth."

"I wasn't running away. I was merely going to visit a friend."

It was certainly a job to steam her off the envelope. She stuck for ten minutes in spite of all Wolfe said, and she didn't loosen up until after I brought the luggage from the dining room and went through it. I had to dig the keys out of her handbag, and at one point I thought she was going to start clawing and kicking, but finally she stopped squealing and only sat in the chair and made holes in me with her eyes.

I did it thoroughly and methodically. When I got through, the suitcase was nearly filled with female garments and accessories, mostly intimate, and piled on Wolfe's desk was a miscellaneous collection not so female. Shirts and ties, three photographs of Harry Gould, a bunch of snapshots, a bundle of letters tied with string, the top one addressed to Rose, various other items, among them a large Manila envelope fastened with a clasp.

I opened the envelope and extracted the contents. There were only two things in it and neither of them made my heart jump. One was a garage job-card with grease smears on it. At the top was printed, "Nelson's Garage, Salamanca, New York," and judging from the list of repairs required the car must have had an argument with a mountain. It was dated 4/11/40. The other item was sheets of printed matter. I unfolded them. They had been torn from the *Garden Journal*, which I would have recognized from the page and type without the running head, and the matter was an article entitled "Kurume Yellows in America" by Lewis Hewitt. I lifted the brows and handed it to Wolfe. Then my eye caught something I had missed on the garage job-card, something written in pencil on the reverse side. It was a name, "Pete Arango," and it was written in a small fine hand quite different from the scribbling on the face of the card. There was another sample of a similar small fine hand there in front of me, on the envelope at the top of the bundle addressed to Rose Lasher, and I untied the string and got out the letter and found that it was signed "Harry."

I passed the outfit to Wolfe and he looked it over.

He grunted. "This will interest the police." His eyes went to Rose. "Even more than your—"

"No!" she cried. She was wriggling. "You won't . . . oh, for God's sake, you mustn't—"

"Where did you hide in that corridor?"

She unloaded. She had hid in the corridor, yes, from the time I saw her there until some time after she had opened the door of the exhibit to look in. She had hid behind the packing cases and shrubs against the rear wall of the corridor. The sound of commotion had alarmed her, and she had sneaked out and gone to the main room and pushed into the crowd around the exhibit and I had returned her bag to her, which she had dropped without knowing it.

What and whom had she seen while hiding in the corridor?

Nothing. Maybe a few people, she didn't know who, passing by. Nothing and no one she remembered, except Fred Updegraff.

Of course she was lying. She must have seen Wolfe and Hewitt and me go by and me pick up the stick. The stick was there at the door that she was watching. And she must have seen someone leave the stick there, stoop down to pass the crook through the loop of the string, probably open the door to get hold of the loop which was ready inside, hidden among the foliage. But Wolfe was handicapped. He didn't dare mention the stick. That was out. But boy, did he want her to mention it, and incidentally mention who had walked in there with it and left it there?

Didn't he? He did. But she wouldn't. She was stuck tight again, and I never saw Wolfe try harder and get nowhere. Finally he pulled the bluff of phoning Cramer, and even that didn't budge her. Then he gave up and rang for Fritz to bring beer.

At that point the phone rang and I answered it, and heard a familiar voice:

"Archie? Saul Panzer. May I speak to Mr. Wolfe?"

Wolfe took it on his phone, and I learned that during my absence he had got hold of Saul and sent him to the Flower Show. After getting a report he told Saul to drop the line he was on and come to the office. He hung up and leaned back and heaved a sigh, and regarded Rose with no sign of esteem.

"That," he said, "was a man I sent to collect facts about Mr. Gould. I'd rather get them from you. I'll allow you until tomorrow to jog your memory about what you saw in that corridor this afternoon, but you'll tell me about him now. We've got all night. How long had you known him?"

"About two years," she said sullenly.

"Are you his wife? His widow?"

She flushed and her lips tightened. "No. He said he wasn't the marrying kind. That's what he said."

"But he lived on Morrow Street with you?"

"No, he didn't. He only came there. He had a room in one of the houses on the Dill place on Long Island. No one ever knew about Morrow Street—I mean no one out there." She suddenly jerked forward and her eyes flashed, and I was surprised at her spunk. "And no one's going to know about it! You hear that? Not while I'm alive they're not!"

"Do you have relatives on Long Island? Do your folks live there?"

"None of your business!"

"Perhaps not," Wolfe conceded. "I wouldn't want it to be. When and where did you meet Mr. Gould?"

She shut her mouth.

"Come," Wolfe said sharply. "Don't irritate me beyond reason. The next time I tell Mr. Goodwin to get Mr. Cramer on the phone it won't be a bluff."

She swallowed. "I was clerking in a store at Richdale and he—I met him there. That was nearly two years ago, when he was working at Hewitt's."

"Do you mean Lewis Hewitt's?"

"Yes, the Hewitt estate."

"Indeed. What did he do there?"

"He was a gardener and he did some chauffering. Then he got fired. He always said he quit, but he got fired."

"When was that?"

"Over a year ago. Winter before last, it was. He was a good green-house man, and it wasn't long before he got another job at Dill's. That's about two miles the other side of Richdale. He went to live there in one of the houses."

"Did you live there with him?"

"Me?" She looked shocked and indignant. "I certainly didn't! I was living at home!"

"I beg your pardon. How long have you been living at the place on Morrow Street?"

She shut her mouth.

"Come, Miss Lasher. Even the janitor could tell me that."

"Look here," she said. "Harry Gould was no good. He never was any good. I knew that all the time. But the trouble is you get started, that's what makes the trouble, you get started and then you keep it up—even if I knew he was no good there was something about him. He always said he wasn't the marrying kind, but when he took me to that place on Morrow Street one day—that was last June, June last year—and said he had rented it, that looked like he wanted a home and maybe to get married after a while, so I quit my job and went there to live. That's how long I've been living there, nine months. At first I was scared, and then I wasn't. There wasn't much money, but there was enough, and then I got scared again on account of the money. I didn't know where he got it."

The seam had ripped and the beans were tumbling out, and Wolfe sat back and let them come.

"He came there one night—he came four or five nights a week—that was one night in December not long before Christmas—and he had over a thousand dollars. He wouldn't let me count it, but it must have been, it might have been two or three thousand. He bought me a watch, and that was all right, but all the money did to me, it scared me. And he began to act different and he didn't come so often. And then about a month ago he told me he was going to get married."

Her lips went tight and after a moment she swallowed.

"Not to you," Wolfe said.

"Oh, no." She made a noise. "Me? Not so you could notice it. But he wouldn't tell me her name. And he kept having money. He didn't show it to me any more, but several times at night I looked in his pockets and he had a bankbook with over three thousand dollars in it and he always had a big roll of bills. Then yesterday I saw a picture of him in the paper, at the Flower Show with that girl. He hadn't said a word to me about it, not a word. And he hadn't been to Morrow Street for nearly a week, and he didn't come last night, so I went there today to see, and there he was in there with her. When I saw him in there with her I wanted to kill him, I tell you that straight, I wanted to kill him!"

"But you didn't," Wolfe murmured.

Her face worked. "I wanted to!"

"But you didn't."

"No," she said, "I didn't."

"But someone did." Wolfe's voice was silky. "He was murdered. And naturally you are in sympathy with the effort to find the murderer. Naturally you intend to help—"

"I do not!"

"But my dear Miss Lasher—"

"I'm not your dear Miss Lasher." She leaned to him from the edge of the chair. "I know what I am, I'm a bum, that's what I am and I know it. But I'm not a complete dumbbell, see? Harry's dead, ain't he? Who killed him I don't know, maybe you did, or maybe it was that ten-cent Clark Gable there that thinks he's so slick he can slide uphill. Whoever it was, I don't know and I don't care, all I care about now is one thing, my folks aren't going to know anything about all this, none of it, and if it gets so I can't help it and they find out about it, all they'll have left to do with me is bury me."

She straightened up. "It's my honor," she said. "It's my family's honor."

Whether that came from the movies or wherever it came from, that's exactly what she said. I suspected the movies, considering her cheap crack about me being a ten-cent Clark Gable, which was ridiculous. He simpers, to begin with, and to end with no one can say I resemble a movie actor, and if they did it would be more apt to be Gary Cooper than Clark Gable.

Anyhow, that's what she said. And apparently she meant it, for although Wolfe went on patiently working at her he didn't get much. She didn't know why Harry had been fired from Hewitt's, or where his sudden wealth had come from, or why he had carefully saved that garage job-card, or why he had been interested in the Kurume yellows, which she had never heard of, and above all she couldn't remember anyone or anything she had seen while she was hiding in the corridor. Wolfe kept at her, and it looked as if she was in for a long hard night.

Around eleven o'clock an interruption arrived in the shape of Saul Panzer. I let him in and he went to the office. With one glance of his sharp gray eyes he added Rose to his internal picture gallery, which meant that she was there for good, and then stood there in his old brown suit—he never wore an overcoat—with his old brown cap in his hand. He looked like a relief veteran, whereas he owned two houses in Brooklyn and was the best head *and* foot detective west of the Atlantic.

"Miss Rose Lasher, Mr. Saul Panzer," Wolfe said. "Archie, get me the atlas."

I shrugged. One of his favorite ways of spending an evening was with the atlas, but with company there? Muttering, "Mine not to reason why," I took it to him, and sat down again while he went on his trip. Pretty soon he closed it and shoved it aside, and addressed Rose:

"Was Mr. Gould ever in Salamanca, New York?"

She said she didn't know.

"Those letters, Archie," Wolfe said.

I got the pile and gave him half and kept half for myself and ran through the envelopes. I was nearly at the bottom when Wolfe emitted a grunt of satisfaction.

"Here's a post card he sent you from Salamanca on December 14th, 1940. A picture of the public library. It says, 'Will be back tomorrow or next day. Love and kisses. Harry.' "

"Then I guess he was there," Rose admitted sullenly.

"Archie, give Saul a hundred dollars." Wolfe handed Saul the post card and the garage job-card. "Go to Salamanca. Take a plane to Buffalo and hire a car. Do you know what Harry Gould looked like?"

"Yes, sir."

"Note the dates—but I don't need to tell you. Go up there and get all you can. Phone me on arrival."

"Yes, sir. If necessary do I pay for it?"

Wolfe grimaced. "Within reason. I want all I can get. Make it two hundred, Archie."

I counted ten twenties into Saul's hand from the stack I got from the safe, and he stuffed it into his pocket and went, as usual, without any foolish questions.

Wolfe resumed with Rose, after ringing for beer. First he spent five minutes trying to get her to remember what Harry had gone to Salamanca for, or anything he had said to her about it, but that was a blank. No savvy Salamanca. Then he returned to former topics, but with a series of flanking movements. He discussed cooking with her. He asked about Harry's abilities and experience as a gardener, his pay, his opinion of Hewitt and Dill, his employers, his drinking habits and other habits.

I was busy getting it down in my notebook, but I certainly wasn't trembling with excitement. I knew that by that method, by the time dawn came Wolfe could accumulate a lot of facts that she wouldn't know he was getting, and one or two of them might even mean something, but among them would not be the thing we wanted most to know, what and whom she had seen in the corridor. As it stood now we didn't dare to let the cops get hold of her even if we felt like it, for fear Cramer would open her up by methods of his own, and if he learned about the stick episode his brain might leap a barricade and spoil everything. And personally I didn't want to toss her to the lions anyhow, even after that Clark Gable crack.

It was a little after midnight when the doorbell rang again, and I went to answer it and got an unpleasant surprise. There on the stoop was Johnny Keems. I never resented any of the other boys being called in to work on a case, and I didn't actually resent Johnny either, only he gave me a pain in the back of my lap with his smirking around trying to edge in on my job. So I didn't howl with delight at sight of him, and then I nearly did howl, not with delight, when I saw he wasn't alone and what it was that kept him from being alone.

It was Anne Tracy standing behind him. And standing behind her was Fred Updegraff.

"Greetings," I said, concealing my emotions, and they all entered. And the sap said to her, "This way, Miss Tracy," and started for the office with her!

I stepped around and blocked him. "Some day," I said, "you'll skin your nose. Wait in the front room."

He smiled at me the way he does. I waited until all three of them had gone through the door to the front room and it had closed behind them, and then returned to the office and told Wolfe:

"I didn't know you had called out the army while I was gone. Visitors. The guy who wants my job and is welcome to it at any time, and my future wife, and the wholesome young fellow with the serious chin."

"Ah," Wolfe said. "That's like Johnny. He should have phoned." He grunted. He leaned back. His eyes rested on Rose an instant, then they closed, and his lips pushed out, and in, and out and in.

His eyes opened. "Bring them in here."

"But—" Rose began, starting from her chair.

"It's all right," he assured her.

I wasn't so darned sure it was all right, but it was him that wanted the black orchids, not me, so I obeyed orders, went to the front room by the connecting doors, and told them to come in. Johnny, who is a gentleman from his skin out, let Anne and Fred pass through ahead of him. She stopped in the middle of the room.

"How do you do," Wolfe said politely. "Forgive me for not rising; I rarely do. May I introduce—Miss Rose Lasher, Miss Anne Tracy. By the way, Miss Lasher has just been telling me that you were engaged to marry Mr. Gould."

"That's a lie," Anne said.

She looked terrible. At no time during the afternoon, when the turmoil had started or when Cramer had announced it was murder or when he had marched her out for examination, had she shown any sign of sag or yellow, but now she looked as if she had taken all she could. At least she did when she entered, and maybe that is why she reacted the way she did to Wolfe's statement and got rough.

"Marry Harry Gould?" she said. "That isn't true!" Her voice trembled with something that sounded like scorn but might have been anything.

Rose was out of her chair and was trembling all over. All right, I thought, Wolfe arranged for it and now he'll get it. She'll scratch Anne's eyes out. I moved a step. But she didn't. She even tried to control her voice.

"You bet it ain't true!" she cried, and that *was* scorn. "Harry wasn't marrying into *your* family! He wasn't marrying any daughter of a thief!"

Anne gawked at her.

Rose spat. "You with your stuckup nose! Why ain't your father in jail where he belongs? And you up there showing your legs like a ten-cent floozie—"

"Archie," Wolfe said sharply. "Take her upstairs."

Rose went on, not even hearing him. I got her suitcase in one hand and gripped her arm with the other and turned her around, and the idea of her nonmarrying Harry marrying another girl, in spite of his being dead, occupied her brain so that she kept right on spitting compliments without even knowing I was propelling her out of the room until we were in the hall. Then she went flat-footed and shut her mouth and glared at me.

"On up two flights," I said. "Or I know how to carry you so you can't bite." I still had her arm. "Up we go, sister."

She came. I took her into the spare room on the same floor as mine, switched on the lights, and put her suitcase on a chair.

I pointed. "Ten-cent bathroom there. Ten-cent bed there. You won't be needed—"

She sat down on the bed and started to bawl.

I went down to the kitchen and told Fritz, "Lady guest in the south room. She has her own nightie, but would you mind seeing about towels and flowers in her room? I'm busy."

7

ANNE SLEPT IN MY BED THAT NIGHT.

It went like this. When I got back to the office Anne was in my chair with her elbows on the desk and her hands covering her eyes. That was a favorite trick of Johnny's, putting someone else in my chair. He hadn't tried putting himself in it again since the day a couple of years back when I found him there looking at my notebook and sort of lost my temper.

Fred Updegraff was on a chair against the wall and Johnny was standing in front of Wolfe's desk. Evidently Wolfe had made some pointed remarks, for Johnny didn't look at all cocky.

"Yes, sir," he was saying in a hurt tone, "but the Tracys live in humble circumstances and have no phone, so I used my best judgment—"

"You were at the Tracy home? Where is it?"

"In Richdale, Long Island, sir. My instructions were to investigate Anne Tracy. I learned that she lives in Richdale, where the Dill nurseries and offices are. You know she works there—"

"I was aware of that. Be brief."

"Yes, sir. I went out to Richdale and made inquiries. I contacted a young woman—as you know, I am especially effective with young women—"

"Contact is not a verb and I said be brief."

"Yes, sir. The last time you told me that I looked it up in the dictionary and I certainly don't want to contradict you but it says contact is a verb. Transitive or intransitive."

"Contact is not a verb under this roof."

"Yes, sir. I learned that Miss Tracy's father had worked at Dill's for many years, up to about a year ago. He was assistant superintendent in charge of broad-leaved evergreens. Dill discovered he was kiting shipments and fired him."

"Kiting shipments?"

"Yes, sir. On shipments to a big estate in Jersey, the Cullen place. He would ship two hundred rhododendrons instead of one hundred and collect from Cullen for the extra hundred personally, at half price. It amounted to several thousand dollars."

Anne lifted her head and turned it and made a noise of protest.

"Miss Tracy says it was only sixteen hundred dollars," Johnny said. "I'm telling you what I was told. People exaggerate, and this never was made public, and Tracy wasn't arrested. He stole it to pay a specialist for fixing his son's eyes, something wrong with his son's eyes. He can't get another job. His daughter was Dill's secretary and still is. She gets fifty a week and pays back twenty on what her father stole, so I was told. She refuses to verify those figures."

Wolfe looked at Anne.

"It doesn't matter," Anne said, looking at me. "Does it?"

"I suppose not," Wolfe said, "but if it's wrong, correct it."

"It's wrong. I get twenty dollars a week and I pay back ten."

"Good God," I blurted, "you need a union."

That was probably Freudian. Probably subconsciously I meant she needed a union with me. So I added hastily, "I mean a labor union. Twenty bucks a week!"

Johnny looked annoyed. He's a conservative. "So of course that gave me an in. I went to Miss Tracy's home and explained to her confidentially the hole she was in. That this murder investigation would put the police on to her father's crime, and that she and Dill were compounding a felony, which is against the law, and that the police would have to be fixed or they'd all be in jail, and there was only one man I knew of who could fix it because he was on intimate terms with high police officials, and that was Mr. Nero Wolfe. I said she'd better come and see you immediately, and she came. It was nearly eleven o'clock and there was no train in from Richdale, so we took a taxi."

Johnny shot me a glance, as much as to say, "Try and match that one."

"How far is it to Richdale?" Wolfe demanded.

"From here? Oh, twenty-five miles."

"How much was the taxi fare?"

"Eight dollars and forty cents counting the tip. The bridge—"

"Don't put it on expense. Pay it yourself."

"But—but, sir—Archie always brings people here—"

"Pay it yourself. You are not Archie. Thank God. One Archie is enough. I sent you to get facts, not Miss Tracy—certainly I didn't send you to coerce her with preposterous threats and fables about my relations with the police. Go to the kitchen—no. Go home."

"But, sir—"

"Go home. And for God's sake quit trying to imitate Archie. You'll never make it. Go home."

Johnny went.

Wolfe asked the guests if they would like some beer and they shook their heads. He poured a glass for himself, drank some, wiped his lips, and leaned back.

"Then—" Anne began, but it got caught on the way out. She cleared her throat and swallowed, and tried again. "Then what he said—you said his threat was preposterous. You mean the police won't do that—won't arrest my father?"

"I couldn't say, Miss Tracy. The police are unpredictable. Even so, that is highly improbable." Wolfe's eyes left her. "And you, Mr. Updegraff? By what bold stroke did Mr. Keems bring you along?"

"He didn't bring me." Fred stood up. "I came."

"By pure coincidence? Or automatism?"

Fred moved forward and put a hand on the back of my chair, which Anne was still sitting in. "I'm protecting Miss Tracy."

"Oh. From what?"

"From everything," he said firmly. He appeared to have a tendency to talk too loud, and he looked more serious than ever, and the more serious he looked the younger he looked. At that moment he might even have passed for Anne's younger brother, which was okay, since I had no objection if she wanted to be a sister to him.

"That's quite a job," Wolfe said. "Are you a friend of hers?"

"I'm more than a friend!" Fred declared defiantly. Suddenly he got as red as a peony. "I mean I—she let me take her home."

"You were there when Mr. Keems arrived?"

"Yes. We had just got there. And I insisted on coming along. It sounded to me like a frame-up. I thought he was lying; I didn't think he was working for you. It didn't sound—I've heard my father talk about you. He met you once—you probably don't remember—"

Wolfe nodded. "At the Atlantic States Exposition. How is he?"

"Oh, he's—not very good." Fred's color was normal again. "He gave up when we lost the plantation of rhodaleas—he just sat down and quit. He had spent his whole life on it, and of course it was an awful wallop financially, too. I suppose you know about it."

"I read of it, yes. The Kurume yellows." Wolfe was sympathetic but casual. "And by the way, someone told me, I forget who, that your father was convinced that his plantation was deliberately infected by Lewis Hewitt, out of pique—or was it Watson or Dill he suspected?"

"He suspected all of them." Fred looked uncomfortable. "Everybody. But that was just—he was hardly responsible, it broke him up so. He had been holding back over thirty varieties, the best ones, for ten years, and was going to start distribution this spring. It was simply too much for Dad to take."

Wolfe grunted. "It seems to be still on your mind, too. Mr. Goodwin tells me you invaded Rucker and Dill's exhibit this afternoon and made off with an infected twig. As a souvenir?"

"I—" Fred hesitated. "I guess that was dumb. Of course it's still on my mind—it darned near ruined us. I wanted to test that twig and see if it was Kurume yellows that had somehow got into the exhibits."

"And investigate the how?"

"I might have. I might have tried to."

"You never traced the infection of your plantation?"

"No. We hadn't had a thing for two years from any of the people that had had Kurume yellows, except a few Ilex crenata as a gift from Hewitt, and they were from nowhere near his infected area and we had them half a mile from the rhodaleas." Fred gestured impatiently. "But that's old prunings. What I was saying, I didn't think you'd pull a trick like that on Miss Tracy." A look came into his eyes. "Now I can take her back home."

The look in his eye took me back to high school days. It was the hand-holding look. Flutter, my heart, bliss looms and ecstasy, I shall hold her little hand in mine! I looked at Anne with pride. A girl who could enkindle Lewis Hewitt to the extent of a black orchid and a dinner on Tuesday, and on Thursday foment the hand-holding hankering in a pure young peony-grower—a girl with a reach like that was something.

At that moment, I admit, she wasn't so overwhelming. She looked pretty dilapidated. She said to Wolfe, "I have to be at the District Attorney's office at ten in the morning. I said I would. I don't mind them asking me questions about that—what happened there today— but what I'm afraid of now, I'm afraid they'll ask me about my father. If they do, what am I going to say? Am I going to admit—" She stopped and her lip started to tremble and she put her teeth on it.

"You need a lawyer," Fred declared. "I'll get one. I don't know any in New York—"

"I do," Wolfe said. "Sit down, Mr. Updegraff." His eyes moved to Anne. "There's a bed here, Miss Tracy, and you'd better use it. You look tired. I doubt if the police will ask you about your father. If they do, don't answer. Refer them to Mr. Dill. They're much more apt to be inquisitive about your engagement to marry Mr. Gould."

"But I wasn't!"

"Apparently he thought you were."

"But he couldn't! He knew very well I didn't like him! And he—" She stopped.

"He what?"

"I won't say that. He's dead."

"Had he asked you to marry him?"

"Yes, he had."

"And you refused?"

"Yes."

"But you consented to perform that rustic charade at the Flower Show with him?"

"I didn't know he was going to be in it—not when Mr. Dill asked me to do it, about two months ago, when he first thought of it. It was going to be another man, a young man in the office. Then Mr. Dill told me Harry Gould was going to do it. I didn't like him, but I didn't want to object because I couldn't afford to offend—I mean Mr. Dill had been so kind about my father—not having him arrested and letting me pay it off gradually—"

"Call it kind if you want to," Fred blurted indignantly. "My lord, your father had worked for him for twenty years!"

Wolfe ignored him. "Was Mr. Gould pestering you? About marrying him?"

"Not pestering me, no. I was—" Anne bit her lip. "I just didn't like him."

"Had you known him long?"

"Not very long. I'm in the office and he was outside. I met him, I don't know, maybe three months ago."

"Did your father know him?"

She shook her head. "I don't think they ever met. Father was— had left before Harry came to work there. Harry used to work on the Hewitt estate on the other side of Richdale."

"So I understand. Do you know why he quit?"

"No, I didn't know him then."

"Have you any idea who killed him?"

"No," she said.

I lifted a brow, not ostentatiously. She said it too quick and she shaded it wrong. There was enough change in tempo and tone to make it at least ten to one that she was telling a whopper. That was bad. Up to that everything had been wholesome and straightforward, and all of a sudden without any warning that big fly plopped in the milk. I cocked an eye at Fred, and of course he hadn't caught it. But Wolfe had. His eyes had gone nearly shut.

He started after her. He kept it polite and friendly, but he went at her from every angle and direction. And for the second time that night he got the can sent back empty by a juvenile female. After a solid hour of it he didn't have even a hint of what it was she was keeping tucked away under her hair, whether it was a suspicion or a fact or a deduction she had made from a set of circumstances. Neither did I. But she was sitting on some kind of lid, and she was smart enough to see that Wolfe knew it and was trying to jostle her off.

It was half past one when Fred Updegraff looked at his watch and stood up again and said it was late and he would take Miss Tracy home.

Wolfe shook his head. "She's exhausted and it's twenty-five miles and there are no trains. She can sleep here. I want to speak to her in the morning before she goes to the District Attorney's office. Archie, will you please see that the north room is in order?"

That meant my room and my bed. Anne started to protest, but not with much spirit, and I went and got Fritz and took him upstairs with me to help change sheets and towels. As I selected a pajama suit for her from the drawer, tan with brown stripes, and put it on the turned down sheet, I reflected that things were moving pretty fast, considering that it was less than ten hours since she had first spoken to me and we never had actually been introduced. Fritz took my sheets and pillow and a blanket downstairs and I went up one flight to the plant rooms and cut three black orchids, one from each plant, and returned and put them in a vase on the bed table. Hewitt had given her one.

On my way downstairs I stopped at the door to the south room and listened. No sound. I tried the door; it was bolted on the inside. I knocked, not very loud. Rose's voice came:

"Who is it?"

"Clark Gable," I called. "Good night, Ruby."

In the lower hall I met Anne coming out of the office, escorted by Fritz. I suppose it would have been more genteel to take her up myself, but it would have been a temptation to get sentimental there among my own furniture, so I told her good night and let her go. In the office Wolfe was alone, in his chair with his arms folded and his chin down; evidently Fred had departed. I began taking cushions from the couch and tossing them into a corner, getting ready to fix my bed.

"Two of them," Wolfe growled.

"Two of what?"

"Women. Nannygoats."

"Not Anne. She's more like a doe. More like a gazelle."

"Bah."

"More like a swan." I flipped a sheet over the couch and tucked it in. "I put three black orchids at her bedside. One from each plant."

"I told Theodore to put them in the fumigating room."

"He did. That's where I found them." I spread the blanket. "I thought we might as well get all the pleasure we can out of them before they're returned to Hewitt."

"They're not going to be returned."

"Oh, I expect they are." I hung my coat and vest over a chair back and sat down to take off my shoes. "It seems a pity. Two girls up there in bed, and if you knew what they know, or probably what either one of them knows, you'd have it sewed up. Rose actually saw the murderer set the trap. I don't know what Anne saw or heard, but she sure does. It's a darned shame. With all your finesse . . ." I got my pants off. ". . . all your extraordinary gifts . . ." I removed my shirt. ". . . all your acknowledged genius, your supreme talent in the art of inquest . . ."

He got up and stalked from the room without a word. I called a cheery good night after him but heard no reply, and after performing a few bedtime chores such as bolting the front door, I laid me down to sleep.

I overdid it. With the house full of company, I intended to be up and about bright and early, but when something jangled my brain alive and I realized it was the phone ringing, I opened my eyes and glanced at my wrist and saw it was after eight o'clock. It was Saul Panzer on the phone calling from Salamanca. I put him through to Wolfe's room and was told by Wolfe that no record would be required, which was his polite way of telling me to hang up, so I did. A trip to Fritz in the kitchen got me the information that Wolfe already had his breakfast tray, and so did Anne and Rose. I washed and dressed in a hurry, returned to the kitchen for my morning refreshment of grapefruit, ham and eggs, muffins and coffee, and was finishing my second cup when the doorbell rang. Fritz was upstairs at the moment, so I went for it, and through the glass panel saw it was Inspector Cramer, unattended.

The situation had aspects. Rose might come trotting downstairs any minute, and if she chose the minute that Cramer was in the hall, that would be the last we would see of Rose. But any delay in opening up would make Cramer suspicious. I swung the door open.

"Law and order forever," I said cordially. "Come in."

"Nuts," he said, entering.

So for that incivility I let him hang up his hat and coat himself. By the time he had done that I had the door closed and was on the other side of him. He screwed up his face at me and demanded:

"Where is she?"

8

I GRINNED TO THE BEST OF MY ABILITY.

"Now wait a minute," I said in a grieved tone. "I've been up less than an hour and my brain's not warmed up. In the first place, how could I know she was married? In the second—"

He made a noise and moved. I moved, sort of backward. The maneuver ended with me covering the foot of the stairs, which was across the hall from the door to the office, and him pressing forward without actually touching me. There I stopped and he had to.

"I'm going up to see Wolfe," he said as if he meant it. "I am aware that he spends the morning with his goddam posies and refuses to come down before eleven o'clock. So I'm going up. Stand aside."

He moved again and we made contact (noun), but I merely held it. "This," I said, "is pretty damn silly. I didn't have to let you in and you know it, but I did. What do you think this is, the den of the White Slave King? This is Nero Wolfe's home, and there's his office where he receives callers, and for last year his income tax was eleven thousand four hundred and twelve dollars and eighty-three cents and he paid it last week. Do you remember what happened the time Purley took me down and charged me with interfering with an officer in the performance of his duty? Wasn't that a picnic?"

He swung on his heel and tramped into the office. I followed, and shut the door, and stayed between him and it until he had sat down. Then, knowing I could move at least twice as fast as he could, I went to my desk.

"Now," I inquired pleasantly, "where is who?"

He regarded me with a mean eye. "Last night," he said, "one of Wolfe's men took Anne Tracy from her home in Richdale. My man

covering the house recognized him and phoned in. I had a man out
front when they arrived here. Your man soon left, and so did the
Updegraff boy, later, but she hasn't left up to now. Where is she?"

So our little Rose was still safe. I locked my relief in my breast
and looked crestfallen.

"I guess it's your trick, Inspector," I admitted. "Miss Tracy is
upstairs in my bed. She spent the night there."

He got red. He's a terrible prude. "See here, Goodwin—"

"No no no no," I said hastily. "Rinse your mind out. I slept here
on the couch. And I doubt if she's in my bed at that, because she's
probably up and dressed. She has a date at the D.A.'s office at ten
o'clock, and it's nine thirty now."

"Then you admit she's here."

"Admit it? I'm proud of it."

"Where is she, up with Wolfe?"

"I don't know. I got up late. I just finished breakfast."

"Find out. Tell her the appointment at the D.A.'s office is off. I
want to see her as soon as I finish with you."

I plugged in the plant room extension and gave it a buzz. In a
minute Wolfe's voice was in my ear:

"Archie? It's about time. Get Mr. Hewitt—"

"Hold it," I put in. "Reporting bad luck. Inspector Cramer is sitting
here glaring at me. Johnny was spotted last night, and Miss Tracy is
not to go to the D.A.'s office because Cramer wants to see her as soon
as he gets through with me. He seems to be disgruntled about something."

"Does he know who slept in the south room?"

"I think not. I'm sure not."

"Very well. I'll attend to that. Miss Tracy is here with me. She
can go down whenever Mr. Cramer is ready for her. Get Mr. Hewitt
on the phone."

"Right out loud?"

"Certainly."

I disconnected and told Cramer, "Miss Tracy is up helping with
the orchids and will be available when wanted. Excuse me." I found
Hewitt's Long Island number and requested it, and finally got him via
two butlers and a secretary, and put him through to Wolfe. Then I
swiveled around and crossed my legs and clasped my hands back of
my head.

"Okay, Inspector. I'm disengaged for the moment. What shall we
talk about?"

"Murder."

"Fine. Any particular murder?"

Cramer took a cigar from his pocket and put it in his mouth and took it out again. He was controlling himself. "I hand it to you," he said. "For barefaced lying I'd play you on the nose. Up there yesterday. You didn't know anyone or anything. But—" He put the cigar back in his mouth. "But you've been hanging around there all week. Every day. And then a man gets murdered and there you are. You *and* Nero Wolfe."

I nodded sympathetically. "I admit it looks sinister. But as I told you yesterday, Wolfe sent me there to look at orchids."

"There were no orchids in the Rucker and Dill exhibit."

"No, but there was—you know what there was. You've seen her. And I'm only a man after all—"

"All right, clown it. Yesterday afternoon about twenty minutes past four you were seen by young Updegraff, with Wolfe and Lewis Hewitt, in the corridor back of the Rucker and Dill exhibit. What were you doing there?"

"Well." I hesitated. "If I told you I was pulling the string that fired the shot that killed Harry Gould, would you believe me?"

"No."

"Then I won't. We were walking from one place to another place."

"You didn't mention yesterday that you were in that corridor at that time."

"Excuse it. Oversight."

"Maybe. What were you saying to Ruby Lawson yesterday?"

"Ruby—?" I frowned. "Oh. Her. You mean after I told Purley she was a Chinese spy. I was trying to date her up. You see, looking at Miss Tracy so much had aroused—"

"I'll bet it had. Did you date her?"

"Yes."

"When is it?"

"Not is it, was it. She didn't keep it."

"That's too bad. What was in the note Miss Tracy's father gave you to take to her?"

"Now, Inspector," I said reprovingly. "I didn't write the note and it wasn't addressed to me."

"Had you met her father before?"

"Never. Didn't know him from Adam."

"Wasn't it peculiar that he entrusted a perfect stranger with an important message to his daughter at a time like that?"

"Not very. He saw me entering the office. People trust me on sight. It's my face, especially my eyes."

"I see. That talk Wolfe had to have with Lewis Hewitt. So important he had to have it then and there, murder or no murder."

Cramer chewed his cigar.

"Yes, sir," I said.

"So important he had to have you to take notes of it."

"Yes, sir."

"I'd like to see the notes you took."

I shook my head regretfully. "Sorry, confidential business. Ask Wolfe."

"I intend to. You won't show me the notes?"

"Certainly not."

"Very well. Now. Last but not least. Why did Wolfe send a man out to Richdale last night to get Anne Tracy?"

"Search me. I wasn't here when he sent him."

"Were you here when she came?"

"Yes."

"Well?"

I grinned at him. "When I was a kid out in Ohio we had a swell comeback for that. If someone said 'Well?' to you, you said, 'Enough wells will make a river.' Wasn't that a stunner?"

"You bet it was. Had Lewis Hewitt engaged Wolfe to arrange for payment to W. G. Dill of the amount Anne Tracy's father had stolen, and get a release?"

I stared at him. "By golly, that's an idea," I said enthusiastically. "That's pretty cute. Hewitt took her to dinner—"

The door opened and Fritz entered. I nodded at him.

"A young man," Fritz said, being discreet.

"Who?" I asked. "Don't mind the Inspector; he already knows everything in the world—"

Fritz didn't get a chance to tell me, because the young man came bouncing in. It was Fred Updegraff. He stopped in the middle of the room, saw Cramer, said, "Oh," looked at me and demanded:

"Where's Miss Tracy?"

I surveyed him disapprovingly. "That's no way to behave," I told him. "Inspector Cramer is grilling me. Go to the front room and wait your turn—"

"No." Cramer stood up. "Get Miss Tracy down here and I'll take her to the front room. I want to see her before I have a talk with Wolfe, and then we can all go to the D.A's office together.

"The hell we can," I remarked.

"The hell we can. Send for her."

I sent Fritz. He used the elevator, since a lady was involved. In the office you could hear it creaking and groaning up, and pretty soon it came down again and jolted to a stop. When Anne entered Fred looked at her the way a blind man looks at the sun. I hoped I wasn't that obvious, and anyway she wasn't very sunny. She tried to greet us with a kind of smile, but with the red-rimmed eyes and the corners of the mouth down it certainly wasn't the face that had stolen the show from a million flowers.

Cramer took her to the front room and shut the soundproof door behind him. I went to my desk and took advantage of this first chance to open the morning mail. Fred wandered around restlessly, looking at the titles of books on the shelves, and finally sat down and lit a cigarette.

"Am I in the way?" he asked.

"Not at all," I assured him.

"Because if I am I can wait outdoors. Only I got a little chilly. I've been out there since eight o'clock."

I abandoned the mail to swivel around and stare at him in awe.

"Good God," I said, stupefied. "You win." I waved a hand. "You can have her."

"Have her?" He flushed. "What are you talking about? Who do you think you are?"

"Brother," I said, "who I am can be left to the worms that eventually eat me, but I know who I am not. I am not a guy who swims the Hellespont, nor him who—he who flees the turmoil of battle to seek you know what on the silken cushions of Cleopatra's barge. I'm not the type—"

The phone rang and I put the receiver to my ear and heard Wolfe's voice: "Archie, come up here."

"Right away," I said, and arose and asked Fred, "Which do you want, whisky or hot coffee?"

"Coffee, if it's not—"

"Righto. Come with me."

I turned him over to Fritz in the kitchen and mounted the three flights to the plant rooms. It was a sunny day and some of the mats were drawn, but mostly the glass was clear, especially in the first two rooms, and the glare and blaze of color was dazzling. In the long stretch where the germinating flasks were, of course the glass was painted. Theodore Horstmann was there examining the flasks. I opened the door into the potting room, and after taking one step stopped and sniffed. My nose is good and I knew that odor. One glance at Wolfe there on his special stool, which is more like a throne, showed me that he was alive, so I dived across to the wall and grabbed the valve to turn it. It was shut tight.

"What's the matter?" Wolfe inquired peevishly.

"I smelled ciphogene. I still do."

"I know. Theodore fumigated those plants a little while ago and opened the door too soon. There's not enough to do any harm."

"Maybe not," I muttered, "but I wouldn't trust that stuff on top of the Empire State Building on a windy day." The door to the fumigating room was standing open and I glanced inside. The benches were empty, as well as I could tell in the half dark. It had no glass. The smell didn't seem any stronger inside. I returned to Wolfe.

"How's Mr. Cramer?" he asked. "Stewing?"

I looked at him suspiciously. His asking that, and the tone of his voice, and the expression on his face—any one would have been enough for me the way I knew him, and the three together made it so obvious that the only question was how he got that way.

I confronted him. "Which one did you crack?" I demanded. "Rose or Anne?"

"Neither," he replied complacently. "I had an hour's talk with Miss Lasher while you were still sleeping, and later some conversation with Miss Tracy. They still clutch their secrets. When Mr. Hewitt—"

"Then where did you lap up all the cream? What are you gloating about?"

"I'm not gloating." He cocked his massive head on one side and rubbed his nose with a forefinger. "It is true that I have conceived a little experiment."

"Oh, you have. Goody. Before or after Cramer carts us off to the D.A.'s office?"

Wolfe chuckled. "Is that his intention? Then it must be before. Is Miss Tracy with him?"

"Yes. The youthful Updegraff is in the kitchen. He's going to marry Anne provided your experiment doesn't land him in the coop for murder."

"I thought you were affianced to Miss Tracy."

"That's off. If I married her he'd stand around in front of the house and make me nervous. He's started it already."

"Well, that saves us the trouble of sending for him. Keep him. When Mr. Hewitt arrives send him up to me immediately. Go down and get Mr. Dill on the phone and put him through to me. On your way make sure that Miss Lasher is in her room and going to stay there and not have hysterics. Except for Mr. Dill, and Mr. Hewitt when he comes, don't disturb me. I have some details to work out. And by the way, do not mention ciphogene."

His tone and look of smug self-satisfaction were absolutely insufferable. Not only that, as I well knew, they were a sign of danger for everyone concerned. When he was in that mood God alone could tell what was going to happen.

I went back through the plant rooms to the door to the stairs with my fingers crossed.

9

IT WAS NEARLY AN HOUR LATER, 11:45, AND I WAS ALONE in the office, when the door to the front room opened and Anne and Cramer entered. She looked mad and determined, and Cramer didn't appear to be exactly exultant, so I gathered that no great friendship had burst its bud.

"Where's Updegraff?" Cramer asked.

"Upstairs."

"I want to see Wolfe."

I buzzed the house phone, got an answer, held a brief conversation, and told the Inspector:

"He says to come up. Hewitt and Dill are up there."

"I'd rather see him down here."

That irritated me, and anyway I was already jumpy, waiting for Wolfe's experiment to start exploding. "My God," I said, "you're fussy. On arrival you insist on going upstairs right through me or over me. Now you have to be coaxed. If you want him down here go up and get him."

He turned. "Come, Miss Tracy, please."

She hesitated. I said, "Fred's up there. Let's all go."

I led the way and they followed. I took the elevator because the stairway route went within ten feet of the door to the south room and Rose might pick that moment to sneeze.

I was half expecting to see one of the peony-growers tied up and the other three applying matches to his bare feet, but not at all. We single-filed through twenty thousand orchids in the four plant rooms and entered the potting room, and there they were in the fumigating room, with the lights turned on, chatting away like pals. In the potting room Theodore was sloshing around with a hose, washing old pots.

"Good morning, Mr. Cramer!" Wolfe called. "Come in!"

Theodore was so enthusiastic with the hose that spray was flying around, and we all stepped into the fumigating room. Fred and Dill were there, seated on the lower tier of a staggered bench, and Wolfe was showing Hewitt a sealed joint in the wall. He was leaning on the handle of an osmundine fork, like a giant shepherd boy resting on his staff, and was expounding with childish enthusiasm:

". . . so we can stick them in here and close the door, and do the job with a turn of the valve I showed you in the potting room, and go on with our work outside. Twice a year at the most we do the whole place, and we use ciphogene for that too. It's a tremendous improvement over the old methods. You ought to try it."

Hewitt nodded. "I think I will. I've been tempted to, but I was apprehensive about it, such deadly stuff."

Wolfe shrugged. "Anything you use is dangerous. You can't kill bugs and lice and eggs and spores with incense. And the cost of installation is a small item, unless you include a sealed chamber, which I would certainly advise—"

"Excuse *me*," Cramer said sarcastically.

Wolfe turned. "Oh, yes, you wanted to speak to me." He sidled around the end of a bench, sat down on a packing box, gradually giving it his weight, and kept himself upright with nothing to lean against, holding the osmundine fork perpendicular, with the handle-end resting on the floor, like Old King Cole with his scepter. He simpered at the Inspector, if an elephant can simper. "Well, sir?"

Cramer shook his head. "I want you and Goodwin and Miss Tracy. So does the District Attorney. At his office."

"You don't mean that, Mr. Cramer."

"And why the hell—why don't I mean it?"

"Because you know I rarely leave my home. Because you know that citizens are not obliged to regulate their movements by the caprice of the District Attorney or to dart around frantically at your whim. We've had this out before. Have you an order from a court?"

"No."

"Then if you have questions to ask, ask them. Here I am."

"I can get an order from a court. And the D.A. is sore and probably will."

"We've had that out before too. You know what you'll get if you try it." Wolfe shook his head regretfully. "Apparently you'll never learn. Confound you, you can't badger me. No one on earth can badger me except Mr. Goodwin. Why the devil do you rile me by trying it? It's a pity, because I'm inclined to help you. And I could help you. Do you want me to do you a favor?"

If the man who knew Wolfe best was me, next to me came Inspector Cramer. Over and over again through the years, he tried bluster because it was in his system and had to come out, but usually he knew when to drop it. So after narrowing his eyes at Wolfe without answering, he kicked a packing box a couple of feet to where there was more leg room, sat down and said calmly:

"Yeah, I'd love to have you do me a favor."

"Good. Archie, bring Miss Lasher up here."

I went. On my way downstairs I thought, so here she goes to the wolves. I didn't like it. I wasn't especially fond of her, but my pride was hurt. It wasn't like Wolfe; it wasn't like us at all.

She was standing looking out of a window, biting her nails. The minute she saw me she started on a torrent. She couldn't stand it any longer, cooped up like that, she had to get out of there, she had to use a telephone—

"Okay," I said, "come up and say good-bye to Wolfe."

"But where am I going—what am I going—"

"Discuss it with him."

I steered her up the one flight and through to the potting room. I had left the door to the fumigating room nearly closed so she couldn't see the assemblage until she was on the threshold, and as I opened it and ushered her in I took a better hold on her arm as a precaution in case she decided to go for Wolfe's eyes as souvenirs. But the reaction was the opposite of what I expected. She saw Cramer and went stiff. She stood stiff three seconds and then turned her head to me and said between her teeth:

"You lousy bastard."

They all stared at her.

Especially Cramer. Finally he spoke not to her but to Wolfe, "This is quite a favor. Where did you get her?"

"Sit down, Miss Lasher," Wolfe said.

"You might as well," I told her. "It's a party."

Her face white and her lips tight, she went and dropped onto a bench. The others were all sitting on benches or packing boxes.

"I told you this morning," Wolfe said, "that unless you told me what you saw in that corridor I would have to turn you over to the police."

She didn't say anything and didn't look as if she intended to.

"So your name's Lasher," Cramer growled. "You might as well—"

"I think," Wolfe put in, "I can save you some time. Details can be supplied later. Her name is Rose Lasher. Yesterday at the Flower Show she saw Miss Tracy and Mr. Gould in Mr. Dill's exhibit. She wished to discuss an extremely important matter with Miss Tracy, so—"

"With me?" It popped out of Anne. She looked indignant. "There was nothing she could possibly—"

"Please, Miss Tracy." Wolfe was peremptory. "This will go better without interruptions. So, to intercept Miss Tracy on her exit, Miss Lasher found her way to the corridor and hid among the shrubs and packing cases along the rear wall opposite the door labeled 'Rucker and Dill.' That was at or about half past three. She remained concealed there until after half past four, and she was watching that door. Therefore she must have seen whatever went on there during that hour or more."

There were stirrings and sounds, then silence, except for the hissing of Theodore's hose in the potting room and the slapping and sloshing of the water against the pots. Wolfe told me to shut the door, and I did so, and then sat on the bench next to W. G. Dill.

"Okay," Cramer said dryly, "details later. What did she see?"

"She prefers not to say. Will you tell us now, Miss Lasher?"

Rose's eyes moved to him and away again, and that was all.

"Sooner or later you will," Wolfe declared. "Mr. Cramer will see to that. He can be—persuasive. In the meantime, I'll tell you what you saw, at least part of it. You saw a man approach that door with a cane in his hand. He was furtive, he kept an eye on the corridor in both directions, and he was in a hurry. You saw him open the door and close it again, and kneel or stoop, doing something with his hands, and when he went away he left the cane there on the floor, its crook against the crack at the bottom of the door. You saw that, didn't you?"

Rose didn't even look at him.

"Very well. I don't know what time that happened, except that it was between four and four-twenty. Probably around four o'clock. The next episode I do know. At twenty minutes past four you saw three men come along the corridor. They saw the cane and spoke about it. One of them picked it up, brushed a loop of green string from the crook, and handed it to one of the others. I don't know whether you saw the string or not. I'm certain that you didn't know that it was part of a longer string that had been tied to the trigger of a revolver, and that by picking up the cane the man had fired the revolver and killed Harry Gould. Nor did you know their names, though you do now. Mr. Goodwin picked up the cane and handed it to Mr. Hewitt. The man with them was myself."

Wolfe took something from his vest pocket, with his left hand, because his right was holding the osmundine fork for support. "Here's the piece of string that was looped on the cane. Not that I would expect you to identify it. I may as well say here that the cane was handed to Mr. Hewitt because it was his property."

He handed the string to Cramer.

I was sunk. Ordinarily, in such circumstances, I would have been watching faces and movements, and hearing what sounds were made or words blurted, but this time he had me. He looked as if he was in his right mind, with all the assured arrogance of Nero Wolfe salting away another one, but either he was cuckoo or I was. He was not only spilling the beans; he was smashing the dish. In any conceivable case it was good-bye orchids. I looked at Hewitt.

And Hewitt should have been half astonished and half sore, and he wasn't. He was pale, and he was trying to pretend he wasn't pale. He was staring at Wolfe, and he licked his lips—the end of his tongue came out and went in, and then came out again.

Uh-uh, I thought. So that's it. But my God, then—

Cramer was looking at the string. W. G. Dill asked, "May I see it?" and held out a hand, and Cramer gave it to him but kept his eyes on it.

"Of course," Wolfe said, "the point is, not who picked the cane up, but who put it there. Miss Lasher, who saw him do it, could tell us but prefers not to. She claims she didn't see him. So we'll have to get at it by indirection. Here are some facts that may help—but it isn't any too comfortable in here. Shall we move downstairs?"

"No," Hewitt said. "Go ahead and finish."

"Go ahead," Cramer said. He reached for the string and Dill handed it to him and he stuffed it in his pocket.

"I'll make it as brief as possible," Wolfe promised. "Harry Gould had an employer. One day he found a garage job-card in one of his employer's cars—possibly it had slipped under a seat and been forgotten—I don't know. Anyhow he found it and he kept it. I don't know why he kept it. He may have suspected that his employer had been on a trip with a woman, for the card was from a garage in Salamanca, New York, which is quite a distance from Long Island. A man with the blackmailing type of mind is apt to keep things. It is understandable that he kept the card. It is less understandable that his employer had been careless enough to leave it in the car." Wolfe turned his head suddenly and snapped at Hewitt:

"Was it just an oversight, Mr. Hewitt?"

But Hewitt had stuff in him at that. He was no longer pale and he wasn't licking his lips. His eyes were steady and so was his voice:

"Finish your story, Mr. Wolfe. I am inclined—but no matter. Finish your story."

"I prefer to use your name instead of clumsy circumlocutions like 'his employer.' It's neater."

"By all means keep it neat. But I warn you that merely because I acknowledged ownership of that cane—"

"Thank you. I appreciate warnings. So I'll say Hewitt hereafter. The time came when Harry Gould's suspicions regarding the card became more definite. Again I don't know why, but my surmise is that he learned about the loss of the most valuable plantation of broad-leaved evergreens in the country—the rhodalea plantation of the Updegraff Nurseries of Erie, Pennsylvania—by an attack of the Kurume yellows. He knew that Hewitt was inordinately proud of his own broad-leaved evergreens, and that he was capable of abnormal extremes in horticultural pride and jealousy. He also, being a gardener, knew how easy it would be, with a bag or two of contaminated peat mulch, to infect another plantation if you had access to it. At any rate, his suspicion became definite enough to cause him to go to Salamanca, which is in the western part of New York near the Pennsylvania border, not far from Erie, and see the proprietor of the Nelson Garage. That was in December. He learned that when Hewitt had gone there with his car months before, damaged in an accident, he had been accompanied not by a woman, but by a man of a certain description, with a cast in his eye. He went to Erie and found the man among the employees of the Updegraff Nurseries. His name was Pete Arango."

Fred Updegraff started up with an ejaculation.

Wolfe showed him a palm. "Please, Mr. Updegraff, don't prolong this." He turned. "And Mr. Hewitt, I'm being fair. I'm not trying to stampede you. I admit that much of this detail is surmise, but the main fact will soon be established beyond question. I sent a man to Salamanca last night, partly to learn why Harry Gould had so carefully preserved an old garage job-card, and partly because he had written on the back of it that name Pete Arango, and I knew that Pete Arango was in the employ of the Updegraff Nurseries. My man phoned me this morning to say that he will be back here at one o'clock, and the proprietor of the Nelson Garage will be with him. He'll tell us whether you were there with Pete Arango. Do you suppose you'll remember him?"

"I'll—" Hewitt swallowed. "Go ahead."

Wolfe nodded. "I imagine you will. I wouldn't be surprised if Gould even got a written confession from Pete Arango that you had bribed him to infect the rhodalea plantation, by threatening to inform Mr. Updegraff that he had been at Salamanca, not far away, in your company. At least he got something that served well enough to put the screws on you. You paid him something around five thousand dollars. Did he turn the confession over to you? I suppose so. And then—may I hazard a guess?"

"I think," Hewitt said evenly, "you've done too much guessing already."

"I'll try one more. Gould saw Pete Arango at the Flower Show, and the temptation was too much for him. He threatened him again, and made him sign another confession, and armed with that made another demand on you. What this time? Ten thousand? Twenty? Or he may even have got delusions of grandeur and gone to six figures. Anyhow, you saw that it couldn't go on. As long as ink and paper lasted for Pete Arango to write confessions with, you were hooked. So you—by the way, Mr. Updegraff, he's up there at your exhibit, isn't he, and available? Pete Arango? We'll want him when Mr. Nelson arrives."

"You're damn right he's available," Fred said grimly.

"Good."

Wolfe's head pivoted back to Hewitt. He paused, and the silence was heavy on us. He was timing his climax, and just to make it good he decorated it.

"I suppose," he said to Hewitt in a tone of doom, "you are familiar with the tradition of the drama? The three traditional knocks to herald the tragedy?"

He lifted the osmundine fork and brought it down again, thumping the floor with it, once, twice, thrice.

Hewitt gazed at him with a sarcastic smile, and it was a pretty good job with the smile.

"So," Wolfe said, "you were compelled to act, and you did so promptly and effectively. And skillfully, because, for instance, Mr. Cramer has apparently been unable to trace the revolver, and no man in the world is better at that sort of thing. As Honorary Chairman of the Committee, naturally you had the run of the exhibit floors at any hour of the day; I suppose you chose the morning, before the doors were opened to the public, to arrange that primitive apparatus. I don't pretend to be inside of your mind, so I don't know when or why you decided to use your own cane as the homicide bait for some unsus-pecting passer-by. On the theory that—"

The door opened and Theodore Horstmann was on the threshold.

"Phone call for Mr. Hewitt," he said irritably. Theodore resented his work being interrupted by anything whatever. "Pete Arango or something."

Hewitt stood up.

Cramer opened his mouth, but Wolfe beat him to it by saying sharply, "Wait! You'll stay here, Mr. Hewitt! Archie—no, I suppose he would recognize your voice. Yours too, Mr. Cramer. Mr. Dill. You can do it if you pitch your voice low. Lead him on, get him to say as much as you can—"

Hewitt said, "That phone call is for me," and was moving for the door. I got in front of him. Dill arose, looking uncertain.

"I don't know whether I can—"

"Certainly you can," Wolfe assured him. "Go ahead. The phone is there on the potting bench. Theodore, confound it, let him by and come in here and close the door."

Theodore obeyed orders. When Dill had passed through Theodore pulled the door shut and stood there resenting us. Hewitt sat down again and put his elbows on his knees and covered his face with his hands. Anne had her head turned not to look at him. That made her face Fred Updegraff, who was next to her, and I became aware for the first time that he was holding her hand. Hardly as private as in a taxi, but he had her hand.

"While we're waiting," Wolfe observed, "I may as well finish my speculations about the cane. Mr. Hewitt may have decided to use it on the theory that the fact of its being his cane would divert suspicion away from him instead of toward him. Was that it, Mr. Hewitt? But in that case, why did you submit to my threat to divulge the fact that it was your cane? I believe I can answer that too. Because you mistrusted my acumen? Because you were afraid my suspicions would be aroused if you failed to conform to the type of the eminent wealthy citizen zealously guarding his reputation from even the breath of scandal? Things like that gather complications as they go along. It's too bad."

Wolfe looked at Hewitt, and shook his head as though regretfully. "But I have no desire to torment you. Theodore, try the door."

"I don't have to," Theodore said, standing with his back to the door. "I heard the bolt. The lower one squeaks."

I stood up. Not that there was anything I intended to do or could do, but I was coming to in a rush and I couldn't stay sitting. Cramer did, but his eyes, on Wolfe, were nothing but narrow slits.

"Try it anyway," Wolfe said quietly.

Theodore turned and lifted the latch and pushed, and turned back again. "It's bolted."

"Indeed," Wolfe said with a tingle in his voice. His head turned. "Well, Miss Lasher, what do you think of it?" His eyes swept the faces. "I ask Miss Lasher because she knew all along that I was lying. She knew it couldn't have been Mr. Hewitt who put that cane there on the floor of the corridor, because she saw Mr. Dill do it. Mr. Hewitt, let me congratulate you on a superb performance—you can't force it, Mr. Cramer, it's a sturdy door—"

Cramer was at it, lifting the latch, assaulting the panel with his shoulder. He turned, his face purple, blurted, "By God, I might have known—," jumped across and grabbed up a heavy packing-box.

"Archie!" Wolfe called sharply.

In all my long and varied association with Inspector Cramer I had never had an opportunity to perform on him properly. This, at last, was it. I wrapped myself around him like cellophane around a tooth-brush and turned on the pressure. For maybe five seconds he wriggled, and just as he stopped Fred Updegraff sprang to his feet and gasped in horror:

"Ciphogene! For God's sake—"

"Stop it!" Wolfe commanded. "I know what I'm doing! There is no occasion for panic. Mr. Cramer, there is an excellent reason why that door must not be opened. If Archie releases you, will you listen to it? No? Then, Archie, hold him. This is a fumigating room where we use ciphogene, a gas which will kill a man by asphyxiation in two minutes. The pipe runs from a tank in the potting room and the valve is in there. This morning I closed the outlet of the pipe in this room, and removed the plug from an outlet in the potting room. So if Mr. Dill has opened that valve in the potting room, he is dead, or soon will be. And if you batter a hole in that door I won't answer for the consequences. We might get out quickly enough and we might not."

"You goddam balloon," Cramer sputtered helplessly. It was the first and only time I ever heard him cuss in the presence of ladies.

I unwrapped myself from him and stepped back. He shook himself and barked at Wolfe:

"Are you going to just sit there? Are we going to just sit here? Isn't there—can't you call someone—"

"I'll try," Wolfe said placidly. He lifted the osmundine fork and thumped the floor with it, five times, at regular intervals.

Lewis Hewitt murmured, believe it or not, apparently to Theodore, "I was in the dramatic club at college."

10

"ALL RIGHT, I'LL BUY YOU A MEDAL," INSPECTOR Cramer said in utter disgust.

Five hours had passed. It was six thirty that evening, and the three of us were in the office. I was at my desk, Cramer was in the red leather chair, and Wolfe was seated behind his own desk, leaning back with his fingertips touching on top of his digestive domain. He looked a little creasy around the eyes, which were almost open.

Cramer went on sputtering: "Dill was a murderer, and he's dead, and you killed him. You maneuvered him into the potting room with a fake phone call, and he took the bait and bolted the door to the fumigating room and opened the valve. And then why didn't he walk out and go on home? How did you know he wouldn't do that?"

"Pfui," Wolfe said lazily. He grunted. "Without waiting four minutes to make sure the ciphogene had worked? And leaving the door bolted, and the valve open? Mr. Dill was a fool, but not that big a fool. After a few minutes he would have closed the valve and opened the door, held his nose long enough to take a look at us and make sure we were finished, and departed, leaving the door closed but not bolted to give it the appearance of an accident. And probably leaving the valve a bit loose so it would leak a little." Wolfe grunted again. "No. That wasn't where the thin ice was. It was next thing to a certainty that Mr. Dill wouldn't decamp without having a look inside at us."

"You were sure of that."

"I was."

"You admit it."

"I do."

"Then you murdered him."

"My dear sir." Wolfe wiggled a finger in exasperation. "If you are privately branding me to relieve your feelings, I don't mind. If you are speaking officially, you are talking gibberish. I could be utterly candid even to a jury, regarding my preparations. I could admit that I plugged the outlet in the fumigating room, and opened the one in the potting room, so that it would be the latter, and not the former, that would be filled with ciphogene if Mr. Dill bolted that door and opened that valve. I could admit that I arranged with Mr. Hewitt to play his part, appealing to him in the interest of justice. He is a public-spirited man. And I discovered his weakness; he has always wanted to be an actor. He even gave me permission to mention his cane, and to recite that wild tale about him—which of course was true, though not true about him, but about Mr. Dill.

"I could admit that I arranged with Theodore also to play his part. He works for me and obeyed orders. I could admit that I had Fritz stationed in the room below, and my three thumps on the floor were a signal to him to make the telephone call for Mr. Hewitt, and the five thumps, later, told him to come upstairs and start the ventilating blowers in the potting room, which can be done from the hall. I could admit that I deliberately postponed the second signal to Fritz for three minutes after I learned that the door had been bolted; that I had previously released a minute quantity of ciphogene in the potting room and fumigating room so that Mr. Dill's nose would be accustomed to the smell and would not take alarm at any sudden odor in the potting room after he turned on the valve; that all my arrangements were made with the idea that if Mr. Dill should open that valve, thinking to murder all eight of us, he would die. I could admit all that to a jury."

Wolfe sighed. "But the fact would remain that Mr. Dill opened the valve of his own volition, intending to exterminate eight people, including you. No jury would find against me even for damage to your self-esteem."

"To hell with my self-esteem," Cramer growled. "Why don't you send a bill to the State of New York for the execution of a murderer f.o.b. your potting room? That's the only thing you've left out. Why don't you?"

Wolfe chuckled. "I wonder if I could collect. It's worth trying. I may tell you privately, Mr. Cramer, that there were several reasons why it would have been unfortunate for Mr. Dill to be brought to trial. One, it might have been difficult to convict him. Only a fairly good case. Two, the part played by Mr. Hewitt's cane would have been made public, and I had undertaken to prevent that. Three, Archie would have been embarrassed. He pulled the trigger and killed the man. Four, Miss Lasher would have committed suicide, or tried to. She's not very bright, but she's stubborn as the devil. She had decided that if she admitted having seen anything from her hiding-place in the corridor, she would have to testify to it publicly, her relations with Mr. Gould would have been exposed, and her family would have been dishonored."

"They would have been exposed anyway."

"Certainly, once you got hold of her. When Archie brought her to the potting room, with you there, she was a goner. That was the beauty of it, Mr. Dill knew she was bound to crack, and that coupled with the threat of being confronted with the garage man was what cracked him. It was a delicate situation. Among many others was the danger that during my recital Miss Lasher might blurt out that it was Dill, not Hewitt, who had placed the cane there by the door, and that would have spoiled everything."

"Wasn't it Hewitt's cane?"

"Yes. A fact, as I have told you, not for publication."

"Where did Dill get it?"

"I don't know. Hewitt had mislaid it, and no doubt Dill spied it and decided to make use of it. By the way, another item not for publication is Miss Lasher's statement. Don't forget you promised that. I owe it to her. If she hadn't included that garage job-card when she packed Mr. Gould's belongings in her suitcase I wouldn't have got anywhere."

"And another thing," I put in. "A public airing of the little difficulty Miss Tracy's father got into wouldn't get you an increase in salary."

"Nothing in God's world would get me an increase in salary," Cramer declared feelingly. "And Miss Tracy's father—" He waved it away.

Wolfe's eyes came to me. "I thought you were no longer affianced to her."

"I'm not. But I'm sentimental about my memories. My lord, but she'll get sick of Fred. Peonies! Incidentally, while you're sweeping up, what was Anne's big secret?"

"Not so big." Wolfe glanced up at the clock, saw that it would be nearly an hour till dinner, and grimaced. "Miss Tracy admitted the soundness of my surmises this morning. Mr. Gould was as devious as he was ruthless. He told her that unless she married him he would force Mr. Dill to have her father arrested, and assured her that he had it in his power to do that. He also spoke of large sums of money. So naturally, when he was murdered Miss Tracy suspected that Mr. Dill was concerned in it, but she refused to disclose her suspicions for obvious reasons—the fear of consequences to her father."

Wolfe put his fingertips together again. "It is surprising that Mr. Gould lived as long as he did, in view of his character. He bragged to Miss Lasher that he was going to marry another girl. That was silly and sadistic. He let Miss Tracy know that he had a hold on Mr. Dill. That was rashly indiscreet. He even infected the Rucker and Dill exhibit with Kurume yellows, doubtless to dramatize the pressure he was exerting on Dill for his big haul—at least I presume he did. That was foolish and flamboyant. Of course Dill was equally foolish when he tried to engage me to investigate the Kurume yellows in his exhibit. He must have been unbalanced by the approaching murder he had arranged for, since bravado was not in his normal character. I suppose he had a hazy idea that hiring me to investigate in advance would help to divert suspicion from him. He really wasn't cut out for a murderer. His nerves weren't up to it."

"Yours are." Cramer stood up. "I've got to run. One thing I don't get, Dill's going clear to Pennsylvania to bribe a guy to poison some bushes. I know you spoke about extremes in horticultural jealousy, but have they all got it? Did Dill have it too?"

Wolfe shook his head. "I was then speaking of Mr. Hewitt. What Mr. Dill had was a desire to protect his investment and income. The prospect of those rhodaleas appearing on the market endangered the biggest department of his business." He suddenly sat up and spoke in a new tone. "But speaking of horticultural jealousy—I had a client, you know. I collected a fee in advance. I'd like to show it to you. Archie, will you bring them down, please?"

I was tired after all the hubbub and the strain of watching Wolfe through another of his little experiments, but he had said please, so I went up to the plant rooms and got them, all three of them, and brought them down and put them side by side on Wolfe's desk. He stood up and bent over them, beaming.

"They're absolutely unique," he said as if he was in church. "Matchless! Incomparable!"

"They're pretty," Cramer said politely, turning to go. "Kind of drab, though. Not much color. I like geraniums better."

That's the first of the two cases. That's how he got the black orchids. And what do you suppose he did with them? I don't mean the plants; it would take the lever Archimedes wanted a fulcrum for to pry one of those plants loose from him (just last week Cuyler Ditson offered him enough for one to buy an antiaircraft gun); I mean a bunch of the blossoms. I saw them myself there on a corner of the casket, with a card he had scribbled his initials on, "N. W." That was all.

I put this case here with the other one only on account of the orchids. As I said, it's a totally different set of people. If, when you finish it, you think the mystery has been solved, all I have to say is you don't know a mystery when you see one.

A. G.

CORDIALLY INVITED TO MEET DEATH

PART II

1

THAT WASN'T THE FIRST TIME I EVER SAW BESS HUD-dleston.

A couple of years previously she had phoned the office one afternoon and asked to speak to Nero Wolfe, and when Wolfe got on the wire she calmly requested him to come at once to her place up at Riverdale to see her. Naturally he cut her off short. In the first place, he never stirred out of the house except in the direction of an old friend or a good cook; and secondly, it hurt his vanity that there was any man or woman alive who didn't know that.

An hour or so later here she came, to the office—the room he used for an office in his old house on West 35th Street, near the river—and there was a lively fifteen minutes. I never saw him more furious. It struck me as an attractive proposition. She offered him two thousand bucks to come to a party she was arranging for a Mrs. Somebody and be the detective in a murder game. Only four or five hours' work, sitting down, all the beer he could drink, and two thousand dollars. She even offered an extra five hundred for me to go along and do the leg work. But was he outraged! You might have thought he was Napoleon and she was asking him to come and deploy the tin soldiers in a nursery.

After she had gone I deplored his attitude. I told him that after all she was nearly as famous as he was, being the most successful party-arranger for the upper brackets that New York had ever had, and a combination of the talents of two such artists as him and her would have been something to remember, not to mention what I could do in the way of fun with five hundred smackers, but all he did was sulk.

That had been two years before. Now, this hot August morning with no air conditioning in the house because he distrusted machinery, she phoned around noon and asked him to come up to her place at Riverdale right away. He motioned to me to dispose of her and hung up. But a little later, when he had gone to the kitchen to consult with Fritz about some problem that had arisen in connection with lunch, I looked up her number and called her back. It had been as dull as a blunt instrument around the office for nearly a month, ever since we had finished with the Nauheim case, and I would have welcomed even tailing a laundry boy suspected of stealing a bottle of pop, so I phoned and told her that if she was contemplating a trip to 35th Street I wanted to remind her that Wolfe was incommunicado upstairs with his orchid plants from nine to eleven in the morning, and from four to six in the afternoon, but that any other time he would be delighted to see her.

I must say he didn't act delighted, when I ushered her in from the hall around three o'clock that afternoon. He didn't even apologize for not getting up from his chair to greet her, though I admit no reasonable person would have expected any such effort after one glance at his dimensions.

"You," he muttered pettishly, "are the woman who came here once and tried to bribe me to play the clown."

She plopped into the red leather chair I placed for her, got a hand-kerchief out of her large green handbag, and passed it across her forehead, the back of her neck, and her throat. She was one of those people who don't look much like their pictures in the paper, because her eyes made her face and made you forget the rest of it when you looked at her. They were black and bright and gave you the feeling they were looking at you when they couldn't have been, and they made her seem a lot younger than the forty-seven or forty-eight she probably was.

"My God," she said, "as hot as this I should think you would sweat more. I'm in a hurry because I've got to see the Mayor about a Defense Pageant he wants me to handle, so I haven't time to argue, but your saying I tried to bribe you is perfectly silly. Perfectly silly! It would have been a marvelous party with you for the detective, but I had to get a policeman, an inspector, and all he did was grunt. Like this." She grunted.

"If you have come, madam, to—"

"I haven't. I don't want you for a party this time. I wish I did. Someone is trying to ruin me."

"Ruin you? Physically, financially—"

"Just ruin me. You know what I do. I do parties—"

"I know what you do," Wolfe said curtly.

"Very well. My clients are rich people and important people, at least they think they're important. Without going into that, they're important to me. So what do you suppose the effect would be—wait, I'll show it to you—"

She opened her handbag and dug into it like a terrier. A small bit of paper fluttered to the floor, and I stepped across to retrieve it for her, but she darted a glance at it and said, "Don't bother, wastebasket," and I disposed of it as indicated and returned to my chair.

Bess Huddleston handed an envelope to Wolfe. "Look at that. What do you think of that?"

Wolfe looked at the envelope, front and back, took from it a sheet of paper which he unfolded and looked at, and passed them over to me.

"This is confidential," Bess Huddleston said.

"So is Mr. Goodwin," Wolfe said dryly.

I examined the exhibits. The envelope, stamped and postmarked and slit open, was addressed on a typewriter:

Mrs. Jervis Horrocks,
902 East 74th Street,
New York City.

The sheet of paper said, also typewritten:

Was it ignorance or something else that caused Dr. Brady to prescribe the wrong medicine for your daughter? Ask Bess Huddleston. She can tell you if she will. She told me.

There was no signature. I handed the sheet and envelope back to Wolfe.

Bess Huddleston used her handkerchief on her forehead and throat again. "There was another one," she said, looking at Wolfe but her eyes making me feel she was looking at me, "but I haven't got it. That one, as you see, is postmarked Tuesday, August 12th, six days ago. The other one was mailed a day earlier, Monday, the 11th, a week ago today. Typewritten, just like that. I've seen it. It was sent to a very rich and prominent man, and it said—I'll repeat it. It said: 'Where and with whom does your wife spend most of her afternoons? If you knew you would be surprised. My authority for this is Bess Huddleston. Ask her.' The man showed it to me. His wife is one of my best—"

"Please." Wolfe wiggled a finger at her. "Are you consulting me or hiring me?"

"I'm hiring you. To find out who sent those things."

"It's a mean kind of a job. Often next to impossible. Nothing but greed could induce me to tackle it."

"Certainly." Bess Huddleston nodded impatiently. "I know how to charge too. I expect to get soaked. But where will I be if this isn't stopped and stopped quick?"

"Very well. Archie, your notebook."

I got it out and got busy. She reeled it off to me while Wolfe rang for beer and then leaned back and closed his eyes. But he opened one of them halfway when he heard her telling me about the stationery and the typewriter. The paper and envelopes of both the anonymous letters, she said, were the kind used for personal correspondence by a girl who worked for her as her assistant in party-arranging, named Janet Nichols; and the letters and envelopes had been typed on a typewriter that belonged to Bess Huddleston herself which was used by another girl who worked for her as her secretary, named Maryella Timms. Bess Huddleston had done no comparing with a magnifying glass, but it looked like the work of that typewriter. Both girls lived with her in her house at Riverdale, and there was a large box of that stationery in Janet Nichols' room.

Then if not one of the girls—one of the girls? Wolfe muttered, "Facts, Archie." Servants? No use to bother about the servants, Bess Huddleston said; no servant ever stayed with her long enough to develop a grudge. I passed it with a nod, having read about the alligators and bears and other disturbing elements in newspaper and magazine pieces. Did anyone else live in the house? Yes, a nephew, Lawrence Huddleston, also on the payroll as an assistant party-arranger, but, according to Aunt Bess, not on any account to be suspected. That all? Yes. Any persons sufficiently intimate with the household to have had access to the typewriter and Janet Nichols' stationery?

Certainly, as possibilities, many people.

Wolfe grunted impolitely. I asked, for another fact, what about the insinuations in the anonymous letters? The wrong medicine and the questionable afternoons? Bess Huddleston's black eyes snapped at me. She knew nothing about those things. And anyway, they were irrelevant. The point was that some malicious person was trying to ruin her by spreading hints that she was blabbing guilty secrets about people, and whether the secrets happened to be true or not had nothing to do with it. Okay, I told her, forget about where Mrs. Rich Man spends her afternoons, maybe at the ball game, but as a matter of record did Mrs. Jervis Horrocks have a daughter, and had she been sick, and had Dr. Brady attended her? Yes, Bess Huddleston said impatiently, Mrs. Horrocks' daughter had died a month ago and Dr. Brady had been her doctor. Died of what? Tetanus. How had she got tetanus? By scratching her arm on a nail in a riding-academy stable.

Wolfe muttered, "There is no wrong medicine—"

"It was terrible," Bess Huddleston interrupted, "but it has nothing to do with this. I'm going to be late for my appointment with the Mayor. This is perfectly simple. Someone wanted to ruin me and conceived this filthy way of doing it, that's all. It has to be stopped, and if you're as smart as you're supposed to be, you can stop it. Of course, I ought to tell you, I know who did it."

I cocked my head at her. Wolfe's eyes opened wide. "What? You know?"

"Yes, I think I know. No, I do know."

"Then why, madam, are you annoying me?"

"Because I can't prove it. And she denies it."

"Indeed." Wolfe shot a sharp glance at her. "You seem to be less intelligent than you look. If, having no proof, you charged her with it."

"Did I say I charged her with it? I didn't. I discussed it with her, and also with Maryella, and my nephew, and Dr. Brady, and my brother. I asked them questions. I saw I couldn't handle it. So I came to you."

"By elimination—the culprit is Miss Nichols."

"Yes."

Wolfe was frowning. "But you have no proof. What do you have?"

"I have—a feeling."

"Pfui. Based on what?"

"I know her."

"You do." Wolfe continued to frown, and his lips pushed out, once, and in again. "By divination? Phrenology? What specific revelations of her character have you observed? Does she pull chairs from under people?"

"Cut the glitter," Bess Huddleston snapped, frowning back at him. "You know quite well what I mean. I say I know her, that's all. Her eyes, her voice, her manner—"

"I see. Flatly, you don't like her. She must be either remarkably stupid or extremely clever, to have used her own stationery for anonymous letters. Had you thought of that?"

"Certainly. She is clever."

"But knowing she did this, you keep her in your employ, in your house?"

"Of course I do. If I discharged her, would that stop her?"

"No. But you say you think her guilty because you know her. That means you knew a week ago, a month ago, a year ago that she was the sort of person who would do this sort of thing. Why didn't you get rid of her?"

"Because I—" Bess Huddleston hesitated. "What difference does that make?" she demanded.

"It makes a big difference to me, madam. You've hired me to investigate the source of those letters. I am doing so now. I am considering the possibility that you sent them yourself."

Her eyes flashed at him. "I? Nonsense."

"Then answer me." Wolfe was imperturbable. "Since you knew what Miss Nichols was like, why didn't you fire her?"

"Because I needed her. She's the best assistant I've ever had. Her ideas are simply . . . take the Stryker dwarf and giant party . . . that was her idea . . . this is confidential . . . some of my biggest successes . . ."

"I see. How long has she worked for you?"

"Three years."

"Do you pay her adequately?"

"Yes. I didn't, but I do now. Ten thousand a year."

"Then why does she want to ruin you? Just cussedness? Or has she got it in for you?"

"She has—she thinks she has a grievance."

"What about?"

"Something . . ." Bess Huddleston shook her head. "That's of no importance. A private matter. It wouldn't help you any. I am willing to pay your bill for finding out who sent those letters and getting proof."

"You mean you will pay me for fastening the guilt on Miss Nichols."

"Not at all. On whoever did it."

"No matter who it is?"

"Certainly."

"But you're sure it's Miss Nichols."

"I am not sure. I said I have a feeling." Bess Huddleston stood up and picked up her handbag from Wolfe's desk. "I have to go. Can you come up to my place tonight?"

"No. Mr.—"

"When can you come?"

"I can't. Mr. Goodwin can go—" Wolfe stopped himself. "No. Since you have already discussed it with all of those people, I'd like to see them. First the young women. Send them down here. I'll be free at six o'clock. This is a nasty job and I want to get it over with."

"My God," Bess Huddleston said, her eyes snapping at him, "you would have made a wonderful party! If I could sell it to the Crowthers I could make it four thousand—only there won't be many more parties for me if we don't get these letters stopped. I'll phone the girls—"

"Here's a phone," I said.

She made the call, gave instructions to one she called Maryella, and departed in a rush.

When I returned to the office after seeing the visitor to the door, Wolfe was out of his chair. There was nothing alarming about that, since it was one minute to four and therefore time for him to go up to the orchids, but what froze me in my tracks was the sight of him stooping over, actually bending nearly double, with his hand in my wastebasket.

He straightened up.

"Did you hurt yourself?" I inquired anxiously.

Ignoring that, he moved nearer the window to inspect an object he held between his thumb and forefinger. I stepped over and he handed it to me and I took a squint at it. It was a snapshot of a girl's face, nothing special to my taste, trimmed off so it was six-sided in shape and about the size of a half dollar.

"Want it for your album?" I asked him.

He ignored that too. "There is nothing in the world," he said, glaring at me as if I had sent him an anonymous letter, "as indestructible as human dignity. That woman makes money killing time for fools. With it she pays me for rooting around in mud. Half of my share goes for taxes which are used to make bombs to blow people to pieces. Yet I am not without dignity. Ask Fritz, my cook. Ask Theodore, my gardener. Ask you, my—"

"Right hand."

"No."

"Prime minister."

"No."

"Pal."

"No!"

"Accomplice, flunkey, Secretary of War, hireling, comrade . . ."
He was on his way out to the elevator. I tossed the snapshot onto my desk and went to the kitchen for a glass of milk.

2   "YOU'RE LATE," I TOLD THE GIRLS REPROACHFULLY AS I showed them into the office. "Mr. Wolfe supposed you would be here at six o'clock, when he comes down from the plant rooms, and it's twenty after. Now he's gone to the kitchen and started operations on some corned beef hash."

They were sitting down and I was looking them over.

"You mean he's eating corned beef hash?" Maryella Timms asked.

"No. That comes later. He's concocting it."

"It's my fault," Janet Nichols said. "I didn't get back until after five, and I was in riding clothes and had to change. I'm sorry."

She didn't look much like a horseback rider. Not that she was built wrong, she had a fairly nice little body, with good hips, but her face was more of a subway face than a bridle-path face. Naturally I had been expecting something out of the ordinary, one way or another, since according to Bess Huddleston she was an anonymous letter writer and had thought up the Stryker dwarf and giant party, and to tell the truth I was disappointed. She looked more like a school teacher—or maybe it would be more accurate to say that she looked like what a school teacher looks like before the time comes that she absolutely looks like a school teacher and nothing else.

Maryella Timms, on the other hand, was in no way disappointing, but she was irritating. Her hair started far back above the slant of her brow, and that made her brow look even higher and broader than it was, and noble and spiritual. But her eyes were very demure, which didn't fit. If you're noble and spiritual you don't have to be demure. There's no point in being demure unless there's something on your mind to be demure about. Besides, there was her accent. Cawned beef ha-a-sh. I am not still fighting the Civil War, and anyway my side won, but these Southern belles—if it sounds like a deliberate come-on to me then it does. I was bawn and braht up in the Nawth.

"I'll see if I can pry him loose," I said, and went to the hall and through to the kitchen.

The outlook was promising for getting Wolfe to come and attend to business, because he had not yet got his hands in the hash. The mixture, or the start of it, was there in a bowl on the long table, and Fritz, at one side of the table, and Wolfe, at the other, were standing there discussing it. They looked around at me as I would expect to be looked at if I busted into a Cabinet meeting at the White House.

"They're here," I announced. "Janet and Maryella."

From the expression on his face as his mouth opened it was a safe bet that Wolfe was going to instruct me to tell them to come back tomorrow, but he didn't get it out. I heard a door open behind me and a voice floated past:

"Ah heah yawl makin' cawned beef ha-a-sh. . . ."

That's the last time I try to reproduce it.

The owner of the voice floated past me too, right up beside Wolfe. She leaned over to peer into the bowl.

"Excuse me," she said, which I couldn't spell the way she said it anyhow, "but corned beef hash is one of my specialties. Nothing in there but meat, is there?"

"As you see," Wolfe grunted.

"It's ground too fine," Maryella asserted.

Wolfe scowled at her. I could see he was torn with conflicting emotions. A female in his kitchen was an outrage. A woman criticizing his or Fritz's cooking was an insult. But corned beef hash was one of life's toughest problems, never yet solved by anyone. To tone down the corned flavor and yet preserve its unique quality, to remove the curse of its dryness without making it greasy—the theories and experiments had gone on for years. He scowled at her, but he didn't order her out.

"This is Miss Timms," I said. "Mr. Wolfe. Mr. Brenner. Miss Nichols is in—"

"Ground too fine for what?" Wolfe demanded truculently. "This is not a tender fresh meat, with juices to lose—"

"Now you just calm down." Maryella's hand was on his arm. "It's not ruined, only it's better if its coarser. That's far too much potatoes for that meat. But if you don't have chitlins you can't—"

"Chitlins!" Wolfe bellowed.

Maryella nodded. "Fresh pig chitlins. That's the secret of it. Fried shallow in olive oil with onion juice—"

"Good heavens!" Wolfe was staring at Fritz. "I never heard of it. It has never occurred to me. Fritz? Well?"

Fritz was frowning thoughtfully. "It might go," he conceded. "We can try it. As an experiment."

Wolfe turned to me in swift decision. "Archie, call up Kretzmeyer and ask if he has pig chitlins. Two pounds."

"You'd better let me help," Maryella said. "It's sort of tricky. . . ."

That was how I came to get so well acquainted with Janet that first day. I thought I might as well have company driving down to the market for chitlins, and Maryella was glued to Wolfe, and as far as that's concerned Wolfe was glued to her for the duration of the experiment, so I took Janet along. By the time we got back to the house I had decided she was innocent in more ways than one, though I admit that didn't mean much, because it's hard for me to believe that anyone not obviously a hyena could pull a trick like anonymous letters. I also admit there wasn't much sparkle to her, and she seemed to be a little absent-minded when it came to conversation, but under the circumstances that wasn't surprising, if she knew why she had been told to go to Nero Wolfe's office, as she probably did.

I delivered the chitlins to the hash artists in the kitchen and then joined Janet in the office. I had been telling her about orchid hybridizing on the way back uptown, and when I went to my desk to get a stack of breeding cards I was going to show her, I noticed something was missing. So I gave her the cards to look at and excused myself and returned to the kitchen, and asked Wolfe if anyone had been in the office during my absence. He was standing beside Maryella, watching Fritz arrange the chitlins on a cutting board, and all I got was a growl.

"None of you left the kitchen?" I insisted.

"No," he said shortly. "Why?"

"Someone ate my lollipop," I told him, and left him with his playmates and returned to the office. Janet was sitting with the cards in her lap, going through them. I stood in front of her and inquired amiably:

"What did you do with it?"

She looked up at me. That way, with her head tilted up, from that angle, she looked kind of pretty.

"What did I—what?"

"That snapshot you took from my desk. It's the only picture I've got of you. Where did you put it?"

"I didn't—" Her mouth closed. "I didn't!" she said defiantly.

I sat down and shook my head at her. "Now listen," I said pleasantly. "Don't lie to me. We're comrades. Side by side we have sought the chitlin in its lair. The wild boar chitlin. That picture is my property and I want it. Let's say it fluttered into your bag. Look in your bag."

"It isn't there." With a new note of spunk in her voice, and a new touch of color on her cheeks, she was more of a person. Her bag was beside her on the chair, and her left hand was clutching it.

"Then I'll look in your bag." I started for her.

"No!" she said. "It isn't there!" She put a palm to her stomach. "It's here."

I stopped short, thinking for a second she had swallowed it. Then I returned to my chair and told her, "Okay. You will now return it. You have three alternatives. Either dig it out yourself, or I will, or I'll call in Maryella and hold you while she does. The first is the most ladylike. I'll turn my back."

"Please." She kept her palm against her stomach. "Please! It's my picture!"

"It's a picture of you, but it's not your picture."

"Miss Huddleston gave it to you."

I saw no point in denying the obvious. "Say she did."

"And she told you . . . she . . . she thinks I sent those awful letters! I know she does!"

"That," I said firmly, "is another matter which the boss is handling. I am handling the picture. It is probably of no importance except as a picture of the girl who thought up the Stryker dwarf and giant party. If you ask Mr. Wolfe for it he'll probably give it to you. It may even be that Miss Huddleston stole it; I don't know. She didn't say where she got it. I do know that you copped it from my desk and I want it back. You can get another one, but I can't. Shall I call Maryella?" I turned my head and looked like a man about to let out a yell.

"No!" she said, and got out of her chair and turned her back and went through some contortions. When she handed me the snapshot I tucked it under a paperweight on Wolfe's desk and then went to help her collect the breeding cards from the floor where they had tumbled from her lap.

"Look what you did," I told her, "mixed them all up. Now you can help me put them in order again. . . ."

It looked for a minute as if tears were going to flow, but they didn't. We spent an hour together, not exactly jolly, but quite friendly. I avoided the letter question, because I didn't know what line Wolfe intended to take.

When he finally got at it there was no line to it. That was after nine o'clock, when we assembled in the office after the hash and trimmings had been disposed of. The hash was okay. It was good hash. Wolfe had three helpings, and when he conversed with Maryella, as he did through most of the meal, he was not only sociable but positively respectful. There was an unpleasant moment at the beginning, when Janet didn't take any hash and Fritz was told to slice some ham for her, and Maryella told her resentfully:

"You won't eat it because I cooked it."

Janet protested that that wasn't so, she just didn't like corned beef.

In the office, afterwards, it became apparent that there was no love lost between the secretary and the assistant party-arranger. Not that either accused the other of writing the poison-pen letters; there were no open hostilities, but a few glances I observed when I looked up from my notebook, and tones of voice when they addressed each other, sounded as if there might be quite a blaze if somebody touched a match to it. Wolfe didn't get anything, as far as I could see, except a collection of unimportant facts. Both the girls were being discreet, to put it mildly. Bess Huddleston, according to them, was a very satisfactory employer. They admitted that her celebrated eccentricities made things difficult sometimes, but they had no kick coming. Janet had worked for her three years, and Maryella two, and they hadn't the slightest idea who could have sent those dreadful letters, and Bess Huddleston had no enemies that they knew of . . . oh, of course, she had hurt some people's feelings, but what did that amount to, and there were scores of people who could have got at Janet's stationery during the past months but they couldn't imagine who, and so forth and so on. Yes, they had known Mrs. Jervis Horrocks' daughter, Helen; she had been a close friend of Maryella's. Her death had been a shock. And yes, they knew Dr. Alan Brady quite well. He was fashionable and successful and had a wonderful reputation for his age. He often went horseback riding with one of them or with Bess Huddleston. Riding academy? No, Bess Huddleston kept horses in her stable at her place at Riverdale, and Dr. Brady would come up from the Medical Center when he got through in the afternoon—it was only a ten-minute drive.

And Bess Huddleston had never been married, and her brother Daniel was some kind of a chemist, not in society, very much not, who showed up at the house for dinner about once a week; and her nephew, Larry, well, there he was, that was all, a young man living there and getting paid for helping his aunt in her business; and there were no other known relatives and no real intimates, except that Bess Huddleston had hundreds of intimates of both sexes and all ages. . . .

It went on for nearly two hours.

After seeing them out to their car—I noticed Maryella was driving—I returned to the office and stood and watched Wolfe down a glass of beer and pour another one.

"That picture of the culprit," I said, "is there under your paper-weight if you want it. She did. I mean she wanted it. In my absence she swiped it and hid it in a spot too intimate to mention in your presence. I got it back—no matter how. I expected her to ask you for it, but she didn't. And if you think you're going to solve this case by—"

"Confound the case." Wolfe sighed clear to the beer he had swallowed. "I might have known better. Tomorrow go up there and look around. The servants, I suppose. Make sure of the typewriter. The nephew. Talk with him and decide if I must see him; if so, bring him. And get Dr. Brady here. After lunch would be best."

"Sure," I said sarcastically.

"Around two o'clock. Please get your notebook and take a letter. Get it off tonight, special delivery. To Professor Martingale at Harvard. Dear Joseph. I have made a remarkable discovery, comma, or rather, comma, have had one communicated to me. You may remember our discussion last winter regarding the possibility of using pig chitlins in connection with . . ."

3   Ever since an incident that occurred when Wolfe sent me on an errand in February, 1935, I automatically ask myself, when leaving the office on a business chore, do I take a gun? I seldom do; but if I had done so that Tuesday afternoon I swear I would have found use for it. As sure as my name is Archie and not Archibald, I would have shot that goddam orangoutang dead in his tracks.

Formerly it took a good three-quarters of an hour to drive from 35th Street to Riverdale, but now, with the West Side Highway and the Henry Hudson Bridge, twenty minutes was ample. I had never seen the Huddleston place before, but since I read newspapers and magazines the trick fence was no surprise to me. I parked the roadster at a wide space on the drive which ran parallel with the fence, got a gate open and went through, and started up a path across the lawn towards the house. There were trees and bushes around, and off to the right an egg-shaped pool.

About twenty paces short of the house I suddenly stopped. I don't know where he had appeared from, but there he was straddling the path, big and black, his teeth flashing in a grin if you want to call it that. I stood and looked at him. He didn't move. I thought to myself, nuts, and moved forward, but when I got closer he made a certain kind of a noise and I stopped again. Okay, I thought, if this is your private path why didn't you say so, and I sashayed off to the right, seeing there was another path the other side of the pool. I didn't actually turn but went sort of sidewise because I was curious to see what he was going to do, and what he did was stalk me, on all fours. So it happened that my head was twisted to keep an eye on him when I backed into a log there on the grass at the edge of the pool and went down flat, nearly tumbling into the water, and when I sprang to my feet again the log was crawling along the ground lengthwise towards me. It was one of the alligators. The orangoutang was sitting down laughing. I don't mean he was making a laughing noise, but by his face he was laughing. That's when I would have shot him. I circled around the pool and got to the other path and headed for the house, but there he was, straddling the path ten yards ahead of me, making the noise again, so I stopped.

A man's voice said, "He wants to play tag."

I had been too preoccupied to see the man, and anyway he had just stepped from behind a shrub at the end of a terrace. With a glance I saw that he was clad in a green shirt and brick-colored slacks, was about my age or a little younger, and seemed to be assuming a supercilious attitude.

He said, "He wants to play tag."

I said, "I don't."

He said, "If you offend him he'll bite you. Start past him on the grass and dodge when he goes to touch you. Dodge three times and then let him tag you, and say 'Mister' in an admiring voice. That's all. His name is Mister."

"I could turn around and go home."

"I wouldn't try that. He would resent it."

"I could sock him one."

"You might. I doubt it. If you hurt him and my aunt ever catches you . . . I suppose you're Archie Goodwin? I'm Larry Huddleston. I didn't send those letters and don't know who did or who might. My aunt will be down later, she's upstairs arguing with Brother Daniel. I can't invite you in until you get past Mister."

"Does everyone who comes here have to play tag with this damn overgrown orangoutang?"

"He's not an orangoutang; he's a chimpanzee. He doesn't often play with strangers. It means he likes you."

I had to go through with it. I took to the grass, was intercepted, dodged three times, said 'Mister' in as admiring a tone of voice as I could manage, and was by. Mister emitted a little squeal and scampered off to a tree and bounded up to a limb. I looked at the back of my hand and saw blood. The nephew asked, not with great concern:

"Did he bite you?"

"No, I fell down and must have scratched it. It's just a scratch."

"Yeah, I saw you trip over Moses. I'll get you some iodine."

I said it wasn't worth bothering about, but he took me across the terrace into the house, into a large living room, twice as long as it was broad, with big windows and a big fireplace, and enough chairs and divans and cushions for a good-sized party right there. When he opened a cupboard door in the wall near the fireplace a shelf was disclosed with a neat array of sterilized gauze, band-aids, adhesive tape, and salve. . . .

As I dabbed iodine on the scratch I said, for something to say, "Handy place for a first-aid outfit."

He nodded. "On account of Mister. He never bites deep, but he often breaks somebody's skin. Then Logo and Lulu, sometimes they take a little nip—"

"Logo and Lulu?"

"The bears."

"Oh, sure. The bears." I looked around and then put the iodine bottle on the shelf and he closed the door. "Where are they now?"

"Having a nap somewhere. They always nap in the afternoon. They'll be around later. Shall we go out to the terrace? What'll you have, scotch, rye, bourbon?"

It was a nice spot, the terrace, on the shady side of the house, with large irregular flagstones separated by ribbons of turf. I sat there for an hour with him, but about all I got out of it was three highballs. I didn't cotton to him much. He talked like an actor; he had a green handkerchief in the breast pocket of his shirt, to match the shirt, he mentioned the Social Register three times in less than an hour; and he wore an hexagonal wrist watch, whereas there's no excuse for a watch to be anything but round. He struck me as barely bright enough for life's simplest demands, but I admit he might have been a darb at a party. I must say he didn't turn loose any secrets. He was pretty indignant about the letters, but about all I learned from him was that he knew how to use a typewriter, that Maryella had gone downtown on some errands, and that Janet was out horseback riding with Dr. Brady. He seemed to be a little cynical about Dr. Brady, but I couldn't get the slant.

When it got five o'clock and his aunt hadn't come down, he went to inquire, and in a moment returned and said I was to go up. He led me upstairs and showed me a door and beat it. I entered and found I was in an office, but there was no one there. It was a mess. Phone books were heaped on a chair. The blotters had been used since the Declaration of Independence. The typewriter wasn't covered. I was frowning around when I heard steps, and Bess Huddleston trotted in, with a skinny specimen behind her. His eyes were as black as hers, but everything else about him was shrunk and faded. As she breezed past me she said:

"Sorry. How are you. My brother. Mr. Goldwyn."

"Goodwin," I said firmly, and shook brother's hand. I was surprised to find he had a good shake. Sister was sitting at a desk, opening a drawer. She got out a checkbook, took a pen from a socket, made out a check, tried to blot it and made a smudge, and handed it to Brother Daniel. He took one look at it and said:

"No."

"Yes," she snapped.

"I tell you, Bess, it won't—"

"It will have to, Dan. At least for this week. That's all there is to it. I've told you a thousand times—"

She stopped, looked at me, and looked at him.

"All right," he said, and stuck the check in his pocket, and sat down on a chair, shaking his head and looking thoughtful.

"Now," Bess turned to me, "what about it?"

"Nothing to brag about," I told her. "There's a slew of fingerprints on that letter and envelope, but since you discussed it with your brother and nephew and the girls and Dr. Brady, I suppose they all handled it. Did they?"

"Yes."

I shrugged. "So. Maryella showed Mr. Wolfe how to make corned beef hash. The secret is chitlins. Aside from that, nothing to report. Except that Janet knows that you think she's it. Also she wanted that picture."

"What picture?"

"The snapshot of her you told me to throw in the wastebasket. It caught her eye and she wanted it. Is there any objection to her having it?"

"Certainly not."

"Is there anything you want to say about it? That might help?"

"No, that picture has nothing to do with it. I mean that wouldn't help you any."

"Dr. Brady was requested to call at our office at two o'clock today but was too busy."

Bess Huddleston went to a window and looked out and came back. "He wasn't too busy to come and ride one of my horses," she said tartly. "They ought to be back soon—I thought I heard them at the stable. . . ."

"Will he come to the house?"

"He will. For cocktails."

"Good. Mr. Wolfe told me to say that there is a remote chance there might be prints on the other letter. The one the rich man got."

"It isn't available."

"Couldn't you get it?"

"I don't think so."

"Has he turned it over to the police?"

"Good heavens, no!"

"Okay. I've played tag with Mister and had a talk with your nephew. Now if I could see where Janet keeps her stationery, and take a sample from that typewriter. Is that the one?"

"Yes. But first come to Janet's room. I'll show you."

I followed her. It was at the other end of the house, on that floor, one flight up, a pleasant little room and nice and neat. But the stationery was a washout. It wasn't in a box. It was in a drawer of a writing table with no lock on it, and all you had to do was open the drawer with a metal ring for a puller, which couldn't possibly have had a print, and reach in and take what you wanted, paper and envelopes both. Bess Huddleston left me there, and after a look around where there was nothing to look for, I went back to the office. Daniel was still there on the chair where we had left him. I ran off some sample lines on the typewriter, using a sheet of Janet's paper, and was putting it in my pocket when Daniel spoke:

"You're a detective."

I nodded. "That's what they tell me."

"You're finding out who sent those anonymous letters."

"Right." I snapped my fingers. "Just like that."

"Anyone who sends letters like that deserves to be immersed to the chin in a ten per cent solution of hydrofluoric acid."

"Why, would that be painful?"

Daniel shuddered. "It would. I stayed here because I thought you might want to ask me something."

"Much obliged. What shall I ask you?"

"That's the trouble." He looked dismal. "There's nothing I can tell you. I wish to God there was. I have no information to offer, even no suspicions. But I would like to offer a comment. Without prejudice. Two comments."

I sat down and looked interested. "Number one?" I said receptively.

"You can pass them on to Nero Wolfe."

"I can and will."

Daniel eyed me, screwing up his lips. "You mentioned five people to my sister just now. Her nephew, Larry—mine too—Miss Nichols and Miss Timms, Dr. Brady, and me. It is worth considering that four of us would be injured by anything that injured my sister. I am her

brother and I have a deep and strong affection for her. The young
ladies are employed by her and they are well paid. Larry is also well
paid. Frankly—I am his uncle—too well. But for his aunt, he might
earn four dollars a day as a helper on a coal barge. I know of no other
occupation that would not strain his faculties beyond their limit. But
the point is, his prosperity depends entirely on hers. So it is conceivable—I offer this merely as a comment—that we four may properly
be eliminated from suspicion."

"Okay," I said. "That leaves one."

"One?"

"Sure, Doc Brady. Of the five I mentioned, you rule out four.
Pointing straight at him."

"By no means." Daniel looked distressed. "You misunderstand me.
I know very little about Dr. Brady, though it so happens that my
second comment concerns him. I insist it is merely a comment. You
have read the letter received by Mrs. Horrocks? Then you have probably realized that while it purports to be an attack on Dr. Brady, it is
so manifestly absurd that it couldn't possibly damage him. Mrs. Horrocks' daughter died of tetanus. There is no such thing as a wrong
medicine for tetanus, nor a right one either, once the toxin has reached
the nerve centers. The antitoxin will prevent, but never, or very rarely,
will it cure. So the attack on Dr. Brady was no attack at all."

"That's interesting," I admitted. "Are you a doctor?"

"No, sir. I'm a research chemist. But any standard medical trea-
tise—"

"Sure. I'll look it up. What reason do you suppose Doc Brady
might have for putting your sister on the skids?"

"So far as I know, none. None whatever."

"Then that lets him out. With everyone else out, there's no one
left but your sister."

"My sister?"

I nodded. "She must have sent the letters herself."

That made him mad. In fact he rather blew up, chiefly because it
was too serious a matter to be facetious about, and I had to turn on
the suavity to calm him down. Then he went into a sulk. After fooling
around with him for another ten minutes and getting nothing for my
trouble, I decided to move on and he accompanied me downstairs and
out to the terrace, where we heard voices.

If that was a sample of a merry gathering arranged by Bess Huddleston, I'll roll my own, though I admit that isn't fair, since she hadn't
done any special arranging. She was lying on a porch swing with her
dress curled above her knees by the breeze, displaying a pair of bare

legs that were merely something to walk with, the feet being shod with high-heeled red slippers, and I don't like shoes without stockings, no matter whose legs they are. Two medium-sized black bears were sitting on the flagstones with their backs propped against the frame of the swing, licking sticks of candy and growling at each other. Maryella Timms was perched on the arm of a chair with her hand happening to rest on the shoulder of Larry Huddleston, who was sitting at careless ease in the chair the way John Barrymore would. Janet Nichols, in riding clothes, was in another chair, her face hot and flushed, which made her look better instead of worse as it does most people, and standing at the other end of the swing, also in riding clothes, was a wiry-looking guy with a muscular face.

When Bess Huddleston introduced us, Dr. Brady and me, I started to meet him halfway for the handshake, but I had taken only two and a half steps when the bears suddenly started for me as if I was the meal of their dreams. I leaped sideways half a mile in one bound and their momentum carried them straight on by, but as I whirled to face them another big black object shot past me from behind like a bat out of hell and I jumped again, just at random. Laughter came from two directions, and from a third Bess Huddleston's voice:

"They weren't after you, Mr. Goldwin, they smelled Mister coming and they're afraid of him. He teases them."

The bears were not in sight. The orangoutang jumped up on the swing and off again. I said savagely, "My name is Goolenwangel."

Dr. Brady was shaking my hand. He said with a laugh, "Don't mind her, Mr. Goodwin. It's a pose. She pretends she can't remember the name of anyone not in the Social Register. Since her entire career is founded on snobbery—"

"Snob yourself," Bess Huddleston snorted. "You were born to it and believe in it. With me it's business. But for heaven's sake let's not—Mister, you devil, don't you dare tickle my feet!"

Mister went right ahead. He already had the red slippers off, and, depositing them right side up on a flagstone, he proceeded to tickle the sole of her right foot. She screamed and kicked him. He tickled the other foot, and she screamed again and kicked him with that. That appeared to satisfy him, for he started off, but his next performance was unpremeditated. A man in a butler's jacket, approaching with a tray of glasses and bottles, had just reached the end of the swing when Mister bumped him, and bumped him good. The man yelled and lost control, and down went the works. Dr. Brady caught one bottle on the fly, and I caught another, but everything else was shattered on the stones. Mister went twenty feet through the air and landed in a chair and sat there and giggled, and the man was trembling all over.

"For God's sake, Haskell," Bess Huddleston said, "don't leave now, with guests coming for dinner. Go to your room and have a drink and lie down. We'll clean this up."

"My name is Hoskins," the man said in a hollow tone.

"So it is. Of course it is. Go and have a drink."

The man went, and the rest of us got busy. When Mister got the idea, which was at once, he waddled over to help, and I'll say this much for him, he was the fastest picker-up of pieces of broken glass I have ever seen. Janet went and came back with implements, among them a couple of brooms, but the trouble was that you couldn't make a comprehensive sweep of it on account of the strips of turf between the flagstones. Larry went for another outfit of drinks, and finally Maryella solved the problem of the bits of glass in the grass strips by bringing a vacuum cleaner. Bess Huddleston stayed on the swing. Dr. Brady carried off the debris, and eventually we got back to normal, everybody with a drink, including Mister, only his was nonalcoholic, or I wouldn't have stayed. What that bird would have done with a couple of Martinis under his fur would have been something to watch from an airplane.

"This seems to be a day for breaking things," Bess Huddleston said, sipping an old-fashioned. "Someone broke my bottle of bath salts and it splattered all over the bathroom and just left it that way."

"Mister?" Maryella asked.

"I don't think so. He never goes in there. I didn't dare ask the servants."

But apparently at the Huddleston place there was no such thing as settling down for a social quarter of an hour, whether Mister was drunk or sober, only the next disturbance wasn't his fault, except indirectly. The social atmosphere was nothing to brag about anyhow, because it struck me that certain primitive feelings were being felt and not concealed with any great success. I'm not so hot at nuances, but it didn't take a Nero Wolfe to see that Maryella was working on Larry Huddleston, that the sight of the performance was giving Dr. Brady the fidgets in his facial muscles, that Janet was embarrassed and trying to pretend she didn't notice what was going on, and that Daniel was absentmindedly drinking too much because he was worrying about something. Bess Huddleston had her ear cocked to hear what I was saying to Dr. Brady, but I was merely dating him to call at the office. He couldn't make it that evening, but tomorrow perhaps . . . his schedule was very crowded. . . .

The disturbance came when Bess Huddleston said she guessed she had better go and see if there was going to be any dinner or anyone to serve it, and sat up and put on her slippers. That is, she put one on; the second one, she stuck her foot in, let out a squeak, and jerked the foot out again.

"Damn!" she said. "A piece of glass in my slipper! Cut my toe!"

Mister bounced over to her, and the rest of us gathered around. Since Brady was a doctor, he took charge of matters. It didn't amount to much, a shallow gash half an inch long on the bottom of her big toe, but it bled some, and Mister started whining and wouldn't stop. Brother Daniel brought first-aid materials from the living room, and after Brady had applied a good dose of iodine he did a neat job with gauze and tape.

"It's all right, Mister," Bess Huddleston said reassuringly. "You don't—hey!"

Mister had swiped the iodine bottle, uncorked it, and was carefully depositing the contents, drop by drop, onto one of the strips of turf. He wouldn't surrender it to Brady or Maryella, but he gave it to his mistress on demand, after re-corking it himself, and she handed it to her brother.

It was after six o'clock, and I wasn't invited to dinner, and anyway I had had enough zoology for one day, so I said good-bye and took myself off. When I got the roadster onto the highway and was among my fellows again, I took a long deep breath of the good old mixture of gasoline and air and the usual odors.

When I got back to the office Wolfe, who was making marks on a big map of Russia he had bought recently, said he would take my report later, so, after comparing the type on my sample with that on the Horrocks letter and finding they were written on the same machine, I went up to my room for a shower and a change. After dinner, back in the office, he told me to make it a complete recital, leaving out nothing, which meant that he had made no start and formed no opinion. I told him I preferred a written report, because when I delivered it verbally he threw me off the track by making faces and irritating me, but he leaned back and shut his eyes and told me to proceed.

It was nearly midnight when I finished, what with the usual interruptions. When he's doing a complete coverage, he thinks nothing of asking such a question as, "Did the animal pour the iodine on the grass with its right paw or its left?" If he were a movable object and went places himself it would save me a lot of breath, but then that's what I get paid for. Partly.

He stood up and stretched, and I yawned. "Well," I asked offensively, "got it sewed up? Including proof?"

"I'm sleepy," he said, starting off. At the door he turned. "You made the usual quantity of mistakes, naturally, but probably the only one of importance was your failure to investigate the matter of the broken bottle in Miss Huddleston's bathroom."

"Pah," I said. "If that's the best you can do. It was not a bottle of anonymous letters. Bath salts."

"All the same it's preposterous. It's even improbable. Break a bottle and simply go off, leaving it scattered around? No one would do that."

"You don't know that orangoutang. I do."

"Not orangoutang. Chimpanzee. It might have done it, yes. That's why you should have investigated. If the animal did not do it, there's something fishy about it. Highly unnatural. If Dr. Brady arrives by eight fifty-nine, I'll see him before I go up to the plant rooms. Good night."

4 THAT WAS TUESDAY NIGHT, AUGUST 19TH. ON FRIDAY the 22nd Bess Huddleston got tetanus. On Monday the 25th she died. To show how everything from war to picnics depends on the weather, as Wolfe remarked when he was discussing the case with a friend the other day, if there had been a heavy rainfall in Riverdale between the 19th and 26th it would have been impossible to prove it was murder, let alone catch the murderer. Not that he showed any great—oh, well.

On Wednesday the 20th Dr. Brady came to the office for an interview with Wolfe, and the next day brother Daniel and nephew Larry came. About all we got out of that was that among the men nobody liked anybody. In the meantime, upon instructions from Wolfe, I was wrapping my tentacles about Janet, coaxing her into my deadly embrace. It really wasn't an unpleasant job, because Wednesday afternoon I took her to a ball game and was agreeably surprised to find that she knew a bunt from a base on balls, and Friday evening we went to the Flamingo Roof and I learned that she could dance nearly as well as Lily Rowan. She was no cuddler and a little stiff, but she went with the music and always knew what we were going to do. Saturday morning I reported to Wolfe regarding her as follows:

1. If she was toting a grievance against Bess Huddleston, it would take a smarter man than me to find out what it was.

2. There was nothing fundamentally wrong with her except that she would rather live in the country than the city.

3. She had no definite suspicion about who had sent the anonymous letters or anyone's motive for sending them.

Wolfe said, "Try Miss Timms for a change."

. I didn't try to date Maryella for Saturday or Sunday, because Janet had told me they were all going to Saratoga for the weekend. Monday morning, I thought, was no time to start a romance, so I waited until afternoon to phone, got Maryella, and got the news. I went up to the plant rooms, where Wolfe was a sight to behold in his undershirt, cutting the tops from a row of vandas for propagation, and told him:

"Bess Huddleston is dead."

"Let me alone," he said peevishly. "I'm doing all I can. Someone will probably get another letter before long, and when—"

"No, sir. No more letters. I am stating facts. Friday evening tetanus set in from that cut on her toe, and about an hour ago she died. Maryella's voice was choked with emotion as she told me."

Wolfe scowled at me. "Tetanus?"

"Yes, sir."

"That would have been a five thousand dollar fee."

"It would have been if you had seen fit to do a little work instead of—"

"It was no good and you know it. I was waiting for another letter. File it away, including the letter to Mrs. Horrocks, to be delivered to her on request. I'm glad to be rid of it."

I wasn't. Down in the office, as I checked over the folder, consisting of the Horrocks letter, the snapshot of Janet, a couple of reports I had made and some memos Wolfe had dictated, I felt as if I was leaving a ball game in the fourth inning with the score a tie. But it looked as if nothing could be done about it, and certainly there was no use trying to badger Wolfe. I phoned Janet to ask if there was anything I could do, and she told me in a weak tired voice that as far as she knew there wasn't.

According to the obit in the *Times* the next morning, the funeral service was to be Wednesday afternoon, at the Belford Memorial Chapel on 73rd Street, and of course there would be a big crowd, even in August, for Bess Huddleston's last party. Cordially invited to meet death. I decided to go. Not merely, if I know myself, for curiosity or another look at Janet. It is not my custom to frequent memorial chapels to look at girls even if they're good dancers. Call it a hunch. Not that I saw anything criminal, only something incredible. I filed past the casket with the throng because from a distance I had seen it and couldn't believe it. But when I got close there it was. Eight black orchids that could have come from nowhere else in the world, and a card with his initials the way he scribbled them, "N.W."

When I got home, and Wolfe came down from the plant rooms at six o'clock, I didn't mention it. I decided it wasn't advisable. I needed to devote some thought to it.

It was that evening, Wednesday evening after the funeral, that I answered the doorbell, and who should I see on the stoop but my old colleague Inspector Cramer of the Homicide Squad. I hailed him with false enthusiasm and ushered him into the office, where Wolfe was making more marks on the map of Russia. They exchanged greetings, and Cramer sat in the red leather chair, took out a handkerchief and wiped perspiration from his exposed surfaces, put a cigar between his lips and sank his teeth in it.

"Your hair's turning gray," I observed. "You look as if you weren't getting enough exercise. A brainworker like you—"

"God knows why you keep him," he said to Wolfe.

Wolfe grunted. "He saved my life once."

"Once!" I exclaimed indignantly. "Beginning—"

"Shut up, Archie. What can I do for you, Inspector?"

"You can tell me what you were doing for Bess Huddleston."

"Indeed." Wolfe's brows went up a shade. "You? The Homicide Bureau? Why do you want to know?"

"Because a guy is making himself a pest down at Headquarters. Her brother. He says she was murdered."

"He does?"

"Yes."

"Offering what evidence?"

"None at all."

"Then why bother me about it? Or yourself either?"

"Because we can't shut him up. He's even been to the Commissioner. And though he has no evidence, he has an argument. I'd like to tell you his argument."

Wolfe leaned back and sighed. "Go ahead."

"Well. He started on us last Saturday, four days ago. She got tetanus the day before. I don't need to tell you about that cut on her toe, since Goodwin was there—"

"I've heard about it."

"I'll bet you have. The brother, Daniel, said she couldn't have got tetanus from that cut. He said it was a clean piece of glass that dropped into her slipper when that tray of glasses fell on the terrace. He saw it. And the slipper was a clean house slipper, nearly new and clean. And she hadn't been walking around barefooted. He claimed there couldn't possibly have been any tetanus germs in that cut, at least not enough to cause so violent an attack so soon. I sent a man up there

Saturday night, but the doctor wouldn't let him see her, and of course he had no evidence—"

"Dr. Brady?"

"Yes. But the brother kept after us, especially when she died, and yesterday morning I sent a couple of men up to rub it off. I want to ask you, Goodwin, what was the piece of glass like? The piece in her slipper that cut her?"

"I knew you really came to see me," I told him genially. "It was a piece from one of the thick blue glasses that they had for old-fashioneds. Several of them broke."

Cramer nodded. "So they all say. We sent the slippers to the laboratory, and they say no tetanus germs. Of course there was another possibility, the iodine and the bandage. We sent all the stuff on that shelf to the laboratory, and the gauze was sterile, and it was good iodine, so naturally there were no germs in it. Under the circum—"

"Subsequent dressings," Wolfe muttered.

"No. The dressing Brady found on it when he was called up there Friday night was the one he had put on originally."

"Listen," I put in, "I know. By God. That orangoutang. He tickled her feet. He rubbed germs on her—"

Cramer shook his head. "We went into that too. One of them suggested it—the nephew. That seems to be a possibility. It sounds farfetched to me, but of course it's possible. Now what the doctor says. Brady."

"Excuse me," Wolfe said. "You talked to those people. Had Miss Huddleston nothing to say to them before she died? Any of them?"

"Not much. Do you know what tetanus does?"

"Vaguely."

"It does plenty. Like strychnine, only worse because there are no periods of relaxation and it lasts longer. When Brady got there Friday night her jaw was already locked tight. He gave her avertin to relieve her, and kept it up till the end. When my man was there Saturday night she was bent double backwards. Sunday she told Brady through her teeth she wanted to tell people good-bye, and he took them in one at a time. I've got their statements. Nothing significant, what you'd expect. Of course she only said a few words to each one—she was in bad shape. Her brother tried to tell her that her approaching death wasn't an accident, it was murder, but Brady and the nurse wouldn't let him."

"She herself had no such suspicion?"

"Not in evidence. You realize what she was like." Cramer shifted the cigar to the other side of his mouth. "What Brady says about the tetanus, one three-hundredth of a grain of the toxin is fatal. The bacilli and spores are more or less around everywhere, but of course especially in the neighborhood of horses. The soil around a barnyard reeks with it. I asked Brady what about his infecting the cut or the bandage with his own fingers when he dressed it, since he had just been riding, but he said he had washed his hands, and so had the Nichols girl, and she corroborated it. He said it was highly unlikely that there should have been tetanus bacilli on the piece of glass or her slipper or the skin of her toe or that animal's paw, at least enough of them to cause such a quick and virulent attack, but he said it was also unlikely that when a man walks across a street at a corner with a green light he should get run over, but sometimes he does. He says that he deeply regrets he didn't return Tuesday evening or Wednesday and give her an injection of antitoxin, but he doesn't blame himself because no doctor alive would have done so. After the poison reached the nerve centers, as it had when Brady arrived Friday night, it was too late for antitoxin, though he tried it. Everything Brady said has been checked with the Examiner and is okay."

"I don't like his analogy," Wolfe declared. "A man crossing a street is extremely likely to get run over. That's why I never undertake it. However, that doesn't impeach Dr. Brady. I ask you again, Mr. Cramer, why do you bother me with all this, or yourself either?"

"That's what I came here to find out."

"Not the proper place. Try the inside of your head."

"Oh, that's all right," Cramer asserted. "I'm satisfied. It was accidental. But that damn brother won't let go. And before I get tough with him and toss him out on his ear, I thought I'd better have a word with you. If there was anyone around there with murder in his heart, you ought to know. You would know. Since you had just started on a job for her. You're not interested in petty larceny. So I'd like to know what the job was."

"No doubt," Wolfe said. "Didn't any of those people tell you?"

"No."

"None of them?"

"No."

"Then how did you know she had hired me?"

"The brother told me about Goodwin being there, and that led me to question him. But he doesn't seem to know what your job was about."

"Neither do I."

Cramer took the cigar from his mouth and said vehemently, "Now look! How's it going to hurt you? Loosen up for once! I want to cross this off, that's all. I've got work to do! All I want to know—"

"Please!" Wolfe said curtly. "You say you are satisfied that the death was accidental. You have no shred of evidence of a crime. Miss Huddleston hired me for a confidential job. Her death does not release me, it merely deprives me of the job. If you had an action you could summon me, but you haven't. Will you have some beer?"

"No." Cramer glared. "My God, you can be honorable when you want to be! Will you answer a plain question? Do you think she was murdered?"

"No."

"Then you think it was purely accidental?"

"No."

"What the hell do you think?"

"Nothing at all. About that. I know nothing about it. I have no interest in it. The woman died, as all women do, may she rest in peace, and I lost a fee. Why don't you ask me this: if you knew what I know, if I told you all about the job she hired me for, would you feel that her death required further investigation?"

"Okay. I ask it."

"The answer is no. Since you have discovered no single suspicious circumstance. Will you have some beer?"

"Yes, I will," Cramer growled.

He consumed a bottle, got no further concessions either in information or in hypothetical questions, and departed.

I saw him to the door, returned to the office, and remarked:

"Old Frizzle-top seems to be improving with age. Of course he has had the advantage of studying my methods. He seems to have covered the ground up there nearly as well as I could."

"Pfui." Wolfe pushed the tray aside to make room for the map. "Not that I don't agree with you. Nearly as well as you could, yes. But either he didn't have sense enough to learn everything that happened that afternoon, or he missed his best chance to expose a crime, if there was one. It hasn't rained the past week, has it? No."

I cocked an eye at him. "You don't say. How many guesses can I have?"

But he left it at that and got busy with the map, ignoring my questions. It was one of the many occasions when it would have been a pleasure to push him off of the Empire State Building, if there had been any way of enticing him there. Of course there was a chance that he was merely pulling my leg, but I doubted it. I know his tones of voice.

It ruined my night for me. Instead of going to sleep in thirty seconds it took me thirty minutes, trying to figure out what the devil he meant, and I woke up twice with nightmares, the first time because it was raining on me through the roof and each raindrop was a tetanus germ, and the second time I was lost in a desert where it hadn't rained for a hundred years. Next morning, after Wolfe had gone up to the plant rooms at nine o'clock, I got stubborn. I sat at my desk and went over that party at Riverdale in my mind, second by second, as I had reported it to Wolfe. And I got it. I would have hit it sooner if it hadn't been for various interruptions, phone calls and so on, but anyway finally there it was, as obvious as lipstick.

Provided one thing. To settle that I phoned Doc Vollmer, whose home and office were in a house down the street, and learned that tetanus, which carried death, had a third as many lives as a cat—one as a toxin, one as a bacillus, and one as a spore. The bacillus or the spore got in you and manufactured the toxin, which did the dirty work, traveling not with the blood but with the nerves. The bacillus and spore were both anaerobic, but could live in surface soil or dust for years and usually did, especially the spore.

And now what? Just forget it? Wolfe had, but then he wasn't human, whereas I was and am. Besides, it would be very neat if it got results, and it would teach Wolfe a lesson. It was nearly eleven o'clock, and I wanted to get out before he came downstairs, so I phoned up to him that I was leaving on an errand, and walked to the garage on Tenth Avenue and got the roadster. Heading uptown, I stopped at a hardware store near 42nd Street and went in and bought a long-bladed kitchen knife, a narrow garden trowel, and four paper bags. Then I went to a phone booth in a drug store at the corner and called the Huddleston number.

Maryella's voice answered, and I asked to speak to Miss Nichols. In a minute she was on, and I told her I was thinking she might be leaving there soon and I'd like to have her address.

"It's nice of you to call," she said. "It's a—pleasant surprise. Naturally I thought you—last week, I mean—I thought you were just being a detective."

"Don't kid me," I told her. "Anyone that dances the way you do being surprised at a phone call. Not that I suppose you're doing any dancing at present."

"Not now. No."

"Will you be leaving there soon?"

"Not this week. We're trying to help Mr. Huddleston straighten things up."

"Will you send me your address when you go?"

"Why—yes. Certainly. If you want it."

"I do, you know. How would it be if I drove up there? Just to say hello?"

"When? Now?"

"Right now. I can be there in twenty minutes. I'd kind of like to see you."

"Why—" Silence. "That would be all right. If you want to take the trouble."

I told her it would be no trouble at all, hung up, went out to the roadster, and made for the entrance to the West Side Highway at 46th Street.

I admit my timing was terrible. If I had arrived, say, between twelve thirty and one, they might have been in the house having lunch, and I could have said I had already eaten and waited for Janet on the terrace, which would have been a perfect opportunity. Of course as it turned out that would have made a monkey of me, so it was just as well that I dubbed it. As it was, leaving the car outside the fence, with the knife in one hip pocket and the trowel in the other, and the folded paper bags in the side pocket of my coat, I walked across the lawn to where Larry stood near the pool, glowering at it. When he heard me coming he transferred the glower to me.

"Hello," I said amiably. "What, no alligators?"

"No. They're gone."

"And Mister? And the bears?"

"Yes. What the hell are you doing here?"

I suppose it would have been sensible to appease him, but he was really quite irritating. Tone and look both. So I said, "I came to play tag with Mister," and started for the house, but Janet appeared, cutting across the lawn. She looked prettier than I remembered her, or maybe not so much prettier as more interesting. Her hair was done differently or something. She said hello to me and let me have a hand to shake, and then told Larry:

"Maryella says you'll have to help her with those Corliss bills. Some of them go back before she came, and she doesn't seem to trust my memory."

Larry nodded at her, and, moving, was in front of me. "What do you want?" he demanded.

"Nothing special," I said. "Freedom of speech, freedom of religion, freedom—"

"If you've got a bill, mail it. You'll get about three per cent."

I suppressed impulses and shook my head. "No bill. I came to see Miss Nichols."

"Yes you did. You came to snoop—"

But Janet had her hand on his arm. "Please, Larry. Mr. Goodwin phoned and asked to see me. Please?"

I would have preferred smacking him, and it was irritating to see her with her hand on his arm looking up at him the way she did, but when he turned and marched off towards the house I restrained myself and let him go.

I asked Janet, "What's eating him?"

"Well," she said, "after all, you are a detective. And his aunt has died—terrible, it was terrible—"

"Sure. If you want to call that grief. What was the crack about three per cent?"

"Oh . . ." She hesitated. "But there's nothing secret about it, good-ness knows. Miss Huddleston's affairs are tangled up. Everybody thought she was rich, but apparently she spent it as fast as she made it."

"Faster, if the creditors are going to get three per cent." I got started towards the terrace, and she came beside me. "In that case, the brother and the nephew are out of luck. I apologize to Larry. He's probably overcome by grief, after all."

"That's a mean thing to say," Janet protested.

"Then I take it back." I waved it away. "Let's talk about something else."

I was thinking the best plan was to sit with her on the terrace, with the idea of getting her to leave me alone there for a few minutes, which was all I needed, but the hot noon sun was coming straight down, and she went on into the house with me behind her. She invited me to sit on a couch with her, but with the tools in my hip pockets I thought it was safer to take a chair facing her. We had a conversation.

Of course the simplest thing would have been to tell her what I wanted to do and then go ahead and do it, and I deny that it was any suspicion of her, either as a letter writer or as a murderess, that kept me from doing that. It was the natural desire I had not to hurt her feelings by letting her know that my real purpose in coming was not just to see her. If things should develop it was good policy to have her friendly. So I played it for a solo. I was thinking it was about time to get on with it, and was figuring out an errand for her, preferably upstairs, that would be sure to keep her five minutes, when suddenly I saw something through the window that made me stare.

It was Daniel Huddleston on the terrace with a newspaper bundle under his arm and a long-bladed knife in one hand and a garden trowel in the other!

I stood up to see better.

"What is it?" Janet asked, and stood up too. I shushed her and whispered in her ear, "First lesson for a detective. Don't make any noise."

Brother Daniel stopped near the center of the terrace, in front of the swing, knelt down on a flagstone, deposited the newspaper bundle and some folded newspapers beside him, and the trowel, and plunged the knife into the strip of turf at the edge of the flagstone. There was nothing furtive about it; he didn't do any glancing over his shoulder, but he worked fast. With the trowel he scooped out a hunk of the turf, the width of the strip, about six inches long and three inches deep, and rolled it in a piece of newspaper. Then a second one, to the right of the first hole, and then a third one, to the left, wrapping each separately.

"What on earth does he think he's doing?" Janet whispered. I squeezed her arm.

He was about done. Opening the package he had brought with him, he produced three strips of turf the size and shape of those he had just dug out, fitted them into the trench he had made, pressed them with his foot until they were level with the flagstones, remade the package with the three hunks he had removed, and the knife and trowel, and went off as if he were bound somewhere.

I took Janet's hand and gave her an earnest eye. "Listen, girlie," I said, "my one fault is curiosity. Otherwise I am perfect. Don't forget that. It's time for your lunch anyway."

She said something to my back as I made for the door. I emerged onto the terrace cautiously, slid across and into the hedge of shrubbery, made a hole and looked through. Daniel was forty paces away, going across the lawn, not in the direction of the drive where my car was but the other way, off to the right. I decided to give him another twenty paces before emerging, and it was well that I did, for suddenly a voice sounded above me:

"Hey, Uncle Dan! Where you going?"

Daniel stopped in his tracks and whirled. I twisted my neck, and through the leaves got a glimpse of Larry's head sticking out of an upper window, and Maryella's beside it.

Larry shouted, "We need you!"

"See you later!" Daniel yelled.

"But it's time for lunch!" Maryella called.

"See you later!" Daniel turned and was off.

"Now that's a performance," Maryella said to Larry.

"Cuckoo," Larry declared.

Their heads went in. But they might still have been looking out, so I scooted along the side of the house to the corner, and from there circled wide around evergreens and similar obstructions before swinging into the direction Daniel had taken. He wasn't in sight. This part of the premises was new to me, and the first thing I knew I ran smack into the fence in the middle of a thicket. I couldn't fight my way through on account of noise, so I doubled around, dashed along the edge of the thicket, and pretty soon hit a path. No sight of Daniel. The path took me to a series of stone steps up a steep bank, and up I went. Getting to the top, I saw him. A hundred feet ahead was a gate in the fence, and he was shutting the gate and starting down a lane between rows of little trees. The package was under his arm. In a way I was more interested in the package than I was in him. What if he threw it down a sewer? So I closed up more than I would have for an ordinary tailing job, and proceeding through the gate, followed him down the lane. At the end of the lane, not far ahead, he stopped, and I dived into the trees.

He had stopped at a curb, a paved street. The way cars were rolling by, apparently it was a main traffic street; and that point was settled when a double-decker bus jerked to a stop right square in front of Daniel, and he climbed on and off the bus went.

I hotfooted it to the corner. It was Marble Avenue. Riverdale is like that. The bus was too far away to read its number, and no taxi was in sight in either direction. I stepped into the street, into the path of the first car coming, and held up a commanding palm. By bad luck it was occupied by the two women that Helen Hokinson uses for models, but there was no time to pick and choose. I hopped into the back seat, gave the driver a fleeting glimpse of my detective license, and said briskly:

"Police business. Step on it and catch up with a bus that's ahead."

The one driving emitted a baby scream. The other one said, "You don't look like a policeman. You get out. If you don't we'll drive to a police station."

"Suit yourself, madam. While we sit and talk the most dangerous gangster in New York is escaping. He's on the bus."

"Oh! He'll shoot at us."

"No. He isn't armed."

"Then why is he dangerous?"

"For God's sake," I reached for the door latch, "I'll take a car with a man in it!"

But the car started forward. "You will not," the driver said fiercely. "I'm as good a driver as any man. My husband says so."

She was okay at that. Within a block she had it up to fifty, and she was good at passing, and it wasn't long before we caught up with the bus. At least, a bus. When it stopped at a corner I told her to get alongside, which she did neatly, and with my hand over my face I looked for him and there he was.

"I'm shadowing him," I told the ladies. "I think he's on his way to meet a crooked politician. The first empty taxi we see you can let me out if you want to, but of course he might suspect a taxi, whereas he never would suspect a car like this with two good-looking well-dressed women in it."

The driver looked grim. "In that case," she declared, "it is our duty."

And by gum she crawled along behind that bus for a good three-quarters of an hour, to Riverside Drive, the whole length of the Drive, over to Broadway, and on downtown. I thought the least I could do was furnish diversion, which I did with tales of my experiences with gangsters and kidnappers and so forth. When Daniel was still on the bus after crossing 42nd Street I decided in disgust that he was probably bound for Headquarters, and I was so deeply considering the feasibility of intercepting him before he got there that I nearly missed it when he hopped to the sidewalk at 34th Street. Paying the ladies with thanks and a cordial smile, I jumped out and dodged through the midday shopping mob, and almost lost him. I picked him up going west on 34th.

At Eighth Avenue he turned uptown. I kept twenty yards behind. At 35th he turned west again.

That was when I got suspicious. Naturally. On he went, straight as a bullet. When he kept on west of Ninth Avenue, there was no question about it. I closed up. He began looking at the numbers on buildings, and came to the stoop and started up. Boy, I'm telling you, they don't get away from me. I get my man. I had trailed this one the length of New York, hanging on like a bulldog, right to Nero Wolfe's door.

5   I HAD BEEN THINKING FAST THE LAST TWO BLOCKS. I HAD considered, and rejected, three different maneuvers to keep Wolfe from finding out. They all seemed good, but I knew damn well none of them was good enough. He would find out all right, no matter what I did. So I bounded up the steps past Daniel, greeted him, let us in with my key, and took him to the office.

Wolfe, at his desk, frowned at us. "How do you do, Mr. Huddleston. Archie. Where have you been?"

"I know," I said, "it's about lunch time, so I'll make it brief. First cast a glance at this." I took the knife, the trowel, and the paper bags from my pockets and put them on his desk.

Daniel stared and muttered something.

"What is this flummery?" Wolfe demanded.

"No flummery," I asserted. "Tools. It still didn't rain last night. So I went to Riverdale to get the piece of turf where the orangoutang poured the iodine. Brother Daniel had the same idea. He was just ahead of me. He's got it in that newspaper. I thought he might be going to toss it in the river, so I tailed him and he led me here. So I look foolish but not dumb. Now you can laugh."

He didn't. He looked at Daniel. "Is that what you have in that package, Mr. Huddleston?"

"It is," Daniel said. "I want—"

"Why did you bring it to me? I'm not a chemist. You are."

"Because I want to authenticate it. I want—"

"Take it to the police."

"No." Daniel looked and sounded determined. "They think I'm

nothing but a nuisance. Maybe I am. But if I analyze this myself, without someone to—"

"Don't analyze it yourself. You have colleagues, friends, haven't you?"

"None I would want to give this to."

"Are you sure you have the piece where the iodine was poured?"

"I am. A few drops were on the edge of the flagstone. I also have pieces taken from each side of that piece, for comparison."

"Naturally. Who suggested this step to you?"

"No one. It occurred to me this morning, and I immediately went up there—"

"Indeed. I congratulate you. Take it to the Fisher Laboratories. You know them, don't you?"

"Certainly." Daniel flushed. "I happen not to have any cash at the moment. They are expensive."

"Establish credit. Your sister's estate. Aren't you her nearest relative?"

"There is no estate. The liabilities greatly exceed the assets."

Wolfe looked annoyed. "You are careless not to have cash. Confound it, you should have cash. You understand, sir, my finger is not in this pie. I am not concerned. My lunch is ready. I should bid you good day. But you seem to be capable of using your brains, and that is so rare a phenomenon it is a pity to waste it. Archie, phone Mr. Weinbach at the Fisher Laboratories. Tell him to expect Mr. Huddleston, to rush the analysis he requires, and to charge it to me. You can pay the bill, sir, at your convenience."

Daniel hesitated. "I have a habit—I am extremely backward about paying bills—"

"You'll pay this one. I'll see that you do. What is argyrol?"

"Argyrol? Why—it's a silver-protein compound. Silver vitellin."

"It stains like iodine. Could tetanus bacilli live in it?"

Daniel considered. "I believe they could. It's far weaker—"

Wolfe nodded impatiently. "Tell Mr. Weinbach to try for it." He got up. "My lunch is waiting."

After I had finished the phone call and ushered Daniel out, with his package, I joined Wolfe in the dining room. Since no discussion of business was permitted at meals, I waited until we were back in the office again before observing:

"I ought to tell you that Janet saw him lifting that turf, and Mary-ella and the nephew—"

"There is no reason to tell me. I am not concerned." He pointed to the knife and trowel, still on his desk. "Where did you get those things?"

"Bought them."

"Please put them somewhere. They are not to appear on the expense account."

"Then I'll keep them in my room."

"Do so. By all means. Please take a letter to Mr. Hoehn."

His tone said, and that's the end of Miss Huddleston and her affairs for this office, for you, and for me.

No doubt it would have been, except for his vanity. Or perhaps it wasn't vanity; it may be that the reason he permitted his privacy to be invaded again by brother Daniel was that he wanted to impress on him the desirability of getting the bill of the Fisher Laboratories paid as soon as possible. At any rate, when Daniel turned up some hours later, a little before seven that evening, Fritz was told to bring him to the office. At first sight of him I knew he had something, by the look in his eye and the set of his jaw. He tramped over to Wolfe's desk and announced:

"My sister was murdered."

He got an envelope from his pocket, took out a paper and unfolded it, and fumbled the job because his hands were trembling. He swayed a little, steadied himself with a hand on the edge of the desk, looked around for a chair, and sat down.

"I guess I'm a little weak from excitement," he said apologetically. "Then I had only an apple for breakfast, and I haven't eaten anything since."

It was probably the one thing in the world he could have said to keep Wolfe from telling him to go to the police and telling me to bounce him out. The one kind of man that never gets the gate at that house is one with an empty stomach. Glaring at him, not sympathetically but indignantly, Wolfe pushed a button and, when Fritz appeared, inquired:

"How far along is the soup?"

"Quite ready, sir, except for the mushrooms."

"Bring a bowl of it, crackers, cottage cheese, and hot tea."

Daniel tried to protest, but Wolfe didn't even listen. He heaved a deep sigh and leaned back and shut his eyes, a man who had eaten nothing but an apple for twenty-four hours being too painful an object to look at. When Fritz came with the tray I had a table ready in front of Daniel, and he wolfed a couple of crackers and then blew on a spoonful of soup and swallowed it.

I had acquired the sheet of paper he had taken from the envelope, a report sheet from Fisher Laboratories, and was looking it over. After some more spoonfuls Daniel said:

"I knew it. I was sure of it. There couldn't—"

"Eat!" Wolfe commanded sternly.

"I'm eating. I'm all right. You were correct about the argyrol. That was a good guess. Argyrol and nothing else." A fork conveyed a hunk of cottage cheese to Daniel's mouth, but he went on, "Not a trace of iodine. And millions of tetanus bacilli, hundreds of millions. Weinbach said he never saw anything like it. And they were all concentrated on the one piece of turf, on the grass stems and the soil surface. The other two pieces had no sign either of the silver vitellin or the tetanus. Weinbach said . . ."

The doorbell rang, but I kept my seat and left it for Fritz because I had no reason to expect any undesirable intrusions. As it turned out, however, it was exactly the kind of invasion Wolfe resents more than anything else. An insurance salesman or a wife wanting her husband tailed is merely a mosquito to be brushed off, with me to do the brushing, but this wasn't as simple as that. The sound of Fritz's voice came from the hall, in indignant protest, and then the door flew open and Inspector Cramer strode in. I mean strode. His first glance caught me, and was it withering. Then he saw who Daniel was, emitted a triumphal grunt, spread his feet apart, and rasped out:

"Come along, you!" And to me: "You too, bud! Come on!"

I grinned at him. "If you ever find time to glance over an interesting document called the Constitution of the United—"

"Shut up, Archie," Wolfe snapped. "Mr. Cramer. What in the name of heaven is the matter with you?"

"Not a thing," Cramer said sarcastically. "Matter with me? Not a damn thing." I never saw him sorer or sourer. "Listen!" he said. He stepped to the desk and tapped a heavy finger on it, sounding like a hammer. "Last night, sitting right at this desk, what did you say? What did you tell me?"

Wolfe was grimacing with distaste. "Your tone and manner, Mr. Cramer—"

"You said, in case you've forgotten, that you weren't interested in the death of Bess Huddleston! Knew nothing about it! Weren't interested!" Cramer went on tapping the desk. "Well, this afternoon somebody in my office got an idea—we do that once in a while! I sent a man up there, and young Huddleston showed him where the monkey poured some of that iodine, and when he went to take some of that turf for analysis, he found it had already been taken! It had been carefully filled up with other turf, but the grass didn't match. He asked questions, and he learned that Daniel Huddleston had done it, taken the turf away, and Goodwin had been there and gone with him!"

"Not with him," I corrected emphatically. "After him."

Cramer ignored me. "We went for Huddleston and couldn't find him. So I come to see you. You and Goodwin. And what do I find? By God! I find Huddleston! Sitting here eating! This is the rawest one you've ever pulled! Removing evidence, destroying evidence—"

"Nonsense," Wolfe said curtly and coldly. "Stop shouting. If you wish to know the purpose of Mr. Huddleston's visit—"

"Not from you I don't! I'll get it from him! And from Goodwin! And separately! I'm taking them downtown."

"No," Wolfe said. "Not from my office."

That was the central point of the situation. Twenty minutes earlier Daniel's empty stomach was all that had kept Wolfe from chasing him to the police, and it wouldn't have hurt his appetite any if I had gone along to keep Daniel company, but this was different. For a cop to remove persons from the house, any person whatever, with or without a charge or a warrant, except at Wolfe's instigation, was an intolerable insult to his pride, his vanity, and his sense of the fitness of things. So as was to be expected, he acted with a burst of energy amounting to violence. He sat up straight in his chair.

"Mr. Cramer," he said, "sit down."

"Not a chance." Cramer meant it. "You're not going to take me in with one of your goddam—"

"Archie, show Mr. Cramer that report from the Fisher Laboratories."

I stuck it under his nose. His impulse was to push it away, but no cop, not even an Inspector, dares to refuse to look at a paper. So he snatched it and scowled at it. Daniel started to say something, but Wolfe shushed him, and Daniel finished off the cheese and the last cracker, and put sugar in his tea and began to stir it.

"So what?" Cramer growled. "How do I know—"

"I sometimes doubt if you know anything," Wolfe said shortly. "I was not and am not interested in Miss Huddleston's death, though you and Mr. Huddleston and Archie keep pestering me about it. I have no client. My client died. You are even affronted to find Mr. Huddleston here eating. If he's hungry, why the devil shouldn't he eat? When he appeared here at one o'clock with that turf, I told him to take it to the police. He said they regarded him as a nuisance. Why he returned here with the laboratory report, I do not know; I only know he was hungry. If you are disgruntled because you have no assurance that the piece of turf examined by the laboratory is the piece onto which the chimpanzee poured some of the contents of the bottle of supposed iodine, I can't help it. Why didn't you get the turf yourself when Mr. Huddleston first called on you, five days ago? It was an obvious thing to do."

"I didn't know then that the chimpanzee had poured—"

"You should have. Proper questioning would have got it. Either it was worth investigating competently, or not at all. Well, sir, there's your report. Keep it. You'll get a bill for it from the Fisher Laboratories. Archie, make a note of that. It wasn't iodine in that bottle; it was argyrol, and it was reeking with tetanus bacilli. An uncommonly ugly thing to do. I have never heard of a more objectionable way of committing murder, nor of an easier or simpler one. I trust, sir, that you'll make an arrest. You should, since you have only five people to deal with—the five who were there, not counting Archie—"

"Wait a minute," Daniel protested. "You're wrong. That bottle could have been put there any time—"

Wolfe shook his head. "No. Only that afternoon. If we had to we could argue that it is not credible that it was left in the cupboard for an extended period, for just anyone to use, but we don't have to. The bottle in that cupboard contained good iodine at four o'clock that afternoon."

Cramer growled. Daniel demanded, "How do you know that?"

"Because it was used at that hour. By Archie. He tripped on an alligator and scratched his hand."

"By God," Cramer said, and sat down. Daniel looked at me, and I nodded at him.

Daniel looked at Wolfe, his jaw hanging open and his face gray. "Then it c-couldn't have been—" he stammered.

"Couldn't have been what?" Cramer demanded.

"It couldn't have been someone—" Daniel shook his head weakly, as if trying to reject something. Suddenly he exclaimed fiercely, "I can't believe that! One of them? Those two girls or Larry or Brady?"

"Or you, sir," Wolfe said dryly. "You were there. As for your trying to get the police started on it, you may be more devious than you look. Save your indignation. Calm yourself. Your digestive processes will make a botch of that soup and cheese if you don't. So, Mr. Cramer, I give you that. It was an impromptu job. Not that it was unpremeditated; far from it; it was carefully prepared; an iodine bottle had been emptied and washed and replenished with argyrol and an army of tetanus germs."

Wolfe compressed his lips. "Very ugly. It would take an extremely unattractive person to think of that, let alone do it. It was done. I presume a situation was to be created requiring the use of the iodine; in fact, there is reason to believe that it had been created, or was in process; but the accident on the terrace provided an opportunity too good to be missed. From the standpoint of technique, it was brilliantly conceived and managed. Only two things needed to be done: drop a piece of glass into Miss Huddleston's slipper, which was quite simple with everyone jostling around picking up the pieces, and substitute the bottle of bogus iodine for the one that was in the cupboard. With no risk whatever. If Miss Huddleston shook the glass out of her slipper before putting it on, if for any reason she didn't cut herself, the bottle could be switched again and nothing lost. There is a point, of course: if the bottle in the cupboard had a different kind of label—"

"They all had the same label," Cramer rumbled.

"All?"

"Yes. There were seven bottles of iodine in that house, counting the kitchen, and they were all the same, size and shape and label."

"They bought it wholesale," I explained, "on account of Mister and the bears."

"That," Wolfe said, "is precisely the sort of thing you would know, Mr. Cramer. Seven. Not eight. Seven. And of course you had it all analyzed and it was all good iodine."

"It was. And what the hell is there in that to be sarcastic about? It clears up your point, don't it? And I might mention another point. The murderer had to leave the terrace, go in the house, between the time the glasses got broken and the time Miss Huddleston cut herself, to switch the iodine bottles."

Wolfe shook his head. "That offers nothing. They all went in the house during that period. Miss Nichols went for brooms and pans. The nephew went for another tray of supplies. Miss Timms went for a vacuum cleaner. Dr. Brady carried off the debris."

Cramer stared at him in exasperation. "And you know nothing about it! Jesus. You're not interested!"

"I didn't," Daniel put in. "I didn't leave the terrace during that period."

"So far as I know," Wolfe agreed, "that is correct. But if I were you I wouldn't brag about it. You went for the iodine. It was the bottle you handed to Dr. Brady that he used. Your jaw is loose again. You bounce, Mr. Huddleston, from wrath to indignation, with amazing agility. Frankly, I doubt if it is possible to suspect you of murdering your sister. If you did it, your facial dexterity surpasses anything in my experience. If you'll stay and dine with me, I'll reach a decision on that before the meal is finished. Partridges in marinade. *En escabecha*."

His eyes gleamed. "They are ready for us." He pushed back his chair and got himself onto his feet. "So, Mr. Cramer, it seems likely that it is limited to four, which simplifies your task. You'll excuse me, I'm sure—"

"Yeah," Cramer said, "glad to." He was up too. "But you'll enjoy your partridges alone. Huddleston and Goodwin are going with me." His glance took us in. "Let's go."

Wolfe looked displeased. "I have already cleared away the brush for you. If you insist on seeing them this evening, they can call at your office—say at ten o'clock?"

"No. They're coming now."

Wolfe's chin went up. His mouth opened and then closed again. It was an interesting sight, especially for me, knowing as I do how hard he is to flabbergast, next to impossible, but I can't truthfully say I enjoyed it, because of who was doing it. So I spoke up:

"I'm staying for the partridges. And I may or may not show up at ten o'clock, depending—"

"To hell with you," Cramer rumbled. "I'll deal with you later. We'll go, Mr. Huddleston."

Wolfe took a step, and his voice was as close to trembling with rage as it ever got. "Mr. Huddleston is my invited guest!"

"I've uninvited him. Come, Mr. Huddleston."

Wolfe turned to Daniel. He was controlling himself under insufferable provocation. "Mr. Huddleston. I have invited you to my table. You are under no compulsion, legal or moral, to accompany this man on demand. He struts and blusters. Later Mr. Goodwin will drive you—"

But Daniel said firmly, "I guess I'll go along with him, Mr. Wolfe. After the days I've spent trying to get them started on this . . ."

The partridge was swell, and I ate nearly as much as Wolfe did. Otherwise it was one of the dullest meals I had ever had under Wolfe's roof. He didn't say a word, clear to the coffee.

6

I DESCRIBED THAT SCENE IN DETAIL, BECAUSE IF IT hadn't been for that I doubt if the murderer of Bess Huddleston would ever have been caught. One of Cramer's bunch might possibly have doped it out, but they never in the world would have got enough evidence for an arrest. And Wolfe, with no client and no commitment, was through with it, or would have been if Cramer hadn't kidnapped a dinner guest right under his nose and made him so damn mad he had to take amphojel twice that evening.

Twice. The first dose was right after dinner, when he sent me up to his room for the bottle. The second was long after midnight, when I got home after my call on Inspector Cramer downtown. I sneaked quietly up the two flights to my room, but was just starting to undress when the house phone on my table buzzed, and, answering it and getting a summons, I descended to Wolfe's room and entered. The light was on and he wasn't in his bed, and, proceeding to his bathroom, I found him taking another shot of amphojel, with a scowl on his face that would have scared Joe Louis right out of the ring. He was a spectacle anyway, draped in the ten yards of yellow silk that it took to make him a suit of pajamas.

"Well?" he demanded.

"Nothing. Routine. Questions and a signed statement."

"He'll pay for this." Wolfe made a face like an infuriated gargoyle and put the amphojel bottle back in the cabinet. "I haven't had to take this stuff since that hideous experiment with eels in the spring. He'll pay for it. Go to Riverdale early in the morning. Consult the stableman and learn—"

"I doubt if there is one. The horses are gone. The creditors get three per cent."

"Find him. Wherever he is. I wish to know whether anyone has recently removed anything, any material, from the vicinity of the stable. A small paper bag filled at the manure pile would have been ideal. Question him. If he's difficult, bring him here. Also—is there a servant on the place?"

I nodded. "The butler. I think he's hanging on hoping to get paid."

"Ask him about that bottle that Miss Huddleston found broken in her bathroom. Whatever he knows about it. Ask any other servant who was there at the time. All details possible—"

"The others too? Maryella, Janet, Larry—"

"No. Mention it to no one but the servants. Phone before returning. Before you go, leave phone numbers on my desk—Riverdale, Mr. Huddleston, Dr. Brady—that's all. He'll pay for this. Good night."

So we had a case. We had no client, no retainer, and no fee in sight, but at least we had a case, which was better than sitting around on my tail listening to the radio.

I made six hours' sleep do me, and before eight o'clock next morning I was up at Riverdale. I didn't phone in advance, since I had to go anyway to get my car which I had left on the driveway the day before. Greeted at the door by Hoskins, I was told that the stableman was gone and maybe Maryella had his address. I would have preferred asking Janet or even Larry, but Hoskins said they were both late sleepers and Maryella was already eating breakfast, so I got the address from her, and by good luck it wasn't Bucyrus, Ohio, but merely Brooklyn. Whatever else you want to say about Brooklyn, and so do I, it does have one big advantage, it's close.

That errand was one of the simplest I have ever performed, once I found the address and the stableman. His name was Tim Lavery and a scar on his cheek made him look mean until he grinned. I started with him cautiously, pretending that my mind was on something else, but soon saw that it wasn't necessary to sneak up on him, and put it to him straight.

"Sure," he said, "one day about a month ago, maybe a little more, Doc Brady filled up a box he brought, an empty candy box. I helped him. He said he wanted it for a test. One of his patients had died of tetanus—I forget her name—"

I pretended there was nothing to be excited about. "Where'd he take it from? The stall?"

"No, the pile. I dug into the middle of the pile for him."

"Who was with him that day? One of the girls?"

Tim shook his head. "He was alone when he did that. They had been riding—I forget who was with him that day—and they went to the house and then he came back alone with that box and said what he wanted."

"Do you remember the day? The date?"

The best he could do on that was the last week in July. I got the details all filled in, made sure that he would be available if and when needed, and, leaving, stopped at the first phone booth and called Wolfe. Answering from the plant rooms and therefore with his mind occupied, he displayed no exultation, which he wouldn't anyway, and informed me that my discovery made no change in the rest of my assignment.

Arriving at the Huddleston place in Riverdale a little after ten o'clock, my luck still held. Instead of stopping by the side gate, I continued along the drive, where another gate opened onto a path leading to the back door, and Hoskins was there in the kitchen having a conversation with a depressed-looking female in a maid's uniform. They acted reserved but not hostile; in fact, Hoskins invited me to have a cup of coffee, which I accepted. Taking an inventory as a precaution against any unwelcome interruptions, I was told that Larry and Maryella had both gone out, Daniel hadn't shown up that morning, no city employees were on the premises, and Janet had just had breakfast in bed. The field was clear, but I had a hunch that a delegation from Cramer's office might be appearing any minute, so I got down to business without wasting any time.

They both remembered all about it. Shortly after lunch that Tuesday afternoon Hoskins had been summoned to Miss Huddleston's room upstairs and requested to take a look at the bathroom. Broken glass was everywhere, in the tub, on the floor, the remnants of a large bottle of bath salts that had been kept on a high shelf above the bathtub. Miss Huddleston hadn't done it. Hoskins hadn't done it. The maid, summoned, said she hadn't done it, and then she and Hoskins cleaned up the mess. I asked what about the orangoutang. Possibly, they said, with that beast anything was possible, but it had not been permitted upstairs and seldom went there, and had not been observed inside the house that day.

I filled in details all I could, even asking to view the remains of the broken bottle, which they said had been thick and heavy and creamy yellow in color, but that had been carted away. Then I asked Hoskins to let me take a look at the bathroom, and when we started for the stairs the maid came along, mumbling something about Miss Nichols' breakfast tray. Bess Huddleston's room was more like a museum than a bedroom, the walls covered with framed autographed photographs and letters, and all the available space filled with everything from a lady manikin in an Eskimo suit to a string of Chinese lanterns, but what I was interested in was the bathroom. It was all colors, the World War camouflage type, or Devil's Rainbow. It made me too dizzy to do a decent job of inspection, but I managed to note such details as the position of the shelf on which the bottle of bath salts had stood. There was a new bottle there, nearly full, and I was reaching for it to take it down to look at it when I suddenly jerked around and cocked an ear and stepped to the door. Hoskins was standing in the middle of the room in a state of suspended animation, his back to me.

"Who screamed?" I demanded.

"Down the hall," he said without turning. "There's nobody but Miss Nichols—"

There had been nothing ear-piercing about it, in fact I had barely heard it, and there were no encores, but a scream is a scream. I marched past Hoskins and through the door, which was standing open, to the hall, and kept going.

"Last door on the right," Hoskins said behind me. I knew that, having been in Janet's room before. The door was shut. I turned the knob and went in, and saw no one, but another door, standing open, revealed a corner of a bathroom. As I started for it the maid's voice came out:

"Who is it?"

"Archie Goodwin. What—"

The maid appeared in the doorway, looking flustered. "You can't come in! Miss Nichols isn't dressed!"

"Okay." I halted out of delicacy. "But I heard a scream. Do you need any rescuing, Janet?"

"Oh, no!" the undressed invisible Janet called, in a voice so weak I could just hear it. "No, I'm all right!" The voice was not only weak, it was shaky.

"What happened?" I asked.

"Nothing serious," the maid said. "A cut on her arm. She cut herself with a piece of glass."

"She what?" I goggled. But without waiting for an answer, I stepped across and walked through the maid into the bathroom. Janet, undressed in the fullest sense of the word and wet all over, was seated on a stool. Ignoring protests and shaking off the maid, who was as red as a beet having her modesty shocked by proxy, I got a towel from a rack and handed it to Janet.

"Here," I said, "this will protect civilization. How the dickens did you do that?"

I lifted her left arm for a look. The cut, nearly an inch long, halfway between the wrist and the elbow, looked worse than it probably was on account of the mixture of blood and iodine. It certainly didn't seem to be worth fainting for, but Janet's face looked as if she might be going to faint. I took the iodine bottle out of her hand and put the cork in it.

"I never scream," Janet said, holding the towel up to her chin. "Really, I never do. But it seemed so . . . cutting myself with glass . . . so soon after Miss Huddleston . . ." She swallowed. "I didn't scream when I cut myself; I'm not quite that silly, really I'm not. I screamed when I saw the piece of glass in the bath brush. It seemed so—"

"Here it is," the maid said.

I took it. It was a piece of jagged glass, creamy yellow, not much bigger than my thumbnail.

"It's like a piece of that bottle that was broke in Miss Huddleston's room that you was asking about," the maid said.

"I'll keep it for a souvenir," I announced, and dropped it into the pocket where I had put the iodine bottle, and picked up the bath brush from the floor. It was soaking wet. "You mean you got in the tub and got soaped, and started to use the brush and cut yourself, and looked at the brush and saw the piece of glass wedged in the bristles, and screamed. Huh?"

Janet nodded. "I know it was silly to scream—"

"I was in the room," the maid said, "and I ran in and—"

"Okay," I cut her off. "Get me some gauze and bandages."

"There in the cabinet," Janet said.

I did a neat job on her, using plenty of gauze because the cut was still trying to bleed. Where she needed the blood was in her face, which was still white and scared, though she tried to smile at me when she thanked me.

I patted her on a nice round shoulder. "Don't mention it, girlie. I'll wait downstairs until you get dressed. I like you in that towel, but I think it would be sensible to go to a doctor and get a shot of antitoxin. I'll drive you. When you—"

"Antitoxin?" she gasped.

"Sure." I patted her again. "Just a precaution. Nothing to worry about. I'll be waiting downstairs."

Hoskins, hovering around in the hall, was relieved when I told him there was nothing for him to do except to get me a piece of paper to wrap the bath brush in. I waited till I was alone, down in the living room, to take the iodine bottle from my pocket, uncork it, and smell it. Whatever it was, it wasn't iodine. I put the cork back in good and tight, went to a lavatory across the hall and washed my hands, and then found a telephone and dialed Wolfe's number.

He answered himself, from the plant rooms since it wasn't eleven o'clock yet, and I gave it to him, all of it. When I finished he said immediately and urgently:

"Get her away from there!"

"Yes, sir, that is my intention—"

"Confound it, at once! Why phone me? If Mr. Cramer goes—"

"Please," I said firmly. "She was naked. I have no white horse, and she hasn't got much hair, at least not that much. As soon as she's dressed we're off. I was going to suggest that you phone Doc Vollmer and tell him to have a dose of antitoxin ready. We'll be there in about half an hour. Or I can phone him from here—"

"No. I will. Leave as soon as possible."

"Righto."

I went upstairs to the door of Janet's room and called to her that I'd be waiting by the side gate, and then went out and turned the car around and took it that far back down the drive. I was debating what course to follow if a police car put in an appearance, when here she came down the path, a little wobbly on her pins and far from pert but her buttons all buttoned. I helped her in and tore out of there with the gravel flying.

She didn't seem to feel like talking. I explained to her about Doc Vollmer being an old friend of ours, with his home and office in the same block as Nero Wolfe's house, so I was taking her there, and I tried a few leading questions, such as whether she had any idea how the piece of glass got into the bristles of her bath brush, but she didn't seem to be having any ideas. What she needed was a strong man to hold her hand, but I was driving. She had simply had the daylights scared out of her.

I had no explaining to do at Doc Vollmer's, since Wolfe had talked to him on the phone, and we weren't in there more than twenty minutes altogether. He cleaned the cut thoroughly, applied some of his own iodine, gave her the antitoxin in that arm, and then took me to an inside room and asked me for the iodine bottle I had. When I gave it to him he uncorked it, smelled it, frowned, poured a little of the contents into a glass vial, corked it again even tighter than I had, and handed it back to me.

"She'll be all right," he said. "What a devilish trick! Tell Mr. Wolfe I'll phone him as soon as possible."

I escorted Janet back out to the car. It was only a couple of hundred feet from there to Wolfe's door, and I discovered that I couldn't drive the last thirty of them because two cars were parked in front. Janet hadn't even asked why I was taking her to Wolfe's house. Apparently she was leaving it up to me. I gave her a reassuring grin as I opened the door with my key and waved her in.

Not knowing who the callers might be, the owners of the cars in front, instead of taking her straight to the office I ushered her into the front room. But one of them was there, sprawled in a chair, and when Janet saw him she emitted an exclamation. It was Larry Huddleston. I greeted him, invited Janet to sit, and, not wanting to use the connecting door to the office, went around by the hall. Wolfe wasn't in the office, but two more visitors were, and they were Dr. Brady and Daniel Huddleston, evidently, judging from their attitudes, not being chummy.

Oho, I thought, we're having a party, and went to the kitchen, and there was Wolfe.

He was standing by the long table, watching Fritz rub a spice mixture into slices of calf's liver, and watching with him, standing beside him, closer to him than I had ever seen any woman or girl of any age tolerated, with her hand slipped between his arm and his bulk, was Maryella.

Wolfe gave me a fleeting glance. "Back, Archie? We're doing mock terrapin. Miss Timms had a suggestion." He leaned over to peer at the liver, straightened, and sighed clear to the bottom. He turned to me: "And Miss Nichols?"

"In front. Doc Vollmer took a sample and will phone as soon as possible."

"Good. On the coldest shelf, Fritz; the time is uncertain; and leave the door to Archie. Archie, we are busy and not available. All of us. Come, Miss Timms."

She couldn't cling to him as they went through the door, because there wasn't room.

7 DR. BRADY SAID SHARPLY, "I'VE BEEN WAITING HERE over half an hour. How long will this take? I'm due at my office at one o'clock."

I was at my desk and he was nearby, on one of the straight-backed chairs. Next to him was Maryella, in the wing chair that I like to read in, and on the other side of her was Larry. Then Daniel Huddleston; and ending the arc was Janet in the red leather chair, her shoulders sagging, looking as if she were only about half there. As far as that goes, none of them looked very comfortable, not even Maryella; she would glance at one of them and then look back at Wolfe, and set her teeth on her lip and clear her throat again.

Wolfe's half-open eyes were directed at Brady. "I'm afraid you may be a little late at your office, doctor. I'm sorry—"

"But what kind of a performance is this? You said on the telephone—"

"Please," Wolfe interrupted sharply. "I said that to get you here." His glance went around. "The situation is no longer as I represented it on the phone, to any of you. I told you that it was definitely known that Miss Huddleston had been murdered. Now we're a little further along. I know who murdered her."

They stared at him. Maryella's teeth went deeper into her lip. Janet gripped the arms of her chair and stopped breathing. Daniel leaned forward with his chin stuck out like a halfback waiting for a signal. Brady made a noise in his throat. The only one who uttered anything intelligible was Larry. He said harshly:

"The hell you do."

Wolfe nodded. "I do. That is one change in the situation. The other is that an attempt has been made to murder Miss Nichols.—Please! There is no cause for alarm. The attempt was frustrated—"

"When?" Brady demanded. "What kind of an attempt?"

"To murder Janet!" Maryella exclaimed incredulously.

Wolfe frowned at them. "This will go more quickly and smoothly with no interruptions. I'll make it as brief as possible; I assure you I have no wish to prolong the unpleasantness. Especially since I find less than enjoyable the presence in this room of an extremely unattractive person. I shall call that person X. As you all know, X began with an effort to injure Miss Huddleston by sending anonymous letters—"

"Nothing of the sort!" Larry blurted indignantly. "We don't know that one of us sent those letters! Neither do you!"

"Put it this way, Mr. Huddleston." Wolfe wiggled a finger at him. "I make statements. You suspend belief. In the end there will be a verdict, and you will concur or not. X sent those letters. Then he—I am forced thus to exclude women, at least temporarily, by the pronominal inadequacy of our language—then he became dissatisfied with the results, or something happened, no matter which. In any case, X decided on something more concrete and conclusive. Murder. The technique was unquestionably suggested by the recent death of Miss Horrocks by tetanus. A small amount of material procured at the stable, immersed in water, furnished the required emulsion. It was strained and mixed with argyrol, the mixture was put in a bottle with an iodine label, and the bottle was substituted for the iodine bottle in the cabinet in Miss Huddleston's bathroom. But—"

"Her bathroom?" Maryella was incredulous again.

"Yes, Miss Timms. But X was not one to wait indefinitely for some accidental disjunction in Miss Huddleston's skin. He carried the preparations further, by smashing her bottle of bath salts and inserting a sliver of glass among the bristles of her bath brush. Beautifully simple. It would be supposed that the sliver lodged there when the bottle broke. If she saw it and removed it, no harm done, try again. If she didn't see it, she would cut herself, and there was the iodine bottle—"

"Nuts!" Larry exploded. "You can't possibly—"

"No?" Wolfe snapped. "Archie, if you please?"

I took it from my pocket and handed it to him, and he displayed it to them between his thumb and forefinger. "Here it is. The identical piece of glass."

They craned their necks. Brady stretched clear out of his chair, demanding, "How in the name of God—"

"Sit down, Dr. Brady. How did I get it? We'll come to that. Those were the preparations. But chance intervened, to make better ones. That very afternoon, on the terrace, a tray of glasses was upset and the pieces flew everywhere. X conceived a brilliant improvisation on the spot. Helping to collect the pieces, he deposited one in Miss Huddleston's slipper, and, entering the house on an errand, as all of you did in connection with that minor catastrophe, he ran upstairs and removed the sliver of glass from the bath brush, and got the bogus bottle of iodine, took it downstairs, and placed it in the cupboard in the living room, removing the genuine one kept there. For an active person half a minute, at most a minute, did for that."

Wolfe sighed. "As you know, it worked. Miss Huddleston stuck her foot in the slipper and cut her toe, her brother brought the iodine, Dr. Brady applied it, and she got tetanus and died." His eyes darted to Brady. "By the way, doctor, that suggests a question. Is it worthy of remark that you failed to notice the absence of the characteristic odor of iodine? I merely ask."

Brady was looking grim. "As far as I am concerned," he said acidly, "it remains to be proven that the bottle did not contain iodine, and therefore—"

"Nonsense. I told you on the phone. The piece of turf where the chimpanzee poured some of the contents has been analyzed. Argyrol, no iodine, and a surfeit of tetanus germs. The police have it. I tell you, I tell all of you, that however disagreeable you may find this inquiry as I pursue it, it would be vastly more disagreeable if the police were doing it. Your alternative—"

The doorbell called me away, since Fritz had been told to leave it to me. I dashed out, not wanting to miss anything crucial, and naturally took the precaution, under the circumstances, of pulling the curtain aside for a peek through the glass. It was well that I did. I never saw the stoop more officially populated. Inspector Cramer, Lieutenant Rowcliff, and Sergeant Stebbins! I slipped the chain bolt in place, which would let the door come only five inches, turned the lock and the knob and pulled, and spoke through the crack:

"They don't live here any more."

"Listen, you goddam squirt," Cramer said impolitely. "Open the door!"

"Can't. The hinge is broke."

"I say open up! We know they're here!"

"You do in a pig's eye. The things you *don't* know. If you've got one, show it. No? No warrant? And all the judges out to lunch—"

"By God, if you think—"

"I don't. Mr. Wolfe thinks. All I have is brute force. Like this—"

I banged the door to, made sure the lock had caught, went to the kitchen and stood on a chair and removed a screw, bolted the back door and told Fritz to leave it that way, and returned to the office. Wolfe stopped talking to look at me. I nodded, and told him as I crossed to my chair:

"Three irate men. They'll probably return with legalities."

"Who are they?"

"Cramer, Rowcliff, Stebbins."

"Ha." Wolfe looked gratified. "Disconnect the bell."

"Done."

"Bolt the back door."

"Done."

"Good." He addressed them: "An inspector, a lieutenant, and a sergeant of police have this building under siege. Since they are investigating murder, and since all of the persons involved have been collected here by me and they know it, my bolted doors will irritate them almost beyond endurance. I shall let them enter when I am ready, not before. If any of you wish to leave now, Mr. Goodwin will let you out to the street. Do you?"

Nobody moved or spoke, or breathed.

Wolfe nodded. "During your absence, Archie, Dr. Brady stated that outdoors on that terrace, with a breeze going, it is not likely that the absence of the iodine odor would have been noticed by him, or by anyone. Is that correct, doctor?"

"Yes," Brady said curtly.

"Very well. I agree with you." Wolfe surveyed the group. "So X's improvisation was a success. Later, of course, he replaced the genuine iodine in the cupboard and removed the bogus. From his standpoint, it was next to perfect. It might indeed have been perfect, invulnerable to any inquest, if the chimpanzee hadn't poured some of that mixture on the grass. I don't know why X didn't attend to that; there was plenty of time, whole days and nights; possibly he hadn't seen the chimpanzee doing it, or maybe he didn't realize the danger. And we know he was foolhardy. He should certainly have disposed of the bogus iodine and the piece of glass he had removed from Miss Huddleston's bath brush when it was no longer needed, but he didn't. He—"

"How do you know he didn't?" Larry demanded.

"Because he kept them. He must have kept them, since he used them. Yesterday he put the bogus iodine in the cabinet in Miss Nichols' bathroom, and the piece of glass in her bath brush."

I was watching them all at once, or trying to, but he or she was too good for me. The one who wasn't surprised and startled put on so good an imitation of it that I was no better off than I was before. Wolfe was taking them in too, his narrowed eyes the only moving part of him, his arms folded, his chin on his necktie.

"And," he rumbled, "it worked. This morning. Miss Nichols got in the tub, cut her arm, took the bottle from the cabinet, and applied the stuff—"

"Good God!" Brady was out of his chair. "Then she must—"

Wolfe pushed a palm at him. "Calm yourself, doctor. Antitoxin has been administered."

"By whom?"

"By a qualified person. Please be seated. Thank you. Miss Nichols does not need your professional services, but I would like to use your professional knowledge. First—Archie, have you got that brush?"

It was on my desk, still wrapped in the paper Hoskins had got for me. I removed the paper and offered the brush to Wolfe, but instead of taking it he asked me:

"You use a bath brush, don't you? Show us how you manipulate it. On your arm."

Accustomed as I was to loony orders from him, I merely obeyed. I started at the wrist and made vigorous sweeps to the shoulder and back.

"That will do, thank you.—No doubt all of you, if you use bath brushes, wield them in a similar manner. Not, that is, with a circular motion, or around the arm, but lengthwise, up and down. So the cut on Miss Nichols' arm, as Mr. Goodwin described it to me, runs lengthwise, about halfway between the wrist and the elbow. Is that correct, Miss Nichols?"

Janet nodded, cleared her throat, and said, "Yes," in a small voice.

"And it's about an inch long. A little less?"

"Yes."

Wolfe turned to Brady. "Now for you, sir. Your professional knowledge. To establish a premise invulnerable to assault. Why did Miss Nichols carve a gash nearly an inch long on her arm? Why didn't she jerk the brush away the moment she felt her skin being ruptured?"

"Why?" Brady was scowling at him. "For the obvious reason that she didn't feel it."

"Didn't feel it?"

"Certainly not. I don't know what premise you're trying to establish, but with the bristles rubbing her skin there would be no feeling of the sharp glass cutting her. None whatever. She wouldn't know she had been cut until she saw the blood."

"Indeed." Wolfe looked disappointed. "You're sure of that? You'd testify to it?"

"I would. Positively."

"And any other doctor would?"

"Certainly."

"Then we'll have to take it that way. Those, then, are the facts. I have finished. Now it's your turn to talk. All of you. Of course this is highly unorthodox, all of you together like this, but it would take too long to do it properly, singly."

He leaned back and joined his finger tips at the apex of his central magnificence. "Miss Timms, we'll start with you. Talk, please."

Maryella said nothing. She seemed to be meeting his gaze, but she didn't speak.

"Well, Miss Timms?"

"I don't know—" she tried to clear the huskiness from her voice— "I don't know what you want me to say."

"Nonsense," Wolf said sharply. "You know quite well. You are an intelligent woman. You've been living in that house two years. Is it likely that ill feeling or fear, any emotion whatever, was born in one of these people and distended to the enormity of homicide, and you were totally unaware of it? I don't believe it. I want you to tell me the things that I would drag out of you if I kept you here alone all afternoon firing questions at you."

Maryella shook her head. "You couldn't drag anything out of me that's not in me."

"You won't talk?"

"I can't talk." Maryella did not look happy. "When I've got nothing to say."

Wolfe's eyes left her. "Miss Nichols?"

Janet shook her head.

"I won't repeat it. I'm saying to you what I said to Miss Timms."

"I know you are." Janet swallowed and went on in a thin voice, "I can't tell you anything, honestly I can't."

"Not even who tried to kill you? You have no idea who tried to kill you this morning?"

"No, I—I haven't. That's what frightened me so much. I don't know who it was."

Wolfe grunted, and turned to Larry. "Mr. Huddleston?"

"I don't know a damn thing," Larry said gruffly.

"You don't. Dr. Brady?"

"It seems to me," Brady said coolly, "that you stopped before you were through. You said you know who murdered Miss Huddleston. If—"

"I prefer to do it this way, doctor. Have you anything to tell me?"

"No."

"Nothing with any bearing on any aspect of this business?"

"No."

Wolfe's eyes went to Daniel. "Mr. Huddleston, you have already talked, to me and to the police. Have you anything new to say?"

"I don't think I have," Daniel said slowly. He looked more miserable than anyone else. "I agree with Dr. Brady that if you—"

"I would expect you to," Wolfe snapped. His glance swept the arc. "I warn all of you, with of course one exception, that the police will worm it out of you and it will be a distressing experience. They will make no distinction between relevancies and irrelevancies. They will, for example, impute significance to the fact that Miss Timms has been trying to captivate Mr. Larry Huddleston with her charms—"

"I have not!" Maryella cried indignantly. "Whatever—"

"Yes, you have. At least you did on Tuesday, August 19th. Mr. Goodwin is a good reporter. Sitting on the arm of his chair. Ogling him—"

"I wasn't! I wasn't trying to captivate him—"

"Do you love him? Desire him? Fancy him?"

"I certainly don't!"

"Then the police will be doubly suspicious. They will suspect that you were after him for his aunt's money. And speaking of money, some of you must know that Miss Huddleston's brother was getting money from her and dissatisfied with what he got. Yet you refuse to tell me—"

"I wasn't dissatisfied," Daniel broke in. His face flushed and his voice rose. "You have no right to make insinuations—"

"I'm not making insinuations." Wolfe was crisp. "I am showing you the sort of thing the police will get their teeth into. They are quite capable of supposing you were blackmailing your sister—"

"Blackmail!" Daniel squealed indignantly. "She gave it to me for research—"

"Research!" his nephew blurted with a sneer. "Research! The Elixir of Life! Step right up, gents . . ."

Daniel sprang to his feet, and for a second I thought his intention was to commit mayhem on Larry, but it seemed he merely was arising to make a speech.

"That," he said, his jaw quivering with anger, "is a downright lie! My motivation and my methods are both strictly scientific. Elixir of Life is a romantic and inadmissible conception. The proper scientific term is 'catholicon.' My sister agreed with me, and being a woman of imagination and insight, for years she generously financed—"

"Catholicon!" Wolfe was staring at him incredulously. "And I said you were capable of using your brains!"

"I assure you, sir—"

"Don't try. Sit down." Wolfe was disgusted, "I don't care if you wasted your sister's money, but there are some things you people know that I do care about, and you are foolish not to tell me." He wiggled a finger at Brady. "You, doctor, should be ashamed of yourself. You ought to know better. It is idiotic to withhold facts which are bound to be uncovered sooner or later. You said you had nothing to tell me with any bearing on any aspect of this business. What about the box of stable refuse you procured for the stated purpose of extracting tetanus germs from it?"

Daniel made a noise and turned his head to fix Brady with a stare. Brady was taken aback, but not as much as might have been expected. He regarded Wolfe a moment and then said quietly, "I admit I should have told you that."

"Is that all you have to say about it? Why didn't you tell the police when they first started to investigate?"

"Because I thought there was nothing to investigate. I continued to think so until this morning, when you phoned me. It would have served no useful purpose—"

"What did you do with that stuff?"

"I took it to the office and did some experiments with two of my colleagues. We were settling an argument. Then we destroyed it. All of it."

"Did any of these people know about it?"

"I don't—" Brady frowned. "Yes. I remember—I discussed it. Telling them how dangerous any small cut might be—"

"Not me," Daniel said grimly. "If I had known you did that—"

They glared at each other. Daniel muttered something and sat down.

The phone rang, and I swiveled and got it. It was Doc Vollmer, and I nodded to Wolfe and he took it. When he hung up he told them:

"The bottle from which Miss Nichols treated her wound this morning contained enough tetanus germs to destroy the population of a city, properly distributed." He focused on Brady. "You may have some idea, doctor, how the police would regard that episode, especially if you had withheld it. It would give you no end of trouble. In a thing like this evasion or concealment should never be attempted without the guidance of an expert. By the way, how long had you known Miss Huddleston?"

"I had known her casually for some time. Several years."

"How long intimately?"

"I wouldn't say I knew her intimately. A couple of months ago I formed the habit of going there rather often."

"What made you form the habit? Did you fall in love with her?"

"With whom?"

"Miss Huddleston."

"Certainly not." Brady looked not only astonished but insulted. "She was old enough to be my mother."

"Then why did you suddenly start going there?"

"Why—a man goes places, that's all."

Wolfe shook his head. "Not in an emotional vacuum. Was it greed or parsimony? Free horseback rides? I doubt it; your income is probably adequate. Mere convenience? No; it was out of your way, quite a bother. My guess, to employ the conventional euphemism, is love. Had you fallen in love with Miss Nichols?"

"No."

"Then what? I assure you, doctor, I am doing this much more tactfully than the police would. What was it?"

A funny look appeared on Brady's face. Or a series of looks. First it was denial, then hesitation, then embarrassment, then do or die. All the time his eyes were straight at Wolfe. Suddenly he said, in a voice louder than he had been using, "I had fallen in love with Miss Timms. Violently."

"Oh!" Maryella exclaimed in amazement. "You certainly never—"

"Don't interrupt, please," Wolfe said testily. "Had you notified Miss Timms of your condition?"

"No, I hadn't." Brady stuck to his guns. "I was afraid to. She was so—I didn't suppose—she's a terrible flirt—"

"That's not true! You know mighty well—"

"Please!" Wolfe was peremptory. His glance shot from right to left and back again. "So all but one of you knew of Dr. Brady's procuring that box of material from the stable, and all withheld the information from me. You're hopeless. Let's try another one, more specific. The day Miss Huddleston came here, she told me that Miss Nichols had a grievance against her, and she suspected her of sending those anonymous letters. I ask all of you—including you, Miss Nichols—what was that grievance?"

No one said a word.

"I ask you individually. Miss Nichols?"

Janet shook her head. Her voice was barely audible. "Nothing. It was nothing."

"Mr. Huddleston?"

Daniel said promptly, "I have no idea."

"Miss Timms?"

"I don't know," Maryella said, and by the way Wolfe's eyes stayed with her an instant, I saw that he knew she was lying.

"Dr. Brady?"

"If I knew I'd tell you," Brady said, "but I don't."

"Mr. Huddleston?"

Larry was waiting for him with a fixed smile that twisted a corner of his mouth. "I told you before," he said harshly, "that I don't know a damn thing. That goes right down the line."

"Indeed. May I have your watch a moment, please?"

Larry goggled at him.

"That hexagonal thing on your wrist," Wolfe said. "May I see it a moment?"

Larry's face displayed changes, as Brady's had shortly before. First it was puzzled, then defiant, then he seemed to be pleased about something. He snarled:

"What do you want with my watch?"

"I want to look at it. It's a small favor. You haven't been very helpful so far."

Larry, his lips twisted with the smile again, unbuckled the strap and arose to pass the watch across the desk to Wolfe, whose fingers closed over it as he said to me:

"The Huddleston folder, Archie."

I went and unlocked the cabinet and got out the folder and brought it. Wolfe took it and flipped it open and said:

"Stay there, Archie. As a bulwark and a witness. Two witnesses would be better. Dr. Brady, if you will please stand beside Mr. Goodwin and keep your eyes on me? Thank you."

Wolfe's eyes went through the gap between Brady and me to focus on Larry. "You are a very silly young man, Mr. Huddleston. Incredibly callow. You were smugly gratified because you thought I was expecting to find a picture of Miss Nichols in your watch case and would be chagrined not to. You were wrong. Now, doctor, and Archie, please observe. Here is the back of the watch. Here is a picture of Miss

Nichols, trimmed to six sides, and apparently to fit. The point could be definitely determined by opening the watch case, but I'm not going to, because it will be opened later and microscopically compared with the picture to prove that it did contain it—Archie!"

I bulwarked. I owed Larry a smack anyhow, for bad manners if nothing else, but I didn't actually deliver it, since all he did was shoot off his mouth and try to shove through Brady and me to make a grab for the watch. So I merely stiff-armed him and propelled him backwards into his chair and stood ready.

"So," Wolfe went on imperturbably, "I put the watch and picture into separate envelopes for safekeeping. Thus. If, Mr. Huddleston, you are wondering how I got that picture, your aunt left it here. I suggest that it is time for you to help us a little, and I'll start with a question that I can make a test of. When did your aunt take that picture from you?"

Larry was trying to sneer, but it wasn't working very well. His face couldn't hold it because some of the muscles were making movements of their own.

"Probably," Wolfe said, "it's time to let the police in. I suppose they'll get along faster with you—"

"You fat bastard!" But the snarl in Larry's voice had become a whine.

Wolfe grimaced. "I'll try once more, sir. You are going to answer these questions, if not for me then for someone less fat but more importunate. Would you rather have it dug out of the servants and your friends and acquaintances? It's shabby enough as it is; that would only make it worse. When did your aunt take that picture from you?"

Larry's jaw worked, but his tongue didn't. Wolfe waited ten seconds, then said curtly:

"Let them in, Archie."

I took a step, but before I took another one Larry blurted:

"Goddam you! You know damn well when she took it! She took it the day she came down here!"

Wolfe nodded. "That's better. But that wasn't the first time she objected to your relations with Miss Nichols. Was it?"

"No."

"Did she object on moral grounds?"

"Hell, no. She objected to our getting married. She ordered me to break off the engagement. The engagement was secret, but she got suspicious and questioned Janet, and Janet told her, and she made me call it off."

"And naturally you were enraged." Wolfe's voice was smooth, silky. "You burned for revenge—"

"I did not!" Larry leaned forward, having trouble to control his jaw. "You can come off that right now! You're not going to pin anything on me! I never really wanted to marry her, and what's more, I never intended to! I can prove that by a friend of mine!"

"Indeed." Wolfe's eyes were nearly shut. "A man like you has friends? I suppose so. But after your aunt made you break the engagement you still kept the picture in your watch?"

"Yes. I had to. I mean I had Janet to deal with too, and it wasn't easy, living right there in the house. I was afraid of her. You don't know her. I opened the watch case purposely in front of my aunt so she'd take that damn picture. Janet seemed to think the picture meant something, and I thought when she knew it was gone—"

"Did you know that Miss Nichols sent the anonymous letters?"

"No, I didn't. Maybe I suspected, but I didn't know."

"Did you also suspect, when your aunt—"

"Stop! Stop it!"

It was Janet.

She didn't raise her voice. She didn't have to. The tone alone was enough to stop anything and anybody. It was what you would expect to come out of an old abandoned grave, if you had such expectations. Except her mouth, no part of her moved. Her eyes were concentrated on Wolfe's face, with an expression in them that made it necessary for me to look somewhere else. Apparently it had the same effect on the others, for they did the same as me. We gazed at Wolfe.

"Ha," he said quietly. "A little too much for you, is it, Miss Nichols?"

She went on staring at him.

"As I expected," he said, "you're all rubble inside. There's nothing left of you. The simplest way is for me to dictate a confession and you sign it. Then I'll send a copy of it to a man I know, the editor of the *Gazette*, and it will be on his front page this evening. He would like an exclusive picture of you to go with it, and Mr. Goodwin will be glad to take it. I know you'll like that."

Uh-huh, I thought, he's not only going to make a monkey of Cramer, he's going to give him a real black eye. Daniel muttered something, and so did Brady, but Wolfe silenced them with a gesture.

"For your satisfaction," he went on, "I ought to tell you, Miss Nichols, that your guilt was by no means obvious. I became aware of it only when Mr. Goodwin telephoned me from Riverdale this morning, though I did of course notice Mr. Larry Huddleston's hexagonal watch when he came here nine days ago, and I surmised your picture had been in it. But your performance today was the act of a nitwit. I presume you were struck with consternation yesterday when you saw that turf being removed, realized what the consequences would be, and attempted to divert suspicion by staging an attack on yourself. Did you know what I was getting at a while ago when I asked Dr. Brady why you didn't jerk the brush away the instant you felt the glass puncture your skin? And he replied, as of course he would, that you didn't feel the glass cutting you?"

She didn't answer.

"That," Wolfe said, "was precisely the point, that you did jerk the brush away when you had pulled it along your arm less than an inch, because you knew the glass was there and was cutting you, having put it there yourself. Otherwise the cut would have been much longer, probably half the length of your arm. You saw Mr. Goodwin wield the brush as an illustration, sweeping from wrist to shoulder. Everyone does that. At least, no one moves the brush less than an inch and stops. But even without that, your performance today was fantastic, if you meant—as you did—to make it appear as an attempt by some other person to kill you. Such a person would have known that after what had happened, even if you used the bogus iodine, you would certainly have antitoxin administered, which would have made the attempt a fiasco. Whereas you, arranging the affair yourself, knew that a dose of antitoxin would save you from harm. You really—"

"Stop it!" Janet said, in exactly the same tone as before. I couldn't look at her.

But that was a mistake, not looking at her. For completely without warning she turned into a streak of lightning. It was so sudden and swift that I was still in my chair when she grabbed the sliver of glass from Wolfe's desk, and by the time I got going she had whirled and gone through the air straight at Larry Huddleston, straight at his face with the piece of glass in her fingers. Everyone else moved too, but no one fast enough, not even Larry. Daniel got his arms around her, her left arm pinned against her, and I got her other arm, including the wrist, but there was a red streak across Larry's cheek from beneath his eye nearly to his chin.

Everybody but Janet was making noises, some of which were words.

"Shut up!" Wolfe said gruffly. "Archie, if you've finished your nap—"

"Go to hell," I told him. "I'm not a genius like you." I gave Janet's wrist a little pressure. "Drop it, girlie."

She let the piece of glass fall to the floor and stood rigid, watching Brady examine Larry's cheek.

"Only skin deep," Brady said, unfolding a handkerchief. "Here, hold this against it."

"By God," Larry blurted, "if it leaves a scar—"

"That was a lie," Janet said. "You lied!"

"What?" Larry glared at her.

"She means," Wolfe put in, "that you lied when you said you neither desired nor intended to marry her. I agree with her that the air was already bad enough in here without that. You fed her passion and her hope. She wanted you, God knows why. When your aunt intervened, she struck. For revenge? Yes. Or saying to your aunt, preparing to say, 'Let me have him or I'll ruin you?' Probably. Or to ruin your aunt and then collect you from the debris? Possibly. Or all three, Miss Nichols?"

Janet, her back to him, still facing Larry, did not speak. I held onto her.

"But," Wolfe said, "your aunt came to see me, and that frightened her. Also, when she herself came that evening and found that picture here, the picture you had carried in your watch, she was not only frightened but enraged. Being a very sentimental young woman—"

"Good God," Brady muttered involuntarily. "Sentimental!"

A shudder ran over Janet from top to bottom. I pulled her around by the arm and steered her to the red leather chair and she dropped into it. Wolfe said brusquely:

"Archie, your notebook. No—first the camera—"

"I can't stand it!" Maryella cried, standing up. She reached for something to hold onto, and as luck would have it, it was Brady's arm. "I can't!"

Wolfe frowned at them. "Take her up and show her the orchids, doctor. Three flights. And take that casualty along and patch it up. Fritz will get what you need. I advise you to smell the iodine."

At six o'clock that evening I was at my desk. The office was quiet and peaceful. Wolfe had done it up brown. Cramer had come like a lion with a squad and a warrant, and had departed like a lamb with a flock of statements, a confession, a murderer, and apoplexy. Despite all of which, loving Cramer as I do, when I heard the elevator bringing Wolfe down from the plant rooms I got too busy with my desk work to turn around. Intending not even to acknowledge his presence. The excuse he had given for keeping Maryella there was that it was impossible for her to return to Riverdale as things stood, and there was no place else for her to go. Phooey.

But I got no chance to freeze them out, for they went right on by the office door, to the kitchen. I stuck to my desk. Time went by, but I was too irritated to get any work done. Towards seven o'clock the bell rang, and I went to the front door and found Doc Brady. He said he had been invited, so I took him to the kitchen.

The kitchen was warm, bright, and full of appetizing smells. Fritz was slicing a ripe pineapple. Wolfe was seated in the chair by the window, tasting out of a steaming saucepan. Maryella was perched on one end of the long table with her legs crossed, sipping a mint julep. She fluttered the fingers of her free hand at Brady for a greeting. He stopped in astonishment, and stood and blinked at her, at Wolfe and Fritz, and back at her.

"Well," he said. "Really. I'm glad you can be so festive. Under the circumstances—"

"Nonsense!" Wolfe snapped. "There's nothing festive about it; we're merely preparing a meal. Miss Timms is much better occupied. Would you prefer hysterics? We had a discussion about spoon bread, and there are two batches in the oven. Two eggs, and three eggs. Milk at a hundred and fifty degrees, and boiling. Take that julep she's offering you. Archie, a julep?"

Brady took the julep from her, set it down on the table without sampling it, wrapped his arms around her, and made it tighter. She showed no inclination to struggle or scratch. Wolfe pretended not to notice, and placidly took another taste from the saucepan. Fritz started trimming the slices of pineapple.

Maryella gasped, "Ah think Ah'd bettah breathe."

Wolfe asked amiably, "A julep, Archie?"

I turned without answering, went to the hall and got my hat, slammed the door from the outside, walked to the corner and into Sam's place, and climbed onto a stool at the counter. I didn't know I was muttering to myself, but I must have been, for Sam, behind the counter, demanded:

"Spoon bread? What the hell is spoon bread?"

"Don't speak till you're spoken to," I told him, "and give me a ham sandwich and a glass of toxin. If you have no toxin, make it milk. Good old wholesome orangoutang milk. I have been playing tag with an undressed murderess. Do you know how to tell a murderess when you see one? It's a cinch. Soak her in iodine over night, drain through cheesecloth, add a pound of pig chitlins—what? Oh. Rye and no pickle. Ah think Ah'd bettah breathe."

I have never mentioned it to him, and I don't intend to. I've got a dozen theories about it. Here are a few for samples:

1. He knew I would go to the funeral, and he sent that bunch of orchids purely and simply to pester me.

2. Something from his past. When he was young and handsome, and Bess Huddleston was ditto, they might have been—uh, acquainted. As for her not recognizing him, I doubt if his own mother would, as is. And there's no doubt he has fifteen or twenty pasts; I know that much about him.

3. He was paying a debt. He knew, or had an idea, that she was going to be murdered, from something someone said that first day, and was too damn lazy, or too interested in corned beef hash with chitlins, to do anything about it. Then when she was ready for burial he felt he owed her something, so he sent her what? Just some orchids, any old orchids? No, sir. Black ones. The first black orchids ever seen on a coffin anywhere on the globe since the dawn of history. Debt canceled. Paid in full. File receipted bills.

4. I'll settle for number three.

5. But it's still a mystery, and when he catches me looking at him a certain way he knows darned well what's on my mind.

                                                              A. G.

CHAMPAGNE FOR ONE

1

IF IT HADN'T BEEN RAINING AND BLOWING THAT RAW
Tuesday morning in March I would have been out, walking to the
bank to deposit a couple of checks, when Austin Byne phoned me,
and he might have tried somebody else. But more likely not. He would
probably have rung again later, so I can't blame all this on the weather.
As it was, I was there in the office, oiling the typewriter and the two
Marley .38's, for which we had permits, from the same can of oil,
when the phone rang and I lifted it and spoke.

"Nero Wolfe's office, Archie Goodwin speaking."

"Hello there. This is Byne. Dinky Byne."

There it is in print for you, but it wasn't for me, and I didn't get
it. It sounded more like a dying bullfrog than a man.

"Clear your throat," I suggested, "or sneeze or something, and try
again."

"That wouldn't help. My tubes are all clogged. Tubes. Clogged.
Understand? Dinky Byne—B-Y-N-E."

"Oh, hello. I won't ask how you are, hearing how you sound. My
sympathy."

"I need it. I need more than sympathy, too." It was coming through
slightly better. "I need help. Will you do me a hell of a favor?"

I made a face. "I might. If I can do it sitting down and it doesn't
cost me any teeth."

"It won't cost you a thing. You know my Aunt Louise. Mrs. Robert Robilotti."

"Only professionally. Mr. Wolfe did a job for her once, recovered
some jewelry. That is, she hired him and I did the job—and she didn't
like me. She resented a remark I made."

"That won't matter. She forgets remarks. I suppose you know about the dinner party she gives every year on the birthday date of my Uncle Albert, now resting in peace perhaps?"

"Sure. Who doesn't?"

"Well, that's it. Today. Seven o'clock. And I'm to be one of the chevaliers, and listen to me, and I've got some fever. I can't go. She'll be sore as the devil if she has to scout around for a fill-in, and when I phone her I want to tell her she won't have to, that I've already got one. Mr. Archie Goodwin. You're a better chevalier than me any day. She knows you, and she has forgotten the remark you made, and anyhow she has resented a hundred remarks I've made, and you'll know exactly how to treat the lady guests. Black tie, seven o'clock, and you know the address. After I phone her, of course she'll ring you to confirm it. And you can do it sitting down, and I'll guarantee nothing will be served that will break your teeth. She has a good cook. My God, I didn't think I could talk so long. How about it, Archie?"

"I'm chewing on it," I told him. "You waited long enough."

"Yeah, I know, but I kept thinking I might be able to make it, until I pried my eyes open this morning. I'll do the same for you someday."

"You can't. I haven't got a billionaire aunt. I doubt if she has forgotten the remark I made because it was fairly sharp. What if she vetoes me? You'd have to ring me again to call it off, and then ring someone else, and you shouldn't talk that much, and besides, my feelings would be hurt."

I was merely stalling, partly because I wanted to hear him talk some more. It sounded to me as if his croak had flaws in it. Clogged tubes have no effect on your esses, as in "seven" and "sitting," but he was trying to produce one, and he turned "long" into "lawd" when it should have been more like "lawg." So I was suspecting that the croak was a phony. If I hadn't had my full share of ego I might also have been curious as to why he had picked on me, since we were not chums, but of course that was no problem. If your ego is in good shape you will pretend you're surprised if a National Chairman calls to tell you his party wants to nominate you for President of the United States, but you're not *really* surprised.

I only stalled him long enough to be satisfied that the croak was a fake before I agreed to take it on. The fact was that the idea appealed to me. It would be a new experience and should increase my knowledge of human nature. It might also be a little ticklish, and even dismal, but it would be interesting to see how they handled it. Not to mention how I would handle it myself. So I told him I would stand by for a call from his Aunt Louise.

It came in less than half an hour. I had finished the oiling job and was putting the guns in their drawer in my desk when the phone rang. A voice I recognized said she was Mrs. Robilotti's secretary and Mrs. Robilotti wished to speak with me, and I said, "Is it jewelry again, Miss Fromm?" and she said, "She will tell you what it is, Mr. Goodwin."

Then another voice, also recognized. "Mr. Goodwin?"

"Speaking."

"My nephew Austin Byne says he phoned you."

"I guess he did."

"You *guess* he did?"

"The voice said it was Byne, but it could have been a seal trying to bark."

"He has laryngitis. He told you so. Apparently you haven't changed any. He says that he asked you to take his place at dinner at my home this evening, and you said you would if I invited you. Is that correct?"

I admitted it.

"He says that you are acquainted with the nature and significance of the affair."

"Of course I am. So are fifty million other people—or more."

"I know. I regret the publicity it has received in the past, but I refuse to abandon it. I owe it to my dear first husband's memory. I am inviting you, Mr. Goodwin."

"Okay. I accept the invitation as a favor to your nephew. Thank you."

"Very well." A pause. "Of course it is not usual, on inviting a dinner guest, to caution him about his conduct, but for this occasion some care is required. You appreciate that?"

"Certainly."

"Tact and discretion are necessary."

"I'll bring mine along," I assured her.

"And of course refinement."

"I'll borrow some." I decided she needed a little comfort. "Don't worry, Mrs. Robilotti, I understand the setup and you can count on me clear through to the coffee and even after. Relax. I am fully briefed. Tact, discretion, refinement, black tie, seven o'clock."

"Then I'll expect you. Please hold the wire. My secretary will give you the names of those who will be present. It will simplify the introductions if you know them in advance."

Miss Fromm got on again. "Mr. Goodwin?"

"Still here."

"You should have paper and pencil."

"I always have. Shoot."

"Stop me if I go too fast. There will be twelve at table. Mr. and Mrs. Robilotti. Miss Celia Grantham and Mr. Cecil Grantham. They are Mrs. Robilotti's son and daughter by her first husband."

"Yeah, I know."

"Miss Helen Yarmis. Miss Ethel Varr. Miss Faith Usher. Am I going too fast?"

I told her no.

"Miss Rose Tuttle. Mr. Paul Schuster. Mr. Beverly Kent. Mr. Edwin Laidlaw. Yourself. That makes twelve. Miss Varr will be on your right and Miss Tuttle will be on your left."

I thanked her and hung up. Now that I was booked, I wasn't so sure I liked it. It would be interesting, but it might also be a strain on the nerves. However, I was booked, and I rang Byne at the number he had given me and told him he could stay home and gargle. Then I went to Wolfe's desk and wrote on his calendar Mrs. Robilotti's name and phone number. He wants to know where to reach me when I'm out, even when we have nothing important on, in case someone yells for help and will pay for it. Then I went to the hall, turned left, and pushed through the swinging door to the kitchen. Fritz was at the big table, spreading anchovy butter on shad roes.

"Cross me off for dinner," I told him. "I'm doing my good deed for the year and getting it over with."

He stopped spreading to look at me. "That's too bad. Veal birds in casserole. You know, with mushrooms and white wine."

"I'll miss it. But there may be something edible where I'm going."

"Perhaps a client?"

He was not being nosy. Fritz Brenner does not pry into other people's private affairs, not even mine. But he has a legitimate interest in the welfare of that establishment, of the people who live in that old brownstone on West Thirty-fifth Street, and he merely wanted to know if my dinner engagement was likely to promote it. It took a lot of cash. I had to be paid. He had to be paid. Theodore Horstmann, who spent all his days and sometimes part of his nights with the ten thousand orchids up in the plant rooms, had to be paid. We all had to be fed, and with the kind of grub that Wolfe preferred and provided and Fritz prepared. Not only did the orchids have to be fed, but only that week Wolfe had bought a Coelogyne from Burma for eight hundred bucks, and that was just routine. And so on and on and on, and the only source of current income was people with problems who were able and willing to pay a detective to handle them. Fritz knew we had no case going at the moment, and he was only asking if my dinner date might lead to one.

I shook my head. "Nope, not a client." I got on a stool. "A former client, Mrs. Robert Robilotti—someone swiped a million dollars' worth of rings and bracelets from her a couple of years ago and we got them back—and I need some advice. You may not be as great an expert on women as you are on food, but you have had your dealings, as I well know, and I would appreciate some suggestions on how I act this evening."

He snorted. "Act with women? You? Ha! With your thousand triumphs! Advice from me? Archie, that is upside down!"

"Thanks for the plug, but these women are special." With a fingertip I wiped up a speck of anchovy butter that had dropped on the table and licked it off. "Here's the problem. This Mrs. Robilotti's first husband was Albert Grantham, who spent the last ten years of his life doing things with part of the three or four hundred million dollars he had inherited—things to improve the world, including the people in it. I assume you will admit that a girl who has a baby but no husband needs improving."

Fritz pursed his lips. "First I would have to see the girl and the baby. They might be charming."

"It's not a question of charm, or at least it wasn't with Grantham. His dealing with the problem of unmarried mothers wasn't one of his really big operations, but he took a personal interest in it. He would rarely let his name be attached to any of his projects, but he did with that one. The place he built for it up in Dutchess County was called Grantham House and still is. What's that you're putting in?"

"Marjoram. I'm trying it."

"Don't tell him and see if he spots it. When the improved mothers were graduated from Grantham House they were financed until they got jobs or husbands, and even then they were not forgotten. One way of keeping in touch was started by Grantham himself a few years before he died. Each year on his birthday he had his wife invite four of them to dinner at his home on Fifth Avenue, and also invite, for their dinner partners, four young men. Since his death, five years ago, his wife has kept it up. She says she owes it to his memory—though she is now married to a specimen named Robert Robilotti who has never been in the improving business. Today is Grantham's birthday, and that's where I'm going for dinner. I am one of the four young men."

"No!" Fritz said.

"Why no?"

"You, Archie?"

"Why not me?"

"It will ruin everything. They will all be back at Grantham House in less than a year."

"No," I said sternly. "I appreciate the compliment, but this is a serious matter and I need advice. Consider: these girls are mothers, but they are improved mothers. They are supposed to be trying to get a toehold on life. Say they are. Inviting them to dinner at that goddam palace, with four young men from the circle that woman moves in as table partners, whom they have never seen before and don't expect ever to see again, is one hell of a note. Okay, I can't help that; I can't improve Grantham, since he's dead, and I would hate to undertake to improve Mrs. Robilotti, dead or alive, but I have my personal problem: how do I act? I would welcome suggestions."

Fritz cocked his head. "Why do you go?"

"Because a man I know asked me to. That's another question, why he picked me, but skip it. I guess I agreed to go because I thought it would be fun to watch, but now I realize it may be pretty damn grim. However, I'm stuck, and what's my program? I can try to make it gay, or clown it, or get one of them talking about the baby, or get lit and the hell with it, or shall I stand up and make a speech about famous mothers like Venus and Mrs. Shakespeare and that Roman woman who had twins?"

"Not that. No."

"Then what?"

"I don't know. Anyway, you are just talking."

"All right, you talk a while."

He aimed a knife at me. "I know you so well, Archie. As well as you know me, maybe. This is just talk and I enjoy it. You need no suggestions. Program?" He slashed at it with the knife. "Ha! You will go there and look at them and see, and act as you feel. You always do. If it is too painful you will leave. If one of the girls is enchanting and the men surround her, you will get her aside and tomorrow you will take her to lunch. If you are bored you will eat too much, no matter what the food is like. If you are offended— There's the elevator!" He looked at the clock. "My God, it's eleven! The larding!" He headed for the refrigerator.

I didn't jump. Wolfe likes to find me in the office when he comes down, and if I'm not there it stirs his blood a little, which is good for him, so I waited until the elevator door opened and his footsteps came down the hall and on in. I have never understood why he doesn't make more noise walking. You would think that his feet, which are no bigger than mine, would make quite a business of getting along under his seventh of a ton, but they don't. It might be someone half his weight. I gave him enough time to cross to his desk and get himself settled in his custom-built oversize chair, and then went. As I entered he grunted a good morning at me and I returned it. Our good mornings usually come then, since Fritz takes his breakfast to his room on a tray, and he spends the two hours from nine to eleven, every day including Sunday, up in the plant rooms with Theodore and the orchids.

When I was at my desk I announced, "I didn't deposit the checks that came yesterday on account of the weather. It may let up before three."

He was glancing through the mail I had put on his desk. "Get Dr. Vollmer," he commanded.

The idea of that was that if I let a little thing like a cold gusty March rain keep me from getting checks to the bank I must be sick. So I coughed. Then I sneezed. "Nothing doing," I said firmly. "He might put me to bed, and in all this bustle and hustle that wouldn't do. It would be too much for you."

He shot me a glance, nodded to show that he was on but was dropping it, and reached for his desk calendar. That always came second, after the glance at the mail.

"What is this phone number?" he demanded. "Mrs. Robilotti? That woman?"

"Yes, sir. The one who didn't want to pay you twenty grand but did."

"What does she want now?"

"Me. That's where you can get me this evening from seven o'clock on."

"Mr. Hewitt is coming this evening to bring a Dendrobium and look at the Renanthera. You said you would be here."

"I know, I expected to, but this is an emergency. She phoned me this morning."

"I didn't know she was cultivating you, or you her."

"We're not. I haven't seen her or heard her since she paid that bill. This is special. You may remember that when she hired you and we were discussing her, I mentioned a piece about her I had read in a magazine, about the dinner party she throws every year on her first husband's birthday. With four girls and four men as guests? The girls are unmarried mothers who are being rehabil—"

"I remember, yes. Buffoonery. A burlesque of hospitality. Do you mean you are abetting it?"

"I wouldn't say abetting it. A man I know named Austin Byne phoned and asked me to fill in for him because he's in bed with a cold and can't go. Anyhow, it will give me a fresh outlook. It will harden my nerves. It will broaden my mind."

His eyes had narrowed. "Archie."

"Yes, sir."

"Do I ever intrude in your private affairs?"

"Yes, sir. Frequently. But you think you don't, so go right ahead."

"I am not intruding. If it is your whim to lend yourself to that outlandish performance, very well. I merely suggest that you demean yourself. Those creatures are summoned there for an obvious purpose. It is hoped that they, or at least one of them, will meet a man who will be moved to pursue the acquaintance and who will end by legitimating, if not the infant already in being, the future produce of the womb. Therefore your attendance there will be an imposture, and you know it. I begin to doubt if you will ever let a woman plant her foot on your neck, but if you do she will have qualities that would make it impossible for her to share the fate of those forlorn creatures. You will be perpetrating a fraud."

I was shaking my head. "No, sir. You've got it wrong. I let you finish just to hear it. If that were the purpose, giving the girls a chance to meet prospects, I would say hooray for Mrs. Robilotti, and I wouldn't go. But that's the hell of it, that's not it at all. The men are from her own social circle, the kind that wear black ties six nights a week, and there's not a chance. The idea is that it will buck the girls up, be good for their morale, to spend an evening with the cream and get a taste of caviar and sit on a chair made by Congreve. Of course—"

"Congreve didn't make chairs."

"I know he didn't, but I needed a name and that one popped in. Of course that's a lot of hooey, but I won't be perpetrating a fraud. And don't be too sure I won't meet my doom. It's a scientific fact that some girls are more beautiful, more spiritual, more fascinating, after they have had a baby. Also it would be an advantage to have the family already started."

"Pfui. Then you're going."

"Yes, sir. I've told Fritz I won't be here for dinner." I left my chair. "I have to see to something. If you want to answer letters before lunch I'll be down in a couple of minutes."

I had remembered that Saturday evening at the Flamingo someone had spilled something on the sleeve of my dinner jacket, and I had used cleaner on it when I got home, and hadn't examined it since. Mounting the two flights to my room, I took a look and found it was okay.

2   I WAS WELL ACQUAINTED WITH THE INSIDES OF THE Grantham mansion, now inhabited by Robilottis, on Fifth Avenue in the Eighties, having been over every inch of it, including the servants' quarters, at the time of the jewelry hunt; and, in the taxi on my way uptown, preparing my mind for the scene of action, I had supposed that the pre-dinner gathering would be on the second floor in what was called the music room. But no. For the mothers, the works.

Hackett, admitting me, did fine. Formerly his manner with me as a hired detective had been absolutely perfect; now that I was an invited guest in uniform he made the switch without batting an eye. I suppose a man working up to butler could be taught all the ins and outs of handling the hat-and-coat problem with different grades of people, but it's so darned tricky that probably it has to be born in him. The way he told me good evening, compared with the way he had formerly greeted me, was a lesson in fine points.

I decided to upset him. When he had my hat and coat I inquired with my nose up, "How's it go, Mr. Hackett?"

It didn't faze him. That man had nerves of iron. He merely said, "Very well, thank you, Mr. Goodwin. Mrs. Robilotti is in the drawing room."

"You win, Hackett. Congratulations." I crossed the reception hall, which took ten paces, and passed through the arch.

The drawing room had a twenty-foot ceiling and could dance fifty couples easily, with an alcove for the orchestra as big as my bedroom. The three crystal chandeliers that had been installed by Albert Grantham's mother were still there, and so were thirty-seven chairs—I had counted them one day—of all shapes and sizes, not made by Congreve,

I admit, but not made in Grand Rapids either. Of all the rooms I had seen, and I had seen a lot, that was about the last one I would pick as the place for a quartet of unwed mothers to meet a bunch of strangers and relax. Entering and casting a glance around, I took a walk—it amounted to that—across to where Mrs. Robilotti was standing with a group near a portable bar. As I approached she turned to me and offered a hand.

"Mr. Goodwin. So nice to see you."

She didn't handle the switch as perfectly as Hackett had, but it was good enough. After all, I had been imposed on her. Her pale gray eyes, which were set in so far that her brows had sharp angles, didn't light up with welcome, but it was a question whether they ever had lit up for anyone or anything. The angles were not confined to the brows. Whoever had designed her had preferred angles to curves and missed no opportunities, and the passing years, now adding up to close to sixty, had made no alterations. At least they were covered below the chin, since her dress, pale gray like her eyes, had sleeves above the elbows and reached up to the base of her corrugated neck. During the jewelry business I had twice seen her exposed for the evening, and it had been no treat. The only jewelry tonight was a string of pearls and a couple of rings.

I was introduced around and was served a champagne cocktail. The first sip of the cocktail told me something was wrong, and I worked closer to the bar to find out what. Cecil Grantham, the son by the first husband, who was mixing, was committing worse than murder. I saw him. Holding a glass behind and below the bar top, he put in a half-lump of sugar, a drop or two of bitters, and a twist of lemon peel, filled it half full of soda water, set it on the bar, and filled it nearly to the top from a bottle of Cordon Rouge. Killing good champagne with junk like sugar and bitters and lemon peel is of course a common crime, but the soda water was adding horror to homicide. The motive was pure, reducing the voltage to protect the guests of honor, but faced with temptation and given my choice of self-control or soda water in champagne, I set my jaw. I was going to keep an eye on Cecil to see if he did to himself as he was doing to others, but another guest arrived and I had to go to be introduced. He made up the dozen.

By the time our hostess led the way through the arch and up the broad marble stairs to the dining room on the floor above, I had them sorted out, with names fitted to faces. Of course I had previously met Robilotti and the twins, Cecil and Celia. Paul Schuster was the one with the thin nose and quick dark eyes. Beverly Kent was the one with the long narrow face and big ears. Edwin Laidlaw was the little guy, who hadn't combed his hair, or if he had, it refused to oblige.

I had had a sort of an idea that with the girls the best way would be as an older brother who liked sisters and liked to kid them, of course with tact and refinement, and their reactions had been fairly satisfactory. Helen Yarmis, tall and slender, a little too slender, with big brown eyes and a wide curved mouth that would have been a real asset if she had kept the corners up, was on her dignity and apparently had some. Ethel Varr was the one I would have picked for my doom if I had been shopping. She was not a head-turner, but she carried her own head with an air, and she had one of those faces that you keep looking back at because it changes as it moves and catches different angles of light and shade.

I would have picked Faith Usher, not for my doom, but for my sister, because she looked as if she needed a brother more than the others. Actually she was the prettiest one of the bunch, with a dainty little face and greenish flecks in her eyes, and her figure, also dainty, was a very nice job, but she was doing her best to cancel her advantages by letting her shoulders sag and keeping her face muscles so tight she would soon have wrinkles. The right kind of brother could have done wonders with her, but I had no chance to get started during the meal because she was across the table from me, with Beverly Kent on her left and Cecil Grantham on her right.

At my left was Rose Tuttle, who showed no signs of needing a brother at all. She had blue eyes in a round face, a pony tail, and enough curves to make a contribution to Mrs. Robilotti and still be well supplied; and she had been born cheerful and it would take more than an accidental baby to smother it. In fact, as I soon learned, it would take more than two of them. With an oyster balanced on her fork, she turned her face to me and asked, "Goodwin? That's your name?"

"Right. Archie Goodwin."

"I was wondering," she said, "because that woman told me I would sit between Mr. Edwin Laidlaw and Mr. Austin Byne, but now your name's Goodwin. The other day I was telling a friend of mine about coming here, this party, and she said there ought to be unmarried fathers here too, and you seem to have changed your name—are you an unmarried father?"

Remember the tact, I warned myself. "I'm half of it," I told her. "I'm unmarried. But not, as far as I know, a father. Mr. Byne has a cold and couldn't come and asked me to fill in for him. His bad luck and my good luck."

She ate the oyster, and another one—she ate cheerfully too—and turned again. "I was telling this friend of mine that if all society men are like the ones that were here the other time, we weren't missing anything, but I guess they're not. Anyway, you're not. I noticed the way you made Helen laugh—Helen Yarmis. I don't think I ever did see her laugh before. I'm going to tell my friend about you if you don't mind."

"Not at all." Time out for an oyster. "But I don't want to mix you up. I'm not society. I'm a working man."

"Oh!" She nodded. "That explains it. What kind of work?"

Remember the discretion, I warned myself. Miss Tuttle should not be led to suspect that Mrs. Robilotti had got a detective there to keep an eye on the guests of honor. "You might," I said, "call it trouble-shooting. I work for a man named Nero Wolfe. You may have heard of him."

"I think I have." The oysters gone, she put her fork down. "I'm pretty sure . . . Oh, I remember, that murder, that woman, Susan some-body. He's a detective."

"That's right. I work for him. But I—"

"You too. You're a detective!"

"I am when I'm working, but not this evening. Now I'm playing. I'm just enjoying myself—and I am, too. I was wondering what you meant—"

Hackett and two female assistants were removing the oyster service, but it wasn't that that stopped me. The interruption was from Robert Robilotti, across the table, between Celia Grantham and Helen Yarmis, who was demanding the general ear; and as other voices gave way Mrs. Robilotti raised hers. "Must you, Robbie? That flea again?"

He smiled at her. From what I had seen of him during the jewelry hunt I had not cottoned to him, smiling or not. I'll try to be fair to him, and I know there is no law against a man having plucked eye-brows and a thin mustache and long polished nails, and my suspicion that he wore a girdle was merely a suspicion, and if he had married Mrs. Albert Grantham for her money I freely admit that no man mar-ries without a reason and with her it would have been next to impos-sible to think up another one, and I concede that he may have had hidden virtues which I had missed. One thing sure, if my name were Robert and I had married a woman fifteen years older than me for a certain reason and she was composed entirely of angles, I would not let her call me Robbie.

I'll say this for him: he didn't let her gag him. What he wanted all ears for was the story about the advertising agency executive who did a research job on the flea, and by gum he stuck to it. I had heard it told better by Saul Panzer, but he got the point in, with only fair audience response. The three society men laughed with tact, discretion, and refinement. Helen Yarmis let the corners of her mouth come up. The Grantham twins exchanged a glance of sympathy. Faith Usher caught Ethel Varr's eye across the table, shook her head, just barely moving it, and dropped her eyes. Then Edwin Laidlaw chipped in with a story about an author who wrote a book in invisible ink, and Beverly Kent followed with one about an army general who forgot which side he was on. We were all one big happy family—well, fairly happy— by the time the squabs were served. Then I had a problem. At Wolfe's table we tackle squabs with our fingers, which is of course the only practical way, but I didn't want to wreck the party. Then Rose Tuttle got her fork onto hers with one hand, and with the other grabbed a leg and yanked, which settled it.

Miss Tuttle had said something that I wanted to go into, tactfully, but she was talking with Edwin Laidlaw, on her left, and I gave Ethel Varr, on my right, a look. Her face was by no means out of surprises. In profile, close up, it was again different, and when it turned and we were eye to eye, once more it was new.

"I hope," I said, "you won't mind a personal remark."

"I'll try not to," she said. "I can't promise until I hear it."

"I'll take a chance. In case you have caught me staring at you I want to explain why."

"I don't know." She was smiling. "Maybe you'd better not. Maybe it would let me down. Maybe I'd rather think you stared just because you wanted to."

"You can think that too. If I hadn't wanted to I wouldn't have stared. But the idea is, I was trying to catch you looking the same twice. If you turn your head only a little one way or the other it's a different face. I know there are people with faces that do that, but I've never seen one that changes as much as yours. Hasn't anyone ever mentioned it to you?"

She parted her lips, closed them, and turned right away from me. All I could do was turn back to my plate, and I did so, but in a moment she was facing me again. "You know," she said, "I'm only nineteen years old."

"I was nineteen once," I assured her. "Some ways I liked it, and some ways it was terrible."

"Yes, it is," she agreed. "I haven't learned how to take things yet, but I suppose I will. I was silly—just because you said that. I should have just told you yes, someone did mention that to me once. About my face. More than once."

So I had put my foot in it. How the hell are you going to be tactful when you don't know what is out of bounds and what isn't? Merely having a face that changes isn't going to get a girl a baby. I flopped around. "Well," I said, "I know it was a personal remark, and I only wanted to explain why I had stared at you. I wouldn't have brought it up if I had known there was anything touchy about it. I think you ought to get even. I'm touchy about horses because once I caught my foot in the stirrup when I was getting off, so you might try that. Ask me something about horses and *my* face will change."

"I suppose you ride in Central Park. Was it in the park?"

"No, it was out West one summer. Go ahead. You're getting warm."

We stayed on horses until Paul Schuster, on her right, horned in. I couldn't blame him, since he had Mrs. Robilotti on his other side. But Edwin Laidlaw still had Rose Tuttle, and it wasn't until the dessert came, cherry pudding topped with whipped cream, that I had a chance to ask her about the remark she had made.

"Something you said," I told her. "Maybe I didn't hear it right."

She swallowed pudding. "Maybe I didn't say it right. I often don't." She leaned to me and lowered her voice. "Is this Mr. Laidlaw a friend of yours?"

I shook my head. "Never saw him before."

"You haven't missed anything. He publishes books. To look at me, would you think I was dying to know how many books were published last year in America and England and a lot of other countries?"

"No, I wouldn't. I would think you could make out all right without it."

"I always have. What was it I said wrong?"

"I didn't say you said it wrong. I understood you to say something about the society men that were here the other time, and I wasn't sure I got it. I didn't know whether you meant another party like this one."

She nodded. "Yes, that's what I meant. Three years ago. She throws one every year, you know."

"Yes, I know."

"This is my second one. This friend of mine I mentioned, she says the only reason I had another baby was to get invited here for some more champagne, but believe me, if I liked champagne so much I could get it a lot quicker and oftener than that, and anyway, I didn't have the faintest idea I would be invited again. How old do you think I am?"

I studied her. "Oh—twenty-one."

She was pleased. "Of course you took off five years to be polite, so you guessed it exactly. I'm twenty-six. So it isn't true that having babies makes a girl look older. Of course if you had a lot of them, eight or ten, but by that time you would *be* older. I just don't believe I would look younger if I hadn't had two babies. Do you?"

I was on a spot. I had accepted the invitation with my eyes and ears open. I had told my hostess that I was acquainted with the nature and significance of the affair and she could count on me. I had on my shoulders the responsibility of the moral and social position of the community, some of it anyhow, and here this cheerful unmarried mother was resting the whole problem on the single question, had it aged her any? If I merely said no, it hadn't, which would have been both true and tactful, it would imply that I agreed that the one objection to her career was a phony. To say no and then proceed to list other objections that were not phonies would have been fine if I had been ordained, but I hadn't, and anyway she had certainly heard of them and hadn't been impressed. I worked it out in three seconds, on the basis that while it was none of my business if she kept on having babies, I absolutely wasn't going to encourage her. So I lied to her.

"Yes," I said.

"What?" She was indignant. "You do?"

I was firm. "I do. You admitted that I took you for twenty-six and deducted five years to be polite. If you had had only one baby I might have taken you for twenty-three, and if you had had none I might have taken you for twenty. I can't prove it, but I might. We'd better get on with the pudding. Some of them have finished."

She turned to it, cheerfully.

Apparently the guests of honor had been briefed on procedure, for when Hackett, on signal, pulled back Mrs. Robilotti's chair as she arose, and we chevaliers did likewise for our partners, they joined the hostess as she headed for the door. When they were out we sat down again.

Cecil Grantham blew a breath, a noisy gust, and said, "The last two hours are the hardest."

Robilotti said, "Brandy, Hackett."

Hackett stopped pouring coffee to look at him. "The cabinet is locked, sir."

"I know it is, but you have a key."

"No, sir, Mrs. Robilotti has it."

It seemed to me that that called for an embarrassed silence, but Cecil Grantham laughed and said, "Get a hatchet."

Hackett poured coffee.

Beverly Kent, the one with a long narrow face and big ears, cleared his throat. "A little deprivation will be good for us, Mr. Robilotti. After all, we understood the protocol when we accepted the invitation."

"Not protocol," Paul Schuster objected. "That's not what protocol means. I'm surprised at you, Bev. You'll never be an ambassador if you don't know what protocol is."

"I never will anyway," Kent declared. "I'm thirty years old, eight years out of college, and what am I? An errand boy in the Mission to the United Nations. So I'm a diplomat? But I ought to know what protocol is better than a promising young corporation lawyer. What do you know about it?"

"Not much." Schuster was sipping coffee. "Not much *about* it, but I know what it is, and you used it wrong. And you're wrong about me being a promising young corporation lawyer. Lawyers never promise anything. That's about as far as I've got, but I'm a year younger than you, so there's hope."

"Hope for who?" Cecil Grantham demanded. "You or the corporations?"

"About that word 'protocol,'" Edwin Laidlaw said, "I can settle that for you. Now that I'm a publisher I'm the last word on words. It comes from two Greek words, *prōtos*, meaning 'first,' and *kolla*, meaning 'glue.' Now why glue? Because in ancient Greece a *prōtokollon* was the first leaf, containing an account of the manuscript, glued to a roll of papyrus. Today a protocol may be any one of various kinds of documents—an original draft of something, or an account of some proceeding, or a record of an agreement. That seems to support you, Paul, but Bev has a point, because a protocol can also be a set of rules of etiquette. So you're both right. This affair this evening does require a special etiquette."

"I'm for Paul," Cecil Grantham declared. "Locking up the booze doesn't come under etiquette. It comes under tyranny."

Kent turned to me. "What about you, Goodwin? I understand you're a detective, so maybe you can detect the answer."

I put my coffee cup down. "I'm a little hazy," I said, "as to what you're after. If you just want to decide whether you used the word 'protocol' right, the best plan would be to get the dictionary. There's one upstairs in the library. But if what you want is brandy, and the cabinet is locked, the best plan would be for one of us to go to a liquor store. There's one at the corner of Eighty-second and Madison. We could toss up."

"The practical man," Laidlaw said. "The man of action."

"You notice," Cecil told them, "that he knows where the dictionary is and where the liquor store is. Detectives know everything." He turned to me. "By the way, speaking of detectives, are you here professionally?"

Not caring much for his tone, I raised my brows. "If I were, what would I say?"

"Why—I suppose you'd say you weren't."

"And if I weren't what would I say?"

Robert Robilotti let out a snort. "*Touché*, Cèce. Try another one." He pronounced it "Seese." Cecil's mother called him "Sessel," and his sister called him "Sesse."

Cecil ignored his stepfather. "I was just asking," he told me. "I shouldn't ask?"

"Sure, why not? I was just answering." I moved my head right and left. "Since the question has been asked, it may be in all your minds. If I were here professionally I would let it stand on my answer to Grantham, but since I'm not, you might as well know it. Austin Byne phoned this morning and asked me to take his place. If any of you are bothered enough you can check with him."

"I think," Robilotti said, "that it is none of our business. I know it is none of my business."

"Nor mine," Schuster agreed.

"Oh, forget it," Cecil snapped. "What the hell, I was just curious. Shall we join the mothers?"

Robilotti darted a glance at him, not friendly. After all, who was the host? "I was about to ask," he said, "if anyone wants more coffee. No?" He left his chair. "We will join them in the music room and escort them downstairs, and it is understood that each of us will dance first with his dinner partner. If you please, gentlemen?"

I got up and shook my pants legs down.

3   I'LL BE DARNED IF THERE WASN'T A LIVE BAND IN THE alcove—piano, sax, two violins, clarinet, and traps. A record player and speaker might have been expected, but for the mothers, spare no expense. Of course, in the matter of expense, the fee for the band was about balanced by the saving on liquids—the soda water in the cocktails, the pink stuff passing for wine at the dinner table, and the brandy ban—so it wasn't too extravagant. The one all-out splurge on liquids came after we had been dancing an hour or so, when Hackett appeared at the bar and began opening champagne, Cordon Rouge, and poured it straight, no dilution or adulteration. With only an hour to go, apparently Mrs. Robilotti had decided to take a calculated risk.

As a dancing partner Rose Tuttle was not a bargain. She was equipped for it physically and she had some idea of rhythm, that wasn't it; it was her basic attitude. She danced cheerfully, and of course that was no good. You can't dance cheerfully. Dancing is too important. It can be wild or solemn or gay or lewd or art for art's sake, but it can't be cheerful. For one thing, if you're cheerful you talk too much. Helen Yarmis was better, or would have been if she hadn't been too *damn* solemn. We would work into the rhythm together and get going fine, when all of a sudden she would stiffen up and was just a dummy making motions. She was a good size for me, too, with the top of her head level with my nose, and the closer you got to her wide, curved mouth the better you liked it—when the corners were up.

Robilotti took her for the next one, and a look around showed me that all the guests of honor were taken, and Celia Grantham was heading for me. I stayed put and let her come, and she stopped at arm's length and tilted her head back.

"Well?" she said.

The tact, I figured, was for the mothers, and there was no point in wasting it on the daughter. So I said, "But is it any better?"

"No," she said, "and it never will be. But how are you going to avoid dancing with me?"

"Easy. Say my feet hurt and take my shoes off."

She nodded. "You would, wouldn't you?"

"I could."

"You really would. Just let me suffer. Will I never be in your arms again? Must I carry my heartache to the grave?"

But I am probably giving a false impression, though I am reporting accurately. I had seen the girl—I say "girl" in spite of the fact that she was perhaps a couple of years older than Rose Tuttle, who was twice a mother—I had seen her just four times. Three of them had been in that house during the jewelry hunt, and on the third occasion, when I had been alone with her briefly, the conversation had somehow resulted in our making a date to dine and dance at the Flamingo, and we had kept it. It had not turned out well. She was a good dancer, very good, but she was also a good drinker, and along toward midnight she had raised an issue with another lady, and had developed it to a point where we got tossed out. In the next few months she had phoned me off and on, say twenty times, to suggest a rerun, and I had been too busy. For me the Flamingo has the best band in town, and I didn't want to get the cold stare for good. As for her persisting, I would like to think that, once she had tasted me, no other flavor would do, but I'm afraid she was just too pigheaded to drop it. I had supposed that she had long since forgotten all about it, but here she was again.

"It's not your heart," I said. "It's your head. You're too loyal to yourself. We're having a clash of wills, that's all. Besides, I have a hunch that if I took you in my arms and started off with you, after one or two turns you would break loose and take a swing at me and make remarks, and that would spoil the party. I see the look in your eye."

"The look in my eye is passion. If you don't know passion when you see it you ought to get around more. Have you got a Bible?"

"No, I forgot to bring it. There's one in the library." From my inside breast pocket I produced my notebook, which is always with me. "Will this do?"

"Fine. Hold it flat." I did so and she put her palm on it. "I swear on my honor that if you dance with me I will be your kitten for better or for worse and will do nothing that will make you wish you hadn't."

Anyway, Mrs. Robilotti, who was dancing with Paul Schuster, was looking at us. Returning the notebook to my pocket, I closed with her daughter, and in three minutes had decided that every allowance should be made for a girl who could dance like that.

The band had stopped for breath, and I had taken Celia to a chair, and was considering whether it would be tactful to have another round with her, when Rose Tuttle approached, unaccompanied, and was at my elbow. Celia spoke to her, woman to woman.

"If you're after Mr. Goodwin I don't blame you. He's the only one here that can dance."

"I'm not after him to dance," Rose said. "Anyway I wouldn't have the nerve because I'm no good at it. I just want to tell him something."

"Go ahead," I told her.

"It's private."

Celia laughed. "That's the way to do it." She stood up. "That would have taken me at least a hundred words, and you do it in two." She moved off toward the bar, where Hackett had appeared and was opening champagne.

"Sit down," I told Rose.

"Oh, it won't take long." She stood. "It's just something I thought you ought to know because you're a detective. I know Mrs. Robilotti wouldn't want any trouble, and I was going to tell her, but I thought it might be better to tell you."

"I'm not here as a detective, Miss Tuttle. As I told you. I'm just here to enjoy myself."

"I know that, but you *are* a detective, and you can tell Mrs. Robilotti if you think you ought to. I don't want to tell her because I know how she is, but if something awful happened and I hadn't told anybody I would think maybe I was to blame."

"Why should something awful happen?"

She had a hand on my arm. "I don't say it should, but it might. Faith Usher still carries that poison around, and she has it with her. It's in her bag. But of course you don't know about it."

"No, I don't. What poison?"

"Her private poison. She told us girls at Grantham House it was cyanide, and she showed it to some of us, in a little bottle. She always had it, in a little pocket she made in her skirt, and she made pockets in her dresses. She said she hadn't made up her mind to kill herself, but she might, and if she did she wanted to have that poison. Some of the girls thought she was just putting on, and one or two of them used to kid her, but I never did. I thought she might really do it, and if she did and I had kidded her I would be to blame. Now she's away from there and she's got a job, and I thought maybe she had got over it, but upstairs a while ago Helen Yarmis was with her in the powder room, and Helen saw the bottle in her bag and asked her if the poison was still in it, and she said yes."

She stopped. "And?" I asked.

"And what?" she asked.

"Is that all?"

"I think it's enough. If you knew Faith like I do. Here in this grand house, and the butler, and the men dressed up, and that powder room, and the champagne—this is where she might do it if she ever does." All of a sudden she was cheerful again. "So would I," she declared. "I would drop the poison in my champagne and get up on a chair with it and hold it high, and call out 'Here goes to all our woes'—that's what one of the girls used to say when she drank a Coke—and drink it down, and throw the glass away and get off the chair, and start to sink down to the floor, and the men would rush to catch me—how long would it take me to die?"

"A couple of minutes, or even less if you put enough in." Her hand was still on my arm and I patted it. "Okay, you've told me. I'd forget it if I were you. Did you ever see the bottle?"

"Yes, she showed it to me."

"Did you smell the stuff in it?"

"No, she didn't open it. It had a screw top."

"Was it glass? Could you see the stuff?"

"No, I think it was some kind of plastic."

"You say Helen Yarmis saw it in her bag. What kind of a bag?"

"Black leather." She turned for a look around. "It's there on a chair. I don't want to point—"

"You've already pointed with your eyes. I see it. Just forget it. I'll see that nothing awful happens. Will you dance?"

She would, and we joined the merry whirl, and when the band paused we went to the bar for champagne. Next I took Faith Usher.

Since Faith Usher had been making her play for a year or more, and the stuff in the plastic bottle might be aspirin or salted peanuts, and even if it were cyanide I didn't agree with Rose Tuttle's notion of the ideal spot for suicide, the chance of anything happening was about one in ten million, but even so, I had had a responsibility wished on me, and I kept an eye both on the bag and on Faith Usher. That was simple when I was dancing with her, since I could forget the bag.

As I said, I would have picked her for my sister because she looked as if she needed a brother, but her being the prettiest one of the bunch may have been a factor. She had perked up some too, with her face muscles relaxed, and, in spite of the fact that she got off the beat now and then, it was a pleasure to dance with her. Also now and then, when she liked something I did, there would be a flash in her eyes with the greenish flecks, and when we finished I wasn't so sure that it was a brother she needed. Maybe cousin would be better.

However, it appeared that she had ideas of her own, if not about brothers and cousins, at least about dancing partners. We were standing at a window when Edwin Laidlaw, the publisher, came up and bowed to her and spoke.

"Will you dance with me, Miss Usher?"

"No," she said.

"I would be honored."

"No."

Naturally I wondered why. He had only a couple of inches on her in height, and perhaps she liked them taller—me, for instance. Or perhaps it was because he hadn't combed his hair, or if he had it didn't look it. If it was more personal, if he had said something that offended her, it hadn't been at the table, since they hadn't been close enough, but of course it could have been before or after. Laidlaw turned and went, and as the band opened up I was opening my mouth to suggest that we try an encore, when Cecil Grantham came and got her. He was about my height and every hair on his head was in place, so that could have been it. I went and got Ethel Varr and said nothing whatever about her face changing. As we danced I tried not to keep twisting my head around, but I had to maintain surveillance on Faith Usher and the bag, which was still on the chair.

When something awful did happen I hadn't the slightest idea that it was coming. I like to think that I can count on myself for hunches, and often I can, but not that time, and what made it worse was that I was keeping an eye on Faith Usher as I stood talking with Ethel Varr. If she was about to die, and if I am any damn good at hunches, I might at least have felt myself breathing a little faster, but not even that. I saw her escorted to a chair by Cecil Grantham, fifteen feet away from the chair the bag was on, and saw her sit, and saw him go and return in a couple of minutes with champagne and hand her hers, and saw him raise his glass and say something. I had been keeping her in the corner of my eye, not to be rude to Ethel Varr, but at that point I had both eyes straight at Faith Usher. Not that I am claiming a hunch; it was simply that Rose Tuttle's idea of poison in champagne was fresh in my mind and I was reacting to it. So I had both eyes on Faith Usher when she took a gulp and went stiff, and shook all over, and jerked halfway to her feet, and made a noise that was part scream and part moan, and went down. Going down, she teetered on the edge of the chair for a second and then would have been on the floor if Cecil hadn't grabbed her.

When I got there he was trying to hold her up. I said to let her down, took her shoulders, and called out to get a doctor. As I eased her to the floor she went into convulsion, her head jerking and her legs thrashing, and when Cecil tried to catch her ankles I told him that was no good and asked if someone was getting a doctor, and someone behind me said yes. I was on my knees, trying to keep her from banging her head on the floor, but managed a glance up and around, and saw that Robilotti and Kent and the band leader were keeping the crowd back. Pretty soon the convulsions eased up, and then stopped. She had been breathing fast in heavy gasps, and when they slowed down and weakened, and I felt her neck getting stiff, I knew the paralysis was starting, and no doctor would make it in time to help.

Cecil was yapping at me, and there were other voices, and I lifted my head to snap, "Will everybody please shut up? There's nothing I can do or anyone else." I saw Rose Tuttle. "Rose, go and guard that bag. Don't touch it. Stick there and don't take your eyes off it." Rose moved.

Mrs. Robilotti took a step toward me and spoke. "You are in my house, Mr. Goodwin. These people are my guests. What's the matter with her?"

Having smelled the breath of her gasps, I could have been specific, but that could wait until she was dead, not long, so I skipped it and asked, "Who's getting a doctor?"

"Celia's phoning," someone said.

Staying on my knees, I turned back to her. A glance at my wristwatch showed me five past eleven. She had been on the floor six minutes. There was foam on her mouth, her eyes were glassy, and her neck was rigid. I stayed put for two minutes, looking at her, ignoring the audience participation, then reached for her hand and pressed hard on the nail of the middle finger. When I removed my fingers the nail stayed white; in thirty seconds there was no sign of returning pink.

I stood up and addressed Robilotti. "Do I phone the police or do you?"

"The police?" He had trouble getting it out.

"Yes. She's dead. I'd rather stick here, but you must phone at once."

"No," Mrs. Robilotti said. "We have sent for a doctor. I give the orders here. I'll phone the police myself when I decide it is necessary."

I was sore. Of course that was bad; it's always a mistake to get sore in a tough situation, especially at yourself; but I couldn't help it.

Not more than half an hour ago I had told Rose to leave it to me, I would see that nothing awful happened, and look. I glanced around. Not a single face, male or female, looked promising. The husband and the son, the two guests of honor, the butler, the three chevaliers—none of them was going to walk over Mrs. Robilotti. Celia wasn't there. Rose was guarding the bag. Then I saw the bandleader, a guy with broad shoulders and a square jaw, standing at the entrance to the alcove with his back to it, surveying the tableau calmly, and called to him.

"My name's Goodwin. What's yours?"

"Johnson."

"Do you want to stay here all night, Mr. Johnson?"

"No."

"Neither do I. I think this woman was murdered, and if the police do too you know what that means, so the sooner they get here the better. I'm a licensed private detective and I ought to stay with the body. There's a phone on a stand in the reception hall. The number is Spring seven-three-one-hundred."

"Right." He headed for the arch. When Mrs. Robilotti commanded him to halt and moved to head him off he just sidestepped her and went on, not bothering to argue, and she called to her men, "Robbie! Cecil! Stop him!"

When they failed to react she wheeled to me. "Leave my house!"

"I would love to," I told her. "If I did, the cops would soon bring me back. Nobody is going to leave your house for a while."

Robilotti was there, taking her arm. "It's no use, Louise. It's horrible, but it's no use. Come and sit down." He looked at me. "Why do you think she was murdered? Why do you say that?"

Paul Schuster, the promising young lawyer, spoke up. "I was going to ask that, Goodwin. She had a bottle of poison in her bag."

"How do you know she did?"

"One of the guests told me. Miss Varr."

"One of them told me too. That's why I asked Miss Tuttle to guard the bag. I still think she was murdered, but I'll save my reason for the police. You people might—"

Celia Grantham came running in, calling, "How is she?" and came on, stopping beside me, looking down at Faith Usher. "My God," she said, whispered, and seized my arm and demanded, "Why don't you *do* something?" She looked down again, her mouth hanging open, and I put my hands on her shoulders and turned her around. "Thanks," she said. "My God, she was so pretty. Is she dead?"

"Yes. Did you get a doctor?"

"Yes, he's coming. I couldn't get ours. I got— What good is a doctor if she's dead?"

"Nobody is dead until a doctor says so. It's a law." Some of the others were jabbering, and I turned and raised my voice. "You people might as well rest your legs and there are plenty of chairs, but stay away from the one the bag is on. If you want to leave the room I can't stop you, but I advise you not to. The police might misunderstand it, and you'd only have more questions to answer." A buzzer sounded and Hackett was going, but I stopped him. "No, Hackett, you'd better stay, you're one of us now. Mr. Johnson will let them in."

He was doing so. There was no sound of the door opening because doors on mansions do not make noises, but there were voices in the reception hall, and everybody turned to face the arch. In they came, a pair, two precinct men in uniform. They marched in and stopped, and one of them asked, "Mr. Robert Robilotti?"

"I'm Robert Robilotti," he said.

"This your house? We got—"

"No," Mrs. Robilotti said. "It's my house."

4 WHEN I MOUNTED THE SEVEN STEPS OF THE STOOP OF the old brownstone at twelve minutes after seven Wednesday morning and let myself in, I was so pooped that I was going to drop my topcoat and hat on the hall bench, but breeding told, and I put the coat on a hanger and the hat on a shelf and went to the kitchen.

Fritz, at the refrigerator, turned and actually left the refrigerator door open to stare at me.

"Behold!" he said. He had told me once that he had got that out of his French-English dictionary, many years ago, as a translation of *voilà*.

"I want," I said, "a quart of orange juice, a pound of sausage, six eggs, twenty griddle cakes, and a gallon of coffee."

"No doughnuts with honey?"

"Yes. I forgot to mention them." I dropped onto the chair I occupy at breakfast, groaning. "Speaking of honey, if you want to make a friend who will never fail you, you might employ the eggs in a hedgehog omelet, with plenty— No. It would take too long. Just fry 'em."

"I never fry eggs." He was stirring a bowl of batter. "You have had a night?"

"I have. A murder with all the trimmings."

"Ah! Terrible! A client, then?"

I do not pretend to understand Fritz's attitude toward murder. He deplores it. To him the idea of one human being killing another is insupportable; he has told me so, and he meant it. But he never has the slightest interest in the details, not even who the victim was, or the murderer, and if I try to tell him about any of the fine points it just bores him. Beyond the bare fact that again a human being has done something insupportable, the only question he wants answered is whether we have a client.

"No client," I told him.

"There may be one, if you were there. Have you had nothing to eat?"

"No. Three hours ago they offered to get me a sandwich at the District Attorney's office, but my stomach said no. It preferred to wait for something that would stay down." He handed me a glass of orange juice. "Many, many thanks. That sausage smells marvelous."

He didn't like to talk or listen when he was actually cooking, even something as simple as broiling sausage, so I picked up the *Times*, there on my table as usual, and gave it a look. A murder has to be more than run-of-the-mill to make the front page of the *Times*, but this one certainly qualified, having occurred at the famous unmarried-mothers party at the home of Mrs. Robert Robilotti, and it was there, with a three-column lead on the bottom half of the page, carried over to page 23. But the account didn't amount to much, since it had happened so late, and there were no pictures, not even of me. That settled, I propped the paper on the reading rack and tackled a sausage and griddle cake.

I was arranging two poached eggs on the fourth cake when the house phone buzzed, and I reached for it and said good morning and had Wolfe's voice.

"So you're here. When did you get home?"

"Half an hour ago. I'm eating breakfast. I suppose it was on the seven-thirty newscast."

"Yes. I just heard it. As you know, I dislike the word 'newscast.' Must you use it?"

"Correction. Make it the seven-thirty radio news broadcast. I don't feel like arguing, and my cake is getting cold."

"You will come up when you have finished."

I said I would. When I had cradled the phone Fritz asked if he was in humor, and I said I didn't know and didn't give a damn. I was still sore at myself.

I took my time with the meal, treating myself to three cups of coffee instead of the usual two, and was taking the last swallow when Fritz returned from taking up the breakfast tray. I put the cup down, got up, had a stretch and a yawn, went to the hall, mounted the flight of stairs in no hurry, turned left, tapped on a door, and was told to come in.

Entering, I blinked. The morning sun was streaking in and glancing off the vast expanse of Wolfe's yellow pajamas. He was seated at a table by a window, barefooted, working on a bowl of fresh figs with cream. When I was listing the cash requirements of the establishment I might have mentioned that fresh figs in March, by air from Chile, are not hay.

He gave me a look. "You are disheveled," he stated.

"Yes, sir. Also disgruntled. Also disslumbered. Did the broadcast say she was murdered?"

"No. That she died of poison and the police are investigating. Your name was not mentioned. Are you involved?"

"Up to my chin. I had been told by a friend of hers that she had a bottle of cyanide in her bag, and I was keeping an eye on her. We were together in the drawing room, dancing, all twelve of us, not counting the butler and the band, when a man brought her a glass of champagne, and she took a gulp, and in eight minutes she was dead. It was cyanide, that's established, and the way it works it had to be in the champagne, but she didn't put it there. I was watching her, and I'm the one that says she didn't. Most of the others, maybe all of them, would like to have it that she did. Mrs. Robilotti would like to choke me, and some of the others would be glad to lend a hand. A suicide at her party would be bad enough, but a homicide is murder. So I'm involved."

He swallowed a bite of fig. "You are indeed. I suppose you considered whether it would be well to reserve your conclusion."

I appreciated that—his not questioning my eyesight or my faculty of attention. It was a real tribute, and the way I felt, I needed one. I said, "Sure I considered it. But I had to include that I had been told she had cyanide in her bag, since the girl who told me would certainly include it, and Cramer and Stebbins and Rowcliff would know damn well that in that case I would have had my eyes open, so I had no choice. I couldn't tell them yes, I was watching her and the bag, and yes, I was looking at her when Grantham took her the champagne and she drank it, and yes, she might have put something in the champagne before she drank when I was absolutely certain she hadn't."

"No," he agreed. He had finished the figs and taken one of the ramekins of shirred eggs with sausage from the warmer. "Then you're in for it. I take it that we expect no profitable engagement."

"We do not. God knows, not from Mrs. Robilotti."

"Very well." He put a muffin in the toaster. "You may remember my remarks yesterday."

"I do. You said I would demean myself. You did not say I would get involved in an unprofitable homicide. I'll deposit the checks this morning."

He said I should go to bed, and I said if I did it would take a
guided missile to get me up again.

After a shower and shave and tooth brush, and clean shirt and
socks, and a walk to the bank and back, I began to think I might last
the day out. I had three reasons for making the trip to the bank: first,
people die, and if the signer of a check dies before the check reaches
his bank the bank won't pay it; second, I wanted air; and third, I had
been told at the District Attorney's office to keep myself constantly
available, and I wanted to uphold my constitutional freedom of movement. However, the issue wasn't raised, for when I returned Fritz told
me that the only phone call had been from Lon Cohen of the *Gazette*.

Lon has done us various favors over the years, and besides, I like
him, so I gave him a ring. What he wanted was an eyewitness story
of the last hours of Faith Usher, and I told him I'd think it over and
let him know. His offer was five hundred bucks, which would have
been not for Nero Wolfe but for me, since my presence at the party
had been strictly personal, and of course he pressed—journalists always press—but I stalled him. The bait was attractive, five Cs and my
picture in the paper, but I would have to include the climax, and if I
reported that exactly as it happened, letting the world know that I was
the one obstacle to calling it suicide, I would have everybody on my
neck from the District Attorney to the butler. I was regretfully deciding
that I would have to pass when the phone rang, and I answered it and
had Celia Grantham's voice. She wanted to know if I was alone. I told
her yes but I wouldn't be in six minutes, when Wolfe would descend
from the plant rooms.

"It won't take that long." Her voice was croaky, but not necessarily
from drink. Like all the rest of them, including me, she had done a lot
of talking in the past twelve hours. "Not if you'll answer a question.
Will you?"

"Ask it."

"Something you said last night when I wasn't there—when I was
phoning for a doctor. My mother says that you said you thought Faith
Usher was murdered. Did you?"

"Yes."

"Why did you say it? That's the question."

"Because I thought it."

"Please don't be smart, Archie. Why did you think it?"

"Because I had to. I was forced to by circumstances. If you think
I'm dodging, I am. I would like to oblige a girl who dances as well
as you do, but I'm not going to answer your question—not now. I'm
sorry, but nothing doing."

"Do you still think she was murdered?"

"Yes."

"But *why?*"

I don't hang up on people. I thought I might have to that time, but she finally gave up, just as Wolfe's elevator jolted to a stop at the bottom. He entered, crossed to his chair behind his desk, got his bulk arranged in it to his satisfaction, glanced through the mail, looked at his calendar, and leaned back to read a three-page letter from an orchid-hunter in New Guinea. He was on the third page when the doorbell rang. I got up and stepped to the hall, saw, through the one-way glass panel of the front door, a burly frame and a round red face, and went and opened the door.

"Good Lord," I said, "don't you ever sleep?"

"Not much," he said, crossing the sill.

I got the collar of his coat as he shed it. "This is an honor, since you must be calling on me. Why not invite me down—Cramer!"

He had headed for the office. My calling him "Cramer" instead of "Inspector" was so unexpected that he stopped and about-faced. "Why," I demanded, "don't you ever learn? You know damn well he hates to have anyone march in on him, even you, or especially you, and you only make it harder. Isn't it me you want?"

"Yes, but I want him to hear it."

"That's obvious, or you would have sent for me instead of coming. If you will kindly—"

Wolfe's bellow came out to us. "Confound it, come in here!"

Cramer wheeled and went, and I followed. Wolfe's only greeting was a scowl. "I cannot," he said coldly, "read my mail in an uproar."

Cramer took his usual seat, the red leather chair near the end of Wolfe's desk. "I came," he said, "to see Goodwin, but I—"

"I heard you in the hall. You would enlighten me? That's why you want me present?"

Cramer took a breath. "The day I try to enlighten you they can send me to the loony house. It's just that I know Goodwin is your man and I want you to understand the situation. I thought the best way would be to discuss it with him with you present. Is that sensible?"

"It may be. I'll know when I hear the discussion."

Cramer aimed his sharp gray eyes at me. "I don't intend to go all over it again, Goodwin. I've questioned you twice myself and I've read your statement. I'm only after one point, the big point. To begin with, I'll tell you something that is not to be repeated. There is not a thing, not a word, in what any of the others have said that rules out suicide. Not a single damn thing. And there's a lot that makes suicide plausible, even probable. I'm saying that if it wasn't for you suicide would be a reasonable assumption, and it seems likely, I only say likely, that that would be the final verdict. You see what that means."

I nodded. "Yeah. I'm the fly in the soup. I don't like it any better than you do. Flies don't like being swamped in soup, especially when it's hot."

He got a cigar from a pocket, rolled it in his palms, put it between his teeth, which were white and even, and removed it. "I'll start at the beginning," he said. "Your being there when it happened. I know what you say, and it's in your statement—the phone call from Austin Byne and the one from Mrs. Robilotti. Of course that happened. When you say anything that can be checked it will always check. But did you or Wolfe help it to happen? Knowing Wolfe, and knowing you, I have got to consider the possibility that you wanted to be there, or Wolfe wanted you to, and you made arrangements. Did you?"

I was yawning and had to finish it. "I beg your pardon. I could just say no, but let's cover it. How and why I was there is fully explained in my statement. Nothing related to it was omitted. Mr. Wolfe thought I shouldn't go because I would demean myself."

"None of the people who were there was or is Wolfe's client?"

"Mrs. Robilotti was a couple of years ago. The job was finished in nine days. Except for that, no."

His eyes went to Wolfe. "You confirm that?"

"Yes. This is gratuitous, Mr. Cramer."

"With you and Goodwin it's hard to tell what is and what isn't." He came back to me. "I'm going to tell you how it stands up to now. First, it was cyanide. That's settled. Second, it was in the champagne. It was in what spilled on the floor when she dropped the glass, and anyway it acts so fast it must have been. Third, a two-ounce plastic bottle in her bag was half full of lumps of sodium cyanide. The laboratory calls them amorphous fragments; I call them lumps. Fourth, she had shown that bottle to various people and told them she wanted to kill herself; she had been doing that for more than a year."

He shifted in the chair. He always sat so as to have Wolfe head on, but now he was at me. "Since the bag was on a chair fifteen feet away from her, and the bottle was in it, she couldn't have taken a lump from it when Grantham brought her the champagne, or just before, but she could have taken it any time during the preceding hour or so and had it concealed in her handkerchief. Testing the handkerchief for traces is out because she dropped it and it fell in the spilled champagne—or rather, it's not out but it's no help. So that's the setup for suicide. Do you see holes in it?"

I killed a yawn. "Certainly not. It's perfect. I don't say she mightn't have committed suicide, I only say she didn't. As you know, I have good eyes, and she was only twenty feet from me. When she took the champagne from Grantham with her right hand her left hand was on her lap, and she didn't lift it. She took the glass by the stem, and when Grantham raised his glass and said something she raised hers a little higher than her mouth and then lowered it and drank. Are you by any chance hiding an ace? Does Grantham say that when he handed her the glass she dropped something in it before she took hold of it?"

"No. He only says she might have put something in it before she drank; he doesn't know."

"Well, I do. She didn't."

"Yeah. You signed your statement." He pointed the cigar at me. "Look, Goodwin. You admit there are no holes in the setup for suicide; how about the setup for murder? The bag was there on the chair in full view. Did someone walk over and pick it up and open it and take out the bottle and unscrew the cap and shake out a lump and screw the cap back on and put the bottle back in the bag and drop it on the chair and walk away? That must have taken nerve."

"Nuts. You're stacking the deck. All someone had to do was get the bag—of course before I started watching it—and take it to a room that could be locked on the inside—there was one handy—and get a lump and conceal it in his or her handkerchief—thank you for suggesting the handkerchief—and return the bag to the chair. That would take care, but no great nerve, since if he had any reason to think he had been seen taking the bag or returning it he wouldn't use the lump. He might or might not have a chance to use it, anyway." A yawn got me.

He pointed the cigar again. "And that's the next point, the chance to use it. The two glasses of champagne that Grantham took were poured by the butler, Hackett; he did all the pouring. One of them had been sitting on the bar for four or five minutes, and Hackett poured the other one just before Grantham came. Who was there, at the bar, during those four or five minutes? We haven't got that completely straight yet, but apparently everybody was, or nearly everybody. You were. By your statement, and Ethel Varr agrees, you and she went there and took two glasses of champagne of the five or six that were there waiting, and then moved off and stood talking, and soon after—you say three minutes—you saw Grantham bring the two glasses to Faith Usher. So you were there. So you might have dropped cyanide in one of the glasses? No. Even granting that you are capable of poisoning somebody's champagne, you would certainly make sure that the right one got it. You wouldn't just drop it in one of the glasses on the bar and walk away, and that applies to all the others, except Edwin Laidlaw, Helen Yarmis, and Mr. and Mrs. Robilotti. They hadn't walked away. They were there at the bar when Grantham came and got the two glasses. But he took *two* glasses. If one of those four people saw him coming and dropped the cyanide in one of the glasses, you've got to assume that he or she didn't give a damn whether Grantham got it or Faith Usher got it, which is too much for me. But not for you?" He clamped his teeth on the cigar. He never lit one.

"As you tell it," I conceded, "I wouldn't buy it. But I have two comments. The first one is that there is one person who did know which glass Faith Usher would get. He handed it to her."

"Oh? You put it on Grantham?"

"I don't put it on anybody. I merely say that you omitted a detail."

"Not an important one. If Grantham dropped the poison in at the bar before he picked up the glasses, there were five people right there, and that *did* take nerve. If he dropped it in while he was crossing to Faith Usher it was quite a trick, with a glass in each hand. If he dropped it in after he handed her the glass you would have seen him. What's your second comment?"

"That I have not implied, in my sessions with you and the others, that I have the slightest notion who did it, or how or why. What you have just told me was mostly news to me. My attention was divided between my companion, Ethel Varr, and the bag, and Faith Usher. I didn't know who was at the bar when Grantham came and got the champagne, or who had been there since Hackett poured the glasses that Grantham took. And I still have no notion who did it, or why or how. I only know that Faith Usher put nothing whatever in the champagne before she drank it, and therefore if it was poison in the champagne that killed her she did not commit suicide. That's the one thing I know."

"And you won't discuss it."

"I won't? What are we doing?"

"I mean you won't discuss the possibility that you're wrong."

"That, no. You wouldn't expect me to discuss the possibility that I'm wrong in thinking you're Inspector Cramer, you're Willie Mays."

He regarded me a long moment with narrowed eyes, then moved to his normal position in the red leather chair, confronting Wolfe. "I'm going to tell you," he said, "exactly what I think."

Wolfe grunted. "You often have."

"I know I have, but I hoped it wouldn't come to this. I hoped

Goodwin had realized that it wouldn't do. I think I know what happened. Rose Tuttle told him that Faith Usher had a bottle of cyanide in her bag, and that she was afraid she might use it right there, and Goodwin told her to forget it, that he would see that nothing happened, and from then on he kept surveillance on both Faith Usher and the bag. That is admitted."

"It is stated."

"Okay, stated. When he sees her drink champagne and collapse and die, and smells the cyanide, what would his reaction be? You know him and so do I. You know how much he likes himself. He would be hit where it hurts. He would hate it. So, without stopping to consider, he tells them that he thinks she was murdered. When the police come, he knows that what he said will be reported, so he repeats it to them, and then he's committed, and when Sergeant Stebbins and I arrive he repeats it to us. But to us he has to give a reason, so he has one, and a damn good one, and as long as there was a decent possibility that she *was* murdered we gave it full weight. But now— You heard me explain how it is. I was hoping that when he heard me and realized the situation he would see that his best course is to say that maybe he has been a little too positive. That he can't absolutely swear that she didn't put something in the champagne. He has had time to think it over, and he is too intelligent not to see that. That's what I think. I hope you will agree."

"It's not a question of agreement, it's a question of fact." Wolfe turned to me. "Archie?"

"No, sir. Nobody likes me better than I do, but I'm not that far gone."

"You maintain your position?"

"Yes. He contradicts himself. First he says I acted like a double-breasted sap and then he says I'm intelligent. He can't have his suicide and eat me too. I stand pat."

Wolfe lifted his shoulders an eighth of an inch, lowered them, and turned to Cramer. "I'm afraid you're wasting your time, Mr. Cramer. And mine."

I was yawning.

Cramer's red face was getting redder, a sure sign that he had reached the limit of something and was about to cut loose, but a miracle happened: he put on the brake in time. It's a pleasure to see self-control win a tussle. He moved his eyes to me.

"I'm not taking this as final, Goodwin. Think it over. Of course we're going on with the investigation. If we find anything at all that points to homicide we'll follow it up. You know that. But it's only

fair to warn you. If our final definite opinion is that it was suicide, and
we say so, and you give your friend Lon Cohen of the *Gazette* a
statement for publication saying that you know it was murder, you'll
regret it. That, or anything like it. Why in hell it had to be that *you*
were there, God only knows. Such a statement from you, as an eyewitness—"

The doorbell rang. I arose, asked Cramer politely to excuse me,
stepped to the hall, and through the one-way glass saw a recent social
acquaintance, though it took me a second to recognize him because
his forty-dollar fedora covered the uncombed hair. I went and opened
the door, confronted him, said, "Ssshhh," patted my lips with a forefinger, backed up, and beckoned him in. He hesitated, looking slightly
startled, then crossed the threshold. I shut the door and, without stopping to relieve him of his hat and coat, opened the door to the front
room, which is on the same side of the hall as the office, motioned
him in, followed him, and shut the door.

"It's all right here," I told him. "Soundproofed, doors and all."

"All right for what?" Edwin Laidlaw asked.

"For privacy. Unless you came to see Inspector Cramer of Homicide?"

"I don't know what you're talking about. I came to see you."

"I thought you might have, and I also thought you might prefer
not to collide with Cramer. He's in the office chatting with Mr. Wolfe,
and is about ready to go, so I shunted you in here."

"I'm glad you did. I've seen all I want of policemen for a while."
He glanced around. "Can we talk here?"

"Yes, but I must go and see Cramer off. I'll be back soon. Have
a chair."

I went to the door to the hall and opened it, and there was Cramer
heading for the front. He didn't even look at me, let alone speak. I
thought if he could be rude I could too, so I let him get his own hat
and coat and let himself out. When the door had closed behind him I
went to the office and crossed to Wolfe's desk. He spoke.

"I will make one remark, Archie. To bedevil Mr. Cramer for a
purpose is one thing; to do so merely for pastime is another."

"Yes, sir. I wouldn't dream of it. You're asking me if my position
with you, privately, is the same as it was with him. The answer is
yes."

"Very well. Then he's in a pickle."

"That's too bad. Someone else is too, apparently. Yesterday when
I was invited to the party and given the names of the male guests, I
wanted to know who they were and phoned Lon Cohen. One of them,

Edwin Laidlaw, is a fairly important citizen for a man his age. He used to be pretty loose around town, but three years ago his father died and he inherited ten million dollars, and recently he bought a controlling interest in the Malvin Press, book publishers, and apparently he intends to settle down and—"

"Is this of interest?"

"It may be. He's in the front room. He came to see me, and since my only contact with him was last night it *could* be of interest. I can talk with him there, but I thought I should tell you because you might possibly want to sit in—or stand in. At the hole. In case I need a witness."

"Pfui."

"Yeah, I know. I don't want to shove, but we haven't had a case for two weeks."

He was scowling at me. It wasn't so much that he would have to leave his chair and walk to the hall and on to the alcove, and stand at the hole—after all, that amount of exercise would be good for his appetite—as it was that the very best that could come of it, getting a client, would also be the worst, since he would have to work. He heaved a sigh, not letting it interfere with the scowl, muttered, "Confound it," put his palms on the desk rim to push his chair back, and got up and went.

The hole was in the wall, at eye level, eight feet to the right of Wolfe's desk. On the office side it was covered by a picture of a pretty waterfall. On the other side, in a wing of the hall across from the kitchen, it was covered by nothing, and you could not only see through but also hear through. I had once stood there for four solid hours, waiting for someone to appear from the front room to snitch something from my desk. I allowed Wolfe a minute to get himself posted and then went and opened the door to the front room and spoke.

"In here, Laidlaw. It's more comfortable." I moved one of the yellow chairs around to face my desk.

5

LAIDLAW SAT AND LOOKED AT ME. THREE SECONDS. SIX seconds. Evidently he needed priming, so I obliged.

"I thought it was a nice party up to a point, didn't you? Even with the protocol."

"I can't remember that far back." He leaned forward. His hair was still perfectly uncombed. "Look, Goodwin. I want to ask you a straight question, and I hope you'll answer it. I don't see why you shouldn't."

"I may not either. What?"

"About what you said last night, that you thought that girl was murdered. You said it not only to us, but to the police and the District Attorney. I can tell you confidentially that I have a friend, it doesn't matter who or where, who has given me a little information. I understand that they would be about ready to call it suicide and close the investigation if it weren't for you, so your reason for thinking it was murder must be a pretty good one. That's my question. What is it?"

"Your friend didn't tell you that?"

"No. Either he wouldn't, or he couldn't because he doesn't know. He says he doesn't know."

I crossed my legs. "Well, I can't very well say that. So I'll say that I have told only the police and the DA's office and Mr. Wolfe, and for the present that's enough."

"You won't tell me?"

"At the moment, no. Rules of etiquette."

"Don't you think the people who are involved just because they were there—don't you think they have a right to know?"

"Yes, I do. I think they have a right to demand that the police tell them exactly why they are going ahead with a homicide investigation when everything seems to point to suicide. But they have no right to demand that *I* tell them."

"I see." He considered that. "But the police refuse to tell us."

"Yeah, I know. I've had experiences with them. I've just had one with Inspector Cramer."

He regarded me. Four seconds. "You're in the detective business, Goodwin. People hire you to get information for them, and they pay you for it. That's all I want, information, an answer to my question. I'll give you five thousand dollars for it. I have it in my pocket in cash. Of course I would expect a definitive answer."

"You would deserve one, for five grand." I was finding that meeting his eyes halfway, not letting them come on through me, took a little effort. "Five grand in cash would suit me fine, since the salary Mr. Wolfe pays me is far from extravagant. But I'll have to say no even if you double it. This is how it is. When the police make up their minds about it one way or the other, that I'm right or I'm wrong, no matter which, I'll feel free to tell you or anybody else. But if I go spreading it around before then they will say I am interfering with an official investigation, and they will interfere with me. If I lost my license as a private detective your five grand wouldn't last long."

"Ten would last longer."

"Not much."

"I own a publishing business. I'd give you a job."

"You'd soon fire me. I'm not a very good speller."

His eyes were certainly straight and steady. "Will you tell me this? How good is your reason for thinking it was murder? Is it good enough to keep them on it the whole way, in spite of the influence of a woman in Mrs. Robilotti's position?"

I nodded. "Yes, I'll answer that. It was good enough to bring Inspector Cramer here when he hadn't had much sleep. In my opinion it is good enough to keep them from crossing it off as suicide until they have dug as deep as they can go."

"I see." He rubbed his palms together. Then he rubbed them on the chair arms. He had transferred his gaze to a spot on the rug, which was a relief. It was a full minute before he came back to me. "You say you have told only the police, the District Attorney, and Nero Wolfe. I want to have a talk with Wolfe."

I raised my brows. "I don't know."

"You don't know what?"

"Whether . . ." I let it trail, screwing my lips. "He doesn't like to mix in when I'm involved personally. Also he's pretty busy. But I'll see." I arose. "With him you never can tell." I moved.

As I turned left in the hall Wolfe appeared at the corner of the wing. He stood there until I had passed and pushed the swing door, and then followed me into the kitchen. When the door had swung shut I spoke.

"I must apologize for that crack about salary. I forgot you were listening."

He grunted. "Your memory is excellent and you shouldn't disparage it. What does that man want of me?"

I covered a yawn. "Search me. If I had had some sleep I might risk a guess, but it's all I can do to get enough oxygen for my lungs so my brain's doing without. Maybe he wants to publish your autobiography. Or maybe he wants you to make a monkey of me by proving it was suicide."

"I won't see him. You have supplied a reason: that you are involved personally."

"Yes, sir. I am also involved personally in the income of your detective business. So is Fritz. So is the guy who wrote you that letter from New Guinea, or he'd like to be."

He growled, as a lion might growl when it realizes it must leave its cozy lair to scout around for a meal. I admit that for him a better comparison would be an elephant, but elephants don't growl. Fritz, at the table shucking clams, started humming a tune, very low, probably pleased at the prospect of a client. Wolfe glared at him, reached for a clam, popped it into his mouth, and chewed. When I pushed the door open and held it, he waited until the clam was down before passing through.

He doesn't like to shake hands with strangers, and when we entered the office and I pronounced names he merely gave Laidlaw a nod en route to his desk. Before I went to mine I asked Laidlaw to move to the red leather chair so I wouldn't have him in profile as he faced Wolfe. As I sat Laidlaw was saying that he supposed Goodwin had told Wolfe who he was, and Wolfe was saying yes, he had.

Laidlaw's straight, steady eyes were now at Wolfe instead of me. "I want," he said, "to engage you professionally. Do you prefer the retainer in cash, or a check?"

Wolfe shook his head. "Neither, until I accept the engagement. What do you want done?"

"I want you to get some information for me. You know what happened at Mrs. Robilotti's house last evening. You know that a girl named Faith Usher was poisoned and died. You know of the circumstances indicating that she committed suicide. Don't you?"

Wolfe said yes.

"Do you know that the authorities have not accepted it as a fact that she killed herself? That they are continuing with the investigation on the assumption that she might have been murdered?"

Wolfe said yes.

"Then it's obvious that they must have knowledge of some circumstance other than the ones I know about—or that any of us know about. They must have some reason for not accepting the fact that it was suicide. I don't know what that reason is, and they won't tell me, and as one of the people involved—involved simply because I was there—I have a legitimate right to know. That's the information I want you to get for me. I'll give you a retainer now, and your bill can be any amount you think is fair, and I'll pay it."

I was not yawning. I must say I admired his gall. Though he didn't know that Wolfe had been at the hole, he must have assumed that I had reported the offer he had made, and here he was looking Wolfe straight in the eye, engaging him professionally, and telling him he could name his figure, no matter what, whereas with me ten grand had been his limit. The gall of the guy! I had to admire him.

The corners of Wolfe's mouth were up. "Indeed," he said. Laidlaw took a breath, but it came out merely as used air, not as words.

"Mr. Goodwin has told me," Wolfe said, "of the proposal you made to him. I am at a loss whether to respect your doggedness and applaud your dexterity or to deplore your naïveté. In any case I must decline the engagement. I already have the information you're after, but I got it from Mr. Goodwin in confidence and may not disclose it. I'm sorry, sir."

Laidlaw took another breath. "I'm not as dogged as you are," he declared. "Both of you. In the name of God, what's so top secret about it? What are you afraid of?"

Wolfe shook his head. "Not afraid, Mr. Laidlaw, merely discreet. When a matter in which we have an interest and a commitment requires us to nettle the police we are not at all reluctant. In this affair Mr. Goodwin is involved solely because he happened to be there, just as you are, and I am not involved at all. It is not a question of fear or of animus. I am merely detached. I will not, for instance, tell the police of the offers you have made Mr. Goodwin and me, because it would stimulate their curiosity about you, and since I assume you have made the offers in good faith I am not disposed to do you an ill turn."

"But you're turning me down."

"Yes. Flatly. In the circumstances I have no choice. Mr. Goodwin can speak for himself."

Laidlaw's head turned to me and I had the eyes again. I wouldn't have put it past him to renew his offer, with an amendment that he would now leave the figure up to me, but if he had that in mind he abandoned it when he saw my steadfast countenance. When, after regarding me for eight seconds, he left his chair, I thought he was leaving the field and Wolfe wouldn't have to go to work after all, but no. He only wanted to mull, and preferred to have his face to himself. He asked, "May I have a minute?" and, when Wolfe said yes, he turned his back and moseyed across the rug toward the far wall, where the big globe stood in front of bookshelves; and, for double the time he had asked for, at least that, he stood revolving the globe. Finally he about-faced and returned to the red leather chair, not moseying.

"I must speak with you privately," he told Wolfe.

"You are," Wolfe said shortly. "If you mean alone, no. If a confidence weren't as safe with Mr. Goodwin as with me he wouldn't be here. His ears are mine, and mine are his."

"This isn't only a confidence. I'm going to tell you something that no one on earth knows about but me. I'm going to risk telling you because I have to, but I'm not going to double the risk."

"You will not be doubling it." Wolfe was patient. "If Mr. Goodwin left us I would give him a signal to listen to us on a contraption in another room, so he might as well stay."

"You don't make it any easier, Wolfe."

"I don't pretend to make things easier. I only make them manageable—when I can."

Laidlaw looked as if he needed to mull some more, but he got it decided without going to consult the globe again. "You'll have all you can do to manage this," he declared. "I couldn't go to my lawyer with it, or anyhow I wouldn't, and even if I had it would have been too much for him. I thought I couldn't go to anybody, and then I thought of you. You have the reputation of a wizard, and God knows I need one. First I wanted to know why Goodwin thinks it was murder, but evidently you're not going—by the way—"

He took a pen from a pocket and a checkfold from another, put the fold on the little table at his elbow, and wrote. He yanked the check off, glanced it over, got up to put it on Wolfe's desk, and returned to the chair.

"If twenty thousand isn't enough," he said, "for a retainer and advance for expenses, say so. You haven't accepted the job, I know, but I'm camping here until you do. You spoke of managing things. I want you to manage that if they go on with their investigation it doesn't go deep enough to uncover and make public a certain event in my life. I also want you to manage that I don't get arrested and put on trial for murder."

Wolfe grunted. "I could give no guaranty against either contingency."

"I don't expect you to. I don't expect you to pass miracles, either. And two things I want to make plain: first, if Faith Usher was murdered I didn't kill her and don't know who did; and second, my own conviction is that she committed suicide. I don't know what Goodwin's reason is for thinking she was murdered, but whatever it is, I'm convinced that he's wrong."

Wolfe grunted again. "Then why come to me in a dither? If you're convinced it was suicide. Since they are human the police do frequently fumble, but usually they arrive at the truth. Finally."

"That's the trouble. Finally. This time, before they arrive, they might run across the event I spoke of, and if they do, they might charge me with murder. Not they might, they would."

"Indeed. It must have been an extraordinary event. If that is what you intend to confide in me, I make two remarks: that you are not yet my client, and that even if you were, disclosures to a private detective by a client are not a privileged communication. It's an impasse, Mr. Laidlaw. I can't decide whether to accept your job until I know what the event was; but I will add that if I do accept it I will go far to protect the interest of a client."

"I'm desperate, Wolfe," Laidlaw said. He pushed his hair back, but it needed more than a push. "I admit it. I'm desperate. You'll accept the job because there's no reason why you shouldn't. What I'm going to tell you is known to no one on earth but me, I'm pretty sure of that, but not absolutely sure, and that's the devil of it."

He pushed at his hair again. "I'm not proud of this, what I'm telling you. I'm thirty-one years old. In August, nineteen fifty-six, a year and a half ago, I went into Cordoni's on Madison Avenue to buy some flowers, and the girl who waited on me was attractive, and that evening I drove her to a place in the country for dinner. Her name was Faith Usher. Her vacation was to start in ten days, and by the time it started I had persuaded her to spend it in Canada with me. I didn't use my own name; I'm almost certain she never knew what it was. She only had a week, and when we got back she went back to work at Cordoni's, and I went to Europe and was gone two months. When I returned I had no idea of resuming any relations with her, but I had no reason to avoid her, and I stopped in at Cordoni's one day. She was there, but she would barely speak to me. She asked me, if I came to Cordoni's again, to get someone else to wait on me."

"I suggest," Wolfe put in, "that you confine this to the essentials."

"I am. I want you to know just how it was. I don't like to feel that I owe anyone anything, especially a woman, and I phoned her twice to get her to meet me and have a talk, but she wouldn't. So I dropped it. I also stopped buying flowers at Cordoni's, but some months later, one rainy day in April, I went there because it was convenient, and she wasn't there. I didn't ask about her. I include these details because you ought to know what the chances are that the police are going to dig this up."

"First the essentials," Wolfe muttered.

"All right, but you ought to know how I found out that she was at Grantham House. Grantham House is an institution started by—"

"I know what it is."

"Then I don't have to explain it. A few days after I had noticed that she wasn't at Cordoni's a friend of mine told me—his name is Austin Byne, and he is Mrs. Robilotti's nephew—he told me that he had been at Grantham House the day before on an errand for Mrs. Robilotti and had seen a girl there that he recognized. He said I might recognize her too—the girl with the little oval face and green eyes who used to work at Cordoni's. I told him I doubted it, that I didn't remember her. But I—"

"Was Mr. Byne's tone or manner suggestive?"

"No. I didn't think—I'm sure it wasn't. But I wondered. Naturally. It had been eight months since the trip to Canada, and I did not believe that she had been promiscuous. I decided that I must see her and talk with her. I prefer to think that my chief reason was my feeling of obligation, but I don't deny that I also wanted to know if she had found out who I was, and if so whether she had told anyone or was going to. In arranging to see her I took every possible precaution. Shall I tell you exactly how I managed it?"

"Later, perhaps."

"All right, I saw her. She said that she had agreed to meet me only because she wanted to tell me that she never wanted to see me or hear from me again. She said she didn't hate me—I don't think she was capable of hate—but that I meant only one thing to her, a mistake that she would never forgive herself for, and that she only wanted to blot me out. Those were her words: 'blot you out.' She said her baby would be given for adoption and would never know who its parents were. I had money with me, a lot of it, but she wouldn't take a cent. I didn't raise the question whether there could be any doubt that I was the father. You wouldn't either, if it had been you, with her, the way she was."

He stopped and set his jaw. After a moment he released it. "That was when I decided to quit playing around. I made an anonymous contribution to Grantham House. I never saw her again until last night. I didn't kill her. I am convinced she killed herself, and I hope to God my being there, seeing me again, wasn't what made her do it."

He stopped again. Then he went on, "I didn't kill her, but you can see where I'll be if the police go on investigating and dig this up somehow—though I don't know how. They would have me. I was standing at the bar when Cecil Grantham came and got the champagne and took it to her. Even if I wasn't convicted of murder, even if I was never put on trial, this would all come out and that would be nearly as bad. And evidently, if it weren't for Goodwin, for what he has told them, they would almost certainly call it suicide and close it. Can you wonder that I want to know what he told them? At any price?"

"No," Wolfe conceded. "Accepting your account as candid, no. But you have shifted your ground. You wanted to hire me to tell you what Mr. Goodwin has told the police, though you didn't put it that way, and I declined. What do you want to hire me to do now?"

"To manage this for me. You said you manage things. To manage that this is not dug up, that my connection with Faith Usher does not become known, that I am not suspected of killing her."

"You're already suspected. You were there."

"That's nonsense. You're quibbling. I wouldn't be suspected if it weren't for Goodwin. Nobody would be."

I permitted myself an inside grin. "Quibble" was one of Wolfe's pet words. Dozens of people, sitting in the red leather chair, had been told by him that they were quibbling, and now he was getting it back, and he didn't like it.

He said testily, "But you *are* suspected, and you'd be a ninny to hire me to prevent something that has already happened. You have admitted you're desperate, and desperate men can't think straight, so I should make allowances, and I do. That the police will not discover your connection with Faith Usher is a forlorn hope. Surely she knew your real name. Weren't you known at Cordoni's? Didn't you have a charge account?"

"No. I have charge accounts, of course, but not at any florist's. I always paid cash for flowers—in those days. Now it doesn't matter, but then it was more—uh—it was wiser. I don't think she ever knew my name, and even if she did I'm almost certain she never told anyone about me—about the trip to Canada."

Wolfe was skeptical. "Even so," he grumbled. "You appeared with her in public places. On the street. You took her to dinner. If the police persist it's highly probable that they'll turn it up; at that sort of thing they're extremely proficient. The only way to ward that off with any assurance would be to arrange that they do not persist, and that rests with Mr. Goodwin." His head turned. "Archie. Has anything that Mr. Laidlaw has said persuaded you that you might have been mistaken?"

"No," I said. "Now that we can name the figure I admit it's a temptation, but I'm committed. No."

"Committed to *what?*" Laidlaw demanded.

"To my statement that Faith Usher didn't kill herself."

"Why? For God's sake, *why?*"

Wolfe took over. "No, sir. That is still reserved, even if I accept your retainer. If I do, I'll proceed on the hypothesis that your account of your relations with Faith Usher is bona fide, but only as a hypothesis. Over the years I have found many hypotheses untenable. It is quite possible that you did kill Faith Usher and your coming to me is a step in some devious and crafty stratagem. Then—"

"I didn't."

"Very well. That's an item of the hypothesis. Then the situation is this: since Mr. Goodwin is unyielding, and since if the police persist they will surely bare your secret and then harass you, I can do your job only (a) by proving that Faith Usher committed suicide and Mr. Goodwin is wrong, or (b) by identifying and exposing the murderer. That would be a laborious and expensive undertaking, and I'll ask you to sign a memorandum stating that, no matter who the murderer is, if I expose him you'll pay my bill."

Laidlaw didn't hesitate. "I'll sign it."

"With, as I said, no guaranty."

"As I said, I don't expect any."

"Then that's understood." Wolfe reached to pick up the check. "Archie. You may deposit this as a retainer and advance for expenses."

I got up and took it and dropped it in a drawer of my desk.

"I want to ask a question," Laidlaw said. He was looking at me. "Evidently you didn't tell the police what happened when I asked Faith Usher to dance with me, and she refused. If you had told them they would certainly have asked me about it. Why didn't you?"

I sat down. "That's about the only thing I left out. For a reason. From the beginning they were on my neck about my thinking it was murder, and if I had told them about her refusing to dance with you they would have thought I was also trying to pick the murderer, and they already had certain feelings about me on account of former collisions. And if you denied it when they asked you about it, they might think I was playing hopscotch. I could always remember it and report it later, if developments called for it."

Wolfe was frowning. "You didn't report this to me."

"No, sir. Why should I? You weren't interested."

"I am now. But now, conveniently, her refusal is already explained." He turned to the client. "Did you know Miss Usher would be there before you went?"

"No," Laidlaw said. "If I had I wouldn't have gone."

"Did she know you would be there?"

"I don't know, but I doubt it. I think that goes for her too; if she had she wouldn't have gone."

"Then it was a remarkable coincidence. In a world that operates largely at random, coincidences are to be expected, but any one of them must always be mistrusted. Had you attended any of those affairs previously? Those annual dinners?"

"No. It was on account of Faith Usher that I accepted the invitation. Not to see her—as I said, I wouldn't have gone if I had known she would be there—just some feeling about what had happened. I suppose a psychiatrist would call it a feeling of guilt."

"Who invited you?"

"Mrs. Robilotti."

"Were you a frequent guest at her house?"

"Not frequent, no, just occasional. I have known Cecil, her son, since prep school, but we have never been close. Her nephew, Austin Byne, was in my class at Harvard. What are you doing, investigating me?"

Wolfe didn't reply. He glanced up at the wall clock: ten minutes past one. He took in a couple of bushels of air through his nose, and let it out through his mouth. He looked at the client, not with enthusiasm.

"This will take hours, Mr. Laidlaw. Just to get started with you— what you know about those people—since I must proceed, tentatively, on the hypothesis that Mr. Goodwin is right and Miss Usher was murdered, and you didn't kill her, and therefore one of the others did. Eleven of them, if we include the butler—no, ten, since I shall arbitrarily eliminate Mr. Goodwin. Confound it, an army! It's time for lunch, and I invite you to join us, and then we'll resume. Clams hashed with eggs, parsley, green peppers, chives, fresh mushrooms, and sherry. Mr. Goodwin drinks milk. I drink beer. Would you prefer white wine?"

Laidlaw said yes, he would, and Wolfe got up and headed for the kitchen.

6 AT A QUARTER PAST FIVE THAT AFTERNOON, WHEN LAID-law left, I had thirty-two pages of shorthand, my private brand, in my book. Of course Wolfe had gone up to the plant rooms at four o'clock, so for the last hour and a quarter I had been the emcee. When Wolfe came down to the office at six I had typed four pages from my notes and was banging away on the fifth.

Most of it was a waste of time and paper, but there were items that might come in handy. To begin with, there was nothing whatever on the three unmarried mothers who were still alive. Laidlaw had never seen or heard of Helen Yarmis or Ethel Varr or Rose Tuttle before the party. Another blank was Hackett. All I had got on him was that he was a good butler, which I already knew, and that he had been there for years, since before Grantham had died.

Mrs. Robilotti. Laidlaw didn't care much for her. He didn't put it that way, but it was obvious. He called her a vulgarian. Her first husband, Albert Grantham, had had genuine philanthropic impulses and knew what to do with them, but she was a phony. She wasn't actually continuing to support his philanthropies; they had been provided for in his will; she spent a lot of time on them, attending board meetings and so on, only to preserve her standing with her betters. "Betters," for Laidlaw, evidently didn't mean people with more money, which I thought was a broad-minded attitude for a man with ten million of his own.

Robert Robilotti. Laidlaw cared for him even less, and said so. Mrs. Albert Grantham, widow, had acquired him in Italy and brought him back with her luggage. That alone showed she was a vulgarian, but here, it seemed to me, things got confused, because Robilotti was not a vulgarian. He was polished, civilized, and well informed. (In all this I'm merely quoting Laidlaw.) Of course he was also a parasite. When I asked if he looked elsewhere for the female refreshments that were in short supply at home, Laidlaw said there were rumors, but there were always rumors.

Celia Grantham. Here I had got a surprise—nothing startling, but enough to make me lift a brow. Laidlaw had asked her to marry him six months ago and she had refused. "I tell you that," he said, "so you will know that I can't be very objective about her. Perhaps I was lucky. That was when I was getting a hold on myself after what had happened with Faith Usher, and perhaps I was just looking for help. Celia could help a man all right if she wanted to. She has character, but she hasn't decided what to do with it. The reason she gave for refusing to marry me was that I didn't dance well enough." It was while we were on Celia that I learned that Laidlaw had an old-fashioned streak. When I asked him what about her relations with men and got a vague answer, and made it more specific by asking if he thought she was a virgin, he said of course, since he had asked her to marry him. An old fogy at thirty-one.

Cecil Grantham. On him it struck me that Laidlaw was being diplomatic, and I thought I guessed why. Cecil was three years younger than Laidlaw, and I gathered that his interests and activities were along the same lines as Laidlaw's had been three years ago before the event with Faith Usher had pushed his nose in—with qualifications, one being that whereas Laidlaw's pile had been left to him with no strings attached, Cecil's was in a trust controlled by his mother and he had to watch his budget. He had been heard to remark that he would like to do something to earn some money but couldn't find any spare time for it. Each year he spent three summer months on a ranch in Montana.

Paul Schuster. He was a prodigy. He had worked his way through college and law school, and when he had graduated with high honors a clerkship had been offered him by a justice of the United States Supreme Court, but he had preferred to go to work for a Wall Street firm with five names at the top, and a dozen at the side, of its letterhead. Probably a hundred and twenty bucks a week. Even more probably, at fifty he would be raking in half a million a year. Laidlaw knew him only fairly well and could furnish no information about the nature and extent of his intimacies with either sex. The owner of one of the five names at the top of the letterhead, now venerable, had been Albert Grantham's lawyer, and that was probably the connection that had got Schuster at Mrs. Robilotti's dinner table.

Beverly Kent. Of the Rhode Island Kents, if that means anything to you. It didn't to me. His family was still hanging on to three thousand acres and a couple of miles of a river named Usquepaugh. He too had been in Laidlaw's class at Harvard, and had followed a family tradition when he chose the diplomatic service for a career. In Laidlaw's opinion it wasn't likely that he had ever been guilty of an indiscretion, let alone an outrage, with a female.

Edwin Laidlaw. A reformed man, a repentant sinner, and a recovered soul. He said he had more appropriate clichés handy, but I told him those would do. When he had inherited his father's stack, three years ago, he had gone on as before, horsing around, and had caught up with himself only after the Faith Usher affair. He had not, to the best of his knowledge, ever made any other woman a mother, married or unmarried. It had taken more than half of his assets to buy the Malvin Press, and for four months he had been spending ten hours a day at his office, five days a week, not to mention evenings and weekends. He thought he would be on to the publishing business in five years.

As for Faith Usher, his thinking that she had not been promiscuous, and his not raising the question, at his last meeting with her, whether there was any doubt about his being the father of the baby she was carrying, had been based entirely on the impression he had got of her. He knew nothing whatever about her family or background. He hadn't even known where she lived; she had refused to tell him. She had given him a phone number and he had called her at it, but he didn't remember what it was, and he had made a little private ceremony of destroying his phone-number book when he had reformed. When I said that on a week's vacation trip there is time for a lot of talk, he said they had done plenty of talking, but she had shied away from anything about her. His guess was that she had probably graduated from high school.

We had spent a solid hour with him on the party before Wolfe went up to the plant rooms. Wolfe took him through every minute of it, trying to get some faint glimmer of a hint. Laidlaw was sure that neither he nor Faith Usher had said or done anything that could have made anyone suspect they had ever met before, except her refusing to dance with him, and no one had heard that but me. He had asked her to dance because he thought it would be noticed if he didn't.

Of course the main point was when Cecil Grantham came to the bar to get the champagne. Laidlaw had been standing there with Helen Yarmis, with whom he had just been dancing, and Mr. and Mrs. Robilotti. As he and Helen Yarmis approached the bar, Beverly Kent and Celia Grantham were moving away, and Mr. and Mrs. Robilotti were there, and of course Hackett. Laidlaw thought he and Helen Yarmis had been there more than a minute, but not more than two, when Cecil Grantham came; that was what he had told the police. He couldn't say whether, when he had taken two glasses of champagne for Helen Yarmis and himself, there had been other glasses on the bar with champagne in them; he simply hadn't noticed. The police had got him to try to recall the picture, but he couldn't. All he was sure of was that he hadn't poisoned any champagne, but he was almost as sure that Helen Yarmis hadn't either. She had been right at his elbow.

There was more, a lot more, but that's enough for here. You can see why I said that most of it was a waste of time and paper. I might mention that Wolfe had dictated the memorandum, and I had typed it, and Laidlaw had signed it. Also, as instructed by Wolfe, as soon as Laidlaw had gone I phoned Saul Panzer, Fred Durkin, and Orrie Cather, and asked them to drop in at nine o'clock.

At six, on the dot as always, Wolfe entered and crossed to his desk. I collated the originals of the four finished pages, took them to him, and went back to the typewriter. I was rolling out the fifth page when he spoke.

"Archie."

I twisted my neck. "Yes, sir?"

"Your attention, please."

I swiveled. "Yes, sir."

"You will agree that this is a devil of a problem, with monstrous difficulties in a disagreeable context."

"Yes, sir."

"I have asked you three times regarding your contention that Miss Usher did not commit suicide. The first time it was merely civil curiosity. The second time, in the presence of Mr. Cramer, it was merely rhetorical, to give you an opportunity to voice your resolution. The third time, in the presence of Mr. Laidlaw, it was merely by the way, since I knew you wouldn't pull back with him here. Now I ask you again. You know how it stands. If I undertake this job, on the assumption that she was murdered, an assumption based solely on your testimony, you know what it will entail in time, energy, wit, and vexation. The expense will be on Mr. Laidlaw, but the rest will be on me. I don't care to risk, in addition, the chance that I am burrowing in an empty hole. So I ask you again."

I nodded. "I knew this would come. Naturally. I stand pat. I can make a speech if you want one."

"No. You have already explained your ground. I will only remind you that the circumstances as described by Mr. Cramer indicate that it would have been impossible for anyone to poison that glass of champagne with any assurance that it would get to Miss Usher."

"I heard him."

"Yes. There is the same objection to supposing that it was intended for any other particular person, and its getting to Miss Usher was a mishap."

"Right."

"There is also the fact that she was the most likely target, since the poison was in her bag, making it highly probable that the conclusion would be that she had killed herself. But for you, that would be the conclusion. Therefore it was almost certainly intended for her."

"Right."

"But, for the reasons given by Mr. Cramer, it couldn't possibly have been intended for her."

I grinned at him. "What the hell," I said. "I know it's a lulu. I admit I wouldn't know where to start, but I'm not supposed to. That's your part. Speaking of starting, Saul and Fred and Orrie will be here at nine o'clock."

He made a face. He had to cook up chores for them, nine o'clock was less than three hours away, for one of the hours he would be dining, and he would not work his brain at the table.

"I have," he growled, "only this moment committed myself, after consulting you. Mr. Laidlaw's check could have been returned." He flattened his palms on the chair arms. "Then I'm in for it, and so are you. You will go tomorrow morning to that institution, Grantham House, and learn about Faith Usher. How she got there, when she came and when she left, what happened to her infant—everything. Cover it."

"I will if I can get in. I mention as a fact, not an objection, that that place has certainly had a lot of visitors today. At least a dozen assorted journalists, not to mention cops. Have you any suggestions?"

"Yes. You told me yesterday morning that a man you know named Austin Byne had phoned to ask you to take his place at that gathering. Today Mr. Laidlaw said that a man named Austin Byne, Mrs. Robilotti's nephew, had once gone to Grantham House on an errand for his aunt. I suppose the same man?"

"You suppose." I crossed my legs. "It wouldn't hurt you any, and would be good for my morale, if you let me take a trick now and then. Austin Byne had already occurred to me, and I asked for suggestions only to be polite. I already know what your powers of observation and memory are and you didn't have to demonstrate them by remembering that I had mentioned his name on the fly and— Why the snort?"

"At the notion that your morale needs any encouragement. Do you know where to reach Mr. Byne?"

I said I did and, before resuming at the typewriter, dialed his number. No answer. During the next hour and a half I interrupted my typing four times to dial the number, and still no answer. By then it was dinnertime. For himself, Wolfe will permit nothing and no one to interfere with the course of a meal, and, since we dine together in the dining room, my leaving the table is a sort of interference and he doesn't like it, but that time I had to. Three times during dinner I went to the office to dial Byne's number, with no luck, and I tried again when, having finished the baked pears, we transferred to the office and Fritz brought coffee. I accept a "no answer" verdict only after counting thirteen rings, and had got nine when the doorbell rang and Fritz announced Saul Panzer. The other two came a minute later.

That trio, the three that Wolfe always called on when we needed more eyes and ears and legs, were as good as you could get in the metropolitan area. In fact, Saul Panzer, a little guy with a big nose who never wore a hat, compromising on a cap when the weather was rough, was better. With an office and a staff he could have cleaned up, but that wouldn't have left him enough time for playing the piano or playing pinochle or keeping up with his reading, so he preferred to free-lance at seventy bucks a day. Fred Durkin, bulky and bald-headed, had his weak points, but he was worth at least half as much as Saul, which was his price, if you gave him the right kind of errands. If Orrie Cather had been as smart as he was brave and handsome he would have been hiring people instead of being hired, and Wolfe would have had to find someone else, which wouldn't have been easy because good operatives are scarce.

They were on yellow chairs in a row facing Wolfe's desk. We hadn't seen any of them for two months, and civilities had been exchanged, including handshakes. They are three of the nine or ten people to whom Wolfe willingly offers a hand. Saul and Orrie had accepted offers of coffee; Fred had preferred beer.

Wolfe sipped coffee, put his cup down, and surveyed them. "I have undertaken," he said, "to find an explanation for something that can't possibly be explained."

Fred Durkin frowned, concentrating. He had decided long ago that there was a clue in every word Wolfe uttered, and he wasn't going to miss one if he could help it. Orrie Cather smiled to show that he recognized a gag when he heard it, and fully appreciated it. Saul Panzer said, "Then the job is to invent one."

Wolfe nodded. "It may come to that, Saul. Either that or abandon it. Usually, as you know, I merely give you specific assignments, but in this case you will have to be told the situation and the background. We are dealing with the death of a woman named Faith Usher who drank poisoned champagne at the home of Mrs. Robert Robilotti. I suppose you have heard of it."

They all had.

Wolfe drank coffee. "But you should know all that I know, except the identity of my client. Yesterday morning Archie got a phone call from a man he knows, by name Austin Byne, the nephew of Mrs. Robilotti. He asked Archie . . ."

Seeing that I could be spared for a while, and thinking it was time for another try at Byne, I got up, circled around the trio, went to the kitchen, and dialed the number on the extension there. After five rings I was thinking I was going to draw a blank again, but then I had a voice saying hello.

"Byne?" I asked. "Dinky Byne?"

"Who is this?"

"Archie Goodwin."

"Oh, hello there. I've been thinking you might call. To give me hell for getting you into a mess. I don't blame you. Go on and say it."

"I could all right, but I've got another idea. You said you'd return the favor someday, and tomorrow is the day. I want to run up to Grantham House and have a talk with someone there, preferably the woman in charge, and they're probably having too many visitors and won't let me in. So I thought you might say a word for me—on the phone, or write a letter I can take, or maybe even go along. How about it?"

Silence. Then: "What makes you think a word from me would help?"

"You're Mrs. Robilotti's nephew. And I heard somebody say, I forget who, that she has sent you there on errands."

Another silence. "What are you after? What do you want to talk about?"

"I'm just curious about something. Some questions the cops have asked me because I was there last night, the mess you got me into, have made me curious."

"What questions?"

"That's a long story. Also complicated. Just say I'm nosy by nature, that's why I'm in the detective business. Maybe I'm trying to scare up a client. Anyway, I'm not asking you to attend a death by poisoning, as you did me, though you didn't know it. I just want you to make a phone call."

"I can't, Archie."

"No? Why not?"

"Because I'm not in a position to. It wouldn't be— It might look as if— I mean I just can't do it."

"Okay, forget it. I'll have to feed some other curiosity—I've got plenty. For instance, my curiosity about why you asked me to fill in for you because you had such a cold you could hardly talk when you didn't have a cold—at least not the kind you tried to fake. I haven't told the cops about that, your faking the cold, so I guess I'd better do that and ask them to ask you why. I'm curious."

"You're crazy. I did have a cold. I wasn't faking."

"Nuts. Take care of yourself. I'll be seeing you, or the cops will." Silence, a short one. "Don't hang up, Archie."

"Why not? Make an offer."

"I want to talk this over. I want to see you, but I don't want to leave here because I'm expecting a phone call. Maybe you could come here?"

"Where is here?"

"My apartment. Eighty-seven Bowdoin Street, in the Village. It's two blocks south—"

"I know where it is. I'll be there in twenty minutes. Take some aspirin."

When I had hung up, Fritz, who was at the sink, turned to say, "As I thought, Archie. I knew there would be a client, since you were there."

I told him I'd have to think that over to decide how to take it, and went to the office to tell the conference it would have to manage without me for a while.

7

THERE'S NO TELLING WHAT 87 BOWDOIN STREET HAD
been like a few years back—or rather, there is, if you know the neighborhood—but someone had spent some dough on it, and it wasn't at
all bad when you got inside. The tile floor was a nice dark green, the
walls were a lighter green but the same tone, and the frame of the
entrance for the do-it-yourself elevator was outlined with a plain wide
strip of dull aluminum. Having been instructed over the intercom in
the vestibule, I entered the elevator and pushed the button marked 5.

When I emerged on the fifth floor Byne was there to greet me and
ushered me in. After taking my hat and coat he motioned me through
a doorway, and I found myself in a room that I would have been
perfectly willing to move to when the day came that Wolfe fired me
or I quit, with perhaps a few minor changes. The rugs and chairs were
the kind I like, and the lights were okay, and there was no fireplace.
I hate fireplaces. When Byne had got me in a chair and asked if I
would like a drink, and I had declined with thanks, he stood facing
me. He was tall and lanky and loose-jointed, with not much covering
for his face bones except skin.

"That was a hell of a mess I got you into," he said. "I'm damn
sorry."

"Don't mention it," I told him. "I admit I wondered a little why
you picked me. If you want some free advice, free but good, next time
you want to cook up a reason for skipping something, don't overdo it.
If you make it a cold, not that kind of a cold, just a plain everyday
virus."

He turned a chair around and sat. "Apparently you've convinced
yourself that was a fake."

"Sure I have, but my convincing myself doesn't prove anything. The proof would have to be got, and of course it could be if it mattered enough—items like people you saw or talked to Monday evening, or phoned to yesterday or they phoned you, and whoever keeps this place so nice and clean, if she was here yesterday—things like that. That would be for the cops. If I needed any proof personally, I got it when as soon as I mentioned that the cold was a fake you had to see me right away. So why don't we just file that?"

"You said you haven't told the cops."

"Right. It was merely a conclusion I had formed."

"Have you told anyone else? My aunt?"

"No. Certainly not her. I was doing you a favor, wasn't I?"

"Yes, and I appreciate it. You know that, Archie, I appreciate it."

"Good. We all like to be appreciated. I would appreciate knowing what it is you want to talk over."

"Well." He clasped his hands behind his head, showing how casual it was, just a pair of pals chatting free and easy. "To tell the truth, I'm in a mess too. Or I will be if you'd like to see me squirm. Would you like to see me squirm?"

"I might if you're a good squirmer. How do I go about it?"

"All you have to do is spill it about my faking a cold. No matter who you spill it to it will get to my aunt, and there I am." He unclasped his hands and leaned forward. "Here's how it was. I've gone to those damn annual dinners on my uncle's birthday the last three years and I was fed up, and when my aunt asked me again I tried to beg off, but she insisted, and there are reasons why I couldn't refuse. But Monday night I played poker all night, and yesterday morning I was fuzzy and couldn't face it. The question was who to tap. For that affair it can't be just anybody. The first two candidates I picked were out of town, and the next three all had dates. Then I thought of you. I knew you could handle yourself in any situation, and you had met my aunt. So I called you, and you were big-hearted enough to say yes."

He sat back. "That's how it was. Then this morning comes the news of what happened. I said I was sorry I got you into it, and I am, I'm damned sorry, but frankly, I'm damned glad I wasn't there. It certainly wasn't a pleasant experience, and I'm just selfish enough to be glad I missed it. You'll understand that."

"Sure. Congratulations. I didn't enjoy it much myself."

"I'll bet you didn't. So that's what I wanted, to explain how it was, so you'd see it wouldn't help matters any for anyone to know about my faking a cold. It certainly wouldn't help me, because it would get to my aunt sooner or later, and you know how she'd be about a thing like that. She'd be sore as hell."

I nodded. "I don't doubt it. Then it's an ideal situation. You want something from me, and I want something from you. Perfect. We'll swap. I don't broadcast about the phony cold, and you get me an audience at Grantham House. What's that woman's name? Irving?"

"Irwin. Blanche Irwin." He scratched the side of his neck with a forefinger. "You want to swap, huh?"

"I do. What could be fairer?"

"It's fair enough," he conceded. "But I told you on the phone I'm not in a position to do that."

"Yeah, but then I was asking a favor. Now I'm making a deal."

His neck itched again. "I might stretch a point. I might, if I knew what you want with her. What's the idea?"

"Greed. Desire for dough. I've been offered five hundred dollars for an eyewitness story on last night, and I want to decorate it with some background. Don't tell Mrs. Irwin that, though. She's probably down on journalists by now. Just tell her I'm your friend and a good loyal citizen and have only been in jail five times."

He laughed. "That'll do it all right. Wait till you see her." He sobered. "So that's it. It's a funny world, Archie. A girl gets herself in a fix she sees only one way out of, to kill herself, and you're there to see her do it just because I had had all I wanted of those affairs, and here you're going to collect five hundred dollars just because you were there. It's a funny world. So I didn't do you such a bad turn after all."

I had to admit that was one way of looking at it. He said he felt like saluting the funny world with a drink, and wouldn't I join him, and I said I'd be glad to. When he had gone and brought the requirements, a scotch and water for me and bourbon on the rocks for him, and we had performed the salute, he got at the phone and made a person-to-person call to Mrs. Irwin at Grantham House. Apparently there was nothing at all wrong with his position; he merely told her he would appreciate it if she would see a friend of his, and that was all there was to it. She said morning would be better than afternoon. After he hung up we discussed the funny world while finishing the drinks, and when I left one more step had been taken toward the brotherhood of man.

Back home, the conference was over, the trio had gone, and Wolfe was at his desk with his current book, one he had said I must read, *World Peace through World Law*, by Grenville Clark and Louis B. Sohn. He finished a paragraph, lowered it, and told me to enter expense advances to Saul and Fred and Orrie, two hundred dollars each. I went to the safe for the book and made the entries, returned the book, locked the safe, and asked him if I needed to know anything about their assignments. He said that could wait, meaning that he wanted to get on with his reading, and asked about mine. I told him it was all set, that he wouldn't see me in the morning because I would be leaving for Grantham House before nine.

"I now call Austin Byne 'Dinky,' " I told him. "I suppose because he's an inch over six feet, but I didn't ask. I should report that he balked and I had to apply a little pressure. When he phoned yesterday he tried to sound as if his tubes were clogged, but he boggled it. He had no cold. He now says that he had been to three of those affairs and had had enough, and he rang me only after he had tried five others and they weren't available. So we made a deal. He gets me in at Grantham House, and I won't tell his aunt on him. He seems to feel that his aunt might bite."

Wolfe grunted. "Nothing is as pitiable as a man afraid of a woman. Is he guileless?"

"I would reserve it. He is not a dope. He might be capable of knowing that someone was going to kill Faith Usher so that it would pass for suicide, and he wanted somebody there alert and brainy and observant to spot it, so he got me, and he is now counting on me, with your help, to nail him. Or her. Or he may be on the level and merely pitiable."

"You and he have not been familiar?"

"No, sir. Just acquaintances. I have only seen him at parties."

"Then his selecting you is suggestive *per se.*"

"Certainly. That's why I took the trouble to go to see him. To observe. There were other ways of getting to Mrs. Irwin of Grantham House."

"But you have formed no conclusion."

"No, sir. Question mark."

"Very well. Pfui. Afraid of a woman." He lifted his book, and I went to the kitchen for a glass of milk.

At eight-twenty the next morning, Thursday, I was steering the 1957 Heron sedan up the Forty-sixth Street ramp to the West Side Highway. Buying the sedan, the year before, had started an argument that wasn't finished yet. Wolfe pays for the cars, but I do the driving, and I wanted one I could U-turn when the occasion arose, and that clashed with Wolfe's notion that anyone in a moving vehicle was in constant deadly peril, and that the peril was in inverse ratio to the size of the vehicle. In a forty-ton truck he might actually have been able to relax. So we got the Heron, and I must say that I had nothing against it but its size.

I soon had proof of what I had been hearing and reading, that the forty-eight-hour rain in New York had been snow a little to the north. At Hawthorne Circle it was already there at the roadside, and the farther I rolled on the Taconic State Parkway the more there was of it. The sun was on it now, glancing off the slopes of the drifts and banks, and it was very pleasant, fighting the hardships of an old-fashioned winter by sailing along on the concrete at fifty-eight mph with ridges of white four and five feet high only a step from the hubcaps. When I finally left the parkway and took a secondary road through the hills, the hardships closed in on me some for a few miles, and when I turned in at an entrance between two stone pillars, with "Grantham House" on one of them, and headed up a curving driveway climbing a hill, only a single narrow lane had been cleared, and as I rounded a sharp curve the hubcaps scraped the ridge.

Coming out of another curve, I braked and stopped. I was blocked, though not by snow. There were nine or ten of them standing there facing me, pink-faced and bright-eyed in the sunshine, in an assortment of jackets and coats, no hats, some with gloves and some without. They would have been taken anywhere for a bunch of high-school girls except for one thing: they were all too bulky around the middle. They stood and grinned at me, white teeth flashing.

I cranked the window down and stuck my head out. "Good morning. What do you suggest?"

One in front, with so much brown hair that only the middle of her face showed, called out, "What paper are you from?"

"No paper. I'm sorry if I ought to be. I'm just an errand boy. Can you get by?"

Another one, a blonde, had advanced to the fender. "The trouble is," she said, "that you're right in the center. If you edge over we can squeeze past." She turned and commanded, "Back up and give him room."

They obeyed. When they were far enough away I eased the car forward and to the right until the fender grazed the snowbank, and stopped. They said that was fine and started down the alley single file. As they passed the front fender they turned sidewise, every darned one, which seemed to me to be faulty tactics, since their spread fore and aft was more than from side to side. Also they should have had their backs to the car so their fronts would be against the soft snow, but no, they all faced me. A couple of them made friendly remarks as they went by, and one with a sharp little chin and dancing dark eyes reached in and pulled my nose. I stuck my head out to see that they were all clear, waved good-by, and pressed gently on the gas.

Grantham House, which had once been somebody's mansion, sprawled over about an acre, surrounded by evergreen trees loaded with snow and other trees still in their winter skeletons. A space had been cleared with enough room to turn around, barely, and I left the car there, followed a path across a terrace to a door, opened it, entered, crossed the vestibule, and was in a hall about the size of Mrs. Robilotti's drawing room. A man who would never see eighty again came hobbling over, squeaking at me, "What's your name?"

I told him. He said Mrs. Irwin was expecting me, and led me into a smaller room where a woman was sitting at a desk. As I entered she spoke, with a snap. "I hope to goodness you didn't run over my girls."

"Absolutely not," I assured her. "I stopped to let them by."

"Thank you." She motioned to a chair. "Sit down. The snow has tried to smother us, but they have to get air and exercise. Are you a newspaperman?"

I told her no and was going to elaborate, but she had the floor. "Mr. Byne said your name is Archie Goodwin and you're a friend of his. According to the newspaper there was an Archie Goodwin at that party at Mrs. Robilotti's. Was that you?"

I was at a disadvantage. With her smooth hair, partly gray, her compact little figure, and her quick brown eyes wide apart, she reminded me of Miss Clark, my high-school geometry teacher out in Ohio, and Miss Clark had always had my number. I had waited until I saw her to decide just what line to take. First I had to decide whether to say it was me or it was I.

"Yes," I said, "that was me. It also said in the paper that I work for a private detective named Nero Wolfe."

"I know it did. Are you here as a detective?"

She certainly liked to come to the point. So had Miss Clark. But I hoped I was man enough not to be afraid of a woman. "The best way to answer that," I told her, "is to explain why I came. You know what happened at that party and you know I was there. The idea seems to be that Faith Usher committed suicide. I have got the impression that the police may settle for that. But on account of what I saw, and what I didn't see, I doubt it. My personal opinion is that she was murdered, and if she was, I would hate to see whoever did it get away with it. But before I start howling about it in public I want to do a little checking, and I thought the best place to check on Faith Usher herself was here with you."

"I see." She sat straight and her eyes were straight. "Then you're a knight with a plume?"

"Not at all. I'd feel silly with a plume. My pride is hurt. I'm a professional detective and I try to be a good one, and I believe that someone committed murder right before my eyes, and how do you think I like that?"

"Why do you believe it was murder?"

"As I said, on account of what I saw and what I didn't see. A question of observation. I would prefer to let it go at that if you don't mind."

She nodded. "The professional with his secrets. I have them too; I have a medical degree. Did Mrs. Robilotti send you here?"

That decision wasn't hard to make. Grantham House wasn't dependent on Mrs. Robilotti, since it had been provided for by Albert Grantham's will, and it was ten to one that I knew what Mrs. Irwin thought of Mrs. Robilotti. So I didn't hesitate.

"Good heavens, no. To have a suicide in her drawing room was bad enough. If she knew I was here looking for support for my belief that it was murder she'd have a fit."

"Mrs. Robilotti doesn't have fits, Mr. Goodwin."

"Well, you know her better than I do. If she ever did have a fit this would call for one. Of course I may be sticking my neck out. If you prefer suicide to murder as much as she does I've wasted a lot of gas driving up here."

She looked at me, sizing me up. "I don't," she said bluntly.

"Good for you," I said.

She lifted her chin. "I see no reason why I shouldn't tell you what I have told the police. Of course it's possible that Faith did kill herself, but I doubt it. I get to know my girls pretty well, and she was here nearly five months, and I doubt it. I knew about the bottle of poison she had—she didn't tell me, but one of the other girls did—and that was a problem, whether to get it away from her. I decided not to, because it would have been dangerous. As long as she had it and went on showing it and talking about using it, that was her outlet for her nerves, and if I took it away she would have to get some other outlet, and there was no telling what it might be. One reason I doubt if she killed herself is that she still had that bottle of poison."

I smiled. "The police would love that."

"They didn't, naturally. Another reason is that if she had finally decided to use the poison she wouldn't have done it there at that party, with all those people. She would have done it somewhere alone, in the dark, and she would have left a note for me. She knew how I felt about my girls, and she would have known it would hurt me, and she would have left a note. Still another reason is the fact that she was actually pretty tough. That bottle of poison was merely the enemy that she intended to defeat somehow—it was death, and she was going to conquer it. The spirit she had, down deep, showed sometimes in a flash in her eyes. You should have seen that flash."

"I did, Tuesday evening when I was dancing with her."

"Then she still had it, and she didn't kill herself. But how are you going to prove it?"

"I can't. I can't prove a negative. I would have to prove an affirmative, or at least open one up. If she didn't poison her champagne someone else did. Who? That's the target."

"Oh." Her eyes widened. "Good heavens! That's obvious, certainly, but if you'll believe me, Mr. Goodwin, it hadn't occurred to me. My only thought was that Faith had not killed herself. My mind had stopped there." Her lips tightened. She shook her head. "I can't help you," she said emphatically. "I wish you success, anyhow. I would help you if I could."

"You already have," I assured her, "and maybe you can more. If you don't mind a few questions. Since you've read the paper, you know who was there Tuesday evening. About the three girls—Helen Yarmis, Ethel Varr, and Rose Tuttle—they were all here at the time Faith Usher was, weren't they?"

"Yes. That is, the times overlapped. Helen and Ethel left a month before Faith did. Rose came six weeks before Faith left."

"Had any of them known her before?"

"No. I didn't ask them—I ask the girls as few questions as possible about their past—but there was no indication that they had, and there isn't much going on here that I don't know about."

"Did any trouble develop between any of them and her?"

She smiled. "Now, Mr. Goodwin. I said I would help you if I could, but this is ridiculous. My girls have their squabbles and their peeves, naturally, but I assure you that nothing that happened here put murder into the heart of Helen or Ethel or Rose. If it had I would have known it, and I would have dealt with it."

"Okay. If it was one of them I'll have to look elsewhere. Take the three male guests—Edwin Laidlaw, Paul Schuster, and Beverly Kent. Do you know any of them?"

"No. I had never heard their names before."

"You know nothing about them?"

"Nothing whatever."

"What about Cecil Grantham?"

"I haven't seen him for several years. His father brought him twice—no, three times—to our summer picnic, when Cecil was in his middle teens. After his father died he was on our Board of Directors for a year, but he resigned."

"You know of no possible connection between him and Faith Usher?"

"No."

"What about Robert Robilotti?"

"I have seen him only once, more than two years ago, when he came to our Thanksgiving dinner with Mrs. Robilotti. He played the piano for the girls and had them singing songs, and when Mrs. Robilotti was ready to leave, the girls didn't want him to go. My feelings were mixed."

"I'll bet they were. Faith Usher wasn't here then?"

"No."

"Well, we're all out of men. Celia Grantham?"

"I knew Celia fairly well at one time. For a year or so after she finished college she came here frequently, three or four times a month, to teach the girls things and talk with them; then suddenly she quit. She was a real help and the girls liked her. She has fine qualities, or had, but she is headstrong. I haven't seen her for four years. I am tempted to add something."

"Go ahead."

"I wouldn't if I thought you would misunderstand. You are looking for a murderer, and Celia would be quite capable of murder if she thought the occasion demanded it. The only discipline she recognizes is her own. But I can't imagine an occasion that would have led her to kill Faith Usher. I haven't seen her for four years."

"Then if she had had contact with Faith Usher you wouldn't know about it. Last but not least, Mrs. Robilotti."

"Well." She smiled. "She is Mrs. Robilotti."

I smiled back. "I agree. You certainly have known her. She was Mrs. Albert Grantham. I am tempted to add something."

"You may."

"I wouldn't if I thought you would misunderstand. I feel that if you knew anything that would indicate that Mrs. Robilotti might have killed Faith Usher you would think it was your duty to tell me about it. So I can simply ask, do you?"

"That's rather cheeky, Mr. Goodwin. But I simply answer, I do not. Ever since Mr. Grantham died Mrs. Robilotti has been coming here about once a month except when she was traveling, but she has never been at ease with the girls, nor they with her. Of course she came while Faith was here, but as far as I know she never spoke with her except as one of a group. So my answer to your question is no."

"Who picks the girls to be invited to the annual dinner on Grantham's birthday?"

"When Mr. Grantham was alive, I did. The first few years after he died, Mrs. Grantham did, on information I supplied. The last two years she has left it to Mr. Byne, and he consults me."

"Is that so? Dinky didn't mention that."

" 'Dinky'?"

"Mr. Byne. We call him that. I'll ask him about it. But if you don't mind telling me, how does he do it? Does he suggest names and ask you about them?"

"No, I make a list, chiefly of girls who have been here in the past year, with information and comments, and he chooses from that. I make the list with care. Some of my girls would not be comfortable in those surroundings. On what basis Mr. Byne makes his selections, I don't know."

"I'll ask him." I put a hand on her desk. "And now for the main point, what I was mostly counting on if you felt like helping me. It's very likely that the event or the situation, whatever it was, that led to Faith Usher's death dated from before she came here. It could have happened after she left, but you wouldn't know about that anyway. She was here nearly five months. You said you ask the girls as few questions as possible about their pasts, but they must tell you a lot, don't they?"

"Some of them do."

"Of course. And of course you keep it in confidence. But Faith is dead, and you said you'd help me if you could. She must have told you things. She may even have told you the name of the man who was responsible for her being here. Did she?"

I asked that because I had to. Mrs. Irwin was much too smart not to realize that that was the first and foremost question a detective would want answered about Faith Usher's past, and if I hadn't asked it she would have wondered why and might even have been bright enough to suspect that I already knew. There wasn't much chance that she had the answer, in view of her tone and manner when she said that she had never heard of Edwin Laidlaw.

"No," she said. "She never said a word about him to me, and I doubt if she did to any of the girls."

"But she did tell you things?"

"Not very much. If you mean facts, people she had known and things she had done, really nothing. But she talked with me a good deal, and I formed two conclusions about her—I mean about her history. No, three. One was that she had had only one sexual relationship with a man, and a brief one. Another was that she had never known her father and probably didn't know who he was. The third was that her mother was still alive and that she hated her—no, hate is too strong a word. Faith was not a girl for hating. Perhaps the word is repugnance. I formed those three conclusions, but she never stated any of them explicitly. Beyond that I know nothing about her past."

"Do you know her mother's name?"

"No. As I said, I have no facts."

"How did she get to Grantham House?"

"She came here one day in March, just a year ago. She was in her seventh month. No letter or phone call, she just came. She said she had once read about Grantham House in a magazine and she remembered it. Her baby was born on May eighteenth." She smiled. "I don't have on my tongue the dates of all the births here, but I looked it up for the police."

"Is there any possibility that the baby is involved? I mean in her death? Anything or anyone connected with it or its adoption?"

"Not the slightest. Absolutely none. I handle that. You may take my word for it."

"Did she ever have any visitors here?"

"No. Not one."

"You say she was here five months, so she left in August. Did someone come for her?"

"No. Usually the girls don't stay so long after the baby comes, but Faith had rather a bad time and had to get her strength back. Actually someone did come for her—Mrs. James Robbins, one of our directors, drove her to New York. Mrs. Robbins had got a job for her at Barwick's, the furniture store, and had arranged for her to share a room with another girl, Helen Yarmis. As you know, Helen was there Tuesday evening. Helen might know if anything— Yes, Dora?"

I turned my head. The woman who had opened the door—middle-aged and a little too plump for her blue uniform—stood holding the knob. She spoke. "I'm sorry to interrupt, Doctor, but Katherine may be going to rush things a bit. Four times since nine o'clock, and the last one was only twenty minutes."

Mrs. Irwin was out of her chair and moving. By the time she reached me I was up too, to take the hand she offered.

"It may be only a prelude," she said, "but I'd better go and see. I repeat, Mr. Goodwin, I wish you success, in spite of what success would mean. I don't envy you your job, but I wish you success. You'll forgive me for rushing off."

I told her I would, and I could have added that I'd rather have my job than hers, or Katherine's either. As I got my coat from a chair and put it on I figured that if she had been there fifteen years and had averaged one a week Katherine's would be the 780th, or even at two a month it would be the 360th. On my way out to the car I had a worry. If I met the girls on their way back the maneuver would have to be repeated with me headed downhill and them up, and I didn't like the idea of them rubbing their fronts along the side of the car again, with the door handles. But luckily, as I started the engine, here they came, straggling from the tunnel of the driveway into the cleared space. Their faces were even pinker and they were puffing. One of them sang out, "Oh, are you going?" and another one called, "Why don't you stay for lunch?" I told them some other time. I was glad I had turned the car around on arrival. I had an impulse to tell them Katherine was tuning up for her big act to see how they would take it, but decided it wouldn't be tactful, and when they had cleared the way I fed gas and rolled. The only one who didn't tell me good-by was out of breath.

8 WHEN WE HAVE COMPANY IN THE OFFICE I LIKE TO BE
there when they arrive, even if the matter being discussed isn't very
important or lucrative, but that time I missed it by five minutes. When
I got there at five past six that afternoon Wolfe was behind his desk,
Orrie Cather was in my chair, and Helen Yarmis, Ethel Varr, and Rose
Tuttle were there in three of the yellow chairs facing Wolfe. As I
entered, Orrie got up and moved to the couch. He has not entirely
given up the idea that someday my desk and chair will be his for good,
and he likes to practice sitting there when I am not present.

Not that it had taken me six hours to drive back from Grantham
House. I had got back in time to eat my share of lunch, kept warm by
Fritz, and then had given Wolfe a verbatim report of my talk with Mrs.
Irwin. He was skeptical of my opinion that her mind was sound and
her heart was pure, since he is convinced that every woman alive has
a screw loose somewhere, but he had to agree that she had talked to
the point, she had furnished a few hints that might be useful about
some of our cast of characters, and she had fed the possibility that
Austin Byne might not be guileless. Further discourse with Dinky was
plainly indicated. I dialed his number and got no answer, and, since
he might be giving his phone a recess, I took a walk through the
sunshine, first to the bank to deposit Laidlaw's check and then down
to 87 Bowdoin Street.

Pushing Byne's button in the vestibule got no response. I had
suggested to Wolfe that I might take along an assortment of keys so
that if Byne wasn't home I could go on in and pass the time by looking
around, but Wolfe had vetoed it, saying that Byne had not yet aroused
our interest quite to that point. So I spent a long hour and a quarter in

a doorway across the street. That's one of the most tiresome chores in the business, waiting for someone to show when you have no idea how long it will be and you haven't much more idea whether he has anything that will help.

It was twelve minutes past five when a taxi rolled to a stop at the curb in front of 87 and Byne climbed out. When he turned after paying the hackie, I was there.

"We must share a beam," I told him. "I feel a desire to see you, and come, and here you are."

Something had happened to the brotherhood of man. His eye was cold. "What the hell—" he began, and stopped. "Not here," he said. "Come on up."

Even his manners were affected. He entered the elevator ahead of me, and upstairs, though he let me precede him into the apartment, I had to deal with my coat and hat unaided. Inside, in the room that would require only minor changes, my fanny was barely touching the chair seat when he demanded, "What's this crap about murder?"

"That word 'crap' bothers me," I said. "The way we used it when I was a boy out in Ohio, we knew exactly what it meant. But I looked it up in the dictionary once, and there's no—"

"Nuts." He sat. "My aunt says that you're saying that Faith Usher was murdered, and that on account of you the police won't accept the fact that it was suicide. You know damn well it was suicide. What are you trying to pull?"

"No pull." I clasped my hands behind my head, showing it was just a pair of pals chatting free and easy, or ought to be. "Look, Dinky. You are neither a cop nor a district attorney. I have given them a statement of what I saw and heard at that party Tuesday evening, and if you want to know why that makes them go slow on their verdict you'll have to ask them. If I told them any lies they'll catch up with me and I'll be hooked. I'm not going to start an argument with you about it."

"What did you say in your statement?"

I shook my head. "Get the cops to tell you. I won't. I'll tell you this: if my statement is all that keeps them from calling it suicide, I'm the goat. I'll be responsible for a lot of trouble for that whole bunch, and I don't like it but can't help it. So I'm doing a little checking on my own. That's why I wanted to see Mrs. Irwin at Grantham House. I told you I had been offered five hundred bucks for a story on Faith Usher, and I had, but what I was really after was information on whether anyone at that party might have had any reason to kill her. For example, if someone intended to kill her at that party he had to know she would be there. So I wanted to ask Mrs. Irwin how she had been picked to be invited and who had picked her."

I gave him a friendly grin. "And I asked her and she told me, and that was certainly no help, since it was you, and you weren't at the party. You even faked a cold to get out of going—and by the way, I said I wouldn't broadcast that, and I haven't." I thought it wouldn't hurt to remind him that there was still a basis for brotherhood.

"I know," he said, "you've got that to shake at me. About my picking Faith Usher to be invited, I suppose Mrs. Irwin told you how it was done. I know she told the police. She gave me a list of names with comments, and I merely picked four of the names. I've just been down at the District Attorney's office telling them about it. As I explained to them, I had no personal knowledge of any of those girls. From Mrs. Irwin's comments I just picked the ones that seemed to be the most desirable."

"Did you keep the list? Have you got it?"

"I had it, but an assistant district attorney took it. One named Mandelbaum. No doubt he'll show it to you if you ask him."

I ignored the dig. "Anyway," I said, "even if the comments showed that you stretched a point to pick Faith Usher, that wouldn't cross any Ts, since you skipped the party. Did anyone happen to be with you when you were making the selections? Someone who said something like, 'There's one with a nice name, Faith Usher, a nice unusual name, why don't you ask her?' "

"No one was with me. I was alone." He pointed. "At that desk."

"Then that's out." I was disappointed. "If you don't mind my asking, a little point occurred to me as I was driving back from Grantham House—that you were interested enough to take the trouble to pick the girls to be invited, but not enough to go to the party. You even went to a lot of trouble to stay away. That seemed a little inconsistent, but I suppose you can explain it."

"To you? Why should I?"

"Well, explain it to yourself and I'll listen."

"There's nothing to explain. I picked the girls because my aunt asked me to. I did it last year too. I told you last night why I skipped the party." He cocked his head, making the skin even tighter on his right cheekbone. "What the hell are you driving at, anyhow? Do you know what I think?"

"No, but I'd like to. Tell me."

He hesitated. "I don't mean that, exactly, what I think. I mean what my aunt thinks—or I'll put it this way, an idea she's got in her mind. I guess she hasn't forgotten that remark you made once that she resented. Also she feels that Wolfe overcharged her for that job he did. The idea is that if you have sold the police and the District Attorney on your murder theory, and if they make things unpleasant enough for her and her guests, you and Wolfe might figure that she would be willing to make a big contribution to have it stopped. A contribution that would make you remember something that would change their minds. What do you think of that?"

"It *is* an idea," I conceded, "but it has a flaw. If I remembered something now that I didn't put in my statement, no contribution from your aunt would replace my hide that the cops and the DA would peel off. Tell your aunt that I appreciate the compliment and her generous offer, but I can't—"

"I didn't say she made an offer. You keep harping on your damn statement. What's in it?"

That was what was biting him, naturally, as it had bit Celia Grantham and Edwin Laidlaw, and probably all of them. For ten minutes he did the harping on it. He didn't go so far as to make a cash offer, either on his own or on behalf of his aunt, but he appealed to everything from my herd instinct to my better nature. I would have let him go on as long as his breath lasted, on the chance that he might drop a word with a spark of light in it, if I hadn't known that company was expected at the office at six o'clock and I wanted to be there when they arrived. When I left he was so frustrated he didn't even go to the hall with me.

I had shaved it pretty close, and that was the worst time of day for uptown traffic, so I didn't quite make it. It was 6:05 when I climbed out of the taxi and headed for the stoop. If you think I was straining my nerves more than necessary, you don't know Wolfe as I do. I have seen him get up and march out and take to his elevator merely because a woman has burst into tears or started screaming at him, and the expected company, he had told me, was three females, Helen Yarmis, Ethel Varr, and Rose Tuttle, and there was no telling what shape they might be in after the sessions they had been having with various officers of the law.

Therefore I was relieved when I entered the office and found that everything was peaceful, with Wolfe at his desk, the girls in a row facing him, and Orrie in my chair. As I greeted the guests Orrie moved to the couch, and when I was where I belonged Wolfe addressed me.

"We have only exchanged civilities, Archie. Have you anything that should be reported?"

"Nothing that won't wait, no, sir. He is still afraid of a woman."

He went to the company. "As I was saying, ladies, I thank you for coming. You were under no obligation. Mr. Cather, asking you to come, explained that Mr. Goodwin's opinion, expressed in your hearing Tuesday evening, that Faith Usher was murdered, has produced some complications that are of concern to me, and that I wished to consult with you. Mr. Goodwin still believes—"

"I told him," Rose Tuttle blurted, "that Faith might take the poison right there, and he said he would see that nothing happened, but it did." Her blue eyes and round face weren't as cheerful as they had been at the party, in fact they weren't cheerful at all, but her curves were all in place and her pony tail made its jaunty arc.

Wolfe nodded. "He has told me of that. But he thinks that what happened was not what you feared. He still believes that someone else poisoned Miss Usher's champagne. Do you disagree with him, Miss Tuttle?"

"I don't know. I thought she might do it, but I didn't see her. I've answered so many questions about it that now I don't know what I think."

"Miss Varr?"

You may remember my remark that I would have picked Ethel Varr if I had been shopping. Since she was facing Wolfe and I had her in profile, and she was in daylight from the windows, her face wasn't ringing any of the changes in its repertory, but that was a good angle for it, and the way she carried her head would never change. Her lips parted and closed again before she answered.

"I don't think," she said in a voice that wanted to tremble but she wouldn't let it, "that Faith killed herself."

"You don't, Miss Varr? Why?"

"Because I was looking at her. When she took the champagne and drank it. I was standing talking with Mr. Goodwin, only just then we weren't saying anything because Rose had told me that she had told him about Faith having the poison, and he was watching Faith so I was watching her too, and I'm sure she didn't put anything in the champagne because I would have seen her. The police have been trying to get me to say that Mr. Goodwin told me to say that, but I keep telling them that he couldn't because he hasn't said anything to me at all. He hasn't had a chance to." Her head turned, changing her face, of course, as I had it straight on. "Have you, Mr. Goodwin?"

I wanted to go and give her a hug and a kiss, and then go and shoot Cramer and a few assistant district attorneys. Cramer hadn't seen fit to mention that my statement had had corroboration; in fact, he had said that if it wasn't for me suicide would be a reasonable assumption. The damn liar. After I shot him I would sue him for damages.

"Of course not," I told her. "If I may make a personal remark, you told me at the dinner table that you were only nineteen years old and hadn't learned how to take things, but you have certainly learned how to observe things, and how to take your ground and stand on it." I turned to Wolfe. "It wouldn't hurt any to tell her it's satisfactory."

"It is," he acknowledged. "Indeed, Miss Varr, quite satisfactory." That, if she had only known it, was a triumph. He gave me a satisfactory only when I hatched a masterpiece. His eyes moved. "Miss Yarmis?"

Helen Yarmis still had her dignity, but the corners of her wide, curved mouth were apparently down for good, and since that was her best feature she looked pretty hopeless. "All I can do," she said stiffly, "is say what I think. I think Faith killed herself. I told her it was dumb to take that poison along to a party where we were supposed to have a good time, but I saw it there in her bag. Why would she take it along to a party like that if she wasn't going to use it?"

Wolfe's understanding of women has some big gaps, but at least he knows enough not to try using logic on them. He merely ignored her appeal to unreason. "When," he asked, "did you tell her not to take the poison along?"

"When we were dressing to go to the party. We lived in an apartment together. Just a big bedroom with a kitchenette, and the bathroom down the hall, but I guess that's an apartment."

"How long had you and she been living together?"

"Seven months. Since August, when she left Grantham House. I can tell you anything you want to ask, after the way I've been over it the last two days. Mrs. Robbins brought her from Grantham House on a Friday so she could get settled to go to work at Barwick's on Monday. She didn't have many clothes—"

"If you please, Miss Yarmis. We must respect the convenience of Miss Varr and Miss Tuttle. During those seven months did Miss Usher have many callers?"

"She never had any."

"Neither men nor women?"

"No. Except once a month when Mrs. Robbins came to see how we were getting along, that was all."

"How did she spend her evenings?"

"She went to school four nights a week to learn typing and shorthand. She was going to be a secretary. I never saw how she could if she was as tired as I was. Fridays we often went to the movies. Sundays she would go for walks, that's what she said. I was too tired. Anyway, sometimes I had a date, and—"

"If you please. Did Miss Usher have no friends at all? Men or women?"

"I never saw any. She never had a date. I often told her that was no way to live, just crawl along like a worm—"

"Did she get any mail?"

"I don't know, but I don't think so. The mail was downstairs on a table in the hall. I never saw her write any letters."

"Did she get any telephone calls?"

"The phone was downstairs in the hall, but of course I would have known if she got a call when I was there. I don't remember she ever got one. This is kinda funny, Mr. Wolfe. I can answer your questions without even thinking because they're all the same questions the police have been asking, even the same words, so I don't have to stop to think."

I could have given her a hug and kiss too, though not in the same spirit as with Ethel Varr. Anyone who takes Wolfe down a peg renders a service to the balance of nature, and to tell him to his face that he was merely a carbon copy of the cops was enough to spoil his appetite for dinner.

He grunted. "Every investigator follows a routine up to a point, Miss Yarmis. Beyond that point comes the opportunity for talent if any is at hand. I find it a little difficult to accept your portfolio of negatives." Another grunt. "It may not be outside my capacity to contrive a question that will not parrot the police. I'll try. Do you mean to tell me that during the seven months you lived with Miss Usher you had no inkling of her having any social or personal contact— excluding her job and night school and the visits of Mrs. Robbins— with any of her fellow beings?"

Helen was frowning. The frown deepened. "Say it again," she commanded.

He did so, slower.

"They didn't ask that," she declared. "What's an inkling?"

"An intimation. A hint."

She still frowned. She shook her head. "I don't remember any hints."

"Did she never tell you that she had met a man that day that she used to know? Or a woman? Or that someone, perhaps a customer at Barwick's, had annoyed her? Or that she had been accosted on the street? Did she never account for a headache or a fit of ill humor by telling of an encounter she had had? An encounter is a meeting face to face. Did she never mention a single name in connection with some experience, either pleasant or disagreeable? In all your hours together, did nothing ever remind her— What is it?"

Helen's frown had gone suddenly, and the corners of her mouth had lifted a little. "Headache," she said. "Faith never had headaches, except only once, one day when she came home from work. She wouldn't eat anything and she didn't go to school that night, and I wanted her to take some aspirin but she said it wouldn't help any. Then she asked me if I had a mother, and I said my mother was dead and she said she wished hers was. That didn't sound like her and I said that was an awful thing to say, and she said she knew it was but I might say it too if I had a mother like hers, and she said she had met her on the street when she was out for lunch and there had been a scene, and she had to run to get away from her." Helen was looking pleased. "So that was a contact, wasn't it?"

"It was. What else did she say about it?"

"That was all. The next day—no, the day after—she said she was sorry she had said it and she hadn't really meant it, about wishing her mother was dead. I told her if all the people died that I had wished they were dead there wouldn't be room in the cemeteries. Of course that was exaggerated, but I thought it would do her good to know that people were wishing people were dead all the time."

"Did she ever mention her mother again?"

"No, just that once."

"Well. We have recalled one contact, perhaps we can recall another."

But they couldn't. He contrived other questions that didn't parrot the police, but all he got was a collection of blanks, and finally he gave it up.

He moved his eyes to include the others. "Perhaps I should have explained," he said, "exactly why I wanted to talk with you. First, since you had been in close association with Miss Usher, I wanted to know your attitude toward Mr. Goodwin's opinion that she did not kill herself. On the whole you have supported it. Miss Varr has upheld it on valid grounds, Miss Yarmis has opposed it on ambiguous grounds, and Miss Tuttle is uncertain."

That was foxy and unfair. He knew damn well Helen Yarmis wouldn't know what "ambiguous" meant, and that was why he used it.

He was going on. "Second, since I am assuming that Mr. Goodwin is right, that Miss Usher did not poison her champagne and that therefore someone else did, I wanted to look at you and hear you talk. You are three of the eleven people who were there and are suspect; I exclude Mr. Goodwin. One of you might have taken that opportunity to use a lump of the poison that you all knew—"

"But we couldn't!" Rose Tuttle blurted. "Ethel was with Archie Goodwin. Helen was with that publisher, what's-his-name, Laidlaw, and I was with the one with big ears—Kent. So we couldn't!"

Wolfe nodded. "I know, Miss Tuttle. Evidentially, nobody could, so I must approach from another direction, and all eleven of you are suspect. I don't intend to harass you ladies in an effort to trick you into betraying some guarded secret of your relationship with Miss Usher; that's an interminable and laborious process and all night would only start it; and besides, it would probably be futile. If one of you has such a secret it will have to be exposed by other means. But I did want to look at you and hear you talk."

"I haven't talked much," Ethel Varr said.

"No," Wolfe agreed, "but you supported Mr. Goodwin, and that alone is suggestive. Third—and this was the main point—I wanted your help. I am assuming that if Miss Usher was murdered you would wish the culprit to be disclosed. I am also assuming that none of you has so deep an interest in any of the other eight people there that you would want to shield him from exposure if he is guilty."

"I certainly haven't," Ethel Varr declared. "Like I told you, I'm sure Faith didn't put anything in her champagne, and if she didn't, who did? I've been thinking about it. I know it wasn't me, and it wasn't Mr. Goodwin, and I'm sure it wasn't Helen or Rose. How many does that leave?"

"Eight. The three male guests, Laidlaw, Schuster, and Kent. The butler. Mr. Grantham and Miss Grantham. Mr. and Mrs. Robilotti."

"Well, I certainly don't want to shield any of *them.*"

"Neither do I," Rose Tuttle asserted, "if one of them did it."

"You couldn't shield them," Helen Yarmis told them, "if they *didn't* do it. There wouldn't be anything to shield them from."

"You don't understand, Helen," Rose told her. "He wants to find out who it was. Now, for instance, what if it was Cecil Grantham, and what if you saw him take the bottle out of Faith's bag and put it back, or something like that, would you want to shield him? That's what he wants to know."

"But that's just it," Helen objected. "If Faith did it herself, why would I want to shield him?"

"But Faith didn't do it. Ethel and Mr. Goodwin were both looking at her."

"Then why," Helen demanded, "did she take the bottle to the party when I told her not to?"

Rose shook her head, wiggling the pony tail. "You'd better explain it," she told Wolfe.

"I fear," he said, "that it's beyond my powers. It may clear the air a little if I say that a suspicious word or action at the party, like Mr. Grantham's taking the bottle from the bag, was not what I had in mind. I meant, rather, to ask if you know anything about any of those eight people that might suggest the possibility of a reason why one of them might have wanted Miss Usher to die. Do you know of any connection between one of them and Miss Usher—either her or someone associated with her?"

"I don't," Rose said positively.

"Neither do I," Ethel declared.

"There's so many of them," Helen complained. "Who are they again?"

Wolfe, patient under stress, pronounced the eight names.

Helen was frowning again. "The only connection I know about," she said, "is Mrs. Robilotti. When she came to Grantham House to see us. Faith didn't like her."

Rose snorted. "Who did?"

Wolfe asked, "Was there something definite, Miss Yarmis? Something between Miss Usher and Mrs. Robilotti?"

"I guess not," Helen conceded. "I guess it wasn't any more definite with Faith than it was with the rest of us."

"Did you have in mind something in particular that Miss Usher and Mrs. Robilotti said to each other?"

"Oh, no. I never heard Faith say anything to her at all. Neither did I. She thought we were harlots."

"Did she use that word? Did she call you harlots?"

"Of course not. She tried to be nice but didn't know how. One of the girls said that one day when she had been there, she said that she thought we were harlots."

"Well." Wolfe took in air, in and clear down to his middle, and let it out again. "I thank you again, ladies, for coming." He pushed his chair back and rose. "We seem to have made little progress, but at least I have seen and talked with you, and I know where to reach you if the occasion arises."

"One thing I don't see," Rose Tuttle said as she left her chair. "Mr. Goodwin said he wasn't there as a detective, but he *is* a detective, and I had told him about Faith having the poison, and I should think he ought to know exactly what happened. I didn't think anyone could commit a murder with a detective right there."

A very superficial and half-baked way to look at it, I thought, as I got up to escort the ladies out.

9

PAUL SCHUSTER, THE PROMISING YOUNG CORPORATION lawyer with the thin nose and quick dark eyes, sat in the red leather chair at a quarter past eleven Friday morning, with the eyes focused on Wolfe. "We do not claim," he said, "to have evidence that you have done anything that is actionable. It should be clearly understood that we are not presenting a threat. But it is a fact that we are being injured, and if you are responsible for the injury it may become a question of law."

Wolfe moved his head to take the others in—Cecil Grantham, Beverly Kent, and Edwin Laidlaw, lined up on yellow chairs—and to include them. "I am not aware," he said dryly, "of having inflicted an injury on anyone."

Of course that wasn't true. What he meant was that he hadn't inflicted the injury he was trying to inflict. Forty-eight hours had passed since Laidlaw had written his check for twenty thousand dollars and put it on Wolfe's desk, and we hadn't earned a dime of it, and the prospect of ever earning it didn't look a bit brighter. Dinky Byne's cover, if he had anything to cover, was intact. The three unmarried mothers had supplied no crack to start a wedge. Orrie Cather, having delivered them at the office for consultation, had been given another assignment, and had come Thursday evening after dinner, with Saul Panzer and Fred Durkin, to report; and all it had added up to was an assortment of blanks. If anyone had had any kind of connection with Faith Usher, it had been buried good and deep, and the trio had been told to keep digging.

When, a little after ten Friday morning, Paul Schuster had phoned to say that he and Grantham and Laidlaw and Kent wanted to see

Wolfe, and the sooner the better, I had broken two of the standing rules: that I make no appointments without checking with Wolfe, and that I disturb him in the plant rooms only for emergencies. I had told Schuster to be there at eleven, and I had buzzed the plant rooms on the house phone to tell Wolfe that company was coming. When he growled I told him that I had looked up "emergency" in the dictionary, and it meant an unforeseen combination of circumstances which calls for immediate action, and if he wanted to argue either with the dictionary or with me I was willing to go upstairs and have it out. He had hung up on me.

And was now telling Schuster that he was not aware of having inflicted an injury on anyone.

"Oh, for God's sake," Cecil Grantham said.

"Facts are facts," Beverly Kent muttered. Unquestionably a diplomatic way of putting it, suitable for a diplomat. When he got a little higher up the ladder he might refine it by making it "A fact is a fact is a fact."

"Do you deny," Schuster demanded, "that we owe it to Goodwin that we are being embarrassed and harassed by a homicide investigation? And he is your agent, employed by you. No doubt you know the legal axiom, *respondeat superior*. Isn't that an injury?"

"Not only that," Cecil charged, "but he goes up to Grantham House, sticking his nose in. And yesterday a man tried to pump my mother's butler, and he had no credentials, and I want to know if you sent him. And another man with no credentials is asking questions about me among my friends, and I want to know if you sent *him*."

"To me," Beverly Kent stated, "the most serious aspect is the scope of the police inquiry. My work on our Mission to the United Nations is in a sensitive field, very sensitive, and already I have been definitely injured. Merely to have been present when a sensational event occurred, the suicide of that young woman, would have been unfortunate. To be involved in an extended police inquiry, a murder investigation, could be disastrous for me. If in addition to that you are sending your private agents among my friends and associates to inquire about me, that is adding insult to injury. I have no information of that, as yet. But you have, Cece?"

Cecil nodded. "I sure have."

"So have I," Schuster said.

"Have you, Ed?"

Laidlaw cleared his throat. "No direct information, no. Nothing explicit. But I have reason to suspect it."

He handled it pretty well, I thought. Naturally he had to be with them, since if he had refused to join in the attack they would have wondered why, but he wanted Wolfe to understand that he was still his client.

"You haven't answered my question," Schuster told Wolfe. "Do you deny that we owe this harassment to Goodwin, and therefore to you, since he is your agent?"

"No," Wolfe said. "But you owe it to me, through Mr. Goodwin, only secondarily. Primarily you owe it to the man or woman who murdered Faith Usher. So it's quite possible that one of you owes it to himself."

"I knew it," Cecil declared. "I told you, Paul."

Schuster ignored him. "As I said," he told Wolfe, "this may become a question of law."

"I expect it to, Mr. Schuster. A murder trial is commonly regarded as a matter of law." Wolfe leaned forward, flattened his palms on the desk, and sharpened his tone. "Gentlemen. Let's get to the point, if there is one. What are you here for? Not, I suppose, merely to grumble at me. To buy me off? To bully me? To dispute my ground? What are you after?"

"Goddammit," Cecil demanded, "what are *you* after? That's the point! What are you trying to pull? Why did you send—"

"Shut up, Cece," Beverly Kent ordered him, not diplomatic at all. "Let Paul tell him."

The lawyer did so. "Your insinuation," Schuster said, "that we have entered into a conspiracy to buy you off is totally unwarranted. Or to bully you. We came because we feel, with reason, that our rights of privacy are being violated without provocation or just cause, and that you are responsible. We doubt if you can justify that responsibility, but we thought you should have a chance to do so before we consider what steps may be taken legally in the matter."

"Pfui," Wolfe said.

"An expression of contempt is hardly an adequate justification, Mr. Wolfe."

"I didn't intend it to be, sir." Wolfe leaned back and clasped his fingers at the apex of his central mound. "This is futile, gentlemen, both for you and for me. Neither of us can possibly be gratified. You want a stop put to your involvement in a murder inquiry, and my concern is to involve you as deeply as possible—the innocent along with—"

"Why?" Schuster demanded. "Why are you concerned?"

"Because Mr. Goodwin's professional reputation and competence have been challenged, and by extension my own. You invoked *re-*

spondeat superior; I will not only answer, I will act. That the innocent must be involved along with the guilty is regrettable but unavoidable. So you can't get what you want, but no more can I. What I want is a path to a fact. I want to know if one of you has buried in his past a fact that will account for his resort to murder to get rid of Faith Usher, and if so, which. Manifestly you are not going to sit here and submit to a day-long inquisition by me, and even if you did, the likelihood that one of you would betray the existence of such a fact is minute. So, as I say, this is futile both for you and for me. I wish you good day only as a matter of form."

But it wasn't quite that simple. They had come for a showdown, and they weren't going to be bowed out with a "good day" as a matter of form—at least, three of them weren't. They got pretty well worked up before they left. Schuster forgot all about saying that they hadn't come to present a threat. Kent went far beyond the bounds of what I would call diplomacy. Cecil Grantham blew his top, at one point even pounding the top of Wolfe's desk with his fist. I was on my feet, to be handy in case one of them lost control and picked up a chair to throw, but my attention was mainly on our client. He was out of luck. For the sake of appearance he sort of tried to join in, but his heart wasn't in it, and all he could manage was a mumble now and then. He didn't leave his chair until Cecil headed for the door, followed by Kent, and then, not wanting to be the last one out, he jumped up and went. I stepped to the hall to see that no one took my new hat in the excitement, went and tried the door after they were out, and returned to the office.

I expected to see Wolfe leaning back with his eyes closed, but no. He was sitting up straight, glaring at space. He transferred the glare to me.

"This is grotesque," he growled.

"It certainly is," I agreed warmly. "Four of the suspects come to see you uninvited, all set for a good long heart-to-heart talk, and what do they get? Bounced. The trouble is, one of them was our client, and he may think we're loafing on the job."

"Bah. When the men phone tell them to come in at three. No. At two-thirty. No. At two o'clock. We'll have lunch early. I'll tell Fritz." He got up and marched out.

I felt uplifted. That he was calling the men in for new instructions was promising. That he had changed it from three o'clock, when his lunch would have been settled, to two-thirty, when digestion would have barely started, was impressive. That he had advanced it again, to two, with an early lunch, was inspiring. And then to go to tell Fritz instead of ringing for him—all hell was popping.

10

"How many times," Wolfe asked, "have you heard me confess that I am a witling?"

Fred Durkin grinned. A joke was a joke. Orrie Cather smiled. He was even handsomer when he smiled, but not necessarily braver. Saul Panzer said, "Three times when you meant it, and twice when you didn't."

"You never disappoint me, Saul." Wolfe was doing his best to be sociable. He had just crossed the hall from the dining room. With Fred and Orrie he wouldn't have strained himself, but Saul had his high regard. "This, then," he said, "makes four times that I have meant it, and this time my fault was so egregious that I made myself pay for it. The only civilized way to spend the hour after lunch is with a book, but I have just swallowed my last bite of cheese cake, and here I am working. You must bear with me. I am paying a deserved penalty."

"Maybe it's our fault too," Saul suggested. "We had an order and we didn't fill it."

"No," Wolfe said emphatically. "I can't grab for the straw of your charity. I am an ass. If any share of the fault is yours it lies only in this, that when I explained the situation to you Wednesday evening and gave you your assignments none of you reminded me of my maxim that nothing is to be expected of tagging the footsteps of the police. That's what you've been doing, at my direction, and it was folly. There are scores of them, and only three of you. You have been merely looking under stones that they have already turned. I am an ass."

"Maybe there's no other stones to try," Orrie observed.

"Of course there are. There always are." Wolfe took time to

breathe. More oxygen was always needed after a meal unless he relaxed with a book. "I have an excuse, naturally, that one approach was closed to my ingenuity. By Mr. Cramer's account, and Archie didn't challenge it, no one could possibly have poisoned that glass of champagne with any assurance that it would get to Miss Usher. I could have tackled that problem only by a minute examination of everyone who was there, and most of them were not available to me. Sooner or later it must be solved, but only after disclosure of a motive. That was the only feasible approach open to me, to find the motive, and you know what I did. I sent you men to flounder around on ground that the police had already covered, or were covering. Pfui."

"I saw four people," Fred protested, "that the cops hadn't got to."

"And learned?"

"Well—nothing."

Wolfe nodded. "So. The quarry, as I told you Wednesday evening, was evidence of some significant association of one of those people with Miss Usher. That was a legitimate line of inquiry, but it was precisely the one the police were following, and I offer my apologies. We shall now try another line, where you will at least be on fresh ground. I want to see Faith Usher's mother. You are to find her and bring her."

Fred and Orrie pulled out their notebooks. Saul had one but rarely used it. The one inside his skull was usually all he needed.

"You won't need notes," Wolfe said. "There is nothing to note except the bare fact that Miss Usher's mother is alive and must be somewhere. This may lead nowhere, but it is not a resort to desperation. Whatever circumstance in Miss Usher's life resulted in her death, she must have been emotionally involved, and I have been apprised of only two phenomena which importantly engaged her emotions. One was her experience with the man who begot her infant. A talk with him might be fruitful, but if he can be found the police will find him; of course they're trying to. The other was her relationship with her mother. Mrs. Irwin, of Grantham House, told Archie that she had formed the conclusion, from talking with Miss Usher, that her mother was alive and that she hated her. And yesterday Miss Helen Yarmis, with whom Miss Usher shared an apartment the last seven months of her life, told me that Miss Usher had come home from work one day with a headache and had said that she had encountered her mother on the street and there had been a scene, and she had had to run to get away from her; and that she wished her mother was dead. Miss Yarmis's choice of words."

Fred, writing in his notebook, looked up. "Does she spell Irwin with an E or an I?"

Wolfe always tried to be patient with Fred, but there was a limit. "As you prefer," he said. "Why spell it at all? I've told you all she said that is relevant, and all that I know. I will add that I doubt if either Mrs. Irwin or Miss Yarmis mentioned Miss Usher's mother to the police, so in looking for her you shouldn't be jostled."

"Is her name Usher?" Orrie asked. Of course Saul wouldn't have asked it, and neither would Fred.

"You should learn to listen, Orrie," Wolfe told him. "I said that's all I know. And no more is to be expected from either Mrs. Irwin or Miss Yarmis. They know no more." His eyes went to Saul. "You will direct the search, using Fred and Orrie as occasions arise."

"Do we keep covered?" Saul asked.

"Preferably, yes. But don't preserve your cover at the cost of missing your mark."

"I took a look," I said, "at the Manhattan phone book when I got back from Grantham House yesterday. A dozen Ushers are listed. Of course she doesn't have to be named Usher, and she doesn't have to live in Manhattan, and she doesn't have to have a phone. It wouldn't take Fred and Orrie long to check the dozen. I can call Lon Cohen at the *Gazette*. He might have gone after the mother for an exclusive and a picture."

"Sure," Saul agreed. "If it weren't for cover my first stop would be the morgue. Even if her daughter hated her, the mother may have claimed the body. But they know me there, and Fred and Orrie too, and of course they know Archie."

It was decided, by Wolfe naturally, that that risk should be taken only after other tries had failed, and that calling Lon Cohen should obviously come first, and I dialed and got him. It was a little complicated. He had rung me a couple of times to try to talk me into the eyewitness story, and now my calling to ask if he had dug up Faith Usher's mother aroused all his professional instincts. Was Wolfe working on the case, and if so, on behalf of whom? Had someone made me a better offer for a story, and did I want the mother so I could put her in, and who had offered me how much? I had to spread the salve thick, and assure him that I wouldn't dream of letting anyone but the *Gazette* get my by-line, and promise that if and when we had anything fit for publication he would get it, before he would answer my simple question.

I hung up and swiveled to report. "You can skip the morgue. A woman went there Wednesday afternoon to claim the body. Name,

Marjorie Betz. B-E-T-Z. Address, Eight-twelve West Eighty-seventh Street, Manhattan. She had a letter signed by Elaine Usher, mother of Faith Usher, same address. By her instructions the body was delivered this morning to the Metropolitan Crematory on Thirty-ninth Street. A *Gazette* man has seen Marjorie Betz, but she clammed up and is staying clammed. She says Elaine Usher went somewhere Wednesday night and she doesn't know where she is. The *Gazette* hasn't been able to find her, and Lon thinks nobody else has. End of chapter."

"Fine," Saul said. "Nobody skips for nothing."

"Find her," Wolfe ordered. "Bring her. Use any inducement that seems likely to—"

The phone rang, and I swiveled and got it.

"Nero Wolfe's office, Arch—"

"Goodwin?"

"Yes."

"This is Laidlaw. I've got to see Wolfe. Quick."

"He's here. Come ahead."

"I'm afraid to. I just left the District Attorney's office and got a taxi, and I'm being followed. I was on my way to see Wolfe about what happened at the District Attorney's office, but now I can't because they mustn't know I'm running to Wolfe. What do I do?"

"Any one of a dozen things. Shaking a tail is a cinch, but of course you haven't had any practice. Where are you?"

"In a booth in a drugstore on Seventh Avenue near Sixteenth Street."

"Have you dismissed your taxi?"

"Yes. I thought that was better."

"It was. How many men are in the taxi tailing you?"

"Two."

"Then they mean it. Okay, so do we. First, have a Coke or something to give me time to get a car—say, six or seven minutes. Then take a taxi to Two-fourteen East Twenty-eighth Street. The Perlman Paper Company is there on the ground floor." I spelled Perlman. "Got that?"

"Yes."

"Go in and ask for Abe and say to him, 'Archie wants some more candy.' What are you going to say to him?"

"Archie wants some more candy."

"Right. He'll take you on through to Twenty-seventh Street, and when you emerge I'll be there in front, either at the curb or double-parked, in a gray Heron sedan. Don't hand Abe anything, he wouldn't like it. This is part of our personalized service."

"What if Abe isn't there?"

"He will be, but if he isn't don't mention candy to anyone else. Find a booth and ring Mr. Wolfe."

I hung up, scribbled "Laidlaw" on my pad, tore the sheet off, and got up and handed it to Wolfe. "He wants to see you quick," I said, "and needs transportation. I'll be back with him in half an hour or less."

He nodded, crumpled the sheet, and dropped it in his wastebasket; and I wished the trio luck on their mother hunt and went.

At the garage, at the corner of Tenth Avenue, I used the three minutes while Hank was bringing the car down to go to the phone in the office and ring the Perlman Paper Company, and got Abe. He said he had been wondering when I would want more candy and would be glad to fill the order.

The de-tailing operation went fine, without a hitch. Going crosstown on Thirty-fourth Street, it was a temptation to swing down Park or Lexington to Twenty-eighth, so as to pass Number 214 and see if I recognized the two in the taxi, but since they might also recognize me I vetoed it and gave them plenty of room by continuing to Second Avenue before turning downtown, then west on Twenty-seventh. It was at the rear entrance on Twenty-seventh that the Perlman Paper Company did its loading and unloading, but no truck was there when I arrived, and I rolled to the curb at 2:49, just nineteen minutes since Laidlaw had phoned, and at 2:52 here he came trotting across the sidewalk. I opened the door and he piled in.

He looked upset. "Relax," I told him as I fed gas. "A tail is a trifle. They won't go in to ask about you for at least half an hour, if at all, and Abe will say he took you to the rear to show you some stock, and you left that way."

"It's not the tail. I want to see Wolfe." His tone indicated that his plan was to get him down and tramp on him, so I left him to his mood. Crossing town, I considered whether there was enough of a chance that the brownstone was under surveillance to warrant taking him in the back way, through the passage between buildings on Thirty-fourth Street, decided no, and went up Eighth Avenue to Thirty-fifth. As usual, there was no space open in front of the brownstone, so I went on to the garage and left the car, and walked back with him. When we entered the office I was at his heels. He didn't have the build to get Wolfe's bulk down and trample on it without help, but after all, he was the only one of the bunch, as it stood then, who had had dealings with Faith Usher that might have produced a motive for murder, and if a man has once murdered you never know what he'll do next.

He didn't move a finger. In fact, he didn't even move his tongue. He stood at the corner of Wolfe's desk looking down at him, and after five seconds I realized that he was too mad, or too scared, or both, to speak, and I took his elbow and eased him to the red leather chair and into it.

"Well, sir?" Wolfe asked.

The client pushed his hair back, though he must have known by then that it was a waste of energy. "I may be wrong," he croaked. "I hope to God I am. Did you send a note to the District Attorney telling him that I am the father of Faith Usher's child?"

"No." Wolfe's lips tightened. "I did not."

Laidlaw's head jerked to me. "Did you?"

"No. Of course not."

"Have you told anybody? Either of you?"

"Plainly," Wolfe said, "you are distressed and so must be indulged. But nothing has happened to release either Mr. Goodwin or me from our pledge of confidence. If and when it does you will first be notified. I suggest that you retire and cool off a little."

"Cool off, hell." The client rubbed the chair arms with his palms, eying Wolfe. "Then it wasn't you. All right. When I left here this morning I went to my office, and my secretary said the District Attorney's office had been trying to reach me, and I phoned and was told they wanted to see me immediately, and I went. I was taken in to Bowen, the District Attorney himself, and he asked if I wished to change my statement that I had never met Faith Usher before Tuesday evening, and I said no. Then he showed me a note that he said had come in the mail. It was typewritten. There wasn't any signature. It said, 'Have you found out yet that Edwin Laidlaw is the father of Faith Usher's baby? Ask him about his trip to Canada in August nineteen fifty-six.' Bowen didn't let me take it. He held onto it. I sat and stared at it."

Wolfe grunted. "It was worth a stare, even if it had been false. Did you collapse?"

"No! By God, I didn't! I don't think I decided what to do while I sat there staring at it; I think my subconscious mind had already decided what to do. Sitting there staring at it, I was too stunned to decide anything, so I must have already decided that the only thing to do was refuse to answer any questions about anything at all, and that's what I did. I said just one thing: that whoever sent that note had libeled me and I had a right to find out who it was, and to do that I would have to have the note, but of course they wouldn't give it to me. They wouldn't even give me a copy. They kept at me for two hours, and when I left I was followed."

"You admitted nothing?"

"No."

"Not even that you had taken a trip to Canada in August of nineteen fifty-six?"

"No. I admitted *nothing*. I didn't answer a single question."

"Satisfactory," Wolfe said. "Highly satisfactory. This is indeed welcome, Mr. Laidlaw. We have—"

"Welcome!" the client squawked. *"Welcome?"*

"Certainly. We have at last goaded someone to action. I am gratified. If there was any small shadow of doubt that Miss Usher was murdered, this removes it. They have all claimed to have had no knowledge of Miss Usher prior to that party; one of them lied, and he has been driven to move. True, it is still possible that you yourself are the culprit, but I now think it extremely improbable. I prefer to take it that the murderer has felt compelled to create a diversion, and that is most gratifying. Now he is doomed."

"But good God! They know about—about me!"

"They know no more than they knew before. They get a dozen accusatory unsigned letters every day, and have learned that the charges in most of them are groundless. As for your refusal to answer questions, a man of your standing might be expected to take that position until he got legal advice. It's a neat situation, very neat. They will of course make every effort to find confirmation of that note, but it is a reasonable assumption that no one can supply it except the person who sent the note, and if he dares to do so we'll have him. We'll challenge him, but we'll have him." He glanced up at the wall clock. "However, we shall not merely twiddle our thumbs and wait for that. I have thirty minutes. You told me Wednesday morning that no one on earth knew of your dalliance with Miss Usher; now we know you were wrong. We must review every moment you spent in her company when you might have been seen or heard. When I leave, at four o'clock, Mr. Goodwin will continue with you. Start with the day she first attracted your notice, when she waited on you at Cordoni's. Was anyone you knew present?"

When Wolfe undertakes that sort of thing, getting someone to recall every detail of a past experience, he is worse than a housewife bent on finding a speck of dust that the maid overlooked. Once I sat for eight straight hours, from nine in the evening until daylight came, while he took a chauffeur over every second of a drive, made six months before, to New Haven and back. This time he wasn't quite that fussy, but he did no skipping. When four o'clock came, time for him to go up and play with the orchids, he had covered the episode at Cordoni's, two dinners, one at the Woodbine in Westchester and one at Henke's on Long Island, and a lunch at Gaydo's on Sixty-ninth Street.

I carried on for more than an hour, following Wolfe's *modus operandi* more or less, but my pulse wasn't pounding from the thrill of it. It seemed to me that it could have been handled just as well by putting one question: "Did you at any time, anywhere, when she was with you, including Canada, see or hear anyone who knew you?" and then make sure there were no gaps in his memory. As for chances that they had been seen but he hadn't known it, there had been plenty. Aside from restaurants, she had been in his car, in midtown, in daylight, three times. The morning they left for Canada he had parked his car, with her in it, in front of his club, while he went in to leave a message for somebody.

But I carried on, and we were working on the third day in Canada, somewhere in Quebec, when the doorbell rang and I went to the hall for a look through the one-way glass and saw Inspector Cramer of Homicide.

I wasn't much surprised, since I knew there had been a pointer for them if they were interested enough; and just as Laidlaw's subconscious had made his decision in advance, mine had made mine. I went to the rack and got Laidlaw's hat and coat, stepped back into the office, and told the client, "Inspector Cramer is here looking for you. This way out. Come on, move—"

"But how did—"

"No matter how." The doorbell rang. "Damn it, move!"

He came, and followed me to the kitchen. Fritz was at the big table, doing something to a duck. I told him, "Mr. Laidlaw wants to leave the back way in a hurry, and I haven't time because Cramer wants in. Show him quick, and you haven't seen him."

Fritz headed for the back door, which opens on our private enclosed garden if you want to call it that, whose fence has a gate into the passage between buildings which leads to Thirty-fourth Street. As the door closed behind them and I turned, the doorbell rang. I went to the front, not in a hurry, put the chain bolt on, opened the door to the two-inch crack the chain allowed, and spoke through it politely.

"I suppose you want me? Since you know Mr. Wolfe won't be available until six o'clock."

"Open up, Goodwin."

"Under conditions. You know damn well what my orders are: no callers admitted between four and six unless it's just for me."

"I know. Open up."

I took that for a commitment, and he knew I did. Also it was conceivable that some character—Sergeant Stebbins, for instance—was on his way with a search warrant, and if so it would take the edge off to admit Cramer without one. So I said, "Okay, if it's me you want," removed the bolt, and swung the door wide, and he stepped in, marched down the hall, and entered the office.

I shut the door and went to join him, but by the time I arrived he wasn't there. The connecting door to the front room was open, and in a moment he came through and barked at me, "Where's Laidlaw?"

I was hurt. "I thought you wanted me. If I had—"

"Where's Laidlaw?"

"Search me. There's lots of Laidlaws, but I haven't got one. If you mean—"

He made for the door to the hall, passing within arm's length of me en route.

The rules for dealing with officers of the law are contradictory. Whether you may restrain them by force or not depends. It was okay to restrain Cramer from entering the house by the force of the chain bolt. It would have been okay to restrain him from going upstairs if there had been a locked door there and I had refused to open it, but I couldn't restrain him by standing on the first step and not letting him by, no matter how careful I was not to hurt him. That may make sense to lawyers, but not to me.

But that's the rule, and it didn't matter that he had said he knew *our* rules before I let him in. So when he crossed the hall to the stairs I didn't waste my breath to yell at him; I saved it for climbing the three flights, which I did, right behind him. Since he was proving that in a pinch he had no honor and no manners, it would have been no surprise if he had turned left at the first landing to invade Wolfe's room, or right at the second landing to invade mine, but he kept going to the top, and on into the vestibule.

I don't know whether he is off of orchids because Wolfe is on them, or is just color blind, but on the few occasions that I have seen him in the plant rooms he has never shown the slightest sign that he realizes that the benches are occupied. Of course in that house his mind is always buzzing or he wouldn't be there, and that could account for it. That day, in the cool room, long panicles of Odontoglossums, yellow, rose, white with spots, crowded the aisle on both sides; in the tropical room, Miltonia hybrids and Phalaenopsis splashed pinks and greens and browns clear to the glass above; and in the intermediate room the Cattleyas were grandstanding all over the place as always. Cramer might have been edging his way between rows of dried-up cornstalks.

The door from the intermediate room to the potting room was closed as usual. When Cramer opened it and I followed him in, I didn't stop to shut it but circled around him and raised my voice to announce, "He said he came to see me. When I let him in he dashed past me to the office and then to the front room and started yapping, 'Where's Laidlaw?' and when I told him I had no Laidlaw he dashed past me again for the stairs. Apparently he has such a craving for someone named Laidlaw that his morals are shot."

Theodore Horstmann, at the sink washing pots, had twisted around for a look, but before I finished was twisted back again, washing pots. Wolfe, at the potting bench inspecting seedlings, had turned full around to glare. He had started the glare at me, but by the time I ended had transferred it to Cramer. "Are you demented?" he inquired icily.

Cramer stood in the middle of the room, returning the glare. "Someday," he said, and stopped.

"Someday what? You will recover your senses?"

Cramer advanced two paces. "So you're horning in again," he said. "Goodwin turns a suicide into a murder, and here you are. Yesterday you had those girls here. This morning you had those men here. This afternoon Laidlaw is called downtown to show him something which he refuses to discuss, and when he leaves he heads for you. So I know he has been here. So I come—"

"If you weren't an inspector," I cut in, "I'd say that's a lie. Since you are, make it a fib. You do not know he has been here."

"I know he hopped a taxi and gave the driver this address, and when he saw he was being followed he went to a booth and phoned, and took another taxi to a place that runs through the block, and left by the other street. Where would I suppose he went?"

"Correction. You *suppose* he has been here."

"All right, I do." He took another step, toward Wolfe. "Have you seen Edwin Laidlaw in the last three hours?"

"This is quite beyond belief," Wolfe declared. "You know how rigidly I maintain my personal schedule. You know that I resent any attempt to interfere with these two hours of relaxation. But you get into my house by duplicity and then come charging up here to ask me a question to which you have no right to an answer. So you don't get one. Indeed, in these circumstances, I doubt if you could put a question about anything whatever that I *would* answer." He turned, giving us the broad expanse of his rear, and picked up a seedling.

"I guess," I told Cramer sympathetically, "your best bet would be to get a search warrant and send a gang to look for evidence, like cigarette ashes from the kind he smokes. I know where it hurts. You've never forgotten the day you did come with a warrant and a crew to look for a woman named Clara Fox and searched the whole house, including here, and didn't find her, and later you learned she had been in this room in a packing case, covered with osmundine that Wolfe was spraying water on. So you thought if you rushed up before I could give the alarm you'd find Laidlaw here, and now that he isn't you're stuck. You can't very well demand to know why Laidlaw rushed here to discuss something with Wolfe that he wouldn't discuss downtown. You ought to take your coat off when you're in the house or you'll catch cold when you leave. I'm just talking to be sociable while you collect yourself. Of course Laidlaw was here this morning with the others, but apparently you know that. Whoever told you should—"

He turned and was going. I followed.

11

AT FIVE MINUTES PAST SIX SAUL PANZER PHONED. That was routine; when one or more of them are out on a chore they call at noon, and again shortly after six, to report progress or lack of it and to learn if there are new instructions. He said he was talking from a booth in a bar and grill on Broadway near Eighty-sixth Street. Wolfe, who had just come down from the plant rooms, did him the honor of reaching for the phone on his desk to listen in.

"So far," Saul reported, "we're only scouting. Marjorie Betz lives with Mrs. Elaine Usher at the address on Eighty-seventh Street. Mrs. Usher is the tenant. I got in to see Miss Betz by one of the standard lines, and got nowhere. Mrs. Usher left Wednesday night, and she doesn't know where she is or when she'll be back. We have seen two elevator men, the janitor, five neighbors, fourteen people in local shops and stores, and a hackie Mrs. Usher patronizes, and Orrie is now after the maid, who left at five-thirty. Do you want Mrs. Usher's description?"

Wolfe said no and I said yes simultaneously. "Very well," Wolfe said, "oblige him."

"Around forty. We got as low as thirty-three and as high as forty-five. Five feet six, hundred and twenty pounds, blue eyes set close, oval face, takes good care of good skin, hair was light brown two years ago, now blond, wears it loose, medium cut. Dresses well but a little flashy. Gets up around noon. Hates to tip. I think that's fairly accurate, but this is a guess with nothing specific, that she has no job but is never short of money, and she likes men. She has lived in that apartment for eight years. Nobody ever saw a husband. Six of them knew the daughter, Faith, and liked her, but it has been four years since they last saw her and Mrs. Usher never mentions her."

Wolfe grunted. "Surely that will do."

"Yes, sir. Do we proceed?"

"Yes."

"Okay. I'll wait to see if Orrie gets anywhere with the maid, and if not I have a couple of ideas. Miss Betz may go out this evening, and the lock on the apartment door is only a Wyatt."

"The hackie she patronizes," I said. "She didn't patronize him Wednesday night?"

"According to him, no. Fred found him. I haven't seen him. Fred thinks he got it straight."

"You know," I said, "you say *only* a Wyatt, but you need more than a paper clip for a Wyatt. I could run up there with an assortment, and we could go into conference—"

"No," Wolfe said firmly. "You're needed here."

For what, he didn't say. After we hung up all he did was ask how I had disposed of Laidlaw and then ask for a report of the hour and a quarter I had spent with him, and I could have covered that in one sentence just by saying that it had been a washout. But he kept pecking at it until dinnertime. I knew what the idea was, and he knew I knew. It was simply that if I had gone to help Saul with an illegal entry into Elaine Usher's apartment there was a chance, say one in a million, that I wouldn't be there to answer the phone in the morning.

But back in the office after dinner he decided it was about time he exerted himself a little, possibly because he saw my expression when he picked up his book as soon as Fritz had come for the coffee service.

He lowered the book. "Confound it," he said, "I wait to see Mrs. Usher not merely because her daughter said she hated her. There is also the fact that she has disappeared."

"Yes, sir. I didn't say anything."

"You looked something. I suppose you are reflecting that we have had two faint intimations of the possible identity of the person who sent that communication to the District Attorney."

"I wasn't reflecting. That's your part. What are the two intimations?"

"You know quite well. One, that Austin Byne told Laidlaw that he had seen Faith Usher at Grantham House. He didn't name her, and Laidlaw did not regard his tone or manner as suggestive, but it deserves notice. Of course you couldn't broach it with Byne, since that would have betrayed our client's confidence. You still can't."

I nodded. "So we file it. What's the other one?"

"Miss Grantham. She gave Laidlaw a bizarre reason for refusing to marry him, that he didn't dance well enough. It is true that women constantly give fantastic reasons without knowing that they are fantastic, but Miss Grantham must have known that that one was. If her real reason was merely that she didn't care enough for him, surely she would have made a better choice for her avowed one, unless she despises him. Does she despise him?"

"No."

"Then why insult him? It is an insult to decline a proposal of marriage, a man's supreme capitulation, with flippancy. She did that six months ago, in September. It is not idle to conjecture that her real reason was that she knew of his experience with Faith Usher. Is she capable of moral revulsion?"

"Probably, if it struck her fancy."

"I think you should see her. Apparently you do dance well enough. You should be able, without disclosing our engagement with Mr. Laidlaw—"

The phone rang, and I turned to get it, hoping it was Saul to say he needed some keys, but no. Saul is not a soprano. However, it was someone who wanted to see me, with no mention of keys. She just wanted me, she said, right away, and I told her to expect me in twenty minutes.

I hung up and swiveled. "The timing," I told Wolfe, "couldn't have been better. Satisfactory. I suppose you arranged it with her while I was out getting Laidlaw. That was Celia Grantham. She wants to see me. Urgently. Presumably to tell me why she insulted Laidlaw when he asked her to marry him, though she didn't say." I arose. "Marvelous timing."

"Where?" Wolfe growled.

"At her home." I was on my way, and turned to correct it. "I mean her mother's home. You have the number." I went.

Since there were at least twenty possible reasons, excluding personal ones, why Celia wanted to see me, and she had given no hint which it was, and since I would soon know anyhow, it would have been pointless to try to guess, so on the way uptown in a taxi that's what I did. When I pushed the button in the vestibule of the Fifth Avenue mansion I had considered only half of them.

I was wondering which I would be for Hackett, the hired detective or the guest, but he didn't have to face the problem. Celia was there with him and took my coat as I shed it and handed it to him, and then fastened on my elbow and steered me to the door of a room on the

right that they called the hall room, and on through it. She shut the
door and turned to me.

"Mother wants to see you," she said.

"Oh?" I raised a brow. "You said you did."

"I do, but it only occurred to me after Mother got me to decoy
for her. The Police Commissioner is here, and they wanted to see you
but thought you might not come, so she asked me to phone you, and
I realized I wanted to see you too. They're up in the music room, but
first I want to ask you something. What is it about Edwin Laidlaw and
that girl? Faith Usher."

That was turning the tables. Wolfe's idea had been that I might
manage, without showing any cards, to find out if she was onto our
client's secret, and here she was popping it at me and I had to play
ignorant.

"Laidlaw?" I shook my head. "Search me. Why?"

"You don't know about it?"

"No. Am I supposed to?"

"I thought you would, naturally, since it's you that's making all
the trouble. You see, I may marry him someday. If he gets into a bad
jam I'll marry him now, since you've turned out to be a skunk. That's
based on inside information but is not guaranteed. Are you a skunk?"

"I'll think it over and let you know. What about Laidlaw and Faith
Usher?"

"That's what I want to know. They're asking questions of all of
us, whether we have any knowledge that Edwin ever knew her. Of
course he didn't. I think they got an anonymous letter. The reason I
think that, they wanted to type something on our typewriters, all four
of them—no, five. Hackett has one, and Cece, and I have, and there
are two in Mother's office. Are you thwarting me again? Don't you
really know?"

"I do now, since you've told me." I patted her shoulder. "Any time
you're hard up and need a job, ring me. You have the makings of a
lady detective, figuring out why they wanted samples from the typewriters. Did they get them?"

"Yes. You can imagine how Mother liked it, but she let them."

I patted her shoulder again. "Don't let it wreck your marriage
plans. Undoubtedly they got an anonymous letter, but they're a dime
a dozen. Whatever the letter said about Laidlaw, even if it said he was
the father of her baby, that proves nothing. People who send anonymous letters are never—"

"That's not it," she said. "If he was the father of her baby, that
would show that if I married him we could have a family, and I want

one. What I'm worried about is his getting in a jam, and you're no help."

Mrs. Irwin had certainly sized her up. She had her own way of looking at things. She was going on. "So now suit yourself. If you'd rather duck Mother and the Police Commissioner, you know where your hat and coat are. I don't like being used for a decoy, and I'll tell them you got mad and went."

It was a tossup. The idea of chatting with Mrs. Robilotti had attractions, since she might be stirred up enough by now to say something interesting, but with Police Commissioner Skinner present it would probably be just some more ring-around-a-rosy. However, it might be helpful to know why they had gone to the trouble of using Celia for bait, so I told her I would hate to disappoint her mother, and she escorted me out to the reception hall and on upstairs to the music room, where we had joined the ladies Tuesday evening after going without brandy.

The whole family was there—Cecil standing over by a window, and Mr. and Mrs. Robilotti and Commissioner Skinner grouped on chairs at the far end, provided with drinks, not champagne. As Celia and I approached, Robilotti and Skinner arose, but not to offer hands. Mrs. Robilotti lifted her bony chin, but not getting the effect she had in mind. You can't look down your nose at someone when he is standing and you are sitting.

"Mr. Goodwin came up on his own," Celia said. "I warned him you were laying for him, but here he is. Mr. Skinner, Mr. Goodwin."

"We've met," the Commissioner said. His tone indicated that it was not one of his treasured memories. He had acquired more gray hairs above his ears and a couple of new wrinkles since I had last seen him, a year or so back.

"I wish to say," Mrs. Robilotti told me, "that I would have preferred never to permit you in my house again."

Skinner shook his head at her. "Now, Louise." He sat down and aimed his eyes at me. "This is unofficial, Goodwin, and off the record. Albert Grantham was my close and valued friend. He would have hated to have a thing like this happen in his house, and I owe it to him—"

"Also," Celia cut in, "he would have hated to ask someone to come and see him and then not invite him to sit down."

"I agree," Robilotti said. "Be seated, Goodwin." I didn't know he had the spunk.

"It may not be worth the trouble." I looked down at Mrs. Robilotti. From that slant her angles were even sharper. "Your daughter said you wanted to see me. Just to tell me I'm not welcome?"

She couldn't look down her nose, but she could look. "I have just spent," she said, "the worst three days of my life, and you are responsible. I had had a previous experience with you, you and the man you work for, and I should have known better than to have you here. I think you are quite capable of blackmail, and I think that's what you have in mind. I want to tell you that I won't submit to it, and if you try—"

"Hold it, Mom," Cecil called over. "That's libelous."

"Also," Skinner said, "it's useless. As I said, Goodwin, this is unofficial and off the record. None of my colleagues know I'm here, including the District Attorney. Let's assume something, just an assumption. Let's assume that here Tuesday evening, when something happened that you had said you would prevent, you were exasperated—naturally you would be—and in the heat of the moment you blurted out that you thought Faith Usher had been murdered, and then you found that you had committed yourself. It carried along from the precinct men to the squad men, to Inspector Cramer, to the District Attorney, and by that time you *were* committed."

He smiled. I knew that smile, and so did a lot of other people. "Another assumption, merely an assumption. Somewhere along the line, probably fairly early, it occurred to you and Wolfe that some of the people who were involved were persons of wealth and high standing, and that the annoyance of a murder investigation might cause one of them to seek the services of a private detective. If that were a fact, instead of an assumption, it should be apparent to you and Wolfe by now that your expectation is vain. None of the people involved is going to be foolish enough to hire you. There will be no fee."

"Do I comment as you go along," I inquired, "or wait till you're through?"

"Please let me finish. I realize your position. I realize that it would be very difficult for you to go now to Inspector Cramer or the District Attorney and say that upon further consideration you have concluded that you were mistaken. So I have a suggestion. I suggest that you wanted to check, to make absolutely sure of your ground, and came here this evening to inspect the scene again, and found me here. And after a careful inspection—the distances, the positions, and so on— you found that, though you had nothing to apologize for, you had probably been unduly positive. You concede that it is possible that Faith Usher did poison her champagne, and that if the official conclusion is suicide you will not challenge it. I will of course be under an obligation to ensure that you will suffer no damage or inconvenience, that you will not be pestered. I will fulfill that obligation. I know you will probably have to consult with Wolfe before you can give me a definite answer, but I would like to have it as soon as possible. You can phone him from here, or go out to a booth if you prefer, or even go to him. I'll wait here for you. This has gone on long enough. I think my suggestion is reasonable and fair."

"Are you through?" I asked.

"Yes."

"Well. I could make some assumptions too, but what's the use? Besides, I'm at a disadvantage. My mother used to tell me never to stay where I wasn't wanted, and you heard Mrs. Robilotti. I guess I'm too sensitive, but I've stood it as long as I can."

I turned and went. Voices came—Skinner's and Celia's and Robilotti's—but I marched on.

12   IF, TO PASS THE TIME, YOU TRIED TO DECIDE WHAT
was the most conceited statement you ever heard anybody make, or
read or heard of anybody making, what would you pick? The other
evening a friend of mine brought it up, and she settled for Louis XIV
saying *L'état, c'est moi*. I didn't have to go so far back. Mine, I told
her, was "They know me." Of course she wanted to know who said it
and when, and since the murderer of Faith Usher had been convicted
by a jury just the day before and the matter was closed, I told her.

Wolfe said it that Friday night when I got home and reported.
When I finished I made a comment. "You know," I said, "it's pretty
damn silly. A police commissioner and a district attorney and an inspector of Homicide all biting nails just because if they say suicide
one obscure citizen may let out a squeak."

"They know me," Wolfe said.

Beat that if you can. I admit it was justified by the record. They
did know him. What if they officially called it suicide, and then, in a
day or a week or a month, Wolfe phoned WA 9-8241 to tell them to
come and get the murderer and the evidence? Not that they were sure
that would happen, but past experience had shown them that it was at
least an even-money bet that it *might* happen. My point is not that it
wasn't justified, but that it would have been more becoming just to
describe the situation.

He saved his breath. He said, "They know me," and picked up his
book.

The next day, Saturday, we had words. The explosion came right
after lunch. Saul had phoned at eight-thirty, as I was on my second
cup of breakfast coffee, to report no progress. Marjorie Betz had stayed

put in the apartment all evening, so the Wyatt lock had not been tackled. At noon he phoned again; more items of assorted information, but still no progress. But at two-thirty, as we returned to the office after lunch, the phone rang and he had news. They had found her. A man from a messenger service had gone to the apartment, and when he came out he had a suitcase with a tag on it. Of course that was pie. Saul and Orrie had entered a subway car right behind him. The tag read: "Miss Edith Upson, Room 911, Hotel Christie, 523 Lexington Avenue." The initials "EU" were stamped on the suitcase.

Getting a look at someone who is holed up in a hotel room can be a little tricky, but that situation was made to order. Saul, not encumbered with luggage, had got to the hotel first and gone to the ninth floor, and had been strolling past the door of Room 911 at the moment it opened to admit the messenger with the suitcase; and if descriptions are any good at all, Edith Upson was Elaine Usher. Of course Saul had been tempted to tackle her then and there, but also of course, since it was Saul, he had retired to think it over and to phone. He wanted to know, were there instructions or was he to roll his own?

"You need a staff," I told him. "I'll be there in twelve minutes. Where—"

"No," Wolfe said, at his phone. "Proceed, Saul, as you think best. You have Orrie. For this sort of juncture your talents are as good as mine. Get her here."

"Yes, sir."

"Preferably in a mood of compliance, but get her here."

"Yes, sir."

That was when we had words. I cradled the receiver, not gently, and stood up. "This is Saturday," I said, "and I've got my check for this week. I want a month's severance pay."

"Pfui."

"No phooey. I am severing relations. It has been eighty-eight hours since I saw that girl die, and your one bright idea, granting that it was bright, was to collect her mother, and I refuse to camp here on my fanny while Saul collects her. Saul is not ten times as smart as I am; he's only twice as smart. A month's severance pay will be—"

"Shut up."

"Gladly." I went to the safe for the checkbook and took it to my desk.

"Archie."

"I have shut up." I opened the checkbook.

"This is natural. That is, it is in us, and we are alive, and whatever is in life is natural. You are headstrong and I am magisterial. Our tolerance of each other is a constantly recurring miracle. I did not have one idea, bright or not; I had two. We have neglected Austin Byne. It has been two days and nights since you saw him. Since he got you to that party, pretending an ailment he didn't have, and since he told Laidlaw he had seen Miss Usher at Grantham House, and since he chose Miss Usher as one of the dinner guests, he deserves better of us. I suggest that you attend to him."

I turned my head but kept the checkbook open. "How? Tell him we don't like his explanations and we want new ones?"

"Nonsense. You are not so ingenuous. Survey him. Explore him."

"I already have. You know what Laidlaw said. He has no visible means of support, but he has an apartment and a car and plays table-stakes poker and does not go naked. The apartment, by the way, hits my eye. If you hang this murder on him, and if our tolerance miracle runs out of gas, I'll probably take it over. Are you working yourself up to saying that you want to see him?"

"No. I have no lever to use on him. I only feel that he has been neglected. If you approach him again you too will be without a lever. Perhaps the best course would be to put him under surveillance."

"If I postpone writing this check is that an instruction?"

"Yes."

At least I would get out in the air and away from the miracle for a while. I returned the checkbook to the safe, took twenty tens from the expense drawer, told Wolfe he would see me when he saw me, and went to the hall for my coat and hat.

When starting to tail a man it is desirable to know where he is, so I was a little handicapped. For all I knew, Byne might be in Jersey City or Brooklyn, or some other province, in a marathon poker game, or he might be at home in bed with a cold, or walking in the park. I got air by walking the two miles to Bowdoin Street, and at the corner of Bowdoin and Arbor I found a phone booth and dialed Byne's number. No answer. So at least I knew where he wasn't, and again I had to resist temptation. It is always a temptation to monkey with locks, and one of the best ways to test your ears is to enter someone's castle uninvited and, while you are looking here and there for something interesting, listen for footsteps on the stairs or the sound of an elevator. If you don't hear them in time your hearing is defective, and you should try some other line of work when you are out and around again.

Having swallowed the temptation, I moved down the block to a place of business I had noticed Thursday afternoon, with an artistic sign bordered with sweet peas, I think, that said AMY'S NOOK. As I entered, my wristwatch said 4:12. Between then and a quarter past six, slightly over two hours, I ate five pieces of pie, two rhubarb and one each of apple, green tomato, and chocolate, and drank four glasses of milk and two cups of coffee, while seated at a table by the front window, from which I could see the entrance to 87, across the street and up a few doors. To keep from arousing curiosity by either my tenure or my diet, I had my notebook and pencil out and made sketches of a cat sleeping on a chair. In the Village that accounts for anything. The pie, incidentally, was more than satisfactory. I would have liked to take a piece home to Fritz. At six-fifteen the light outside was getting dim, and I asked for my check and was putting my notebook in a pocket when a taxi drew up in front of 87 and Dinky Byne piled out and headed for the entrance. When my change came I added a quarter to the tip, saying, "For the cat," and vacated.

It was nothing like as comfortable in the doorway across from 87, the one I had patronized Thursday, but you have to be closer at night than in the daytime, no matter how good your eyes are. I could only hope that Dinky wasn't set to spend the evening curled up with a book, or even without one, but that didn't seem likely, since he would have to eat and I doubted if he did his own cooking. A light had shown at the fifth-floor windows, and that gave me something to do, bend my head back every half-minute or so to see if it had gone out. My neck was beginning to feel the strain when it finally did go out, at 7:02. In a couple of minutes the subject stepped out of the vestibule and turned right.

Tailing a man solo in Manhattan, even if he isn't wise, is a joke. If he suddenly decides to flag a taxi— There are a hundred ifs, and they are all on his side. But of course any game is more fun if the odds are against you, and if you win it's good for the ego. Naturally it's easier at night, especially if the subject knows you. On that occasion I claim no credit for keeping on Byne, for none of the ifs developed. It was merely a ten-minute walk. He turned left on Arbor, crossed Seventh Avenue, went three blocks west and one uptown, and entered a door where there was a sign on the window: TOM'S JOINT.

That's the sort of situation where being known to the subject cramps you; I couldn't go in. All I could do was hunt a post, and I found a perfect one: a narrow passage between two buildings almost directly across the street. I could go in a good ten feet from the building line, where no light came at all, and still see the front of Tom's Joint. There was even an iron thing to sit on if my feet needed a rest.

They didn't. It didn't last long enough. I hadn't been there more than five minutes when suddenly company came. I was alone, and then I wasn't. A man had slid in, caught sight of me, and was peering in the darkness. A question that had arisen on various occasions, which of us had better eyesight, was settled when we spoke simultaneously. He said, "Archie," and I said, "Saul."

"What the hell," I said.

"Are you on her too?" he asked. "You might have told me."

"I'm on a man. I'll be damned. Where is yours?"

"Across the street. Tom's Joint. She just came."

"This is fate," I said. "It is also a break in a thousand. Of course it could be coincidence. Mr. Wolfe says that in a world that operates largely at random, coincidences are to be expected, but not this one. Have you spoken with her? Does she know you?"

"No."

"My man knows me. His name is Austin Byne. He is six-feet-one, hundred and seventy pounds, lanky, loose-jointed, early thirties, brown hair and eyes, skin tight on his bones. Go in and take a look. If you want a bet, one will get you ten that they're together."

"I never bet against fate," he said, and went. The five minutes that he was gone were five hours. I sat down on the iron thing and got up again three times, or maybe four.

He came, and said, "They're together in a booth in a rear corner. No one is with them. He's eating oysters."

"He'll soon be eating crow. What do you want for Christmas?"

"I have always wanted your autograph."

"You'll get it. I'll tattoo it on you. Now we have a problem. She's yours and he's mine. Now they're together. Who's in command?"

"That's easy, Archie. Mr. Wolfe."

"I suppose so, damn it. We could wrap it up by midnight. Take them to a basement, I know one, and peel their hides off. If he's eating oysters there's plenty of time to phone. You or me?"

"You. I'll stick here."

"Where's Orrie?"

"Lost. When she came out he was for feet and I was for wheels, and she took a taxi."

"I saw it pull up. Okay. Sit down and make yourself at home."

At the bar and grill at the corner the phone booth was occupied and I had to wait, and I was tired of waiting, having done too much of it in the last four days. But in a few minutes the customer emerged, and I entered, pulled the door shut, and dialed the number I knew best. When Fritz answered I told him I wanted to speak to Mr. Wolfe.

"But Archie! He's at dinner!"

"I know. Tell him it's urgent." That was another unexpected pleasure, having a good excuse to call Wolfe from the table. He has too many rules. His voice came, or rather his roar.

"Well?"

"I have a report. Saul and I are having an argument. He thought—"

"What the devil are you doing with Saul?"

"I'm telling you. He thought I should phone you. We have a problem of protocol. I tailed Byne to a restaurant, a joint, and Saul tailed Mrs. Usher to the same restaurant, and our two subjects are in there together in a booth. Byne is eating oysters. So the question is, who is in charge, Saul or me? The only way to settle it without violence was to call you."

"At mealtime," he said. I didn't retort, knowing that his complaint was not that I had presumed to interrupt, but that his two bright ideas had picked that moment to rendezvous.

I said sympathetically, "They should have known better."

"Is anyone with them?" he asked.

"No."

"Do they know they have been seen?"

"No."

"Could you eavesdrop?"

"Possibly, but I doubt it."

"Very well, bring them. There's no hurry, since I have just started dinner. Give them no opportunity for a private exchange after they see you. Have you eaten?"

"I'm full of pie and milk. I don't know about Saul. I'll ask him."

"Do so. He could come and eat— No. You may need him."

I hung up, returned to our field headquarters, and told Saul, "He wants them. Naturally. In an hour will do, since he just started dinner. Do you know what a genius is? A genius is a guy who makes things happen without his having any idea that they are going to happen. It's quite a trick. Our genius wanted to know if you've had anything to eat."

"He would. Sure. Plenty."

"Okay. Now the m.o. Do we take them in there or wait till they come out?"

Both procedures had pros and cons, and after discussion it was decided that Saul should go in and see how their meal was coming along, and when he thought they had swallowed enough to hold them through the hours ahead, or when they showed signs of adjourning, he would come out and wigwag me, go back in, and be near their booth when I approached.

They must have been fast eaters, for Saul hadn't been gone more than ten minutes when he came out, lifted a hand, saw me move, and went back in. I crossed over, entered, took five seconds to adjust to the noise and the smoke screen from the mob, made it to the rear, and there they were. The first Byne knew, someone was crowding him on the narrow seat, and his head jerked around. He started to say something, saw who it was, and goggled at me.

"Hi, Dinky," I said. "Excuse me for butting in, but I want to introduce a friend. Mr. Panzer. Saul, Mrs. Usher. Mr. Byne. Sit down. Would you mind giving him room, Mrs. Usher?"

Byne had started to rise, by reflex, but it can't be done in a tight little booth without toppling the table. He sank back. His mouth opened, and closed. Liquid spilled on the table top from a glass Elaine Usher was holding, and Saul, squeezed in beside her, reached and took it.

"Let me out," Byne said. "Let us out or I'll go out over you. Her name is Upson. Edith Upson."

I shook my head. "If you start a row you'll only make it worse. Mr. Panzer knows Mrs. Usher, though she doesn't know him. Let's be calm and consider the situation. There must be—"

"What do you want?"

"I'm trying to tell you. There must be some good reason why you two arranged to meet in this out-of-the-way dump, and Mr. Panzer and I are curious to know what it is, and others will be too—the press, the public, the police, the District Attorney, and Nero Wolfe. I wouldn't expect you to explain it here in this din and smog. Either Mr. Panzer can phone Inspector Cramer while I sit and chat with you, and he can send a car for you, or we'll take you to talk it over with Mr. Wolfe, whichever you prefer."

He had recovered some. He had played a lot of poker. He put a hand on my arm. "Look, Archie, there's nothing to it. It looks funny, sure it does, us here together, but we didn't arrange it. I met Mrs. Usher about a year ago, I went to see her when her daughter went to Grantham House, and when I came in here this evening and saw her, after what's happened, naturally I spoke to her and we—"

"Save it, Dinky. Saul, phone Cramer."

Saul started to slide out. Byne reached and grabbed his sleeve. "Now wait a minute. Damn it, can't you listen? I'm—"

"No," I said. "No listening. You can have one minute to decide." I looked at my watch. "In one minute either you and Mrs. Usher come along to Nero Wolfe or we phone Cramer. One minute." I looked at my watch. "Go."

"Not the cops," Mrs. Usher said. "My God, not the cops."

Byne began, "If you'd only listen—"

"No. Forty seconds."

If you're playing stud, and there's only one card to come, and the man across has two jacks showing and all you have is a mess, it doesn't matter what his hole card is, or yours either. Byne didn't use up the forty seconds. Only ten of them had gone when he stretched his neck to look for a waiter and ask for his check.

13   Surveying Elaine Usher from my desk as she sat in the red leather chair, I told myself that Saul's picture of her, pieced together from a dozen descriptions he had got, had been pretty accurate. Oval face, blue eyes set close, good skin, medium-cut blond hair, around forty. I would have said 115 pounds instead of 120, but she might have lost a few in the last four days. I had put her in the red leather chair because I had thought it desirable to have Byne closer to me. He was between Saul and me, and Saul was between the two subjects. But my arrangement was soon changed.

"I prefer," Wolfe said, "to speak with you separately, but first I must make sure that there is no misunderstanding. I intend to badger you, but you don't have to submit to it. Before I start, or at any moment, you may get up and leave. If you do, you will be through with me; thenceforth you will deal with the police. I make that clear because I don't want you bouncing up and down. If you want to go now, go."

He took a deep breath. He had just come in from the dining room, having had his coffee there while I reported on the summit conference at Tom's Joint.

"We were forced to come here by a threat," Byne said.

"Certainly you were. And I am detaining you by the same threat. When you prefer that to this, leave. Now, madam, I wish to speak privately with Mr. Byne. Saul, take Mrs. Usher to the front room."

"Don't go," Byne told her. "Stay here."

Wolfe turned to me. "You were right, Archie. He is incorrigible. It isn't worth it. Get Mr. Cramer."

"No," Elaine Usher said. She left the chair. "I'll go."

Saul was up. "This way," he said, and went and opened the door to the front room and held it for her. When she had passed through he followed and closed the door.

Wolfe leveled his eyes at Byne. "Now, sir. Don't bother to raise your voice; that wall and door are soundproofed. Mr. Goodwin has told me how you explained being in that restaurant with Mrs. Usher. Do you expect me to accept it?"

"No," Dinky said.

Of course. He had had time to realize that it wouldn't do. If he had gone to see her because her daughter was at Grantham House, how had he learned that she was Faith's mother? Not from the records and not from Mrs. Irwin. From one of the other girls? It was too tricky.

"What do you substitute for it?" Wolfe asked.

"I told Goodwin that because the real explanation would have been embarrassing for Mrs. Usher. Now I can't help it. I met her some time ago, three years ago, and for about a year I was intimate with her. She'll probably deny it. I'm pretty sure she will. Naturally she would."

"No doubt. And your meeting her this evening was accidental?"

"No," Dinky said. He had also had time to realize that that was too fishy. He went on, "She phoned me this morning and said she was at the Christie Hotel, registered as Edith Upson. She had known that I was Mrs. Robilotti's nephew, and she said she wanted to see me and ask me about her daughter who had died. I told her I hadn't been there Tuesday evening, and she said she knew that, but she wanted to see me. I agreed to see her because I didn't want to offend her. I didn't want it to get out that I had been intimate with Faith Usher's mother. We arranged to meet at that restaurant."

"Had you known previously that she was Faith Usher's mother?"

"I had known that she had a daughter, but not that her name was Faith. She had spoken of her daughter when we—when I had known her."

"What did she ask you about her daughter this evening?"

"She just wanted to know if I knew anything that hadn't been in the papers. Anything about the people there or exactly what had happened. I could tell her about the people, but I didn't know any more about what had happened than she did."

"Do you wish to elaborate on any of this? Or add anything?"

"There's nothing to add."

"Then I'll see Mrs. Usher. After I speak with her I'll ask you in again, with her present. Archie, take Mr. Byne and bring Mrs. Usher."

He came like a lamb. He had thrown away his discard and made his draw and his bets, and was ready for the showdown. I opened the door for him, held it for Mrs. Usher to enter, closed it, and returned to my desk. She went to the red leather chair, so Wolfe had to swivel to face her. Another item of Saul's report on her had been that she liked men, and there were indications that men probably liked her—the way she handled her hips when she walked, the tilt of her head, the hint of a suggestion in her eyes, even now, when she was under pressure and when the man she was looking at was not a likely candidate for a frolic. And she was forty. At twenty she must have been a treat.

Wolfe breathed deep again. Exertion right after a meal was pretty rugged. "Of course, madam," he said, "my reason for speaking with you and Mr. Byne separately is transparent: to see if your account will agree with his. Since you have had no opportunity for collusion, agreement would be, if not conclusive, at least persuasive."

She smiled. "You use big words, don't you?" Something in her tone and her look conveyed the notion that for years she had been wanting to meet a man who used big words.

Wolfe grunted. "I try to use words that say what I mean."

"So do I," she declared, "but sometimes it's hard to find the ones I want. I don't know what Mr. Byne told you, but all I can do is tell you the truth. You want to know how I happened to be with him there tonight, isn't that it?"

"That's it."

"Well, I phoned him this morning and said I wanted to see him and he said he would meet me there at Tom's Joint, I had never heard of it before, at a quarter past seven. So I went. That's not very thrilling, is it?"

"Only moderately. Have you known him long?"

"I don't really *know* him at all. I met him somewhere about a year ago, and I wish I could tell you where, but I've been trying to remember and I simply *can't*. It was a party somewhere, but I can't remember where. Anyhow, it doesn't matter. But yesterday I was sitting at the window thinking about my daughter. My dear daughter Faith." She stopped to gulp, but it wasn't very impressive. "And I remembered meeting a man named Byne, Austin Byne, and someone telling me, maybe he told me himself, that he was the nephew of the rich Mrs. Robilotti who used to be Mrs. Albert Grantham. And my daughter had died at Mrs. Robilotti's house, so maybe he could tell me about her, and maybe he could get Mrs. Robilotti to see me so I could ask her about her. I wanted to learn all I could about my daughter." She gulped.

It didn't look good. In fact, it looked bad. Byne had been smart enough to invent one that she couldn't be expected to corroborate; he had even warned that she would probably deny it; and what was worse, it was even possible that he hadn't invented it. He might have been telling the truth, like a gentleman. The meeting of Wolfe's two bright ideas at Tom's Joint, which had looked so rosy when Saul told me they were together, might fizzle out entirely. Maybe he wasn't a genius after all.

If he was sharing my gloom it didn't show. He asked, "Since your rendezvous with Mr. Byne was innocuous, why were you alarmed by his threat to call the police? What were her words, Archie?"

" 'Not the cops. My God, not the cops.' "

"Yes. Why, Mrs. Usher?"

"I don't like cops. I never have liked cops."

"Why did you leave your home and go to a hotel and register under another name?"

"Because of how I felt, what my daughter had done. I didn't want to see people. I knew newspapermen would come. And cops. I wanted to be alone. You would too if—"

The doorbell rang, and I went. Sometimes I let Fritz answer it when I am engaged, but with her there and Byne in the front room I thought I had better see who it was, and besides, I was having a comedown and felt like moving. It was only Orrie Cather. I opened up and greeted him, and he crossed the sill, and I shut the door. When he removed his coat there was disclosed a leather thing, a zippered case, that he had had under it.

"What's that?" I asked. "Your weekend bag?"

"No," he said. "It's Mrs. Usher's sec—"

My hand darted to clap on his mouth. He was startled, but he can take a hint, and when I headed down the hall and turned right to the dining room he followed.

I shut the door, moved away from it, and demanded, "Mrs. Usher's what?"

"Her secret sin." There was a gleam in his eye. "I want to give it to Mr. Wolfe myself."

"You can't. Mrs. Usher is in the office with him. Where did—"

"She's here? How come?"

"That can wait. Where did you get that thing?"

I may have sounded magisterial, but my nerves were a little raw. It put Orrie on his dignity. His chin went up. "It's a pleasure to report, Mr. Goodwin. Mr. Panzer and I were covering the Christie Hotel. When the subject appeared and hopped a taxi he followed in one before I could join him. That left me loose and I phoned in. Mr. Wolfe asked me if there had been any indication how long she would be gone, and I said yes, since she took a taxi it certainly wouldn't be less than half an hour and probably longer, and he said it would be desirable to take a look at her room, and I said fine. It took a while to get in. Do you want the details?"

"That can wait. What's in it?"

"It was in a locked suitcase—not the one the messenger took today, a smaller one. The suitcase was easy, but this thing had a trick lock and I had to bust it."

I put out a hand. He hated to give it up, but protocol is protocol. I took it to the table, unzipped it, and pulled out two envelopes, one nine by twelve and the other one smaller. Neither was sealed, and hadn't been. I slipped out the contents of the big one.

They were pictures that had been clipped from magazines and newspapers. I would have recognized him even if there had been no captions, since I had been old enough to read for some years, and you often run across a picture of a multimillionaire philanthropist. The one on top was captioned: "Albert Grantham (left) receiving the annual award of the American Benevolent League." They were all of Grantham, twenty or more. I started to turn them over, one by one, to see if anything was written on them.

"To hell with that," Orrie said impatiently. "It's the other one."

It, not so big, held another envelope, smaller, of white rag bond. The engraved return in the corner said "Albert Grantham," with the Fifth Avenue address, and it was addressed in longhand to Mrs. Elaine Usher, 812 West 87th Street, New York, and below was written "By Messenger." Inside were folded sheets. I unfolded them and read:

June 6, 1952

My dear Elaine:

In accordance with my promise, I am confirming in writing what I said to you recently.

I am not accepting the obligations, legal or moral, of paternity of your daughter, Faith. You have always maintained that I am her father, and for a time I believed you, and I now have no evidence to prove you are wrong, but as I told you, I have taken the trouble to inform myself of your method of life for the past ten years, and it is quite clear that chastity is not one of your virtues. It may have been, during that period fifteen years ago when I took advantage of your youth and enjoyed your favors—you say it was—but your subsequent conduct makes it doubtful. I shall not again express my regret for my own conduct during that period. I have done that and you know how I feel about it, and have always felt since I achieved maturity, and I have not been illiberal in supplying the material needs of your daughter and yourself. For a time that was not easy, but since my father's death I have given you $2000 each month, and you have paid no taxes on it.

But I am getting along in years, and you are quite right, I should make provision against contingencies. As I told you, I must reject your suggestion that I give you a large sum outright—large enough for you and your daughter to live on the income. I distrust your attitude toward money. I fear that in your hands the principal would soon be squandered, and you would again appeal to me. Nor can I provide for you through a trust fund, either now or in my will, for the reasons I gave you. I will not risk disclosure.

So I have taken steps that should meet the situation. I have given my nephew, Austin Byne, a portfolio of securities the income from which is tax exempt, amounting to slightly more than two million dollars. The yield will be about $55,000 annually. My nephew is to remit half of it to you and keep the other half for himself.

This arrangement is recorded in an agreement signed by my nephew and myself. One provision is that if you make additional demands, or if you disclose the relationship you and I once had, or if you make any claims on my estate or any member of my family, he is relieved of any obligation to share the income with you. Another provision is that if he fails to make the proper remittances to you with reasonable promptness you may claim the entire principal. In drafting that provision I would have liked to have legal advice, but could not. I am sure it is binding. I do not think my nephew will fail in his performance, but if he does you will know what to do. There is of course the possibility that *he* will squander the principal, but I have known him all his life and I am sure it is remote.

I have herewith kept my promise to confirm what I told you. I repeat that this letter is not to be taken as an acknowledgment by me that I am the father of your daughter, Faith. If you ever show it or use it as the basis of any claim, the remittances from my nephew will cease at once.

I close with all good wishes for the welfare and happiness of your daughter and yourself.

Yours sincerely,
Albert Grantham

As I finished and looked up Orrie said, "I want to give it to Mr. Wolfe myself."

"I don't blame you." I folded the sheets and put them in the envelope. "Quite a letter. *Quite* a letter. I saw a note in the paper the other day that some bozo is doing a biography of him. He would love to have this. You lucky stiff. I'd give a month's pay for the kick you got when you found it."

"It *was* nice. I want to give it to him."

"You will. Wait here. Help yourself to champagne."

I left, crossed to the office, stood until Wolfe finished a sentence, and told him, "Mr. Cather wants to show you something. He's in the dining room." He got up and went, and I sat down. Judging by the expression on Mrs. Usher's face, she had been doing fine. I really would rather not have looked at her, to see the cocky little tilt of her head, the light of satisfaction in her eyes, knowing as I did that she was about to be hit by a ton of brick. So I didn't. I turned to my desk and opened a drawer and got out papers, and did things with them. When she told my back that she was glad I had brought them to Wolfe, she didn't mind a bit explaining to him, I wasn't even polite enough to turn around when I answered her. I had taken my notebook from my pocket and was tearing sketches of cats from it when Wolfe's footsteps came.

As he sat down he spoke. "Bring Mr. Byne, Archie. And Saul."

I went and opened the door and said, "Come in, gentlemen."

As Byne entered his eyes went to Mrs. Usher and saw what I had seen, and then he too was satisfied. They took the seats they had had before. Wolfe looked from one to the other and back again.

"I don't want to prolong this beyond necessity," he said, "but I would like to congratulate you. You were taken in that place by surprise and brought here with no chance to confer, but you have both lied so cleverly that it would have taken a long and costly investigation to impeach you. It was an admirable performance— If you please, Mr. Byne. You may soon speak, and you will need to. Unfortunately, for you, the performance was wasted. Fresh ammunition has arrived. I have just finished reading a document that was not intended for me." He looked at Mrs. Usher. "It states, madam, that if you disclose its contents you will suffer a severe penalty, but you have not disclosed them. On the contrary, you have done your best to safeguard them."

Mrs. Usher had sat up. "What document? What are you talking about?"

"The best way to identify it is to quote an excerpt—say, the fourth paragraph. It goes: 'So I have taken steps that should meet the situation. I have given my nephew, Austin Byne, a portfolio of securities the income from which is tax exempt, amounting to slightly more than two million dollars. The yield will be about fifty-five thousand dollars annually. My nephew is to remit half—' "

Byne was on his feet. The next few seconds were a little confused. I was up, to be between Byne and Wolfe, but the fury in his eyes was for Mrs. Usher. Then, as he moved toward her, Saul was there to block him, so everything was under control. But then, with Saul's back to her and me cut off by Saul and Byne, Mrs. Usher shot out of her chair and streaked for Wolfe. I might have beat her to it by diving across Wolfe's desk, but maybe not, from where I was, and anyway, I was too astonished to move—not by her, but by him. He had been facing her, so his knees weren't under the desk and he didn't have to swivel, but even so, he had a lot of pounds to get in motion. Back went his bulk, and up came his legs, and just as she arrived his feet were there, and one of them caught her smack on the chin. She staggered back into Saul's arms and he eased her onto the chair. And I'll be damned if she didn't put both hands to her jaw and squawk at Wolfe, "You hit me!"

I had hold of Byne's arm, a good hold, and he didn't even know it. When he realized it he tried to jerk loose but couldn't, and for a second I thought he was going to swing with the other fist, and so did he.

"Take it easy," I advised him. "You're going to need all the breath you've got."

"How did you get it?" Mrs. Usher demanded. "Where is it?" She was still clutching her jaw with both hands.

Wolfe was eying her, but not warily. Complacently, I would say. You might think that for a long time he had had a suppressed desire to kick a woman on the chin.

"It's in my pocket," he said. He tapped his chest. "I got it just now from the man who took it from your hotel room. You'll probably get it back in due course; that will depend; it may—"

"That's burglary," Byne said. "That's a felony."

Wolfe nodded. "By definition, yes. I doubt if Mrs. Usher will care to make the charge if the document is eventually returned to her. It may be an exhibit in evidence in a murder trial. If so—"

"There has been no murder."

"You are in error, Mr. Byne. Will you please sit down? This will take a while. Thank you. I'll cover that point decisively with a categorical statement: Faith Usher was murdered."

"No!" Mrs. Usher said. Her hands left her jaw but remained poised, the fingers curved. "Faith killed herself!"

"I'm not going to debate the point," Wolfe told her. "I say merely that I will stake my professional reputation on the statement that she was murdered—indeed, I have done so. That's why I am applying my resources and risking my credit. That's why I must explore the possibilities suggested by this letter." He tapped his chest and focused on Byne. "For instance, I shall insist on seeing the agreement between you and Mr. Grantham. Does it provide that if Faith Usher should die your remittances to her mother are to be materially decreased, or even cease altogether?"

Byne wet his lips. "Since you've read the letter to Mrs. Usher you know what the agreement provides. It's a confidential agreement and you're not going to see it."

"Oh, but I am." Wolfe was assured. "When you came here my threat was only to tell the police of your rendezvous. Now my threat is more imperative and may even be mortal. Observe Mrs. Usher. Note her expression as she regards you. Have you seen the agreement, madam?"

"Yes," she said, "I have."

"Does it contain such a provision as I suggested?"

"Yes," she said, "it does. It says that if Faith dies he can pay me only half as much or even less. Are you telling the truth, that she was murdered?"

"Nuts," Byne said. "It's not the truth he's after. Anyhow, I wasn't even there. Don't look at me, Elaine, look at *him.*"

"I thought," Wolfe said, "that it might save time to see the agreement now, so I sent Mr. Cather to your apartment to look for it. It will expedite matters if you phone him and tell him where it is. He is good with locks and should be inside by this time."

Byne was staring. "By God," he said.

"Do you want to phone him?"

"Not him. By God. You've been threatening to call the police. I'll call them myself. I'll tell them a man has broken into my apartment, and he's there now, and they'll get him."

I left my chair. "Here, Dinky, use my phone."

He ignored me. "It's not the agreement," he told Wolfe. "It's your goddamn nerve. He won't find the agreement because it's not there. It's in a safe-deposit box and it's going to stay there."

"Then it must wait until Monday." Wolfe's shoulders went up an eighth of an inch and down again. "However, Mr. Cather will not have his trouble for nothing. Aside from the chance that he may turn up other interesting items, he will use your typewriter, if you have one. I told him if he found one there to write something with it. I even told him what to write. This: 'Have you found out yet that Edwin Laidlaw is the father of Faith Usher's baby? Ask him about his trip to Canada in August nineteen fifty-six.' He will type that and bring it to me. You smile. You are amused? Because you don't have a typewriter?"

"Sure I have a typewriter. Did I smile?" He smiled again, a poker smile. "At you, dragging Laidlaw in all of a sudden. I don't get it, but I suppose you do."

"I didn't drag him in," Wolfe asserted. "Someone else did. The police received an unsigned typewritten communication which I have just quoted. And you were wrong to smile; that was a mistake. You couldn't possibly have been amused, so you must have been pleased, and by what? Not that you don't have a typewriter, because you have. I'll try a guess. Might it not have been that you were enjoying the idea of Mr. Cather bringing me a sample of typing from your machine when you know it is innocent, and that you know it is innocent because you know where the guilty machine is? I think that deserves exploration. Unfortunately tomorrow is Sunday; it will have to wait. Monday morning Mr. Goodwin, Mr. Panzer, and Mr. Cather will call at places where a machine might be easily and naturally available to you—for instance, your club. Another is the bank vault where you have a safe-deposit box. Archie. You go to my box regularly. Would it be remarkable for a vault customer to ask to use a typewriter?"

"Remarkable?" I shook my head. "No."

"Then that is one possibility. Actually," he told Byne, "I am not sorry that this must wait until Monday, for it does have a drawback. The samples collected from the machines must be compared with the communication received by the police, and it is in their hands. I don't like that, but there's no other way. At least, if my guess is good, I will have exposed the sender of the communication, and that will be helpful. On this point, sir, I do not threaten to go to the police; I am forced to."

"You goddamn snoop," Byne said through his teeth.

Wolfe's brows went up. "I must have made a lucky guess. It's the machine at the vault?"

Byne's head jerked to Mrs. Usher. "Beat it, Elaine. I want to talk to him."

14   AUSTIN BYNE SAT STRAIGHT AND STIFF. WHEN SAUL
had escorted Mrs. Usher to the front room, staying there with her, I
had told Dinky he would be more comfortable in the red leather chair,
but from the way he looked at me I suspected that he had forgotten
what "comfortable" meant.

"You win," he told Wolfe. "So I spill my guts. Where do you want
me to start?"

Wolfe was leaning back with his elbows on the chair arms and his
palms together. "First let's clear up a point or two. Why did you send
that thing about Laidlaw to the police?"

"I haven't said I sent it."

"Pfui." Wolfe was disgusted. "Either you've submitted or you
haven't. I don't intend to squeeze it out drop by drop. Why did you
send it?"

Byne did have to squeeze it out. His lips didn't want to part.
"Because," he finally managed, "they were going on with the investigation and there was no telling what they might dig up. They might
find out that I knew Faith's mother, and about my—about the arrangement. I still thought Faith had killed herself, and I still do, but if she
had been murdered I thought Laidlaw must have done it and I wanted
them to know about him and Faith."

"Why must he have done it? You invented that, didn't you? About
him and Miss Usher?"

"I did not. I sort of kept an eye on Faith, naturally. I don't mean
I was with her, I just kept an eye on her. I saw her with Laidlaw twice,
and the day he left for Canada I saw her in his car. I knew he went

to Canada because a friend got a card from him. I didn't have to invent it."

Wolfe grunted. "You realize, Mr. Byne, that everything you say is now suspect. Assuming that you knew that Laidlaw and Miss Usher had in fact been intimate, why did you surmise that he had killed her? Was she menacing him?"

"Not that I know of. If he had a reason for killing her I didn't know what it was. But he was the only one of the people there that night who had had anything to do with her."

"No. You had."

"Damn it, I wasn't there!"

"That's true, but those who were there can also plead lack of opportunity. In the circumstances as I have heard them described, no one could have poisoned Miss Usher's champagne with any assurance that it would get to her. And you alone, of all those involved, had a motive, and not a puny one. An increase in annual income of twenty-seven thousand dollars or more, tax exempt, is an alluring prospect. If I were you I would accept almost any alternative to a disclosure of that agreement to the District Attorney."

"I am. I'm sitting here while you pile it on."

"So you are." Wolfe looked at his palms and put them on the chair arms. "Now. Did you know that Miss Usher kept a bottle of poison on her person?"

No hesitation. "I knew that she said she did. I never saw it. Her mother told me, and Mrs. Irwin at Grantham House mentioned it to me once."

"Did you know what kind of poison it was?"

"No."

"Was it Mrs. Usher's own idea to seclude herself in a hotel under another name, or did you suggest it?"

"Neither one. I mean I don't remember. She phoned me Thursday—no, Wednesday—and we decided she ought to do that. I don't remember who suggested it."

"Who suggested your meeting this evening?"

"She did. She phoned me this morning. I told you that."

"What did she want?"

"She wanted to know what I was going to do about payments, with Faith dead. She knew that by the agreement it was left to my discretion. I told her that for the present I would continue to send her half."

"Had she been using any of the money you sent her to support her daughter?"

"I don't think so. Not for the last four or five years, but it wasn't her fault. Faith wouldn't take anything from her. Faith wouldn't live with her. They couldn't get along. Mrs. Usher is very—unconventional. Faith left when she was sixteen, and for over a year we didn't know where she was. When I found her she was working in a restaurant. A waitress."

"But you continued to pay Mrs. Usher her full share?"

"Yes."

"Is that fund in your possession and control without supervision?"

"Certainly."

"It has never been audited?"

"Certainly not. Who would audit it?"

"I couldn't say. Would you object to an audit by an accountant of my selection? Now that I know of the agreement?"

"I certainly would. The fund is my property and I am accountable to no one but myself, as long as I pay Mrs. Usher her share."

"I must see that agreement." Wolfe pursed his lips and slowly shook his head. "It is extremely difficult," he said, "to circumvent the finality of death. Mr. Grantham made a gallant try, but he was hobbled by his vain desire to guard his secret even after he became food for worms. He protected you and Mrs. Usher, each against the frailty or knavery of the other, but what if you joined forces in a threat to his repute? He couldn't preclude that." He lifted a hand to brush it aside. "A desire to defeat death makes any man a fool. I must see that agreement. Meanwhile, a few points remain. You told Mr. Goodwin that your selection of Miss Usher to be invited to that party was fortuitous, but now that won't do. Then why?"

"Of course," Byne said. "I knew that was coming."

"Then you've had time to devise an answer."

"I don't have to devise it. I was a damn fool. When I got the list from Mrs. Irwin and saw Faith's name on it—well, there it was. The idea of having Faith as a guest at my aunt's house—it just appealed to me. Mrs. Robilotti is only my aunt by marriage, you know. My mother was Albert Grantham's sister. You've got to admit there was a kick in the idea of having Faith sitting at my aunt's table. And then . . ."

He left it hanging. Wolfe prodded him. "Then?"

"That suggested another idea, to have Laidlaw there too. I know I was a damn fool, but there it was. Laidlaw seeing Faith there, and Faith seeing him. Of course my aunt could cross Faith off and tell Mrs. Irwin—" He stopped. In a second he went on, "I mean you never knew what Faith would do, she might refuse to go, but Laidlaw wouldn't know she had been asked, so what the hell. So I suggested that to my aunt, to invite Laidlaw, and she did."

"Did Miss Usher know that Albert Grantham had fathered her?"

"My God, no. She thought her father had been a man named Usher who had died before she was born."

"Did she know you were the source of her mother's income?"

"No. I think— No, I don't think, I know. She suspected that her mother's income came from friends. From men she knew. That was why she left. About my picking Faith to be invited to that party and suggesting Laidlaw, after I had done that I got cold feet. I realized something might happen. At least Faith might walk out when she saw him, and it might be something worse, and I didn't want to be there, so I decided to get someone to go in my place. The first four or five I tried couldn't make it, and I thought of Archie Goodwin."

Wolfe leaned back and closed his eyes, and his lips started to work. They pushed out and went back in, out and in, out and in. . . . Sooner or later he always does that, and I really should have a sign made, GENIUS AT WORK, and put it on his desk when he starts it. Usually I have some sort of idea as to what genius is working on, but that time not a glimmer. He had cleared away some underbrush, for instance who had sicked the cops on Laidlaw and how Faith and Laidlaw had both got invited to the party, but he had got only one thing to chew on, that he had at last found somebody who had had a healthy motive to kill Faith Usher, and Byne, as he liked to point out himself, hadn't even been at the party. Of course that could have been what genius was at, doping out how Byne could have poisoned the champagne by remote control, but I doubted it.

Wolfe opened his eyes and aimed them at Dinky. "I'm not going to wait until Monday," he said. "If I haven't enough now, I never will have. One thing you have told me, or at least implied, will have to be my peg. If I asked you about it now, you would only wriggle out with lies, so I won't bother. The time has come to attack the central question: if someone had decided to kill Faith Usher, how did he manage it?" He turned. "Archie, get Mr. Cramer."

"No!" Byne was on his feet. "Damn you, after I've spilled—"

I had lifted the receiver, but Byne was there, jostling and reaching. Wolfe's voice, with a snap, turned him. "Mr. Byne! Don't squeal until you're hurt. I've got you and I intend to keep you. Must I call Mr. Panzer in?"

He didn't have to. Dinky backed away a step, giving me elbow room to dial, but close enough, he thought, to pounce. Getting Inspector Cramer at twenty minutes past ten on a Saturday evening can be anything from quick and simple to practically impossible. That time I had luck. He was at Homicide on Twentieth Street, and after a short wait I had him, and Wolfe got on, and Cramer greeted him with a growl, and Wolfe said he would need three minutes.

"I'll take all I can stand," Cramer said. "What is it?"

"About Faith Usher. I am being pestered beyond endurance. Take yesterday. In the morning those four men insisted on seeing me. In the afternoon you barged in. In the evening Mr. Goodwin and I were interrupted by a phone call summoning him to Mrs. Robilotti's house, and when he goes he finds Mr. Skinner there, and he—"

"Do you mean the Commissioner?"

"Yes. He said it was unofficial and off the record, and made an offensive proposal which Mr. Goodwin was to refer to me. I don't complain of that to you, since he is your superior and you presumably didn't know about it."

"I didn't."

"But it was another thorn for me, and I have had enough. I would like to put an end to it. All this hullabaloo has been caused by Mr. Goodwin's conviction, as an eyewitness, that Faith Usher did not kill herself, and I intend to satisfy myself on the point independently. If I decide he is wrong I will deal with him. If I decide he is right it will be because I will have uncovered evidence that may have escaped you. I notify you of my intention because in order to proceed I must see all of the people involved, I must invite them to my office, and I thought you should know about it. Also I thought you might choose to be present, and if so you will be welcome, but in that case you should get them here. I will not ask people to my office for a conference and then confront them with a police inspector. Tomorrow morning at eleven o'clock would be a good time."

Cramer made a noise, something like "Wmgzwmzg." Then he found words. "So you've got your teeth in something. What?"

"It's other people's teeth that are in something. In me. And I'm annoyed. The situation is precisely as I have described it and I have nothing to add."

"You wouldn't have. Tomorrow is Sunday."

"Yes. Since three of them are girls with jobs that is just as well."

"You want all of them?"

"Yes."

"Are any of them with you now?"

"No."

"Is Commissioner Skinner in this?"

"No."

"I'll call you back in an hour."

"That won't do," Wolfe objected. "If I am to invite them I must start at once, and it's late."

Not only that, but he knew darned well that if he gave him an hour Cramer would probably ring our bell in about ten minutes and want in. Anyway, it was a cinch that Cramer would buy it, and after a few more foolish questions he did.

We hung up, and Wolfe turned to Byne, who had returned to his chair. "Now for you," he said, "and Mrs. Usher. I do not intend to let you communicate with anyone, and there is only one way to insure against it. She will spend the night here; there is a spare room with a good bed. It is a male household, but that shouldn't disconcert her. There is another room you may use, or, if you prefer, Mr. Panzer will accompany you home and sleep there, and bring you here in the morning. Mr. Cramer will have the others here at eleven o'clock."

"You can go to hell," Byne said. He stood up. "I'm taking Mrs. Usher to her hotel."

Wolfe shook his head. "I know your mind is in disorder, but surely you must see that that is out of the question. I can't possibly allow you an opportunity to repair any of the gaps I have made in your fences. If you scoot I shall move at once, and you'll find you have no fences left at all. Only by my sufferance can you hope to get out of this mess without disfigurement, and you know it. Archie, bring Saul and Mrs. Usher—no. First ring Mr. Byne's apartment and tell Orrie to come. Also tell him not to be disappointed at not finding the agreement; it isn't there. If he has found any items that seem significant he might as well bring them."

"You goddamn snoop," Dinky said, merely repeating himself.

I turned to the phone.

15

FOR AN HOUR AND A HALF SUNDAY MORNING FRITZ and I worked like beavers, setting the stage. The idea was—that is, Wolfe's idea—to reproduce as nearly as possible the scene of the crime, and it was a damn silly idea, since you could have put seven or eight of that office into Mrs. Robilotti's drawing room. Taking the globe and the couch and the television cabinet and a few other items to the dining room helped a little, but it was still hopeless. I wanted to go up to the plant rooms and tell Wolfe so, and add that if a playback was essential to his program he had better break his rule never to leave the house on business and move the whole performance uptown to Mrs. Robilotti's, but Fritz talked me out of it. To get fourteen chairs we had to bring some down from upstairs, and then it developed later that some of them weren't really necessary. The bar was a table over in the far corner, but it couldn't be against the wall because there had to be room for Hackett behind it. One small satisfaction I got was that the red leather chair had been taken to the dining room with the other stuff, and Cramer wouldn't like that a bit.

Furniture-moving wasn't all. Mrs. Usher kept buzzing on the house phone from the South Room, for more coffee, for more towels, though she had a full supply, for a section she said was missing from the Sunday paper I had taken her, and for an additional list of items I had to get from the drugstore. Then at ten-fifteen here came Austin Byne, escorted by Saul, demanding a private audience with Wolfe immediately, and to get him off my neck I had Saul take him up the three flights to the vestibule of the plant rooms, where they found the door locked, and then Saul had to get physical with him when he wanted to open doors on the upper floors trying to find Mrs. Usher.

I expected more turmoil when, at ten-forty, the bell rang and Inspector Cramer was on the stoop, but it wasn't Wolfe he had come
early for. He merely asked if Mrs. Robilotti had arrived, and, when I
told him no, stayed outside. Theoretically, in a democracy, a police
inspector should react just the same to a dame with a Fifth Avenue
mansion as to an unmarried mother, but a job is a job, and facts are
facts, and one fact was that the Commissioner himself had taken the
trouble to make a trip to the mansion. So I didn't chalk it up against
Cramer that he waited out on the sidewalk for the Robilotti limousine;
and anyway, he was there to greet the three unmarried mothers when
Sergeant Purley Stebbins arrived with them in a police car. The three
chevaliers, Paul Schuster, Beverly Kent, and Edwin Laidlaw, came
singly, on their own.

I had promised myself a certain pleasure, and I didn't let Cramer's
one-man reception committee interfere with it. When the limousine
finally rolled to the curb, a few minutes late, and he convoyed Mrs.
Robilotti up the stoop steps, followed by her husband, son, daughter,
and butler, I held the door for them as they entered and then left them
to Fritz. My objective was the last one in, Hackett. When he had
crossed the sill I put my hands ready for his coat and hat, in the proper
manner exactly.

"Good morning, sir," I said. "A pleasant day. Mr. Wolfe will be
down shortly."

It got him. He darted a glance at the others, saw that no eye was
on him, handed me his hat, and said, "Quite. Thank you, Goodwin."

That made the day for me personally, no matter how it turned out
professionally. I took him to the office and then went to the kitchen,
buzzed the plant rooms on the house phone, and told Wolfe the cast
had arrived.

"Mrs. Usher?" he asked.

"Okay. In her room. She'll stay put."

"Mr. Byne?"

"Also okay. In the office with the others, with Saul glued to him."

"Very well. I'll be down."

I went and joined the mob. They were scattered around, some
seated and some standing. I permitted myself a private grin when I
saw that Cramer, finding the red leather chair gone, had moved one
of the yellow ones to its exact position and put Mrs. Robilotti in it,
and was on his feet beside it, bending down to her. As I threaded my
way through to my desk the sound of the elevator came, and in a
moment Wolfe entered.

No pronouncing of names was required, since he had met the

Robilottis and the Grantham twins and Hackett at the time of the jewelry hunt. He made it to his desk, sent his eyes around, and sat. He looked at Cramer.

"You have explained the purpose of this gathering, Mr. Cramer?"

"Yes. You're going to prove that Goodwin is either wrong or right."

"I didn't say 'prove.' I said I intend to satisfy myself and deal with him accordingly." He surveyed the audience. "Ladies and gentlemen. I will not keep you long—at least, not most of you. I have no exhortation for you and no questions to ask. To form an opinion of Mr. Goodwin's competence as an eyewitness, I need to see, not what he saw, since these quarters are too cramped for that, but an approximation of it. You cannot take your positions precisely as they were last Tuesday evening, or re-enact the scene with complete fidelity, but we'll do the best we can. Archie?"

I left my chair to stage-manage. Thinking that Mrs. Robilotti and her Robert were the most likely to balk, I left them till the last. First I put Hackett behind the table, which was the bar, and Laidlaw and Helen Yarmis at one end of it. Then Rose Tuttle and Beverly Kent, on chairs over where the globe had stood. Then Celia Grantham and Paul Schuster by the wall to the right of Wolfe's desk, with her sitting and him standing. Then I put Saul Panzer on a chair near the door to the hall, and told the audience, "Mr. Panzer here is Faith Usher. The distance is wrong and so are the others, but the relative positions are about right." Then I put an ashtray on a chair to the right of the safe, and told them, "This is Faith Usher's bag, containing the bottle of poison." With all that arranged, I didn't think Mrs. Robilotti would protest when I asked her and her husband to take their places in front of the bar, and she didn't.

That was all, except for Ethel Varr and me, and I got her and stood with her at a corner of my desk, and told Wolfe, "All set."

"Miss Tuttle and I were much farther away," Beverly Kent objected.

"Yes, sir," Wolfe agreed. "It is not presumed that this is identical. Now." His eyes went to the group at the bar. "Mr. Hackett, I understand that when Mr. Grantham went to the bar for champagne for himself and Miss Usher, two glasses were there in readiness. You had poured one of them a few minutes previously, and the other just before he arrived. Is that correct?"

"Yes, sir." Hackett had fully recovered from our brush in the hall and was back in character. "I have stated to the police that one of the glasses had been standing there three or four minutes."

"Please pour a glass now and put it in place."

The bottles in the cooler on the table were champagne, and good champagne; Wolfe had insisted on it. Fritz had opened two of them. Pouring champagne is always nice to watch, but I doubt if any pourer ever had as attentive an audience as Hackett had, as he took a bottle from the cooler and filled a glass.

"Keep the bottle in your hand," Wolfe directed him. "I'll explain what I'm after and then you may proceed. I want to see it from various angles. You will pour another glass, and Mr. Grantham will come and get the two glasses and go with them to Mr. Panzer—that is to say, to Miss Usher. He will hand him one, and Mr. Goodwin will be there and take the other one. Meanwhile you will be pouring two more glasses, and Mr. Grantham will come and get them and go with them to Miss Tuttle, and hand her one, and again Mr. Goodwin will be there and take the other one. You will do the same with Miss Varr and Miss Grantham. Not with Miss Yarmis and Mrs. Robilotti, since they are there at the bar. That way I shall see it from all sides. Is that clear, Mr. Hackett?"

"Yes, sir."

"It's not clear to me," Cecil said. "What's the idea? I didn't do that. All I did was get two glasses and take one to Miss Usher."

"I'm aware of that," Wolfe told him. "As I said, I want to get various angles on it. If you prefer, Mr. Panzer can move to the different positions, but this is simpler. I only request your cooperation. Do you find my request unreasonable?"

"I find it pretty damn nutty. But it's all nutty, in my opinion, so a little more won't hurt, if I can keep a glass for myself when I've performed." He moved, then turned. "What's the order again?"

"The order is unimportant. After Mr. Panzer, Misses Tuttle, Varr, and Grantham, in any order you please."

"Right. Start pouring, Hackett. Here I come."

The show started. It did seem fairly nutty, at that, especially my part. Hackett pouring, and Cecil carrying, and the girls taking—there was nothing odd about that; but me racing around, taking the second glass, deciding what to do with it, doing it, and getting to the next one in time to be there waiting when Cecil arrived—of all the miscellaneous chores I had performed at Wolfe's direction over the years, that took the prize. At the fourth and last one, for Celia Grantham, by the wall to the right of Wolfe's desk, Cecil cheated. After he had handed his sister hers he ignored my outstretched hand, raised his glass, said, "Here's to crime," and took a mouthful of the bubbles. He lowered the glass and told Wolfe, "I hope that didn't spoil it."

"It was in bad taste," Celia said.

"I meant it to be," he retorted. "This whole thing has been in bad taste from the beginning."

Wolfe, who had straightened up to watch the performance, let his shoulders down. "You didn't spoil it," he said. His eyes went around. "I invite comment. Did anyone notice anything worthy of remark?"

"I don't know whether it's worthy of remark or not," Paul Schuster, the lawyer, said, "but this exhibition can't possibly be made the basis for any conclusion. The conditions were not the same at all."

"I must disagree," Wolfe disagreed. "I did get a basis for a conclusion, and for the specific conclusion I had hoped for. I need support for it, but would rather not suggest it. I appeal to all of you: did anything about Mr. Grantham's performance strike your eye?"

A growl came from the door to the hall. Sergeant Purley Stebbins was standing there on the sill, his big frame half filling the rectangle. "I don't know about a conclusion," he said, "but I noticed that he carried the glasses the same every time. The one in his right hand, his thumb and two fingers were on the bowl part, and the one in his left hand, he held that lower down, by the stem. And he kept the one in his right hand and handed them the one in his left hand. Every time."

I had never before seen Wolfe look at Purley with unqualified admiration. "Thank you, Mr. Stebbins," he said. "You not only have eyes but know what they're for. Will anyone corroborate him?"

"I will," Saul Panzer said. "I do." He was still holding the glass Cecil had handed him.

"Will you, Mr. Cramer?"

"I reserve it." Cramer's eyes were narrowed at him. "What's your conclusion?"

"Surely that's obvious." Wolfe turned a hand over. "What I hoped to get was ground for a conclusion that anyone who was sufficiently familiar with Mr. Grantham's habits, and who saw him pick up the glasses and start off with them, would know which one he would hand to Miss Usher. And I got it, and I have two competent witnesses, Mr. Stebbins and Mr. Panzer." His head turned. "That is all, ladies and gentlemen. I wish to continue, but only to Mrs. Robilotti, Mr. Byne, and Mr. Laidlaw—and Mr. Robilotti by courtesy, if he chooses to stay. The rest of you may go. I needed your help for this demonstration and I thank you for coming. It would be a pleasure to serve you champagne on some happier occasion."

"You mean we have to go?" Rose Tuttle piped. "I want to stay."

Judging from the expressions on most of the faces, the others did too, except Helen Yarmis, who was standing by the bar with Laidlaw.

She said, "Come on, Ethel," to Ethel Varr, who was standing by my desk, and they headed for the door. Cecil emptied his glass and put it on Wolfe's desk and announced that he was staying, and Celia said she was too. Beverly Kent, the diplomat, showed that he had picked the right career by handling Rose Tuttle, who was seated beside him. She let him escort her out. Paul Schuster approached to listen a moment to the twins arguing with Wolfe, and then turned and went. Seeing Cramer cross to Mrs. Robilotti, at the bar with her husband, I noted that Hackett wasn't there and then found that he wasn't anywhere. He had gone without my knowing it, one more proof that a detective is no match for a butler.

It was Mrs. Robilotti who settled the issue with the twins. She came to Wolfe's desk, followed by Cramer and her husband, and told them to go, and then turned to her husband and told him to go too. Her pale gray eyes, back under her angled brows, were little circles of tinted ice. It was Celia she looked at.

"This man needs a lesson," she said, "and I'll give it to him. I never have needed you, and I don't need you now. You're being absurd. I do things better alone, and I'll do this alone."

Celia opened her mouth, closed it again, turned to look at Laidlaw, and went, and Cecil followed. Robilotti started to speak, met the pale gray eyes, shrugged like a polished and civilized Italian, and quit. When her eyes had seen him to the door, she walked to the chair Cramer had placed for her when she arrived, sat, aimed the eyes at Wolfe, and spoke.

"You said you wished to continue. Well?"

He was polite. "In a moment, madam. Another person is expected. If you gentlemen will be seated? Archie?"

Saul was already seated, still in Faith Usher's place, sipping champagne. Leaving it to the other four, Laidlaw, Byne, Cramer, and Stebbins, to do their own seating, I went to the hall, mounted the two flights to the South Room, knocked on the door, was told to come in, and did so.

Elaine Usher, in a chair by a window with sections of the Sunday paper scattered on the floor, had a mean look ready for me.

"Okay," I said. "Your cue."

"It's about time." She kicked the papers away from her feet and got up. "Who's there?"

"As expected. Mr. Wolfe. Byne, Laidlaw, Panzer. Inspector Cramer and Sergeant Stebbins. Mrs. Robilotti. She sent her husband home. I take you straight to her."

"I know. I'll enjoy that, I really will, no matter what happens. My hair's a mess. I'll be with you in a minute."

She went to the bathroom and closed the door. I wasn't impatient, since Wolfe would use the time to get Mrs. Robilotti into a proper mood. Mrs. Usher used it too. When she emerged her hair was very nice and her lips were the color that excites a bull. I asked her if she preferred the elevator, and she said no, and I followed her down the two flights. As we entered the office I was at her elbow.

It came out so perfect that you might have thought it had been rehearsed. I crossed with her, passing between Cramer and Byne, turned so we were facing Mrs. Robilotti, right in front of her, and said, "Mrs. Robilotti, let me present Mrs. Usher, the mother of Faith Usher." Mrs. Usher bent at the waist, put out a hand, and said, "It's a pleasure, a great pleasure." Mrs. Robilotti stared a second, shot a hand out, and slapped Mrs. Usher's face. Perfect.

16 YOUR GUESS IS AS GOOD AS MINE, WHETHER WOLFE would have been able to crash through anyway if the confrontation stunt hadn't worked—if Mrs. Robilotti had been quick enough and tough enough to take Mrs. Usher's offered hand and respond according to protocol. He maintains that he would have, but that the question is academic, since with Mrs. Robilotti's nerves already on edge the sudden appearance of that woman, without warning, bending to her and offering a hand, was sure to break her.

I didn't pull Mrs. Usher back in time to dodge the slap, though I might have, but after it landed I acted. After all she was a house guest, and a kick on the chin by the host and a smack in the face by another guest were no credit to our hospitality; and besides, she might try to return the compliment. So I gripped her arm and pulled her back out of range, bumping into Cramer, who had bounced out of his chair. Mrs. Robilotti had jerked back and sat stiff, her teeth pinning her lower lip.

"It might be well," Wolfe told me, "to seat Mrs. Usher near you. Madam, I regret the indignity you have suffered under my roof." He gestured. "That is Mr. Laidlaw. Mr. Cramer, of the police. Mr. Stebbins, also of the police. You know Mr. Byne."

As I was convoying her to the chair Saul had brought, putting her between Laidlaw and me, Cramer was saying, "You stage it and then you regret it." To his right: "I do regret it, Mrs. Robilotti. I had no hand in it." Back to Wolfe: "All right, let's hear it."

"You have seen it," Wolfe told him. "Certainly I staged it. You heard me deliberately bait Mrs. Robilotti, to ensure the desired reaction to Mrs. Usher's appearance. Before commenting on that reaction, I must explain Mr. Laidlaw's presence. I asked him to stay because he has a legitimate concern. As you know, someone sent an anonymous communication making certain statements about him, and that entitles him to hear disclosure of the truth. Why Mr. Byne is here will soon be apparent. It was something he said last evening that informed me that Mrs. Robilotti had known that her former husband, Albert Grantham, was the father of Faith Usher. However—"

"That's a lie," Byne said. "That's a damn lie."

Wolfe's tone sharpened. "I choose my words, Mr. Byne. I didn't say you told me that, but that something you said informed me. Speaking of the people invited to that gathering, you said, 'Of course my aunt could cross Faith off and tell Mrs. Irwin'—and stopped, realizing that you had slipped. When I let it pass, you thought I had missed it, but I hadn't. It was merely that if I had tried to pin you down you would have wriggled out by denying the implication. Now that—"

"There was no implication!"

"Nonsense. Why should your aunt 'cross Faith off'? Why should she refuse to have Miss Usher in her house? Granting that there were many possible explanations, there was one suggested by the known facts: that she would not receive as a guest the natural daughter of her former husband. And I had just learned that Faith Usher was Albert Grantham's natural daughter, and that you were aware of it. So I had the implication, and I arranged to test it. If Mrs. Robilotti, suddenly confronted by Faith Usher's mother extending a friendly hand, took the hand and betrayed no reluctance, the implication would be discredited. I expected her to shrink from it, and I was wrong. I may learn someday that what a woman will do is beyond conjecture. Instead of shrinking, she struck. I repeat, Mrs. Usher, I regret it. I did not foresee it."

"You can't have it both ways," Byne said. "You say my aunt wouldn't have Faith Usher in her house because she knew she was her former husband's natural daughter. But she did have her in her house. She knew she had been invited, and she let her come."

Wolfe nodded. "I know. That's the point. That's my main reason for assuming that your aunt killed her. There are other—"

"Hold it," Cramer snapped. His head turned. "Mrs. Robilotti, I want you to know that this is as shocking to me as it is to you."

Her pale gray eyes were on Wolfe and she didn't move them. "I doubt it," she said. "I didn't know any man could go as low as *this*. This is incredible."

"I agree," Wolfe told her. "Murder is always incredible. I have now committed myself, madam, before witnesses, and if I am wrong

I shall be at your mercy. I wouldn't like that. Mr. Cramer. You are shocked. I can expound, or you can attack. Which do you prefer?"

"Neither one." Cramer's fists were on his knees. "I just want to know. What evidence have you that Faith Usher was Albert Grantham's daughter?"

"Well." Wolfe cocked his head. "That is a ticklish point. My sole concern in this is the murder of Faith Usher, and I have no desire to make unnecessary trouble for people not implicated in it. For example, I know where you can find evidence that the death of Faith Usher meant substantial financial profit for a certain man, but since he wasn't there and couldn't have killed her, I'll tell you about it only if it becomes requisite. To answer your question: I have the statements of two people, Mrs. Elaine Usher and Mr. Austin Byne." His eyes moved. "And, Mr. Byne, you have trimmed long enough. Did your aunt know that Faith Usher was the daughter of Albert Grantham?"

Dinky's jaw worked. He looked left, at Mrs. Usher, but not right, at his aunt. Wolfe had made it plain: if he came through, Wolfe would not tell Cramer about the agreement and where it was. Probably what decided him was the fact that Mrs. Robilotti had already given it away by slapping Mrs. Usher.

"Yes," he said. "I told her."

"When?"

"A couple of months ago."

"Why?"

"Because—something she said. She had said it before, that I was a parasite because I was living on money my uncle had given me before he died. When she said it again that day I lost my temper and told her that my uncle had given me the money so I could provide for his illegitimate daughter. She wouldn't believe me, and I told her the name of the daughter and her mother. Afterward I was sorry I had told her, and I told her so—"

A noise, an explosive noise, came from his aunt. "You liar," she said, a glint of hate in the pale gray eyes. "You sit there and lie. You told me so you could blackmail me, to get more millions out of me. The millions Albert had given you weren't enough. You weren't satisfied—"

"Stop it!" Wolfe's voice was a whip. He was scowling at her. "You are in mortal peril, madam. I have put you there, so I have a responsibility, and I advise you to hold your tongue. Mr. Cramer. Do you want more from Mr. Byne, or more from me?"

"You." Cramer was so shocked he was hoarse. "You say that Mrs.

Robilotti deliberately let Faith Usher come to that party so she could kill her. Is that right?"

"Yes."

"And that her motive was that she knew that Faith Usher was the illegitimate child of Albert Grantham?"

"It could have been. With her character and temperament that could have been sufficient motive. But she has herself just suggested an additional one. Her nephew may have been using Faith Usher as a fulcrum to pry a fortune out of her. You will explore that."

"I certainly will. That show you put on. You say that proved that Mrs. Robilotti could have done it?"

"Yes. You saw it. She could have dropped the poison into the glass that had been standing there for three or four minutes. She stayed there at the bar. If someone else had started to take that glass she could have said it was hers. When her son came and picked up the two glasses, if he had taken the poisoned one in his right hand, which would have meant—to her, since she knew his habits—that he would drink it himself, again she could have said it was hers and told him to get another one. Or she could even have handed it to him, have seen to it that he took the poisoned one in his left hand; but you can't hope to establish that, since neither she nor her son would admit it. The moment he left the bar with the poisoned glass in his left hand Faith Usher was doomed; and the risk was slight, since an ample supply of cyanide was there on a chair in Miss Usher's bag. It would unquestionably be assumed that she had committed suicide; indeed, it was assumed, and the assumption would have prevailed if Mr. Goodwin hadn't been there and kept his eyes open."

"Who told Mrs. Robilotti that Miss Usher had the poison? And when?"

"I don't know." Wolfe gestured. "Confound it, must I shine your shoes for you?"

"No, I'll manage. You've shined enough. You say the risk was slight. It wasn't slight when she got Miss Usher's bag and took out the bottle and took some of the poison."

"I doubt if she did that. I doubt if she ever went near that bag. If she knew that the poison Miss Usher carried around was cyanide, and several people did, she probably got some somewhere else, which isn't difficult, and had it at hand. I suggest that that is worth inquiry, whether she recently had access to a supply of cyanide. You might even find that she had actually procured some." Wolfe gestured again. "I do not pretend that I am showing you a ripened fruit which you need only to pick. I undertook merely to satisfy myself whether Mr. Goodwin was right or wrong. I am satisfied. Are you?"

Cramer never said. Mrs. Robilotti was on her feet. I had the idea then that what moved her was Wolfe's mentioning the possibility that she had got hold of cyanide somewhere else, and learned a few days later that I had been right, when Purley Stebbins told me that they had found out where she got it, and could prove it. Anyhow, she was on her feet, and moving, but had taken only three steps when she had to stop. Cramer and Purley were both there blocking the way, and together they weigh four hundred pounds and are over four feet wide.

"Let me pass," she said. "I'm going home."

I have seldom felt sorry for that pair, but I did then, especially Cramer.

"Not right now," he said gruffly. "I'm afraid you'll have to answer some questions."

17   ONE ITEM. YOU MAY REMEMBER MY MENTIONING that one day, the day after the murderer of Faith Usher was convicted, I was discussing with a friend what was the most conceited remark we had ever heard? It was that same day that I caught sight of Edwin Laidlaw in the men's bar at the Churchill and decided to do a good deed. Besides, I had felt that the amount on the bill we had sent him, which he had paid promptly without a murmur, had been pretty stiff, and he had something coming. So I approached him, and after greetings had been exchanged I performed the deed.

"I didn't want to mention it," I said, "while her mother was on trial for murder, but now I can tell you, in case you're interested. One day during that commotion I was talking with Celia Grantham, and your name came up, and she said, 'I may marry him someday. If he gets into a bad jam I'll marry him now.' I report it only because I thought you might want to take some dancing lessons."

"I don't have to," he said. "I appreciate it, and many thanks, but we're getting married next week. On the quiet. We put it off until the trial was over. Let me buy you a drink."

There you are. I'm one good deed shy.